Praise for *Reclaiming Lily*

"A remarkable layering of intertwined experiences woven together into a truly memorable story. Led by the spirit and the heart, Lacy gives the reader a chance to experience China in a new way. *Reclaiming Lily* is a book to be savored."

—Cindy Champnella, author of *The Waiting Child: How the Faith and Love of One Orphan Saved the Life of Another*

"Patti Lacy bravely ushers the reader across cultural lines to show the power of God to restore all that the locusts have eaten. *Reclaiming Lily* is a moving story of loss, healing, and above all, love."

—Gina Holmes, bestselling author of *Crossing Oceans* and *Dry as Rain*

"The bonds of maternal love and whispered promises are held to a flame and tested in this redemptive story of sacrifice. Patti Lacy's vibrant prose and endearing characters will capture your heart. Bravo!"

—Carla Stewart, author of *Chasing Lilacs* and *Broken Wings*

"Riveting. Powerful. Haunting. *Reclaiming Lily* is a stunning example of just why Patti Lacy is a must-read in Christian fiction today. I dare anyone to pick up this book and not be moved, inspired and changed forever. Truly a talent not to be missed."

—Julie Lessman, award-winning author of *A Hope Undaunted*

Reclaiming *Lily*

Reclaiming *Lily*

A NOVEL

PATTI LACY

BETHANY HOUSE PUBLISHERS
a division of Baker Publishing Group
Minneapolis, Minnesota

Published by Bethany House Publishers
11400 Hampshire Avenue South
Bloomington, Minnesota 55438
www.bethanyhouse.com

Bethany House Publishers is a division of
Baker Publishing Group, Grand Rapids, Michigan

Printed in the United States of America

Library of Congress Cataloging-in-Publication Data
Lacy, Patti.
    Reclaiming Lily / Patti Lacy.
      p.   cm.
    ISBN 978-0-7642-0941-3 (pbk.)
    1. Sisters—Fiction. 2. Genetic disorders—Fiction. 3. Intercountry adoption—China—Fiction. 4. Intercountry adoption—United States—Fiction. I. Title.
PS3612.A3545R43 2011
813'.6—dc22   2011025213

Cover design by Andrea Gjeldum

11 12 13 14 15 16 17   7 6 5 4 3 2 1

Reclaiming *Lily*

Prologue

EASTERN CHINA, 1990

The van jostled its way to the orphanage. Hunkered beside her pastor husband, Andrew, Gloria Powell craned her neck to gaze out the filmy window. Though she'd read books and studied photos until bleary-eyed, nothing—*nothing*—had captured this wild land! Waterfalls cascaded velvet hills, yet garbage carpeted the countryside with tin, paper, and plastic. A naked child squatted to pee near a dismembered dog. Bent-backed peasants formed graceful shadows on rice fields robed in green and silver.

A sigh escaped Gloria. This was a strange land, a magnificent land, the homeland of their baby.

But it sure was a long way from Texas.

The van wheezed to a stop near a crumbling stone wall circling a weathered two-story building. Children streamed from a blistered wooden gate and clustered about Gloria's van window. A bow-legged toddler pointed at her, as did others with rice-bowl haircuts. A gangly child—he or she?

Five or six?—in a striped shirt and flowery pants shuffled to a shade tree.

"Is this it?" Gloria whispered to Sherri and Jim, missionary friends sitting in the seat behind them.

"Yes. We're here."

Gloria leaned against Andrew's shoulder. A picnic on Baylor University's quad, where her engagement ring was presented and eagerly accepted after a cafeteria-cookie dessert, had birthed this China odyssey. Unlike other college marrieds, they had wanted children right away—and had "family-planned" during study breaks in that tiny first apartment. *"Why wait?"* Andrew had whispered. *"A baby'll liven up this place."*

Over ten years I've waited. And still no baby. Gloria thanked God for Andrew, who had always seemed to know what she wanted, like that first time, when he'd approached her at a BSU mixer and asked her to volunteer with him at Waco's Buckner Children's Home. Andrew glimpsed the Gloria hidden behind the façade she'd erected to keep out men who lied and cheated. Men like . . . her daddy. In one evening, Andrew had coaxed trivia from her—favorite color, pink; favorite food, enchiladas; and secret things too.

Soulmate Andrew . . . *Even he doesn't fathom my hunger for a child.* Why, she'd diapered countless Chatty Cathy dolls, waiting for this. Wiped runny noses and dirty bottoms in church nurseries, waiting for this. Were these orphans waiting too? Would the older ones slump away, reluctant to face the heartbreak of not being chosen . . . again?

Like those children, Gloria had borne disappointment with every surgical-gloved examination, every lovemaking session that revolved around a half-degree rise in her body temperature. For a decade she'd waited for phone calls, for paper work . . . for God.

Damming her emotions, she pressed her face against the dusty window. Her heart seized at the sight of a living doll with a lopsided ponytail sprouting off the side of her head. Gloria let the China sun, the Chinese children, ward off her insecurity. *God, with your help, I'll be the best mother in Texas!*

"Is one of them ours?" escaped her lips.

Syllables rat-a-tatted in the front seat. There the civil affairs official, the driver, and their guide were having it out. While their baby waited . . .

"Maybe," Sherri finally whispered.

Gloria bit her lip. If she didn't shush, she'd light a fuse in this powder keg called international adoption, brand-new to China. Things couldn't explode before they got their baby.

Andrew found her hand and squeezed hope into it.

Good thing I married a pastor. His middle name is hope!

"Just hold on," continued Sherri. "It won't be long."

Hurry up and wait. Her theme song, even in this final leg of their journey. They'd languished in Customs and Civil Affairs and train depot cane chairs. They'd flown thousands of miles, rail-traveled hundreds more, road-bumped most of this day away. Would an angel soon nestle in her arms, or would God once again snatch family and future from her?

Arm waves, hisses, and snarls continued from the front seat. Gloria couldn't understand a word, and her confusion intensified her fears.

She propped her elbow against the van door as regret washed over her. The Bertolets had coached her to remain silent, patient. Had she offended those who, with a nod, could vaporize their hopes for a baby? "I shouldn't have asked that," she whispered to Andrew.

Though Andrew pressed two fingers over her lips, his eyes

crinkled like they did when his church kids made a human horse out of him. "It'll be all right." His voice salved her frayed nerves. "At least we're here."

Preachers—especially hers—knew the right things to say. Gloria focused her gaze outside to the children being led into the orphanage by women, looking official in the Party dress of white blouses and navy pants.

Suddenly the still-squawking officials leapt from the van and shoved open the back door. The Bertolets climbed out, stretching and blinking. Tucked under Jim's arm was the folder holding two years of correspondence. Permits. *That folder holds our future.*

"Stay in here." Traffic-cop style, Jim raised his hand. Then the Bertolets joined the officials in a succession of bows and a spattering of strange syllables, though Gloria barely heard for the whooshing in her ears.

Andrew found her hand. "God, we pray that you will guide us, protect . . ."

Blood continued to roar through Gloria and muted Andrew's words. She burrowed into him like she might be swept not just from the van, but off the very continent of Asia if they didn't get their baby soon.

Footfalls signaled a development. Gloria's chin lifted. Progress?

Jim stepped to the van and crouched so she could see his face. "It shouldn't be long. We'll get things rolling."

"Thanks." Andrew's voice became husky.

"Remember." Jim waved that folder. "No pictures." Then Jim rejoined the entourage entrusted with their baby's life.

Gloria craned her neck, taking in every nuance of the place her baby had lived and, Lord willing, the place her baby would *leave*. Later, she'd transcribe it into a journal: their train travel, in berths stacked like pancakes, two hundred passengers in one car! Old men drinking grainy-smelling beer. Women sipping perfumed tea. Students dragging on cigarettes. The smell of soy sauce and rancid oil emanating from cloth seats. Chopsticks that clicked, game tiles that clinked; throats that cleared, mouths that spit. People that laughed and snorted and snored and stood and sat and lay. She'd soaked up every experience, knowing her baby came from China. Her baby *was* China.

She and Andrew would preserve for their baby a history book. She and Andrew would not deny their baby glimpses of its homeland. Its *heart* land.

Her mind whirred to capture the orphanage walls plastered with exotic red Chinese characters. Wood trim had peeled and masonry had fissured. The grassless yard boasted no playground equipment, but the property was free from the excrement and kitten-sized rats they'd seen along China's byways. Gloria clenched her hands. Dared she hope that these caretakers had kept her baby clean? Healthy?

The officials stood in the courtyard, their arms waving, their lips flapping. Jim kept shaking his head. Gloria observed every move while her baby dangled unseen, like catfish bait, between the Americans and the Chinese. She swallowed, fidgeted about in her seat, and resisted the urge to claw her neck, leap from the van, and hightail it into the building, screaming for her daughter.

The world stopped rotating on its axis. *Daughter.* She replayed that word. *Daughter.* They'd have a daughter. Fallout from the one-child policy and the patriarchal bent of the country had tilted the odds toward adoption of a girl, but the Holy Spirit had just doused any doubt. And Gloria believed she'd know that baby girl the minute their eyes met.

Seat springs creaked. Andrew cocked his head toward the crowd. "What's happening?" *Talk about role reversal! He's worried; I'm . . . calm!* "What're they saying?"

She shrugged but kept her focus on those who thought they controlled her future. Prayer had reminded her that God was in charge.

"Can you read their lips?" Andrew blurted out.

"I can barely see their lips."

Andrew forced a laugh.

Waving arms and shrill voices again drew her attention. A woman with choppy bobby-pinned hair thrust her hands on her hips, shook her head, pivoted, and disappeared into the orphanage building.

Though Gloria's stomach heaved, peace battled . . . and prevailed. She breathed slowly. *More waiting. I've* majored *in waiting.*

"Dear Father," Andrew prayed as he massaged her neck, "give us your peace. Help us to accept your will, whatever it may be. . . ."

Calling on her lifelong technique for comfort, Gloria rubbed her thumb against her palm. *Your will. I can, I will accept it.*

Jim strode back to them. Half-moons of sweat darkened his chest and underarms. A tic worked his jaw. "Andrew, could I talk to you? Alone?"

Gloria's spine stiffened, and she dug her fingernail into the fleshy part of her thumb. "I need to hear this." She met Andrew's gaze. "Please."

Jim heaved a sigh, took Gloria's sweaty hand, and helped her from the van. Andrew untangled his long legs and climbed out after her.

Jim drew her and Andrew aside. "Something's come up."

Andrew's brow rutted like the road. "What?"

Gloria locked her knees to keep them from buckling. *God can. God can.*

"We'll work this out." Jim's calm kept Gloria standing. "It just may take a while. Another trip."

Waiting. Waiting. I've spent my whole life—

A white shape blurred in Gloria's peripheral vision. She stole a sideways glance.

Orphanage doors framed Miss Bobby Pins. Next to her stood a girl—perhaps eight, perhaps ten—wearing a red blouse polka-dotted with white. Red. White. Red.

The air around Gloria shimmered and matched glittery sensations in her heart. She wobbled forward.

Andrew reached out . . . trying to rein her in? No one could rein in her wild, wild heart. She inched toward the child wearing the red-and-white clothes.

"There isn't a baby available," Jim mumbled. "Or so they say."

"How can they do this?" Andrew hissed. "After all we've done, the money we've paid . . ."

Gloria's heart pounded a message that these men didn't yet know. Soon she would tell them. . . .

The girl stepped close.

Gloria clapped her hand over her heart, as if to stop the pounding that competed with the slapping sound of worn black shoes. The girl's shoes. The girl wore precious black, worn shoes. The precious girl wore black, worn shoes.

"I'm sorry." Jim leafed through the folder, as if searching for logic. *Poor man . . .*

"*Sorry* doesn't cut it. They promised. It's all there, in black and white." Andrew flailed at the papers and then groped for her hand, as if lost and desperate for a guide. She fought a giggle as elation filled her. Here in China, she'd be strong for Andrew! Why, God hadn't yet told him that the girl in the black shoes was their daughter . . .

"We all thought that. It's what they said. State-sponsored adoption's a new frontier." Jim leaned close. "Technically illegal. What they say and what they do isn't always the same."

Gloria locked eyes with Jim. "Who's that woman?" Her voice jerked, as if her heart spasms had spread. "Who's the woman by the girl in the black shoes?"

"The orphanage director." Jim spoke through clenched teeth. "Who says the only child available is the, um, afterbirth—excuse me, y'all—of counterrevolutionaries."

"So our baby . . ." Words died in homage to a perfect oval face with peach-blossom skin.

"Our baby is somewhere else in China." Andrew tightened his grip on her hand. "Waiting for us to find her . . . or him." His sandpaper voice battled for control.

The girl raised her head and showed eyes heavy with wisdom, sorrow . . . questions.

A million bubbles effervesced inside Gloria and threatened to lift her off the ground. *For once, Andrew, the pastor, doubts. It's me with faith!* She fought an urge to throw back her head and laugh, to dash forward and fling her arms around this perfect child. Her age didn't matter. Neither did her questionable heritage, if that were even true. *God! You've given me the child of my soul, my heart, my mind!*

"Gloria? Gloria!" Andrew grabbed her shoulders, surely to silence the laughter she couldn't contain.

The Bertolets froze, as did the Chinese. Not Gloria. Life had bubbled freedom to every cell. God had freed her from a lifetime of wanting a child, of waiting for a child! "That child, that precious child, is our daughter!"

"Gloria, she's not a baby. I thought we . . . wanted a baby."

"The agency guarantees her health." Jim edged close, an odd light in his eyes. "It's rumored that she has been secretly cared for by her family, former blacks."

Andrew's eyebrows shot toward the sky. "Blacks?"

"China's elite and educated. What they also call 'stinking ninths.'"

"Stinking ninths?"

"Andrew, it doesn't matter." Gloria planted her feet on the sidewalk to keep from floating toward heaven. "She's the one we came for. She is our Joy." Though the bubbles dizzied her, a surprising calm weighted her words.

Andrew seemed to study the child and then Gloria. Spidery lines creased his eyes and the corners of his mouth. "Are you sure, Gloria? Are you very sure?"

"I haven't been this sure since I married you."

He enveloped her into the refuge formed by his shoulders, his chin; the rangy body that the years had form-fitted to her own. She buried her head in his chest, heard that loving heart pound, felt his sweat-dampened shirt. A sob ravaged her throat with exquisite pain. *Oh, God. My man's dedicated, baptized, married, and counseled other people's children. You've given him—given us—our own! A perfect girl named Joy.*

They eased toward Joy, murmuring greetings. Careful not to startle her, they let their entwined fingers graze her shoulder.

The child's eyes tracked wildly; otherwise she stood mannequin-like. "It's okay. Yes. Yes, dear." Gloria bathed each word in soothing tones, as she did with visitors' children entrusted to their church nursery's care.

Something niggled in Gloria's peripheral vision. She risked a sideways glance.

In the road stood a young woman, her rusted bike sprawled

on the ground. Her face was a study in circles—widened eyes, open mouth, flared nostrils. Surely another villager stunned at seeing pale-faced foreigners.

Exhaling a decade of frustration, Gloria refocused on the world's most beautiful child and drew her close. *God! You dreamed bigger than I imagined! Bigger than Texas. Bigger than China! Bigger than the world!*

Andrew's breath tickled her ear. "You sure about calling her Joy?"

"It's her name," she whispered, relaying what the Spirit had told her—was it a moment ago? A decade ago? *God, have I known this, at some level, my entire life?*

⌒⊙⌒

Oh, Lily! Chang Kaiping punished her bike pedals. Billowy grain stalks and the rutted road blurred into a canvas of golds and browns. Slowly, ever so slowly, Fourth Daughter Lily's face appeared, as if a master artist had sketched Father's cheekbones, Mother's bow lips, and Lily's own pearl-drop face into the China landscape. It was that image that had kept her poring over textbooks in her Boston flat, pushing through eighteen-hour shifts at Mass General. There, remembering Mother and Father, she had lavished compassion onto patients.

Kai hunched over, her spine curving forward, her hands gripping the rusted bar. She pedaled even faster, pursuing that elusive wind called fate. It was tricky to capture, but oh, the rewards! In time she would restore the Chang family honor. Reclaim her sister Lily. Today, though, it would be enough to see her.

All Kai had absorbed since 1988—America's technology, Harvard Medical School's biology—faded in the clatter of her rattling spokes as the hope of seeing Lily captured her. She was young. Free. Dr. Kai Chang vanished. In her stead was Second Daughter Kai, soaring on a dragon kite toward the orphanage. Toward Fourth Daughter Lily, who would lean close and whisper *moy moy* and flutter moth lashes in secret sister language. *Dear Lily, who does not know I have returned from America. Dear Lily, who does not know Mother resides on the ancestral burial hill.* Kai's throat tightened like her handlebar grip. *Dear Lily, who knows not her own flesh and blood except as volunteers who thrust Lucky Candies into cupped and grimy orphan hands . . . especially for the girl with Mother's bow lips. Oh, sister Lily!*

Kai blinked away bitter tears and continued her flight. Blood rushed to her limbs, fluttering her strange bike-kite. *Careful!* Kai adjusted her handlebar grip lest the kite careen, like a drunken peasant, and crash, short of its destination.

The oxidized red blur of the orphanage fence seeped onto the countryside canvas. Kai eased her feet off the pedals. The dragon kite fluttered its tails, squealed disappointment at leaving its sky home, and once again became a bicycle. Kai dragged her toe in the dust but lifted her head.

There stood Lily. Precious Fourth Sister. To battle her racing pulse, her melting heart, and mask her love from prying eyes, Kai calibrated Lily's height and weight. Twentieth percentile among ten-year-old females in America. Ninetieth percentile here in the land of "chinks and starving slant-eyes," as David's father described China. Kai dismissed thoughts of her boyfriend's bigoted Boston father and instead noted with ancestral pride the sight of Father's strong jaw, Mother's porcelain skin. Here at the orphanage, Lily was a sweet honey-suckle vine amid scrawny grasses.

A foot drag stopped her bicycle, and Kai plotted how best to see Lily. It was a delicate matter because of the orphanage director's power.

A shadow engulfed Lily.

Gripping her bike for steadiness, Kai scuffed forward. Her eyes widened with horror.

A blond-haired woman towered over Lily.

Blood drained from Kai. Why would a foreigner stalk her sister? Kai sharpened her gaze but kept the mask over her emotions.

Three *lao wai* trailed the woman, an American—her slouchy posture, expensive clothes, and heavy makeup screamed it. Kai's palms became slick with sweat. *These Americans, who strut in their finery past crumbling walls like they own everything and everyone.* Kai's mask slipped. A sneer took hold. Why were they here?

A brown-haired man fixed love-sick eyes on the woman . . . and Lily. Kai darted a glance at the other couple and dismissed their importance. The predators were that blond woman and the man, invading precious *mei mei's feng shui* by touching her head, her shoulder . . .

An icy river of emotion rushed over Kai, obliterating her handlebar grip. The bike clattered onto the packed soil. Why would Fourth Sister be joined with lao wai?

The woman fixed weak, water eyes on Kai. "Let go of Lily," Kai snarled.

The woman's brows arched. Her mouth stretched into a curlicue apple peel, candied and sickly sweet. She took the man's arm. So happy, this couple, as they guided Lily— *my sister*—into a van. Kai padlocked pleasant American memories—her boyfriend, David, her roommate, Cheryl, the Harvard staff. Her mouth yawned to breathe fire on the

Americans. Then she spotted the orphanage director, bowing to the lao wai. A mouse squeak emerged.

The other lao wai and what surely were officials hurried into the van, which chugged to life and disappeared.

Kai flung out her arms, grasping only noxious fumes. Tears streaked her face.

The orphanage director, so smug in her Party uniform, cast a wicked smile at Kai before walking up the orphanage steps. *The steps where I left dear Fourth Sister, ten years ago. The steps that precipitated Mother's slow but sure march to death.*

Despite the chance that her gesture would be noted, Kai shook a fist trembling with hate. Since the Revolution, the director had nursed her smoldering-coal revenge against the Changs. This was a conflagration.

Stop! Stop! Stop! The words enflamed Kai's throat, trapped. She opened her mouth . . . closed it. How dare she think only of herself? China had branded her and her sisters dangerous counterrevolutionaries. As an elite studying overseas, Kai might be awoken from her American dream and detained here in China if she humiliated this woman protected by a Mao jacket, a red scarf, a stiff cap. Determination set Kai's mouth. She could withstand their abuse. Not so poor Father, mourning Mother's departure. First and Third Daughters Ling and Mei—who had sacrificed in ways she could only imagine in the easy-come, easy-go USA—did not deserve such disgrace.

Kai's spine sagged like dying bamboo as she stared down the road. Nothing remained of Lily but van ruts and the memory of her perfect face. Kai swabbed tears, tears stanched even during Mother's funeral procession.

One remaining official hurried inside the orphanage where Lily lived no more. Kai stuffed her fist in her mouth to keep from crying, *Little sister! Our jewel!* But little sister, proof that the Changs had reclaimed fate, was gone.

Second Daughter?

Kai perked her ears to hear the masculine voice. Who called? No men presently worked at the orphanage, according to her sisters' latest gossip.

Little Dragon!

Though she was a grown woman, a medical doctor, she whimpered like a child. Only Old Grandfather had called her Little Dragon, Father abandoning that nickname years ago, along with his belief in Confucius, Mao's Red Book, even the zodiac.

Shivers wracked Kai. She moved her lips but could not summon the strange words Grandfather had whispered a lifetime ago. Oh, but she heard them! Each syllable stirred a cooling breeze. She righted her bicycle. Kai, Second Daughter of the Chang family, Golden Dragon of China, graduate of the world's greatest medical school, would battle the fates to honor Mother's last wish, Grandfather's first legacy. If it took her last breath, she would reclaim Lily. It was her fate.

1

How the fates torture me! Having dressed hours ago, Kai again checked the simple gold watch David had slipped around her wrist during a quiet birthday celebration. Would ten o'clock ever arrive? Kai clutched Lily's medical file, sank into a cowhide love seat, and tried to relax. Others might bask in the luxury of Egyptian weave linens, silk pile carpet, and an unobstructed window view of what slow-talking, slow-walking Texans called Cowtown. Such extravagance mollified one from a remote village. Years ago, a two-hundred-fifty-dollar-a-night room at the Sundance Hotel would have obliterated her savings. But Kai, now a doctor with Massachusetts Renal Associates, could afford all of this . . . and more.

She would trade it all for time with Lily. *Oh, Lily* . . .

To prepare for her meeting, Kai opened the file labeled with the most precious name in the world. Since the fates transported Kai to America, she had begged them to reunite her with Lily. How else would a penniless peasant breach

23

American privacy laws to find one in a land of over two hundred fifty million people? Harvard Medical School and her internship had demanded back-killing, mind-numbing commitments that left little time to implement such a preposterous plan. Yet every framed diploma, every notarized paper, inched her toward what had caused Kai to span seas.

Her mother's last words: *"Reclaim Lily."*

Mother's last wish had echoed down predawn hospital corridors. Shrieked with alley cats in Cambridge midnight alleys. Rode Boston sea breezes on crisp afternoons.

"Reclaim Lily."

With ruthless pursuit, Kai achieved residency, then citizenship, to satisfy the burning drive within her to heal—a force so powerful it flowed to her hand in an undeniably tangible force. But also to reclaim Lily. She shared her secret with no one.

Massachusetts Renal Associates's generous job offer obliterated financial concern. Another step toward reclaiming Lily.

Two years ago, student loan notes arrived stamped *Paid in Full*. Letters—and money—meandered to China and back . . . as did Mother's file. Determined to understand the cause of her mother's death, Kai finally deciphered the complex Chinese characters and spotty medical records the file contained. Translation? In any language, her mother had died from polycystic kidney disease.

After a PKD self-test—found negative—Kai sent word to sisters Ling and Mei, who surely labored to unravel the knotty thread of obtaining sophisticated Western medical procedures for mere village women. *Did they even receive my letter?* Kai wondered. And what of precious Fourth Daughter? Had the fates declared it time to find Lily? *Dare I upset the feng shui of a seventeen-year-old and her American family?*

Kai had barely slept, for thinking of Lily. Had barely eaten, for worrying about Lily. How peculiar that the passage of time had intensified her desire to reclaim the fourth Chang daughter as she'd better grasped the futility of penetrating adoption records and privacy acts to uncover the name of one leaving China in 1991.

"What's wrong?" her roommate Cheryl had asked.

"Tell me," David had demanded.

Cheryl and David had become like family, so she shared with them the story of her heart. Her Lily.

David had called "a friend of a friend," that peculiar American phrase meaning everything and nothing. The former police lieutenant, now a private investigator, demanded an exorbitant fee . . . and promised an out-of-this-universe result.

Kai stared at her image in a gaudy brass mirror. Only Mother's final wish and Kai's passion to conquer fate could have led Kai, a reserved individual, to hire a licensed snoop! But it had to be done. David insisted Lily could be reclaimed in no other way.

Three weeks later, a manila envelope stamped *Personal and Confidential* had arrived at Kai's office.

Now her skin prickled as she unlocked her briefcase and withdrew fate's final assurance that she must find Lily.

3/30/1997. Paducchi & Associates Confidential Report Page 1 of 3

The following is a summary of information re Joy Grace Powell, as requested pursuant to a contract signed by Chang Kai, M.D., a Boston resident.

Joy Powell, a seventeen-year-old Paschal High

```
School junior, resides with her adoptive par-
ents, Reverend and Mrs. Andrew Powell—
```

Papers rustled as Kai flipped the page.

```
An unnamed source states that "when she's not
cutting class . . ." Miss Powell ". . . lives
in the nurse's office" and "tries to hang out
with goths and potheads." The same source
labels Miss Powell "a pimple-faced nerd."
```

Kai had understood the implication of the nurse's office reference but little else about that first paragraph on page 2. David and Cheryl had no such comprehension problem. After her boyfriend's and roommate's translation of the words *goths* and *potheads*, phone calls zipped between Kai and the phone number the PI had provided. A meeting was scheduled. On the night of March 30, Kai charged to her new credit card one round-trip ticket to Fort Worth, Texas.

Minutes stretched to hours and agonized into five days of waiting for an airport voice to announce her flight.

Kai checked her watch. *The wait will soon end.* Her stiff fingers slid the report into the file marked with that lovely name. *Lily.*

Fate affirmed the validity of my quest, and I have answered. So why does anxiety gnaw my insides?

As usual, Kai summoned science to calm her, digging through drug monographs and journal articles from her briefcase. This data not only graded the road ahead, but possessed enough signage to guide even the most emotional Americans to a logical conclusion. Yet to help Lily, the drawl-talking Texan and his wife, Gloria—believers in the Christian God like her boyfriend, David, her roommate, Cheryl—must trust an atheist. The lifeblood of the Changs, of Lily, might depend on it.

Kai's cell phone ring pierced the air, and she dropped Lily's folder. Medical reports swished onto a carpet patterned with stars. Did the Powells think she would brainwash Lily? Whisk her to China? They would not cancel now, would they? Kai grabbed her phone and flipped it open.

"Dr. Kai," she snipped, then bit her tongue in exasperation. Despite her anxiety, she must not use a tone edged with a scalpel's clinical coldness. A pastor and his wife would respond more favorably to humility.

"Doctor. It's Andrew Powell."

Hoarseness cloaked the voice Kai had analyzed in numerous phone conversations. Kai's fingers tensed. The reverend sounded scared. Had something happened to Lily?

"There's been a change in plans."

Kai longed to rail at the whims of these Texans. *Lily's adoptive family*, she reminded herself, *whom you must woo. They have fed her, educated her, and loved her when you could not.* "I see," she replied, though she did not see at all.

"My wife, Gloria, would like to meet . . . at a more neutral location."

Kai's lips curled. So a Chinese woman was not welcome in the Powell home.

"I mean . . ." His chuckle made Kai cringe. She did not like unexpected changes, and certainly did not think them humorous. "Gloria's just worried . . . until we . . . work through things, it might be best if you and Joy don't meet."

Best for Gloria or Joy? A lifetime of surviving fickle political winds sealed Kai's lips, yet inwardly she fumed. Why would they keep Joy from family?

"Could we meet at your hotel?"

"Yes, of course, Reverend."

"Which one was it again?"

She had faxed her itinerary and provided references for the man who'd acted as if she were a Communist agent. Her arrival was a sty in the eye for them, something to suffer through and get rid of as soon as possible. She sighed and expelled such thoughts. They did not know what her folder contained. They did not know. "The Sundance Hotel. Seventh and Main."

There was such a pause, Kai feared her lifeline to Lily had been disconnected. "I could check conference room availability. For privacy," she added. "If everything's booked, there is a sitting area off the lobby."

"Well, sure," exploded in her ears. "That would be great."

"Very good."

"Could we stretch it a bit? Meet later?"

I have traveled thousands of miles, labored hundreds of days for this moment. How can I wait longer? Do you hear me, Reverend Powell, or must I write what I have to tell you in the contrails of your so-called friendly skies? Kai clutched her stomach. The waiting, the lurking diagnosis, this call—it shredded any semblance of her composure. Yet she must not succumb to nerves, not when she was so close. "What is convenient for you?" she managed.

"Give us an hour. Say eleven o'clock?"

Kai agreed and said good-bye. She summoned the front-desk manager with the press of a button on her room phone and booked the Stampede Room at a price that would feed every comrade in her village for a month. She would gladly pay six, ten, a thousand times that cost for a chance to save the sister she had abandoned on the orphanage steps. She would max out her new Visa card, borrow from David—even beg money from his banker father, if necessary—to explain to the Powells why she must meet Lily, help Lily, reclaim Lily as a Chang . . . though she'd never phrase it as such.

She smoothed her tailored suit, double-checked that the briefcase contained the wrapped presents for each Powell, and collected the papers that catalogued and quantified the insidious things of her heritage. Documents that, if accepted and acted upon, could save the life of Fourth Chang Daughter. Could restore Chang loss of face. Could tame the fire-breathing dragon that had resided for years in the depths of Kai's soul.

Gloria rubbed her thumb against her palm, trying to erase another potential setback in Joy's life. "I don't think this is a good idea," she told Andrew for the hundredth time since this doctor—this supposed sister—had called.

Andrew tapped his fingers on the steering wheel. "It's her family." The radio dial became the victim of Andrew's nervous jiggles. "She claims we need to discuss Joy's medical history."

"The National Weather Service has issued a tornado watch—just a watch, y'all—for Parker County, remaining in effect until one p.m."

For five days, the radio had squawked of storms. Her heart heavy, Gloria canvassed the freeway's SUVs, Mercedes, and pickups. With a high-strung teenager—*a troubled teenager*—coloring their sky moody blue, they'd ducked from one temporary refuge—the nurse's office, a counselor, their doctor—like the umbrella-toting folks scurrying along the pedestrian walkways. Had God now sent an Asian storm when health problems, school problems, and church problems already clouded Joy's sky?

Andrew kept fiddling with the dial. Reba McEntire sang of secrets, the Backstreet Boys told them to quit playing games, and a gospel soprano threatened to blow their one good speaker. Gloria half listened while recalling the smells and sights of China that she'd so carefully recorded in "My Baby's Memory Book," then secreted under sweaters in a hope chest and never shown to Joy. The memories birthed the fear that she'd never voiced, yet always felt near: Joy might be taken from them. The memories birthed other unsettling things. Things Gloria had never dared utter.

Not even to Andrew.

Perhaps China could've better provided for Joy than us Powells. Perhaps God is punishing Joy—and us—for our arrogant assumption otherwise.

"I hate you!" Joy's words had glazed their family room— and Gloria—with ice. *"When I'm eighteen, I'm outta here."* Joy had tugged at the sleeves of the canyon-deep V-necked sweater, whose purchase by Joy had slammed yet another thunderstorm into their home. *"I'm going to find them. My real parents."*

Gloria remembered the exact inflection that spewed from Joy's painted-purple lips. Shivering, she now darted a glance at Andrew and heaved a sigh. She couldn't burden poor Andrew with her fears. Not now. It wouldn't stop this meeting, anyway. China—and that real family—had called. Andrew said they must answer.

They exited at Main, mere blocks from the Sundance. Mere minutes from the time when Joy's past might funnel from the sky and suck up the life they'd created. Who, really, was this Dr. Chang Kai? What did she want with Joy? They swerved into a parking lot. Gloria clutched the door handle. She'd been praying for a chance to show Joy how much they loved her.

Andrew said he hoped God had answered the prayer. Though how God could use a mysterious Chinese relative—supposed relative—Gloria couldn't begin to imagine.

⁓

I cannot endure the stares of those dead animals for another minute. Every fiber in Kai's body screamed for her to escape the garish hotel lobby. In an unusual acquiescence to psychological whims, she clicked past a fireplace bigger than her townhouse kitchen. A lion, a cow with gigantic horns, and a grizzly bear stalked her from their trophy mounts. Animals slaughtered, just for show—another strange American custom, like being late to appointments. Ten minutes late. She ducked her head and hurried to the grand Sundance entry. Would she ever get used to this country? Would this country ever get used to her?

"Can I help you, ma'am?" asked the concierge, seated behind a mahogany table.

"No, thank you." Kai fanned her face with Lily's folder. "I just need fresh air." Until she settled this matter, breathing would not come easy.

Outside, she dodged strollers and businessmen and gulped air so hot, so humid, it possessed a cottony texture. Where were her salty Boston sea breezes?

In a parking lot across the street, a lanky man dressed in khaki pants and a wrinkled Oxford shirt helped a woman from a faded blue sedan. It was the woman who still harrowed her nightmares. Hot wind tore through Kai at the sight of the familiar blond hair, though six years had faded it, and the rouged cheeks. Lily's taker wore a gauzy pastel skirt that fluttered around well-formed legs. Her shoulders hunched as if she might blow away. Dared Kai hope she was as compliant as she looked?

The couple joined hands and stepped forward. The man locked kindly eyes on Kai, who managed a smile. Surely he knew who she was, as she was the only Asian standing in front of the Sundance Hotel. Most likely the only Asian *staying* at the Sundance Hotel. To scurry inside now would be improper. Discourteous.

"You must be Dr. . . . um . . ."

"Call me Kai." Another forced smile. Though it rankled, she had dropped her Chinese surname, as her sponsors had suggested, when she deplaned at Logan, insisting Americans just call her Kai. It was less insulting than to hear them butcher her name. Why embarrass those not knowing better? She gripped Lily's file as if it were a shield. Distance between them would buttress her composure.

"Kai, this is my wife, Gloria."

It was difficult to smile while staring into the visage burned into Kai's memory, eyes that had devoured Lily as she'd been guided into that van. Kai forced a bow and adopted the mindset she used with patients who'd asked the receptionist if they could be seen by another doctor, one they could understand. "Hello. Nice to meet you."

Not a muscle on Gloria moved . . . except her fingers, which dug into pale fists.

Gloria's silence crushed Kai's chest. Soon she might asphyxiate. "A meeting room was available," she managed.

"Wonderful," breathed Reverend Powell, perhaps relieved to utter pleasantries and compensate for his wife's silence.

Kai led Lily's parents past enormous Western oil paintings that lined a corridor lit by chandeliers fashioned from antlers. More strange Texas things.

The Stampede Room had been serviced with a soft drink tray, ice bucket and tongs, hockey-puck-sized cookies, plates, and napkins. Everything to make this meeting comfortable, though the well-meaning staff did not realize that was impossible.

Kai waited for the Powells to take seats at a gleaming mahogany table surely designed for oil barons, then settled across from them. *Give the Texans their space, but position yourself to look in their eyes.*

Reverend Powell chatted about the weather, but Kai barely listened for scrutinizing the couple. Andrew's wrinkled shirt—had they properly cared for Lily? Gloria's glacial eyes—had Lily received a mother's compassion?

"Can I get you ladies something to drink?" asked Reverend Powell.

Gloria extended her moratorium on speech.

"No, thank you." Kai placed her hand on Lily's folder and battled emotions threatening to spew all over the table. How hard it was to play what Americans called the waiting game when every tick of the clock could be shortening Lily's life. She debated presenting her gifts in the Chinese way and decided against it. The last impression she wanted to give was that of a fawner, a user, trying to buy respect.

Reverend Powell reached for his wife's hand and cupped it in his. Freckled skin displayed matching gold bands, symbolizing commitment to each other. Did that same commitment extend to Lily?

"Well," the reverend finally said, "would you mind if we begin in prayer?"

Kai shook her head, though exasperation tightened her jaw. How often had David and Cheryl begun festive evenings in this same depressing way?

As the man begged for God to be present, Kai couldn't keep from casing the room and everything in it, including Gloria . . . who pinned her with a narrowed gaze.

So prayer is a sham to her as well. Kai ducked her head and waited for the "Amen" to end the ritual.

Reverend Powell cleared his throat. "Kai, I appreciate you coming all the way from Boston." The man's curly brown hair glistened with sweat. "We are grateful, truly, for your concerns about Joy's health."

Gloria let go of her husband's hand to dig into her palms.

Kai tried not to stare at the woman's frantic gesture. Was the woman—*Lily's mother*—neurotic?

"We're curious why you felt the urgency to find us. To find Joy." The man seemed hypnotized by Kai's folder.

"Yes, we are," echoed the woman, a glazed look in her eyes. Would this woman's demeanor be so cold if she had been in debt up to her frosty blue lids; if she had worked twenty-four-hour shifts and rushed home, not to sleep but to pore over journals, wait on a green card; if she'd had to pay bribes to get records from China, then hire a reputable PI willing to help a Chinese woman find her American sister?

It's behind me now, Kai reminded herself. But it was still painful.

"We're just, um, concerned." Reverend Powell laughed nervously. "I guess we need to shush and let you tell us why you are here."

Kai closed her eyes to visualize the mother of the terminally ill toddler, the husband of the colleague whose inoperable tumor had gobbled up a perfectly healthy liver. With surprising calm, she remembered those who had come for her parents, those who had killed Old Grandfather. She begged every anatomical term, every whim of fate, every unfortunate act that had twisted her world to infuse her speech with kindness and hope. If she did so, the fates might convince these people of her veracity . . . and spare precious Lily.

"I am honored to meet Joy's parents," she lied. It stung to call Fourth Chang Daughter by this American name! "I am here first as a medical doctor, sworn to honor the commitments I made when I took the oath." She opened her file, though there was no need; the words had been stamped into her brain, her soul, her heart. "Secondly, I am here in the role of Joy's birth sister."

The woman named Gloria tightened her jaw. Her forehead creased. Her eyes turned clear as ice. Not a propitious start.

"Six years ago last summer, my blessed mother passed away. I was allowed to return to China for her funeral. It was then that . . . we were fortunate to have you adopt Joy." Despite the bitter taste of the words, Kai managed to say what must be said if this wooing were to be successful.

"When I returned to America I committed myself to the study of kidney disease, which I believe to be the cause of my mother's demise."

The reverend sighed and shook his head. At least *he* displayed sympathy.

Kai battled a dry mouth. "It took years, but I persuaded"—*bribed*—"Chinese officials to release my mother's file. I have spent hours" —*and every spare penny*—"identifying her underlying disease." Her zeal to fight PKD infused her voice with passion.

The woman shuddered and drew back. Was it because of prejudice? Innate dislike?

Kai stemmed a desire to massage her right hand. She'd dealt with such things before and would deal with them again. Stiff fingers pried open the file and withdrew documents. She slid copies to the Powells, who had huddled close, like shivering chicks. "I believe the disease that killed my mother is PKD, polycystic kidney disease."

"You believe or you know?" asked Mrs. Powell.

Kai stiffened at the woman's comment, and then determined to set it aside.

"PKD is a hereditary disorder." Kai's physician's control faltered; she had to envision Lily's perfect oval face to harden her resolve and mask her emotions. "There is a possibility that your Joy"—*my Lily*—"has inherited the abnormal PKD chromosome."

Gloria covered her mouth but failed to stop a sob. "How much of a chance?"

Kai stared at the willowy body, the trembling chin. This was the crux of being a healer: finding a humane yet truthful way to inform patients of their fate. Yet this was not just any patient. This was her long-lost Lily. Kai moistened her lips. "At this point, we do not yet know whether Joy has PKD. Has she manifested symptoms? That is the true sign. If so, she needs to be tested. The sooner, the better."

Silence swallowed every sound save the hum of the hotel's air-conditioning system. Kai replayed her words, sure that the tone and vocabulary had been wrong. She had not presented her case—*Lily's* case—in the proper way. Did she, with the *yin-yang* personality of an Americanized Asian, even *possess* the ability to be both sympathetic physician and Chang family member, desperate to reclaim her youngest sister?

Blond hair cascaded over the woman's eyes. "We'd like to know more about PKD before Joy's subjected to . . . who knows what."

The air-conditioner hummed louder, as if desperate to cool the air, yet heat flashed through Kai. She begged the fates to intervene before a storm clouded her plan.

"Dr. Kai," drawled the reverend, "what are we—what is Joy—facing?"

Kai swallowed down prognoses hovering on her tongue and forced Western optimism onto a palate exposed to death's reality. "Has Joy had unusual symptoms?"

"Such as what?" came from the woman, who grabbed her husband's sleeve and fixed wild-animal eyes on Kai.

To compose herself, Kai lowered her gaze to the star-spangled carpet. Lily had symptoms. Not only did the PI's report hint at it; she could read it in those eyes as clearly as if she held Lily's complete medical history in her hands. Tears welled. Poor Lily, who had endured neglect at the orphanage, must now drink a draught brewed from life's bitter roots. Again Kai moistened her lips. She was mired in what Americans called a lose-lose situation! A good doctor would avoid listing symptoms sure to fertilize anxious parents' imaginations. But these were not just anxious parents. These were her sister's parents. Forget Harvard training and intern mandates. At all cost, she must humor the Powells.

"Signs and symptoms for PKD would include unexplained elevated blood pressure, low back pain, occasional sharp, localized pain in the abdomen—"

Knowing gasps escaped the woman.

An iron vise gripped Kai with such force that she, too, gasped, though she tried to mask it with a cough. *Poor Lily. I must help her!* Could she convince the Powells—mainly the wife—of her concern for Lily? Could they forge an alliance, based on mutual devotion to a teenaged girl?

"Doctor." The reverend's smooth brow and soft drawl demonstrated control; his soft brown eyes, compassion. They exchanged sad smiles. Kai's tightness eased. This was a kind man, accustomed to shouldering others' troubles. Reverend Andrew Powell seemed an ally in this war against PKD. "Assuming our girl's had aches and pains, what's the worst-case scenario here?"

Kai pursed her lips. Americans insisted on leaping to worst case as if with knowledge, they could trump fate. She smoothed her skirt, desperate to hold the hands of these Texans and progress slowly. "PKD can be life-threatening, but science is making great strides toward—"

"Tell me what will happen to my Joy." Mrs. Powell's nostrils flared with anger. Delicate features hardened with dislike.

Heat throttled Kai's cheeks. This woman blamed her for Lily's predicament! Thankfully the words of old Dr. Ward rescued a poisonous retort. *"Patients view you not as physician but as the deadly disease itself. To them you are the enemy. Accept this burden with grace and continue the fight."*

"Yes, Doctor." Urgency sped up Reverend Powell's pulled-taffy drawl. "Cut to the chase here. What will happen to our Joy?"

"Tell us," demanded the woman.

This one suffers from sharp-tongue disease. Though she begged it to leave, the image of that pale hand on Lily's shoulder, leading her toward the van, toward America, infused her clinician's mind with emotion. Dr. Ward had not prepared her for this. "By the time young patients with PKD develop symptoms, there's usually advanced kidney disease." Kai's words came out garbled. "Until I know the specific presentation—"

"Oh, please! Can't you just tell us? In English?" Gloria wailed.

"Speak up!" a patient had hissed on Kai's first night in the ER. *"Can't you talk any better than that? Where are you from, anyway? Are you a Jap?"* Memories of racial slurs stung, though Mrs. Powell, of course, referred to medical-speak and not her foreign accent. Still, pride for China filled her with

indignation. Kai released a sigh. "The worst case is dialysis. Kidney failure. With no transplant, death."

"How can we be sure this is necessary?" Gloria rose from her seat, shoving away her husband's hand, his spluttering protestations. "You appear out of nowhere with this . . . emergency." Her eyes were veiled with . . . dislike? Fear? "Carl—Fort Worth's best internist, I might add—thinks Joy has a nervous stomach. No one's mentioned this . . . poly . . . whatever it is. How do we know you are not using this . . ."

"PKD," Kai supplied.

". . . PKD . . . to worm your way into Joy's life?"

"I do not worm my way in, Mrs. Powell. I have been prepared for this all my life."

"Prepared? What do you mean?"

Papers swished to the floor. The carpet's reds, whites, and blues blurred, as did Kai's vision. How dare this soft American woman question a calling the fates revealed at age five? She would not stand for it. No, she had come too far and accomplished too much to be treated this way. Did not Lily's well-being—perhaps Lily's life—hang on the hope that she could convince these people of her motives, concern, and love?

As she reclaimed the scattered papers, she begged fate to reveal words that would resonate in the hearts of these Texans. She would tell them as much as they—and she—could handle, starting from the beginning.

2

AN EASTERN CHINA VILLAGE, 1967

Five-year-old Kai dashed down an alleyway past neighbor children. Ripening plums perfumed the air with a sweet wine smell. Birds twittered a glorious song. Gentleman Dog growled and chased his tail. Kai's jubilation over Spring Festival threatened to send her airborne, like the kites children released to the winds before sunset. When Father's school gates closed, the two of them would crisscross the field and let their royal red kite rule mountains, birds . . . even puffy white clouds. But first she must purchase new twine.

Peasants in their rough cotton shirts and pants shuffled by, kicking up dust. Two men grumbled and conked each other in the head with bamboo poles.

"Silly little fool," one mumbled, as if Kai were to blame for their bad moods.

"What do you expect from the spoiled child of intellectuals?"

The men afflicted with jealousy's green-skinned disease spat on the ground and glared at her as if their tobacco-stained

40

phlegm belonged on her face. Kai flinched and then puffed out her chest. She would not let the peasants' poor feng shui dim the bright light that was her family's successful wooing of fate, especially during this glorious season. Despite her thoughts, she bowed at the men in the customary way. She was Chang Kai, Second Daughter. To retaliate against villagers who wished her evil might upset life's delicate balance.

Kai reached in her pocket, where she had stashed the last bit of old kite twine and a knife, whose ivory smoothness soothed the men's harsh words. Buoyed by a west wind, she streaked past the workers to the dusty main street of their village. Fluttering crimson-and-gold animal lanterns hung from warped rafters of the store. She hopped up uneven steps to say hello, first to the bulging-eyed frog lantern. Silly thing! Then an elephant lantern waved his trunk and begged a pretend peanut, trumpeting thanks when she flattened her palm to feed it. Saving best for last, she tiptoed to the fire-breather lantern, her very own zodiac symbol, with such splendor in his forked tongue and scaly tail! Pride stretched her legs to reach his shiny crimson back. Up, up—

Chee, chee.

What sound tickled her ears? Had a strange bird coasted on the wind current to attend the festival? She jumped off the porch, threw back her head, and searched a blue sky. Lazy clouds floated by, but no bird.

Chee, chee.

Kai stepped into grass, tilted her head, and peered into a tree. A mother bird flapped into a nest and settled wings about bald chicks whose beaks were closed. Silent.

Chee, chee.

Kai pricked her ears to follow the sound, scrambled onto her hands and knees, and crawled to a flowering jasmine.

The bush shuddered. Out popped a tiny creature, plucked-chicken pink. Beady eyes studied her. Wings flapped like broken fans.

Kai clapped her hands and cooed. What a funny-looking thing!

The chick staggered forward and crashed into a gnarly branch. *"Chee, chee."*

"Chee, chee," Kai whispered. "Greetings, little one."

Silent, the chick stared back, lifted one foot, and toppled over.

Had spring intoxicated the chick? Kai spied an angry red knot on the chick's leg joint. Below the knot, the leg bent like a discarded pipe cleaner. Useless for walking. Flying. Living.

Poor thing! As Kai reached for the chick, her right hand radiated heat to match her sympathy-warmed heart. Fate had cursed this chick! She must try to repair its poor crooked leg. Old Grandfather had taught her to mend broken chairs. Was the principle not similar? "Chee, chee," she whispered, and scooped up the chick.

The bird struggled, then lay still . . . except for a *thump, thump* against Kai's fingers. *Thump. Thump.* Such a strong little heart! Kai tingled with pleasure. A coo escaped her mouth. She had found the chick's life rhythms!

"Chee, chee." Speaking the chick's language, Kai folded her legs underneath her and sat on the ground. "Be still, little one." Kai balanced the chick between her knees and dug in her pocket for the knife and string. Moving slowly, so as not to scare the chick, she slashed the string in two. Her fingers tickled the grass and inched caterpillar-like to a stick. Still whispering, "Chee, chee," she stripped bark from the stick and made a splint for her little friend.

Except for its heartbeat, the chick was silent.

Kai scooped up the chick, used her pulsating right hand to straighten the bent leg against the splint, then looped string round and round until the splint and the leg became one. The chick never struggled, as if it understood exactly what Kai was doing.

"*Chee, chee,*" the chick said in thanks.

Kai transferred the chick into her left hand and spread the fingers of her right hand, half expecting to see steam rising as from a boiling pot. She opened her hand, closed it. Opened it, closed it.

Warmth spread to the funny looped ridges on the back of her fingers that Old Grandfather said made her hand different from everyone else's. The warmth soothed like the *kang* bed on a winter night. Mesmerized, she stretched her fingers and studied her hand's every pore, every crease.

Of its own accord, the right hand moved to massage the chick's fluffy breast.

Thump. Thump. Thump.

The chick's heartbeats matched the heat pulsating through Kai's hand. The hand was magic! Kai, Second Daughter of the Chang family, possessed a Healing Right Hand that somehow connected with hurt creatures!

Kai's heart pattered in a wild rhythm. If the fates allowed, this tiny creature could now hop. Dared she hope it might one day soar high as the festival kites? She stroked the chick's breast in thanks for such a momentous Spring Festival beginning. Perhaps she could help other birds! Oh, never had she dreamed of such a connection with the creatures that she loved! She must tell Old Grandfather! She must—

"What are you doing?" A shrill voice shattered the magic.

Old Ling has found us.

The cranky wife of the shop owner always tottered away

on swollen stubs of feet and refused to wait on the Chang daughters. Old Ling had hated Kai since her first moon. Though Kai had asked Mother why, Mother never responded.

"Stupid girl!" Old Ling plunked down the shop steps. Her jaw gaped to expose the black holes and yellow crags of a filthy cave mouth. She shook a broom at Kai. Bits of straw and mouse dung fluttered in the air. "Why waste time on such frivolity?"

Kai cupped her hand about her new feathered friend to shield it from Old Ling's poor feng shui.

"Why do you not cook and scrub and weed?" Again Old Ling swung the broom, barely missing Kai's head. "And you, devil bird!" Curse words and spit soiled the air. "We should have finished you off when we had the chance! Both of you, scoot!"

Kai wobbled to her feet, the chick still in her hands. She pigeon-toed away from Old Ling. The shop door slammed. Old Ling and her ill temper disappeared, though her strange words lingered.

Kai tiptoed to the chick's nest home. "You will grow strong, little friend." She settled the chick by its brothers and sisters and tried to ignore the flapping and cawing mother trembling a nearby limb. "Good-bye for now."

Thank-you cheeps streamed from the nest.

Wind gusts caught Kai's bubbling laughter and spun it into music. The frog lantern croaked, the elephant lantern trumpeted, the dragon lantern snorted fire. Kai sprinted for home. The alleyways blurred into browns, greens, and slivers of red. Barks, meows, grunts, and mumbles rose from the yards. Animal creatures, all cheering for the work of her healing hand!

When Kai's heart threatened to explode within her chest,

she slowed to a walk. Her heart stopped its punishment, but a question hammered her mind.

She entered her house, which was fragrant with the aroma of garlic and tea.

"Hello, Second Daughter." Wiping her hands on her apron, Mother turned from a simmering pot. Mother balanced cooking, lesson-preparing, and caring for Third Daughter on her shapely shoulders. What harmony she brought to their home! "The Party has called a special meeting," Mother continued. "There will be no kite-flying."

Kites? Because of her adventure with the bird, Kai had forgotten to buy kite twine, had forgotten about kite-flying with Father. She had *not* forgotten Old Ling's strange, hate-tinged words. She held out her arm, as if guiding a kite, but fixed her eyes on the Healing Right Hand. "Old Grandfather?"

Old Grandfather nodded and puffed his pipe. Smoke ringed his head and drifted to his rounded belly.

Kai beamed. What honor Old Grandfather brought their family! Could she bring honor, too, with her discovery of a most unusual gift?

Musty tobacco leaves joined kitchen scents and obliterated the last of Old Ling's sourness. "Mother! Old Grandfather!" Kai waved her arm. "I have a magic right hand!"

Mother frowned. "If it is so magic, have it assemble these dumplings."

"Daughter, let the little one be. She will work soon enough." Old Grandfather patted his knees, held out his arms.

Mother, usually so cheerful, picked up her pot and huffed to the courtyard, most likely to let the stuffing mixture cool.

Ignoring Mother, Kai shrieked. To be coddled by Old Grandfather, a thing rarely allowed? The right hand had brought not only magic, but good fortune. She would ask

Old Grandfather the question flapping about in her mind. She eased into Old Grandfather's lap, mindful of his fragile bones.

"Tell me, Second Daughter, what has put dragon fire in your eyes?"

Kai breathed Old Grandfather's cornstarch-and-smoke smell. "I met a baby bird. With a hurt leg." As she talked, she spread her fingers to show what she had done, then had to poke Old Grandfather twice to open his heavy eyelids. How could a storyteller like Old Grandfather drift away as she recounted such adventure . . . and before her question?

"Old Grandfather!" She raised her voice, clapped her hands.

Life stirred between the folds and creases surrounding his marble eyes.

Kai sat straight, determined to ask the question before Old Grandfather again left for the dream world.

"Old Ling cursed my bird friend. Why?" Questions made Kai rustle about. "She spoke of old days. What did she mean by 'finishing off' birds?"

Her questions hovered in the air, though Kai begged them to vanish since they sagged and shadowed Old Grandfather's seventy-year-old eyelids.

The questions refused to leave. They were stubborn things, just like her.

Pale lips gripped the pipe. Smoke puffs encircled Old Grandfather's nose. "In famine years, Chairman Mao decreed that sparrows gobbled up our crops. A campaign was launched to exterminate the wasteful creatures."

"Exterminate?" Kai's teeth chattered at such an awful-sounding word.

"Rock-hurling peasants stormed the fields. Teachers ordered students to beat washbasins, clang pot lids."

"Why?"

"To disturb the birds' feng shui."

"Just to . . . scare them away?"

Old Grandfather puffed his pipe and shook his head.

Her hand swelled as if ten hornets had attacked. "To . . . kill them?"

Old Grandfather did not say a word. He did not need to.

Chills zipped along Kai's spine. "Our village? They did this here in our village?"

Smoke seeped from Old Grandfather's mouth as he slowly nodded.

"No!" Kai's heart throbbed pain. She struggled out of Old Grandfather's lap.

Though Old Grandfather's lips moved, wings beat so violently against Kai's heart that she could not hear him. The pipe smoke she had once loved swirled to choke her. Images of limp wings and bloodied feathers swooped in to join the attack.

Free from Old Grandfather's lap, Kai tore out of the house, past Mother, still working in the courtyard, through the garden, and to the ladder that leaned against the shed. She had to join her feathered friends in their sky home and leave the horrid ground behind! Sobs shook her body. Who would hurl sticks and stones at innocent birds? Her bare toes curled about ladder rungs as she climbed toward a world where nature's creatures achieved perfect harmony. Her fingers dug into splintery wood. Higher! Higher! With each step she left the nasty killing world of men.

Bird chatter began when she reached the top rung. Huffing, she collapsed onto the shed roof. "Chee, chee!" she cried as she wiped away her tears and pivoted enough to shove the ladder to the ground. "I, Chang Kai," she shouted to the sparrows and gulls and bulbuls and ducks from her shed-top kingdom, "will never threaten your life."

Shouts rose from the yard, but Kai paid them no mind. She twirled to create a wind that would block the low world's sounds. "I, Chang Kai, will honor you as long as the fates allow!"

Oh, what chirping! What singing! The shed roof became her roost. Kai flapped her arms and hopped like the injured chick to show the birds what was in her heart. She hopped as the little bird had. Twirled. Hopped—

Something whooshed, like kite tails battling an angry wind. Kai felt herself falling. She opened her mouth to scream, but the breeze captured her voice.

For the span of two wing flaps, Kai hung in the air. Then she banged against the cold hard ground. The Healing Right Hand clawed the dirt.

Dark descended. Heavy weights pinned her limbs. Someone called from far, far away. Kai tried to talk, but pain allowed only groans.

"Little Kai! Little Kai!" finally penetrated the void.

She pried open heavy lids.

Light streamed in and stabbed her eyes. She shut them tight.

"Second Daughter!"

It was Old Grandfather, out in the light. To avoid stabbing pain to her eyes, she must stay in the dark. But she would signal that she heard. She tried to smile, to shake her limbs, but pain halted even a toe wiggle. Oh, what had happened?

"Second Daughter, get up."

"You must keep her conscious!"

Someone—Father?—slapped her cheeks.

Someone—Mother?—wailed like little Third Daughter.

"Get the doctor!" Father cried.

Feet—Mother's?—scurried away.

"Second Daughter? Little Dragon?"

It was Old Grandfather, his smoky smell near her head.

"Nod if you can hear me."

Though the movement of her neck birthed three groans, she obeyed.

"You will not leave us. Do you understand? You and your Healing Right Hand are destined to journey to a faraway land. You will save many people. Are you listening, Second Daughter? It is your fate to embark on an extraordinary quest and bring honor to the family name."

Fingers probed her head, chest, stomach, limbs, even the Healing Right Hand. Every touch throbbed pain; to battle it, she clung to Old Grandfather's strange words.

"You must wake up," Old Grandfather spoke so naturally, so calmly, Kai imagined that she could see pipe smoke. But she could not see anything.

Shouts and rustles began to drown out the strange prophecy.

"Bruises."

"Maybe a broken arm."

"It is no matter." Old Grandfather's voice soared above the others. Like swallows, conquering rooftops. She tilted her head toward Old Grandfather and his soothing voice.

"She has a Healing Right Hand that will save others . . . and save herself."

Old Grandfather was magic, like her right hand! Though Kai had not explained its powers, Old Grandfather knew. It birthed four groans for Kai to smile. With an ancestor like Old Grandfather, the fates would heal her. Somehow a Healing Right Hand would be involved. She smiled at her good fortune and slipped into darkness.

China . . . so far from . . . Fort Worth. This luxury hotel conference room. Kai blinked away images priceless as Dynasty relics and found her bearings, yet her body trembled, remembering that long-ago fall. Summoning strength, she poured a glass of water and assessed the Powells' reaction to her story.

Reverend Powell drummed the table. His wife pushed back her chair and hugged her arms. *A shield from my story? Do not worry, mother of Joy. I will say no more.* Intuitively, she refrained from overloading these Christians by recounting the atrocities that had plagued their village in the years after her fall. These Christians would close their ears to how she, aged eleven, and First Daughter, aged fifteen, had salved the bloody wounds Father had received in prison, how she had massaged Father's stroke-damaged limbs until he could again walk. These Christians would close their eyes to her shampooing of Mother's yin-yang haircut—half her hair shaved, the other half tangled and thick with lice.

Kai managed to set down her glass without spilling water. She would not tell them that at the ripe old age of eleven, in the shadow of a banyan tree, she had sworn to become a doctor, a profession that seemed best suited to reclaim Chang dignity and provide for Mother and Father.

She gripped Lily's file until her hands ached. She would not tell them about sleepless nights on the kang, sleepless nights in the dormitory, sleepless nights in the study carrel, sleepless weekends on call. They had not opened their ears to hear about her ordeals, her journeys . . . her life. Using every ounce of control she possessed, she smiled sweetly at the Americans. She would tell them no more, for if she saw another smattering of disgust, disbelief, or disinterest on their picture-window American faces, she might shatter into a million pieces. That would not help Lily. No, that would not help Lily at all.

3

Gloria fisted her hands to keep from biting already chewed fingernails. This healing hand tale proved that Joy's sister lived in the outer limits of bizarre. She was supposed to trust the life of *her only child* with a complete stranger who trusted the fates? "I just don't see . . ." A lifetime of acting with social grace spluttered to a halt . . . *what this has to do with Joy . . . if she even is your sister.* This woman couldn't be in God's plan to save Joy. This woman—

Andrew cupped her hand with familiar reassurance, unfamiliar restraint. In her role as a pastor's wife, she'd never dared such bluntness . . . except after the church fire. But this woman threatened their Joy, their peace. What if Joy, still in a snit about getting grounded over the graffiti incident, decided to run off with this woman?

"Thanks for sharing your, um, history," Andrew finally said. "Don't get the wrong idea, Kai. We're not questioning your calling as a physician."

"What is it, then, you question?" A maddening calm coated the doctor's tone.

"We're just wondering, with all Joy's been through, how

51

she'd react to another upheaval. I mean, seventeen's a pretty rough age—"

"To have your world turned upside down." Gloria felt her lips curl into a frown. "Your family torn apart."

"Now, Gloria—"

"Mrs. Powell, I do not intend to tear apart your family." The woman's deep-set eyes burned with intensity. Did sisterly love spark that fire? *Doubtful.* Vengeance? *Perhaps.* A physician's passion to heal? *I don't think so.*

"I would like to partner with you and Reverend Powell," the woman continued.

"We have partners. More partners than we can handle." *Counselors. Teachers. Doctors. Believers. For heaven's sake, the Lord Jesus himself.*

"I can understand why you might not trust me."

Gloria's vision focused on the doctor's smiling bow lips that revealed nothing of the heart. Another woman had once "partnered" with Daddy to destroy Gloria's world . . . and her ability to trust. That scar had knitted together nicely, thanks to Andrew, who'd proved that not all men cheated on their family. Andrew, who had shared her passion to adopt Joy. *This woman won't destroy what Andrew and I have built.*

Gloria rested her elbows on her chair arms and searched the doctor's face as if to discern the motivations of her heart in the flutter of lashes, the narrowing of almond-shaped eyes. How had this woman even managed to *find* them? Surely laws had been broken, privacy acts had been breached . . .

Gloria twisted her wedding ring, desperate to transfer hostility somewhere besides this doctor. Yet she found she could not stop herself as resentment and fear surged. "Tell me, Doctor. Has your life disintegrated in one day? One hour?"

Words escaped in a hiss as Gloria visualized blood-red lipstick smeared all over Daddy's face and neck. "One moment?"

The doctor's eyes widened until her eyelids disappeared. She crossed her arms and sat motionless. "Why, yes, Mrs. Powell. My world has been knocked off its axis. Would you like to hear about it?" The doctor's arms unfolded. Her eyes bulged with . . . Gloria blinked. Was this doctor experiencing fear? Anger? The same emotions that tore at Gloria as she battled to again keep her world—*her Joy*—from falling apart?

Andrew nodded. "Of course, Kai. We would like to hear your story."

As the doctor calmly sipped water and settled into her chair, Gloria fought an urge to scream. Could she sit through another story about China, the land from which they had taken Joy? The land that, through this woman, had returned to reclaim something. What would that something be?

CHINA, 1968

A far-away rooster crowed. Kai stirred from a dream of pale faces with pale eyelashes and pale blue eyes. Why did the gods plant such strangeness in her head? Blinking, she assured herself that she was Number Two Daughter Kai, safe in a still-warm kang. She edged away from the openmouthed breathing of Number One Daughter Ling, sat up straight, and peered out the window. A cool wind whispered a secret . . .

Beaming, Kai jumped off the kang and twirled about. Sun rays painted golden streaks on their wall and promised a masterpiece. A gift by the fates for the most important day of her life!

As if unaware of the miracle sky, villagers puffed up dust

while shuffling to the fields, rusted hoes bobbing on stooped shoulders.

"A Young Pioneer must be prepared." Kai shivered into the uniform so carefully laid out the night before. "A Young Pioneer must study well. Keep fit."

Still-sleepy fingers struggled to knot the red scarf, her badge of honor. How she had coveted this symbol of fallen comrades, of blood flowing in Chairman Mao's veins! Both she and Number One Daughter possessed the scarf . . . but if the fates smiled, today Kai alone would claim the position of class monitor. Mother and Father would beam! Old Grandfather would rock his chair until it, too, creaked with delight!

A groan rose from the kang. Number One Daughter's lashes fluttered as she rolled over. Even in sleep, the delicate arches of her sister's brows mirrored her inner character. Kai grabbed Ling's hand and held it tight. Such beauty, heaped like jewels onto a girl already possessing the loving heart, the loyal ways of one born under the sign of the Dog. The fates had granted riches to their family. Yet Kai must never tempt the fates by speaking of such things. *Modesty brings prosperity. I must work hard. Study hard. Preserve the Chang name.*

Energized by Confucius and Mao, Kai tugged on Number One Daughter's hand. "Get up or we'll be late, you lazy mule!"

"Nasty pig!" Number One Daughter giggled. "Grunting so early in the morning."

Kai stomped her feet and saluted. "I am no pig. I am a Young Pioneer. I love the Motherland and its people. I must work hard. Modesty brings prosperity."

Number One Daughter rolled her eyes. "Slogan saying will not help, you silly pig. But the class-monitor position—yes, I know about it—will remove you from your muddy sty." As if smelling night soil, Ling wrinkled her perfect nose, dangled a dainty foot out of the covers, and shivered into Kai's arms. The two embraced and giggled as they did when cold nights cocooned them under the kang's many layers.

From the other room, Third Daughter Mei wailed. The teapot shrieked. Mother chattered in the old dialect with Grandfather, who chuckled and chattered back.

Mother is still home? Kai held her breath and hurried into the front room.

Her padded Mao jacket nowhere in sight, Mother sat by Old Grandfather and bounced squirming Third Daughter on her knee. Most unusual behavior for Mother on a school day.

"Why are you not at your teacher's desk?" Kai asked. "Is Third Daughter sick? Are you sick?" She tried to slow a mountain stream of words, but ice-cold water had chilled her veins.

"Good morning, young dragon, breathing fire on all in your path." Mother fanned her hand, as if to disperse smoke. Her knowing glance at Old Grandfather further troubled the air. Something had disturbed Chang tranquility. Kai was sure of it.

Third Daughter Mei displayed thumbprint dimples, her contentment stilling Kai's anxiety. Perhaps all was well.

"Put your fire to use," ordered Mother. "Steep the tea."

Kai bowed, mainly for Old Grandfather, who puffed with pride at her display of respect. "A cup for you, Mother? Grandfather?" she asked, a mere formality. *As long as the sun shines, the Changs will drink tea!*

"Thank you, most kind daughter," said Mother.

Old Grandfather chuckled and nodded.

"It is my privilege." Kai bowed low. "But first tell me why you are home. Most honorable Mother," she added, ducking her head to hide a sly smile.

Silence allowed courtyard clucks and crow caws to fill the room. With arched brows and widened eyes, elder talk in the old dialect zipped from Mother to Old Grandfather. Kai pinched her lips tight and leaned against the stove, whose sure, solid warmth slowed her icy streams. Though questions beat against her chest, she waited. It would never do to interrupt elder talk.

Third Daughter squirmed and fussed, angry that Mother had stopped the bouncing. How Kai wished she could squirm in uneasy situations!

Elder talk stopped. Mother studied the floor as if searching for a missing pearl. "Today I will stay home. I have a fever."

"A fever?" Kai asked.

Mother nodded and again galloped her knees for the baby. "Do not fret, Second Daughter. If the fever does not go away, there are remedies."

"There are always remedies." Grandfather picked up his pipe, tamped damp leaves with his thumb, and tried to light the smoke. Over and over he struck the match, but it failed to ignite. *"Gaisi!"* he muttered.

Kai whirled about. Why had Grandfather cursed like a slobbery-nosed drunk? She fought to still her trembling hands so she could prepare four cups of tea. Precious Dragon Needles must be preserved, no matter what ill winds blew.

Tea was served, yet Kai's icy fears could not be melted by Mother's sips, Grandfather's contented sighs. Though she nodded pleasantly, she itched to escape a room chilled by strange glances, unfamiliar words. "First Daughter!" she cried, eager to finish the morning ritual. Her school routine would bring comfort. "Tea awaits!"

First Daughter glided into the room and took her cup. Now that her elders had been served, Kai sipped the fragrant grassy liquid revered for its elements of earth, water, and fire. Feng shui began to return, as did thoughts of today's awaiting honor. "Can we go?" Kai tapped her foot to accelerate First Daughter's slug-like ways.

"Ling?" Mother set Third Daughter on Grandfather's lap and placed her palms on First Daughter's cheeks. Breath puffed between Mother's bow lips.

Mongol winds swirled through Kai. Why was Mother using First Daughter's given name? She pretended to straighten her blouse but studied Mother's every movement.

"Take care of Kai."

"Yes, Mother." First Daughter's cheeks blushed peony pink.

Kai's cup rattled as she set it in a saucer. Did sister's coloring come from the steam or from Mother's strange behavior?

"Good-bye, Second Daughter." Mother cupped Kai's cheeks with her palms.

Kai could not help but smile. Soft as a lotus blossom was Mother's skin. Soft—she shrank from Mother's night-breeze-cool touch. Why, Mother had been holding a steaming teacup and caressing warm daughter cheeks, yet her hands shivered with cold! Mother had no fever! "Good-bye," Kai echoed dully. Mother had lied, but Kai could not ask why and cause Mother to lose face.

First Daughter found Kai's hand. They walked out of the house and toward the alley. "Little swallow," First Daughter sang, "why do you come here?"

The folksong lyrics irritated like cicada dirges. Mother had not missed a day of teaching since Grandmother's death. Until now.

The girls zigzagged through clusters of workers, a woman yoked to her bucket pole, classmates kicking pebbles and chattering like chickens. Kai kept looking east, sure that storm clouds threatened. Clouds that had nothing to do with Mother's health.

⌒∘⌒

"Good morning, Honorable Teacher." Her head cocked for diligence, bowed for humility, Kai waited by the teacher's desk. The dusty smell of chalk and pencil shavings, the sight of paired desks, the crackles and hisses of the cast-iron stove, blanketed her earlier chills. "If it pleases you, may I assist with the chores?"

Her long face pinched and pale, Teacher Zhou rose from her chair and turned to the chalkboard, which bore smudges of yesterday's lessons. Her hair, usually pinned into order, drooped to meet her shirt collar as she wrote on the board.

Kai blinked in astonishment, toe-minced to her front-row table, and sat down. How often had she coaxed First Daughter from bed and hurried past a school yard noisy with children's jump ropes thudding against the earth to assist her second-level teacher? She would sprain her back to draw water for the one who transformed a blackboard into a spidery-character story, the one fluent in a mysterious number language. Kai craned her neck to study every movement of the one who had just dismissed her without a nod. The one who always demanded a clean slate wrote on a dirty board today!

A glance confirmed that the bucket sat, as usual, near the door. The ice river again flowed swift in Kai's veins. Kai rubbed her arms. Despite Teacher's behavior, she would proceed in the customary way. Feng shui must be reversed. Shivering, she grabbed the bucket, grimaced to see yellow-brown water speckled with grit and straw. Kai gripped the handle. Work must be done.

Guoliang, a plump boy who preferred napping to studies, strolled into the room, his shoelaces slapping the dirt floor. Others stomped behind him, breathing down Guoliang's neck. Yet the boy slogged like an ox with a heavy yoke.

To reach the bucket, Kai squeezed between the desk edge and Guoliang.

Guoliang shoved Kai. "You are a dung beetle," he hissed. Beady eyes disappeared into yellow folds of skin.

"The Changs are stinking ninths," others tittered.

Fireworks exploded. Kai tensed to keep from kicking knobby knees, punching snotty noses. How dare they dishonor the Chang name? Why hadn't Teacher Zhou intervened? Her head swiveled to see her instructor. A knot of classmates blocked her view. Perhaps her teacher had stepped away . . .

"You're a filthy pile of night soil," Guoliang muttered.

Kai gritted her teeth, lowered her head, and butted Guoliang's dumpling dough chest. Until Teacher returned, she would battle this herdsman mentality.

A hot wind grabbed the children's voices and transformed titters to snarls.

Though she rammed Guoliang with all her might, his sheer bulk foiled her efforts. As Kai struggled, she stared into his wild-boar eyes. Hate gleamed, a hate that caught Kai's breath. She peeked over Guoliang's shoulder.

Kai's classmates had linked arms with Guoliang and strained like peasants seeking to dislodge a heavy stone. Kai's mouth went slack. She, Second Daughter of the Chang family, was the stone!

Guoliang grabbed her shoulders and slammed Kai into a front-row desk.

Another boy rammed her with an elbow.

Kai cradled her head. Hot needles stabbed her spine. Her

shoulders. She swallowed a cry, commanded achy bones to lift her. Soon Teacher Zhou would return. Soon— Kai blinked. Stared.

Teacher Zhou stood before her. Clapped her hands together once. Twice. Except for the lightning-quick palms, she stood still as a porcelain figurine. "Lazy ones," she hissed. "Get to your seats."

Without another glance at Kai, classmates marched to their desks. Only Guoliang stood before her, triumphant daggers shooting from his eyes.

Kai's insides crumbled into dust. Why had Teacher Zhou not taken a stick to Guoliang's hide? Rained insults on his head?

As the students found their writing tablets, Kai disciplined her breaths to rise and fall. She must play the lute, even for this wild boar. A Young Pioneer could not let trifling matters affect her family's fortune.

Though Guoliang continued his glare, Kai marched toward her chair.

"Chang Kaiping!" Teacher Zhou's forehead rippled like a rushing stream. "I have repositioned the seats. Get your things. Move to the back row."

Kai's fingers froze on her chair back. A hot iron seared her limbs.

Teacher Zhou clapped again.

Kai found the strength to move, though her steps wobbled. Hot and cold sensations warred within her body.

"As the official class monitor, Guoliang, sit in front." Teacher Zhou woodenly approached the board and resumed copying the lesson.

A lazy boy of low character attained the position she deserved? How could this be? Suppressing the desire to act like a wild boar herself and charge everything in sight, Kai opened her tablet, found her pencil, ordered her burning eyes to study the board, urged her numb hand to copy the assignment.

Boundless faith in Chairman Mao, she wrote, pressing so hard her lead snapped. She found another pencil. *Chairman Mao is a blazing sun in our hearts.*

Kai set her pencil down. She darted a glance at her new seat partner, who turned watermelon seed eyes on her, then hunched over her paper as if unaware—or uninterested—in Kai.

What had happened to her class? Her family? Kai rubbed her arms, halfway convinced she had sleep-walked into a nightmare. Habit-changing pronouncements always boomed from village loudspeakers, but they were annoying mosquito bites compared to this. She fought a desire to bolt from her seat, streak out of the school, and study the signs of nature. Did her bird friends fly upside down? Did the neighborhood dogs run against the wind?

"Lazy one." The teacher fixed bright lantern eyes on her. "Reeducate yourself."

Kai dipped her head, picked up her pencil, and ordered the swallows in her stomach to be still. Her feathered friends refused to obey.

The morning dragged. Lunch break brought no release. Friends hurled piercing barbs of "black dog" and "dirty rat." Naptime brought a shove and a kick as her new seat partner huffed atop the desk, leaving her with no blanket to cushion the cold, hard floor. "Please, Father of Time," she whispered, staring at crumbling wasp nests hanging from the underside of her desk, "turn back the hands of this awful day."

"Shut up!" The nap monitor stalked toward Kai and

stomped his foot a hand's length from her face. Tears sprang into eyes unaccustomed to humiliation. Why had the fates overturned Kia's world?

Seconds stretched to minutes; minutes to hours. When lessons resumed, a tear smeared the characters she had toiled to make perfect. No matter how she tried, the fates had turned against her. She could do nothing to stop them. Nothing at all.

⟳

Gloria shifted about, the cushy conference room chair offering no comfort. *She is intelligent . . . like Joy. She has tried but failed to bury her emotions . . . like my girl; tried but failed to bury her past, like . . . me.* She felt a greater discomfort when she recognized a glimmer—tears?—in the doctor's eyes. Gloria couldn't let down her guard until she trusted this woman. *Yet how can I trust her until I let down my guard?*

Andrew sat motionless, as if spellbound by Kai and her history. For one of the few times in their married life, he irritated her. Shouldn't they get to the reason for this meeting? Sure, Kai had a sad story, as did many Cultural Revolution survivors, according to what she'd read. Things she'd promised to tell Joy about . . . but never had. It would only have upset her, confused her.

Could Joy be more confused than she is now?

"Doctor." Andrew's slumped shoulders, the bent of his head, modeled empathy. A must-have pastor trait. Yet Gloria's composure fissured. How could she partner with her husband to both personify Christ's character for a stranger and protect her daughter?

"That was the beginning of the nightmare, wasn't it?" asked Andrew.

Kai lowered her head to nod. Silver glimmered in her hair, silver woven by time, by trials. Life had slammed this woman with sorrow . . . but did that fact earn her passage into Joy's world? *Their* world?

"Could you tell us more?" Andrew asked in his gentle, unhurried way. "It might help us to better understand our Joy."

A thousand pins pricked Gloria, who resisted the urge to scratch the daylights out of her hands. *We already understand Joy, who's a typical moody teenager with pimples and PMS to prove it. We don't know . . . or understand . . . this woman.*

Gloria opened her mouth, but the snippy retort melted. Why had she wadded up the invitation to Our Chinese Family Foundation picnic and thrown it away? Why had she similarly trashed every chance for Joy to explore her culture? Was it fear that she would lose Joy? Fear that Joy had never been hers to lose?

The very thought of Joy not being hers knotted Gloria's insides. She didn't know if she could stand to hear one more word about this woman's past. *What matters is today. Joy's life here in Fort Worth, Texas, U.S. of A.*

"It might help me if we got to the bottom of things. Our daughter." Gloria hugged her arms to combat a sinking sensation. What happened years ago in China would not interfere with Joy's well-being. Any sane person could see they dealt with two separate issues here.

"I apologize for the digression." The doctor opened her file and blinked, as if she were shutting a portal to her past.

A sigh escaped Gloria. *Good.*

With a tight smile, the doctor picked up her paper. "I have summarized the epidemiology of PKD." She dug eyeglasses out of her bag. "You are busy people, Reverend and Mrs. Powell. I will not waste more of your time than necessary."

"You're busy, too, Doctor. Hey, we haven't wasted the day. Far from it." Andrew's soothing tone—which usually salved Gloria's soul—scratched and clawed.

"That is most kind of you to say, Reverend."

"We appreciate hearing about your struggles. Our Joy has had struggles t—"

Gloria's jaw tightened. "Excuse me." She tapped on the doctor's printout to keep from wadding it up and throwing it at Andrew. How could he share Joy's secrets? Personal things. Private things. The piercings. The hair. *Embarrassing* things. "Before we get into Joy's issues, could you tell us more about this PKD?"

Andrew sighed and picked up the paper in front of him.

The doctor's face deflated, though her expression never wavered. "If Joy has not presented with respiratory insufficiency, if her physician has not detected grossly enlarged echogenic kidneys, we can rule out autosomal recessive PKD. However, if Joy has presented with symptoms . . ." The doctor took off her glasses and rubbed the bridge of her nose. She studied Andrew and then replaced her glasses.

Silence yawned maddeningly. Pressure throbbed Gloria's temples. Why had Andrew agreed to this meeting, insisting they hear what this woman had to say?

"As Gloria mentioned earlier, Joy's had a nervous stomach. A few aches and pains. Teenage jitters. Acting out."

"Could you be more specific?"

"About the acting out?"

"Yes."

"Some outbursts at home."

Joy cursing at the top of her lungs.

"Disagreements over . . . her appearance."

A naval stud. That . . . hair. Boobs hanging out of a doll-sized blouse.

"Supposedly Joy vandalized a school wall with graffiti."
During a mandatory pep rally.

A buzzing began in Gloria's ears and drowned Andrew's recital, the woman's murmurs.

Joy, tossing her hair and storming out of church. Joy, locked in the bathroom, refusing to come out. Joy, shaving her eyebrows after some jerk nicknamed her Miss Uni. What had happened to their beautiful little girl? What had happened to the best mother in Texas?

Gloria's chest tightened. She was to blame for not communicating with Joy, though Lord knows, she'd tried. Hadn't she begged God to protect Joy, to coax her back into His flock?

Andrew and the doctor continued to discuss Joy as if they were chatting over coffee at the Paris Café.

Gloria opened her mouth, ready to defend Joy's privacy. Another thought punctured the anger smothering her breath. Had her buttinsky ways—smothering and snooping and eavesdropping—handicapped Joy, as Andrew believed? *Am I, oh, Lord, keeping her from you? Would you use Kai to help Joy?* Gloria straightened, scanned the sheet in front of her, and refocused on the conversation about her daughter, her Joy.

"Those behaviors might indicate PKD?" Andrew surely referred to the behavioral stew named Joy.

"PKD could manifest in psychological and psychosomatic symptoms such as the ones you describe."

"Let me get this straight." A drawn, gray complexion altered Andrew's boyish good looks. "To rule out PKD, we'd have to subject Joy to ultrasound and CT scans and genetic testing?"

Testing would push Joy to an emotional abyss. Just last week she'd balked at a school counseling session! Gloria shoved away the papers and glared at her husband, then the doctor. "We are *not* agreeing to this. Do you hear me, Andrew?"

"I hear you. If you don't calm down, so will everyone in the Sundance Hotel."

"I don't care!" Gloria clenched her fists to keep from shouting. "We're talking about our daughter here. Our Joy."

A loud knock sounded. The conference room doors banged open.

Gloria gripped her thighs. Surely she hadn't disturbed the peace. Surely—

In strode a policeman. The points of his shiny star-shaped badge gleamed a chilling message. What in the world could it be? If the paper in his hand, the set of his jaw, meant anything, she'd soon find out.

4

The policeman blurred into shades of flesh and blue. Andrew stumbled from his chair, as did Gloria. The air thickened so that Gloria could not breathe, could not find her balance, could not think . . . She clutched Andrew's arm. What had Joy done now?

"Reverend Powell, I'm Detective Robbins," Gloria heard dimly. "We've met before."

Gloria's pulse skyrocketed. Joy had skipped school again, had defaced another wall with graffiti. . . .

"Reverend Powell, I responded to that . . . incident behind your church?"

Waves of relief bathed Gloria. She sat down. When her vision stopped swimming, she took in the policeman's expressionless gaze. He'd come about the homeless men who'd dug through the church dumpster for food. Joy was fine.

"Of course." Andrew's babble echoed her relief. "I remember you. Oh, Officer, this is my wife." Andrew darted a look toward the doctor. "And Dr. . . ."

"Kai," the woman said.

Gloria nodded. Everything was fine, just fine.

"Nice to meet y'all." The officer studied his shiny black oxfords, then cleared his throat. "Reverend, your secretary told me where to find you. I'm not here about the church. It's about your daughter . . ."

Nooo! Though his statement confirmed her suspicions, Gloria silently fought reality. *I drove her in today. Last week her counselor hinted at improvement.* "Where is she?" The war between her head and heart propelled her to her feet. "Is she okay?"

Muscled arms folded. "She's been arrested for shoplifting. We're holding her at the detention center." Keys jangled. "I'll drive y'all down, or y'all can meet me there."

The officer gave Andrew directions. Then her own thoughts drowned his voice. Gentle Joy, who loved stray dogs and little babes in the nursery. Generous Joy, who gave away her new jacket, lunch money, and candy bars, with equal aplomb. How could that Joy be accused of a crime? Shoplifting, for heaven's sake, when they'd given her *everything*! It was too much to deal with, too much to think about, too much . . . Gloria faltered under the weight of his revelation and crumbled into blackness.

⌒♭⌒

Ashen pallor. Unsteady gait. Dilated pupils. Ignoring the adrenaline surge brought by news of Lily's predicament, Kai guided Mrs. Powell to a sitting position on the floor while cataloguing her physical condition. Syncope, she believed, likely vasovagal. But she must be sure.

"Gloria!" Reverend Powell dropped to his knees beside Kai. "Are you okay?"

Mrs. Powell's eyes fluttered. A good sign.

"Just lean back." Her right hand throbbing, Kai eased the

woman onto the floor. Practiced fingers found Mrs. Powell's pulse. Kai checked her watch and began to count.

"You good with this?" asked the policeman, who completed a trio of kneelers.

Kai nodded warmly. ER duty at Mass General had schooled her in what Dr. Ward called CWC, Communication With Cops. *"The good cops are on fire to save lives and are comrades in arms. The bad ones must be treated with equal respect, for they can incinerate the lives of everyone they touch."*

"What's wrong?" Fear shrilled the reverend's tone. No wonder; his wife had fainted, the police held his daughter. Kai slowed her breathing. *One thing at a time. Do not alarm this man, who at this moment is not Lily's father but the husband of an ailing woman.*

"It is most likely a simple fainting spell." Kai rubbed Mrs. Powell's arms, patted her cheeks, and tapped her shoulders.

Pale eyes widened. Color tinged wan cheeks. "Where— where am I?" Thin arms flailed.

"It is all right." Kai rocked forward and gently but firmly hugged Mrs. Powell to quell her angst. The woman stiffened but did not resist. Kai again checked the pulse—stronger and slower—and sighed with relief. "Do you have any chest pain?" Kai asked, now that she could trust the woman to answer. "Back pain? Any trouble breathing?"

Mrs. Powell shook her head and tried to sit up.

"Has this happened before?" Kai asked.

Again Mrs. Powell shook her head. "J-Joy," she stammered. "I need to see Joy."

"It's all right, Gloria." Reverend Powell patted his wife's hand and stroked her hair. "We'll see her. I assure you of that."

Kai swallowed hard. Clearly they were devoted to one

another. Did such devotion extend to Lily? She shooed away distraction. *A physician must remain emotionally detached.* "Please rest for a moment, Mrs. Powell. Don't get up until we make sure you're okay. It will not take long."

Mrs. Powell struggled against her husband's and Kai's grasp. "I need to see Joy!"

The policeman offered a glass of water. "Should I call an ambulance?"

Kai shook her head, accepted the drink, and battled prickly resentment. This woman's anxiety surely exacerbated whatever wars raged inside Lily.

"She needs us!" railed Mrs. Powell.

"Gloria, just calm down." Reverend Powell's brows knitted. His lips tightened. "You can't help Joy in this condition."

Kai let out a breath. At least Joy's *father* possessed common sense.

Mrs. Powell's cheeks flamed. *She's recovered emotions, if not logic.* "How dare you talk to me like that, Andrew," she rasped, "after all we've been through?"

Muscles tightened about the reverend's mouth and thinned into a smile. "When you're okay, we'll go to Joy." He glued his eyes on his wife. "Try to relax."

Now Mrs. Powell had tight lips . . . but normal pulse and color. Satisfied her patient was stable, Kai's mind . . . and heart . . . turned to the girl with Mother's bow lips, Father's strong cheekbones. What had the fates done to their Lily? What had this country done to their Lily? Would this family who believed in the Christian God allow her to lend a physician's helping hand? Kai's fingers trembled against the *thrum, thrum* of lifeblood through the body of Lily's mother. Oh, that the fates would turn Mrs. Powell's affections toward the Changs! Lily's real family . . .

70

Kai glanced at her watch and rechecked Mrs. Powell's pulse. Reverend Powell, still kneeling, bowed his head and closed his eyes as if he were praying . . . waiting . . .

The policeman, who had moved toward the conference room door, fidgeted with his keys. He too waited . . . to go to Lily, who was in jail.

We are all waiting. Kai's right hand throbbed with such intensity that she struggled to hold it steady. The fates had presented this fainting spell as an opportunity to assess Lily at the detention center . . . *and comfort her as only a true sister can do.* She masked excitement by furrowing her forehead and rechecking her watch. "It has been long enough, Reverend." She nodded toward a chair.

Reverend Powell scrambled to his feet. "Come on, dear." His voice rang with a falsetto tone. "Let's get you up."

With no indication of weakness, the woman stood. Her husband guided her back to her chair.

Kai massaged her hand and rose from the floor. *She has recovered from a simple fainting spell. But for now, I will keep that to myself. Besides, there is no harm in being ultra-conservative.* "Mrs. Powell, I think you are fine." She spoke lightly, enunciated carefully. "However, you should be monitored." With what she hoped resembled efficiency, she gathered her papers. "For an hour or so."

Mrs. Powell jumped to her feet, dizziness gone. "Please take me to Joy! Now!"

"Of course." Kai tucked her hair behind her ears. "I propose to go with you."

"That's impossible!" the woman spluttered, her face blotchy. She jerked out of her husband's grasp and planted her hands on her hips. "This is a family matter."

The reverend's lips pursed. "Gloria, I just pulled you off

the floor." Kai became the subject of that calm-eyed gaze. "Kai is a doctor, and family to Joy."

"Not really!"

"Yes, Gloria, *really*."

"She doesn't even know Joy."

Kai's muscles tightened. *I wasn't allowed to know Joy.*

"In Joy's present state—"

"Forgive me for interrupting." Kai fought to maintain a courteous tone, despite the woman's insults. "Perhaps my training would permit me to monitor you and evaluate Joy's present state to assess whether her personal physician should be contacted."

"We do not need your help in that decision," spat out Mrs. Powell.

"Gloria!" The reverend's reprimand froze a sneer on his wife's face. "That's enough." He smoothed his pants and straightened his shoulders. Kai battled her own sneer. Imagine, unmasking such emotions in front of a policeman, a doctor, and *her husband*!

"Detective? Kai?" Utter calm had returned to the reverend's countenance. "Could you give me a moment with my wife?"

The detective eyed his watch. "Captain'll have my . . . um . . . I need to get back."

The reverend's hands steepled. "Please. I'll just be a moment."

Kai and the detective stepped into the hall. The detective whipped out his radio. Though the door clicked shut, murmurs seeped around the doorjamb and joined rasps, radio static, and the detective's mutterings to claw at Kai's nerves. She breathed deeply and exhaled. Wisdom and an eerie peace had shone from the reverend's eyes; *wisdom, thank the fates, which hints at a decision to allow me to see Joy at the*

72

detention center. Wisdom that comes, according to Cheryl and David, from those strange Bible texts.

As Kai ran her finger along the edge of Lily's file, she studied the antler chandeliers that splashed the hall with glitzy light. How strange to sacrifice an animal just to fashion a fancy fixture. But it was no stranger than the Christian belief of a god sacrificing his life for humanity. She ground her teeth together and straightened her shoulders, preparing herself to endure yet another wait, suffer another setback. She would endure anything to reclaim Lily, even if it meant humiliation, pain, a masking of self. She owed it to Mother, to Father, to her sisters, and to herself.

The odd Texan light fixtures brightened, as if a spotlight had zeroed in on Kai's life, and she remembered times when the American Dream had not only greeted her but embraced her. Trodding the Harvard stage to claim her diploma. Stepping to the podium at a medical symposium. But none of that mattered now. Kai leaned back and let the wall support her and her doubts. Though she had achieved a modicum of success in this land, would it be enough for the Powells to entrust her with Lily's health?

Such a void struck Kai that she thrust her hand into her jacket pocket to be comforted by her cell phone. She could call David, who was surely swamped with emergency calls, or Pamela, the MRA receptionist who had made Kai promise to leave her office, her patients—her life—behind. Thinking of the Chang strength, she lifted her chin and withdrew her hand from her pocket. She would not trouble busy colleagues and her doctor boyfriend with her little drama.

Kai released her phone, straightened her spine, and continued her battle with doubt. Could a foreigner succeed in

America? In *Texas*? Would fate cede to her efforts and allow her to reclaim Lily? As the lights blinked and winked, Kai clutched Lily's file, her fears, and waited. It was the only thing she knew. It was the only thing she could do.

Who do you think . . . Gloria opened her mouth, then clamped it shut and ground her teeth. To keep from grabbing Andrew and shaking him, she dug her nails into her arms. She, who had never dreamed of hurting another—who had barreled out of the house screaming on that awful day nearly thirty years ago when Mommy slapped Daddy—itched to not only shake her husband but strike him! Anger climaxed as she stared into Andrew's placid cow eyes. How dare he expose their daughter to this woman, to PKD, until they confirmed things? Why, it was downright negligent, when she'd *labored* to keep Joy safe! Not that it had worked.

A sob of frustration puffed the air. She would give her life for Joy . . . not that it had seemed to matter. As a child, Joy had expressed faith in Christ, but years had passed since she'd acknowledged the one who had given His life for her. Despite Andrew's teachings, Gloria's prayers and pleadings, Joy hadn't even been baptized. . . .

"Gloria . . ." Andrew stepped near and held out his arms, offering a hug.

She jerked away, sure his touch would electrocute her. Hadn't his complicity in this matter swelled a spark into a thousand-volt jolt?

"Fine." Andrew's face hardened into flint and sent a chill through Gloria, who wasn't used to seeing fire and ice in his eyes. Andrew hadn't glowered at her—or anyone, to her knowledge—since the cataclysm that shook their church's foundations. "If you're going to act like a two-year-old, I'll treat you like one."

Gloria's lips trembled. Tears pooled. How could Andrew wound a heart bruised by problems with Joy and now this mysterious sister? Though she tried to will it away, a sob slipped from Gloria. *Lord, it's too much.*

Andrew stepped near. A whisper-touch wiped away her tears. "Gloria. It's okay. Really." His calm and sure voice soothed her emotional torrent. "How long have we begged for the Lord to help Joy? How many prayer chains have we contacted, how many counseling sessions have we attended?"

More than I can count—that's for sure. She shook her head, unable to talk.

"Out of the blue, seemingly, this doctor—Joy's *sister*—calls."

Gloria's head hung heavy with regret. *Oh, God. I've been overreacting.*

"She just happens to have an explanation for symptoms that Joy just happens to be having." Andrew's voice quivered. "She nailed it, Gloria. Were you listening?"

Gloria shook her head. She'd been too busy falling apart.

"Joy's sent an SOS." His voice broke. "For . . . years. We've failed. Maybe Kai will succeed." A warm hand cupped her chin. "For heaven's sake, Gloria, she's kin!"

"A woman who *says* she's kin," Gloria added, though her feistiness had evaporated. How many times had she lovingly traced Joy's proud brow, kissed her tiny bow lips? Features so like Kai's? Though she'd tried to ignore it, her soul broadcast the truth. Kai was Joy's sister. Perhaps God had sent her after all.

Someone rapped on the door. The sound—and her regret—propelled Gloria into Andrew's arms. "I'm sorry. Please forgive me," she whispered.

Andrew squeezed her hand. "We can do this. For Joy. For ourselves." He locked her in the Spirit-fired gaze that pulled people down the aisle. "For God."

Her earlier rudeness tolled in Gloria's heart, as did Andrew's reminder of God at the forefront. "With your help," she whispered, looking at Andrew but talking to God.

⌒∞⌒

The reverend darted glances in his rearview mirror. Kai gripped the backseat armrest and tried to ignore stain-splotched upholstery, the balled-up fast-food wrappers and torn magazines that cluttered the floorboards of this storage bin on wheels. How could they raise a child in such a mess?

"So . . . how do you like Boston?" the reverend asked.

Kai measured her response, eager to set the right tone. "Boston is now my home," she managed. Did that sound patriotic . . . or elitist? The former, she hoped.

Andrew wove and maneuvered and zipped down the interstate, Kai clinging to the armrest as if it would protect her. She should have refused the Powells' offer—the *reverend's* offer—and accepted the policeman's. *That would have been awkward as well. But not this awkward.*

"I'm sure Boston's nice," the reverend continued. "But it ain't Texas. There's nothing like the Lone Star State."

Mrs. Powell continued her mannequin-like ways.

Kai scrambled for a witty American colloquialism, though it was all she could do to keep her nerves from rattling like the nuts and bolts of this old clunker. Christians shouldn't drive like *him*, shouldn't act like *her*—should they?

Conversation died. *Thank the fates!* Kai needed clarity, as she approached this pivotal point in her life. Forget Yantai

University, Harvard, Dr. Ward, and Massachusetts Renal. The fates had brought her to Lily. She must do her part.

Noisy vans, custom-painted SUVs, and enough luxury cars to build a bridge to China zoomed past on eight lanes of concrete and embankments, their sounds mingling with the grumble of thunder. During their ride, steely gray clouds had blackened and drooped and mixed with smog to canopy the bustling freeway. Kai battled a storm rising within. What friction would her presence create in Lily? She had been so sure of her plan to accumulate money, accolades, and U.S. citizenship before arranging this reunion. PKD and that PI's report had simplified the decision . . . or had she fooled herself? Had she even the *right* to see Lily? To whom did Lily belong? China, a land ironically boasting ownership by the people? America, founded on the rights of each individual? The Powells? The Changs? Or did fate—nothing more, nothing less—own Lily?

A horn honked. The rolling storage bin darted in front of a truck. Kai clenched Joy's file and squeezed shut her eyes. This might be the last car ride of her life. *Surely the fates won't stop me now. Surely—*

"Whew!"

Kai's eyes gaped. Whew? More like *Thank the fates!*

"Talk about close!" Chuckling, the reverend banged the steering wheel. "Sorry 'bout that."

Kai's heart skittered. Another second and they might have been twisted metal, burning flesh. But fate had intervened. She could trust it. She must trust it.

Mrs. Powell turned her head. Their eyes met. "Um, you'd started to tell us about the beginning of your nightmare."

A tremor raced through Kai. What had brought the mannequin to life? She studied the profile view of a teary eye and a droopy mouth. *Most certainly my presence brings pain to Mrs. Powell.* Had Lily also inflicted pain on this woman? Kai's hand throbbed confirmation. Gloria had not had an easy time.

"I wonder if you'd tell me . . ." Gloria bowed her head, which muffled her voice.

Kai leaned forward, wanting, needing to hear every word. Instead she heard a sob.

Kai caressed her right hand. Dared she hope this woman might understand her motives? "Mrs. Powell." Kai tiptoed every word so as not to misstep. "I do not want to waste your time."

A prominent chin lifted. A head turned. Bleary but determined eyes met her gaze. "It's Gloria. Please. Call me Gloria."

"All right. Gloria." Kai studied the woman as she would an interesting patient. What word, what action, had disseminated the hostile wind and brought calm?

"I want to hear your story," whooshed from Gloria. "For Joy."

Kai leaned against the faded seat cover. Of course. The reverend had talked sense into her. She was just doing her maternal duty. Still, it was an improvement.

Gloria's jaw tightened. "I also want to hear it for me." Though the change was inexplicable, it could not be denied. The woman in the front seat had masked her earlier weaknesses, her earlier resentment. "Please tell us, Kai. Now."

5

I have endured the worst day of my life. Kai found First Daughter and entered the flow of noisy comrades streaming through the school gates. The stretch of blue skies and brown earth offered freedom as never before. The tight sash of earlier insults loosened to let her breathe. She arched her neck, threw back her head, and searched for dainty feathered friends. She saw only a greasy black crow.

Someone banged her shoulder and trampled her heel. Kai reached for First Daughter's lily-petal hand.

"Let go." First Daughter gave a steaming-teapot hiss. "Mask your feelings."

They walked the customary way, past fields cultivated by peasants in baggy trousers and wide-brimmed hats. From his pen, Old Cousin's speckled pig grunted a greeting. Trailing First Daughter like a stray dog, Kai trotted down alleys, past courtyards full of old men sitting in cane chairs, smoking their pipes and rattling *mah-jongg* tiles, past women using brooms to pile trash and shoo away hens. Normal village life. Or so it seemed . . .

79

Kai hurried into their courtyard and breathed deep of hot oil and jasmine blossoms and the hundred scents of home. Should she speak to Mother of the day's unfortunate incidents or hide them behind—

Someone screamed. Mother. Inside their house.

Kai tripped over an invisible block of fear and nearly crashed into First Daughter.

"Don't touch her, I tell you!" shouted Father.

Glass shattered and split a silence, awful after Father's words.

Third Daughter wailed like a monkey gone mad. No normalcy. *Madness has followed us home!*

First Daughter, her breath hot on Kai's hair, yanked Kai around the house. They streaked past the banyan and huddled under the willow's droopy branches. All the while, crashes and smashes and screeches joined the *boom, boom* of Kai's heart and First Daughter's gasps of breath to create a chaotic song.

"You must reform your counterrevolutionary thoughts!" shouted a man.

"We have no such thoughts." Father spoke slowly, as he did when teaching the sayings of Confucius.

"Chang Lao speaks the truth," declared Old Grandfather.

"Truth? Those with black tongue disease speak no truth!"

Kai's back stiffened as she met First Daughter's gaping stare. Who would dare dishonor Old Grandfather, a Long March survivor?

Something crashed. A table? A chair? The very house groaned. Whimpered.

Or was that Mother?

Kai shivered from head to toe.

"You destroyed the vase of my ancestors," Kai heard

Mother say. Third Daughter's wails had been reduced to tired sobs.

Kai bit her lip to keep from crying. Why would anyone destroy Mother's beloved relics? Mother was a most favored teacher. Mother was—

"They are nothing but worthless mementos. Proof of a capitalist bent."

"We have no capitalist bent."

"Do not be quick to defend poor behavior. Chairman Mao offers leniency to those who admit their crimes."

Kai's icy fingers entwined First Daughter's in an effort to keep from crying out. How many men were ransacking their house? Why?

The house fell silent. Kai held her breath and begged her heart to stop its thundering lest they be caught eavesdropping like capitalist spies.

Boots thudded. A door slammed. Men cursed.

First Daughter tore from Kai, who begged her numb legs to follow brave Ling.

"Oh, Mother. Father." Through the back window came First Daughter's sobs.

"Do not cry, Ling." Despite the dreadful denunciations, Father's voice was unwavering.

Kai's heart slowed as she feasted on air. She wobbled along the path Ling had trod, only Kai wobbled like the broken-legged bird that she had doctored not long ago.

"Where is little Kai, Ling?" she heard Mother cry. "Where, oh, where is Second Daughter? They did not detain her at school, did they?"

To relieve Mother, Kai found the strength to span the threshold of their home. With a final surge, she fell into Mother's warmth and sobbed out the pain that knifed her body. After her cries were spent, she peeked through her fingers. What would happen now?

Old Grandfather sat in the rocker with Third Daughter. First Daughter rattled at the stove. Making tea? Father swept up porcelain shards and plucked fragments of Old Grandfather's writings from the dirt. The table was returned to its customary position. As if it were a typical afternoon, Old Grandfather lit his pipe.

But it was not a typical afternoon. No, it was horrid!

The peach pit of fear expanded and scraped Kai's insides. She edged toward Father, who now sat in his chair. As upper school principal and master of their house, Father would understand the sentiments of Kai the student and Kai the child.

Bloodshot eyes met her gaze. Her father, crying?

To avoid a freefall into terror, Kai lunged at Father and seized his hand. Father had not wept since Grandmother's death. "Father," she cried, "why did I lose face at school? Why did those men destroy Mother's things? Why, oh, why has madness visited our house?"

Father managed a droll expression. "Our dragon breathes questions, not fire."

Kai pinched her fingers to stop their twitching. She must wait. Father would explain things in his way, in his time.

"One red ant bite sting can easily be salved," Father finally said. "But an army of red ants can destroy a house. A village."

Why would Father now quote Confucius? Though his sayings had endured like the Great Wall, one whose bones were dust had no antidote for fate's cruel shattering of their lives. Why did the fates suddenly hate them?

"We can endure intermittent stings, my little dragon, by loyalty to Chairman Mao and our comrades. If fate intervenes, we will muster strength to withstand an army of ants."

"An army?" Old Grandfather rattled to his feet. "Monkeys dressed in uniforms are no army." Old Grandfather grabbed a torn *China Daily* and banged his pipe. Damp tobacco clumped on the headlines. "A strong west wind will annihilate them all!" Old Grandfather cleared his throat and spat.

Kai felt her eyes widen. From the lane came the pounding of boots, the rumble of voices. Hair bristled on Kai's neck. Those men had gone, had they not, like a once-in-a-century storm? Surely only workers approached, with their sickles and hoes . . .

"I feared it." Father spoke as if discussing the weather. "They come with an indictment."

"So soon?" whispered Mother.

"They are paper tigers, trying to roar." Father gave Mother a sad smile. "We must endure until real tigers arrive."

Old Grandfather harrumphed, but his limbs trembled like willow leaves. First Daughter grabbed Third Daughter, whose chest heaved, whose limbs clawed.

A snake coiled about Kai's throat and strangled a scream that rose from within. Her legs gave way. She fell in a heap, unable to endure more.

"Mother, go into the bedroom with our daughters," Father hissed. "Now."

As if she had not heard, Mother stood statue-like, her hand against their mud wall.

"You, too, Old Man. Go with them."

His eyes sunk into his face, Old Grandfather slumped back into his chair, perhaps revisiting steppes he had climbed during the war. Kai longed to go with him!

"Now, Old Man!"

"Am I not a Long March survivor?" Old Grandfather spewed bitterness. "Yet I face squawking chickens!"

Father laid a hand on Old Grandfather's arm. "You are a man in a time when white hair has no more value than a rotten egg."

"If it is my fate to be heaped onto garbage, I will accept it."

"Stay then, Old Man." Father yanked Mother's arm. "Take the baby. Go in there. Now!"

Mother did not blink, did not even seem to breathe.

Father reached out to caress Mother's cheek. "May the fates protect you."

The whisper, and Father's touch, revived Mother. She took the baby from First Daughter and disappeared.

"Ling, get Kai. Join Mother and the baby."

First Daughter yanked Kai from the floor and half-dragged, half-carried her to the kang, where Mother lay, clutching the baby. Shadows danced from the teak wardrobe, flashed in the mirror over the washstand, swirled about the little stool, where she had so carefully laid her nightgown this morning, expecting this to be the best day of her life.

The front door thudded open. Voices swallowed the protests of Father and Old Grandfather. They were dreadful, powerful voices that gobbled up Mother's coos and Third Daughter's sniffles.

"Here you sit, you stinking ninths, lazing the day away. You should labor in the fields! Purify your thoughts!"

A slapping sound ended the words.

Old Grandfather groaned. Wood splintered. Moans and clatters shook the house.

"By directive of the Regimental Political Section, you are indicted for . . ."

Whimpers dribbled from Kai and drowned out the shouts. It was one thing to have their house ripped to shreds, but to have Old Grandfather and Father arrested?

"What will happen to them?" Kai whispered.

Number One Daughter pushed Kai into the softness of the kang. "Hush, I tell you, or I will slap your face!"

Kai covered her eyes, but not before glancing at her sister, who blew fire like a dragon. How dreadful! Dogs had become dragons. Boars pretended to be tigers. Monkeys reigned like men. The room spun about like her mind. The world *had* gone mad!

Scuffles and thuds continued their assault. Again the door thudded. Then silence seized the house. Had Father and Old Grandfather been taken away?

Kai felt her mouth form a circle. Her body spasmed as if it belonged to another. Then she thought of her poor elders and staggered toward the door. If she caught up with Father and Grandfather before they rounded the courtyard gate, she could rescue them!

Three men burst into the room and knocked Kai down. Red kerchiefs knotted their scraggly hair. Red armbands bound their right arms. Kai remembered red, pouring from the slit throat of their festival chicken. Red, seeping from open wounds after her fall, oh, so long ago. So much red, the proud color of China; the horrifying color of death . . .

"Come with us, Chang Jiang, enemy of the proletariat!" One man crooked his finger and jabbed Mother's side.

"Possessor of bourgeois frivolities!" A second man hurled one of Mother's books onto the dirt floor. It lay exposed, its pale pages trembling.

The three men lunged for Mother.

A cyclone of anger spun Kai to her feet. They had soiled two of her beloved things: Mother and her writings. She doubled up her fists and growled. "How dare you criticize Mother's books? She has devoted her life to the poets of our land. She has—"

Mother yanked Kai back to the kang and clamped her palm over Kai's mouth.

A swollen-faced man stomped near. "You stinking ninth! What is worse, the child or the parent?" The man flattened his palm and slapped Kai.

Mother screamed.

Third Daughter's cries pierced Kai's ears, yet hot winds surged into her limbs. She broke free from Mother. "You are wrong!" Kai shouted. "My mother writes of beauty, valor, of love for country."

"She must be reeducated . . . or be whacked into pieces!"

Again Kai suffered the clap of Mother's hand and was restrained by Mother's sweaty arms, First Daughter's writhing legs. She struggled with both Mother and First Daughter, her mind spiraling like an escaped kite.

When the swollen-faced man squatted down, a stinking garlic smell pummeled Kai in the face. "Aha!" he snorted. "Another bad root, sending her shoots into the fertile soil of China." Greasy fingers grabbed her arm. "Another bad root, to hack and destroy."

A thin man stepped from the line of three men. Though scars pitted his face, his eyes had a cloudy, sad cast. "Do not punish a Young Pioneer for the misdeeds of her family. With help, this one can be reeducated." The thin man was joined by another, who stepped in front of him and Stinking Garlic. "As can Comrade Chang."

Stinking Garlic beat his fists against Thin Man's back but was paid no mind. "Come, Comrade Chang," continued Thin Man. "If you do not resist, we will leave your daughters alone."

"If you do not obey," growled Stinking Garlic, "we will throw you all in prison."

"I will come with you." The kang shook as Mother rose, her teacher's voice in command. "Leave my daughters alone."

Kai's limbs melted under the pressure of another change. Mother planned to obey these men and leave them here? *Alone?*

Nonchalantly, as though tending to household chores, Mother handed the baby to First Daughter. Her eyes clear, her chin firm, Mother kissed their foreheads and then fixed her gaze on her eldest. "First Daughter, you are in charge. Remember what you have been taught." Her voice was whispery, yet she enunciated each word. "Fate will reunite us. Until then, you must be strong."

"Now!" commanded Stinking Garlic. His two comrades silenced him with shoves.

"Second Daughter," Mother continued, "subdue your fiery ways. Vent your energy into suitable pursuits." Her brow gathered, as if to warn of a storm. "Obey First Daughter. Survival depends on it."

Suddenly Mother's face softened, and she looked like a young girl. "Take care of the baby," she whispered. "Both of you."

Who was this woman, with eyes of thunder, demanding obedience . . . yet leaving them? Tears clouded Kai's vision. *Oh, Mother,* she longed to say. Yet fear and sadness swelled her throat.

"Fanhui."

Mother stepped forward, folded her arms behind her. Stinking Garlic clamped cuffs on her wrists. The three men shoved Mother toward the door. *"Manbuzhai hu!"* Stinking Garlic kicked Mother's wardrobe, swore, rubbed his foot, and kicked again. "Daughters of swine!" He grabbed one of Kai's shoes, wielded it like a scythe, and pummeled the washbasin and mirror.

"Enough, son of a stupid cow!" Thin Man said. "We have followed our directive."

The shoe—Kai's shoe—thudded to the floor. She would never wear it, never touch it again. Even if she must walk barefoot in a pig sty.

Shuffling feet and the baby's whimpers replaced the men's nasty words. Dare Kai breathe?

She sat up and again rubbed her cheek, which smarted from the man's coarse hand. As the door slammed, her gaze fell on the mirror.

A new crack split Kai's reflection in half—or perhaps she had been split in half. She pinched her arms to make sure she had not lost her mind, like the woman who lived in the mountains, ran with the wild boar, and knelt to lap water from a stream.

Mother, Father, Old Grandfather gone? How would they survive? Hot tears coursed from her eyes, her nose, and her mouth. She fell against First and Third Daughters, felt the quivery breathing bodies of her two sisters. With all her might, she clung to what remained of their family. She must fight the red tide that splashed the walls, the wardrobe, the kang, their very bodies, by crying to the fates.

With tears and pleas and promises, Kai begged that her family be rescued. The fates did not answer.

Finally the sun sank below adobe roofs and trumpeted the end of the struggle.

First Daughter rose from the bed, moved to the washbasin, and scrubbed her face. She helped Third Daughter and Kai do the same. Yet filth from the earlier events had burrowed into Kai like nasty leeches and could not be washed away.

"We will survive." Though her face had taken on the color of ash, First Daughter spoke without wavering. "The Chang family will recover its honor."

Kai nodded as she dried her face with her sleeve. Until she died, she would strive to fulfill Mother's and First Daughter's commands. The Chang sisters would blow dragon smoke on the fates until they agreed to help.

The noon-hour traffic of Cowtown disappeared in their rearview mirror when Andrew took Exit 54. Yet Gloria could leave neither China nor the images of three little girls with Joy's delicate features, left to survive while their folks were tossed into prison. "I'm so sorry," she whispered. "How long did it last?"

"They killed Old Grandfather." Hoarseness softened the doctor's businesslike tone. "My parents spent five years languishing in a makeshift prison in the basement of our school."

Gloria twisted about, massaging the crick in her neck as a ruse to watch Kai, whose straight-backed dignity conflicted with a teary gaze. *What grief she's borne! I thought my childhood memories were painful.*

"Being reeducated?" Andrew asked.

A bold light shone from dark eyes. "The prisoners were paraded out during lunch break so we students could humiliate them with sticks, stones . . . and slurs."

Gloria's hand flew to her throat. "You had to denounce your own parents?"

"Or let guards' clubs stripe our backs." The doctor massaged her hand. "First Daughter never relented. I did . . . once. I hit Mother . . . with a rock." Her jaw quivered.

"You were only a child." Andrew white-knuckled the steering wheel.

Kai strained against the seat belt as she sat up straight. "No, Reverend. When they took our parents, we became adults, even Third Daughter. Thank the fates for maturing us." Kai's voice became whispery. "Then hooligans smashed our windows . . . and our last semblance of normalcy. School closed. We boarded up our house, desperate to shut out what China had become." Like a wilted flower, Kai drooped her head. "We survived by eating pillow stuffing, the braids of garlic plants, food left by kind ones. When not a crumb remained, First Daughter crept out in the dead of night to scavenge carcasses of rats, crows, whatever she could find. I scoured the yard for grasses, weeds—anything to woo a young goat so I could milk her for Third Daughter."

Gloria massaged her churning belly. She'd never been hungry . . . except by choice.

"We had made a vow to Mother. Thank the fates, we kept it until our parents returned. Return they did."

Gloria's arms prickled. After what had been done to her, how could Kai trust "the fates"? With another backward glance, she searched the oval face, seeing Joy's strong brow, Joy's steady gaze. There was good in Joy, despite her detour into teenage wasteland. She continued to look at Kai. *Lord, there's good in this face as well. If you will use her to help my daughter, Lord, so be it.*

As Andrew veered into a parking lot, Gloria heard paper rustling. Another glance backward showed Kai digging into her briefcase. Surely not more horrid reports . . .

After they parked, Kai leaned forward. She held two gifts, elaborately wrapped with metallic paper and velvet ribbons. "I would like to present you with tokens of affection from the Chang family. Perhaps these gifts will bring you fortune and please the fates."

"Well, ah, thanks!" Andrew chortled. "We sure do appreciate that."

"How lovely! Thank you." Gloria's southern upbringing brought a pat response to her lips, though she again doubted Kai's motives for finding Joy. Still, Kai should be here. Kai was Joy's sister, Joy's blood. Despite Kai's beliefs in fortune and the fates, God could use her to help Joy. Couldn't He?

6

This may be the most important walk of my life. Make that the most important run. Clutching Lily's file, Kai tracked the Powells' zigzag through the parking lot. Gloria's seeming change of heart paved the way for an alliance centered on one goal: saving Lily.

Kai stopped short. Saving Joy. For now, she must call her beloved sister, Fourth Chang Daughter, Joy. Why further confuse a troubled teenager with a new name? Why risk angering the Powells with an *old* name? Every word, now that Kai neared her goal of reclaiming what was lost, held great import. A slip of her tongue might prove disastrous.

The juvenile detention center, a three-story brick building, sprawled across a prairie-flat lot. Scrubby trees did little to offset windowless sterility and a profound sense of institutionalization. Kai breathed deeply to expand airways constricted by her jog, the unbearable humidity . . . and the unbearable thought of Joy being imprisoned here.

The Powells squeezed into a revolving door, their arms about each other's waists, shoring up one another. Had they supported Joy? Then why had she wound up here?

The door's vacuum-air hiss halted Kai's thoughts. She slipped into the glass compartment and stepped out into a waiting room furnished with blocky module chairs and end tables. A lanky man had buried his face in a ragged copy of *Field & Stream*. A petite woman wearing short shorts screamed into a cell phone. Vents in the low ceiling blasted frigid air. Kai hugged her arms and stood in the middle of the room. There was nothing welcoming about the waiting area. Perhaps that was the point.

A metal clock pulsed seconds; Kai could not tear her eyes from the needle-thin rotating hand. Though she had waited years, suddenly the stretch of even a minute without seeing Joy clawed her heart. Yet she, a doctor, had been trained to wait. If she suffered so, what must this predicament be doing to Joy's parents?

"We're here to see our daughter, Joy." The Powells, still embracing, stepped to a reception counter. "Joy Powell," the reverend continued.

"ID, please." A youthful woman wearing headphones typed their information into a computer and asked Andrew to fill out paper work. Gloria retreated to join Kai and gave her a fleeting, conciliatory smile. *Did I gain her trust by sharing my history, or is the Christian God "transforming her," as David and Cheryl would say?*

"Who's your contacting officer?" the clerk asked Reverend Powell.

"Robbins."

"Hang on. I'll get your JD."

"JD?" Andrew repeated.

"Juvenile director." The clerk never looked up, as if preoccupied with detention work. The thought of her sister in here certainly preoccupied Kai.

Andrew joined them in the center of the foyer. The three of them represented Joy's past and present, Joy's East and West. Surely they could protect Joy. Rescue Joy. Kai battled wobbly knees and bombarding doubts. *What I do not know about American teenagers—about* any *teenagers—fills this building.*

A door adjacent to the registration desk opened. There stood a woman in uniform. "Mr. and Mrs. Powell?"

Gloria brushed Kai's arm. "And Dr. Chang. Joy's sister."

"Hello. I'm Officer Ferguson." The woman's cool eyes flickered, surely trying to discern, with one sweep, what mismoves, misspeaks, and mishaps had brought them here. Kai wondered the same thing.

"Follow me." Officer Ferguson stilled a creaky door. "I'll take you to the director . . . and to your daughter."

They tromped single file down a carpeted path through a community of cubicles, each manned with desk, phone, and computer screen. Kai's field of vision narrowed to follow the blue blur of Gloria's dress, yet her mind expanded to reveal the seas she had spanned, the mountains she had climbed. As she hugged Joy's file, she begged the fates to allow her one final step—into the heart, into the soul . . . into the arms of her sister Joy.

❧

They passed what seemed like the millionth dreary cubicle. Gloria's imagination continued to balloon, envisioning Joy in handcuffs, Joy being harassed. How would even a minute of jail time scar her?

At the end of a dimly lit hall, a young woman stepped from a corner office and nodded, as if expecting them.

"Hey, Barton." Officer Ferguson approached the young

woman. "These are Joy Powell's parents, Reverend and Mrs. Powell, and Joy's sister, Dr. Chang."

"Hi. I'm JD Barton, but just call me Nicole, like the kids do. To my face, anyway." Nicole wore blue jeans, a camisole, and a lightweight jacket. A tied-back ponytail, funky metallic glasses, and multi-studded ears created a hip look. *Not the stereotypical cop. Thank goodness.*

Gloria risked a smile. Joy just might talk to, might trust Nicole.

"I saw your daughter. She's in the back. Chatting with the AO."

"The AO?"

"Arresting officer. Just filling out paper work. Prelims."

"But she's a minor. Surely you could have waited—"

Andrew's hand-squeeze shushed Gloria's rant. How maddening to lose control of their daughter . . . of their life.

Nicole shrugged. "We could've waited, but Joy told us she was nineteen. And had the ID to prove it."

A fake ID? Gloria blinked. How? She'd rifled through Joy's purse, backpack . . .

"So she lied," Andrew said dully.

Again Nicole shrugged. "It's not uncommon."

Sweat trickled down Gloria's back. Their home had disintegrated to the point that lying and stealing were common. *Oh, God, help us. . . .*

Andrew's jaw hardened. "Uncommon or not, I assure you, it's not acceptable. With us, anyway."

Nicole's smile dimpled her cheeks. "I appreciate that, I really do. I want to help y'all get to the bottom of this."

"Thank you." Andrew, ever cordial and gracious, managed small talk, as did Kai. *Yet I can barely breathe.*

They were led into an office. With a hand wave, Nicole

invited them to sit around a table. "Just make yourself comfortable. Joy and Robbins should be here any minute."

Comfortable? To keep from chewing her nails to nubs, Gloria studied a Warhol soup can poster, a bowl overflowing with chocolate of the expensive kind, a metal rack of CDs, and two computer stations. Her stomach muscles loosened enough for her to inhale, exhale. She rested her hands on the table and stared at a framed photo of the Colorado Rockies, praying that the tranquil scene would one day symbolize their family life.

"Water? Coke?" Nicole picked up a pitcher atop an ancient microwave.

Andrew nodded. "Water's fine."

Kai nodded. "Yes, ma'am, that is fine."

Nothing is fine. Gloria's face scrunched up. Tears burned her eyes. *This is my fault.*

"We will help her," Kai whispered, leaning forward.

She knows what I'm thinking . . . and reacts like a saint. Gloria stifled an impulse to touch Kai's shoulder. Hearing congregants criticize Andrew . . . and Joy . . . had perfected Gloria's bent toward cool propriety except with a trusted handful of friends. Joy's situation demanded change, like accepting this Chinese sister.

As Gloria leaned toward Kai, someone knocked on the door, then opened it. There stood the detective who'd come for them at the hotel. By him stood their daughter . . . or a desperately unhappy teenager, masquerading as Joy.

⌒

Something rustled in the hall. Kai tore her gaze from the attractive young policewoman and settled it on the door, which creaked open.

A young woman flanked Officer Robbins. With the help of teased purplish-red hair, she reached the policeman's shoulder. Kai clutched at her haywire heart, noting the arch of the girl's brows, the shape of her face. Despite grungy clothes, that hair, she was looking at Lily. Her Lily.

Kai's mouth opened, though air neither went in nor came out. As she honed in on Father's cheekbones, Mother's bow lips, images from the past and present mingled. The precious little baby she had cupped in her hands while First Daughter cut the umbilical cord stood before her now.

Though Kai said not a word, her heart cried, *Blow, ye winds of fate! I have withstood you! The youngest child of the Chang clan stands before me!*

"Oh, God! Why are y'all here?" Smudged makeup ringed swollen, sullen eyes. Tiny feet clad in laced-tight leather boots stomped a clear message: war.

Kai's internal chorus faded. Joy, who had invoked the name of the Christian God, who had pointed at her parents as if they were hated class enemies, was screaming for rescue. Kai's right hand throbbed as if arthritic. *Have I not come all this way to help her? To recover the stolen years? Fates, just give me the chance. . . .*

A chair scraped against the floor. Gloria, a grayish cast to her skin, wobbled to her feet. "Why . . . are we here? We're your . . . parents, Joy!" Sobs spewed from Gloria's mouth and garbled her words. "I know I haven't done the things I should have. I know . . ." Gloria stumbled toward her daughter, her arms extended, her face slack.

A force akin to a million volts of electricity zapped the particles of air in the room. Kai could not breathe, could not think, could do nothing except stare at flared nostrils, a mouth smeared with purplish-black lipstick, a creamy complexion marred by angry acne breakouts, hair thick as First Daughter's but cheapened by garish dye.

Kai's hands fell limp into her lap. The pain, the distrust, the distance in this room . . . it could slay a hundred families. If fate did not intervene, it would surely slay this fragile American mother, whose composure and gait were deteriorating.

Kai leapt to her feet. *Perhaps I did not catch something earlier.* With effort, she ignored Joy. "Mrs. Powell. Please sit here." Kai guided the mother into a chair while assessing her breathing and general condition: skin pale, cool, slightly clammy; breathing normal. Kai then found Gloria's radial pulse. Mildly tachycardic. Not surprising. Yet combined with her earlier fainting—

"Who is that?" Lily emitted the most obnoxious shriek Kai had ever heard.

As Kai stood frozen, life hovered in a state of inertia. She could not have moved . . . even with the help of the fates.

A chair—the young policewoman's?—scraped, a sound that made Kai grind her teeth. She tried—failed—to raise her head. To be here, to see this, after so much hope, so many trials, and to know she could do nothing to help, was unbearable!

"That, my dear Joy, is your sister, who has traveled across time and space to find you." It was the reverend, who had found his calm voice. "Her name is Dr. Chang Kai."

It took every trial Kai had endured, every procedure she had been taught, to lift her head and meet her sister's eyes. *If my presence in any way wounds you, dear child, blood of my ancestors, may the fates strike me dead.*

"My sister?" A strange lilt infused Lily's voice. So like dear Third Daughter's, Mother's . . . Lily had inherited their sense of melody!

Their eyes locked.

Waves of tenderness muddled Kai's balance. She grabbed for the table. Stared into the eyes of that innocent baby. Eyes like her own. She wobbled toward the one she had sought.

Joy minced forward in those boots, then clicked to a stop. Indifference frosted her eyes. She cocked her head, shoved her hands in the pockets of shredded jeans. "My sister?" A glacial floe had chilled her lilt. "Why are you here now?" She threw back her shoulders. A beaded choker rattled against collarbones exposed by a low-cut top. "Where have you been all these years?"

Kai bit her lip against a torrent of words that might surge like a wave and sweep them away. *Dear child, where shall I start? When Father agreed that Mother did not have to abort you? Where shall I end? One minute ago, when a glance at your face made my life worth living . . . but nearly killed me?* The denim-and-lace vision that broke Kai's heart . . . and made her whole . . . blurred into blues and whites.

The policewoman made her way to Joy and held out her hand. "I'm Nicole, the Juvenile Division officer who'll work with y'all."

If Joy heard, she gave no sign of it.

Nicole joined Officer Robbins, who stood by the door. "It looks like y'all could use a minute together. Take five. Maybe ten. We'll be right over there." Nicole pointed through the glass door. "In a waiting room."

Joy dangled her hands. "You're going to leave me in here with them?"

"It's either that or book you." Officer Robbins jingled those keys. "Fingerprints, a mug shot, the whole shebang."

Nicole harrumphed and laid a hand on Joy's shoulder. "You'll be fine. Just take a minute. Straighten things out."

Gray eyes seemed to land on each of them, then settled on Joy. "We want what's best for everyone, Joy. Especially you."

"Yeah, right," Joy muttered, but her voice had lost its edge.

Perhaps sensing familial fireworks, the officers scurried away, leaving Kai with Andrew, Gloria, Joy, and the deafening roar of silence. As Kai took her seat, unable to do anything else, she begged the fates to whisper her next move. The axis that spun Joy's world, the Powells' world, her world, depended on their help!

The fates—oh, those capricious things . . . hateful one moment, joyful the next—refused to answer.

7

"Like, what in . . . is going on?" Joy raked her hands through her latest dye job, which was red-purple, black-purple, purple-hideous.

At the sound of cursing, Gloria clutched her stomach, which roiled with abandon. "Joy . . ." she began. Bleary, narrowed eyes and a chin-dimpling smirk halted further words.

Instead, Gloria made a list of her faults. She hadn't exposed Joy to her culture. She'd changed the subject when Joy asked about her "other" family. That last time China had been mentioned, as Joy's runaway destination, Gloria had diluted Joy's angst with words about counseling. About God.

Joy doesn't want—or need—my words. Gloria sealed her lips and prayed that her stomach—and her heart—would settle.

"Joy, just calm down, okay?" Gloria noted how Andrew's gentle voice and godly demeanor soothed Joy. *He builds a bridge to Joy while I flounder on the shore.* If anyone could revitalize this teenage wasteland—their family's wasteland—it would be her Andrew.

"Recently your sister—Dr. Kai, here—contacted us."

"Like, how recently?"

"Last week," Andrew continued.

Curses again stained the air. Gloria hugged herself, as if warding off the vile words. When had Joy begun talking like this, *thinking* like this?

"*My sister* contacted you *last week?* Like, *seven days* ago? I'm the last to know?"

"We planned to tell you, Joy."

"Like, when? Next century?"

"Perhaps I can explain things" came from behind her. It was Kai.

Gloria swallowed a bitter taste . . . a bitter truth. Never had a voice infused such concern, such humility. To think, two hours ago, she'd . . . *hated* Kai.

"I'm listening." Joy planted her hands on her hips, tapped her boot toe, and eyed her sister with curiosity. "If you'll step on it, that is."

Again Gloria tried to swallow the frustration and bitterness Joy's words evoked, but this time, it didn't budge. Suddenly she whirled from Joy, scrunched her shoulders, and clamped both hands over her mouth. Too late. She heaved, unable to hold back the contents of her stomach.

"Mrs. Powell." Kai, a sudden hovering presence, offered a paper towel, murmured kindnesses, and led her back to her chair. Andrew, with similar ministrations, helped her sit, took another towel from Kai, and cleaned off her hands.

Gloria kept darting glances toward the mess on the floor, the mess on her hands, the mess she'd made with Joy, the mess she'd made with Joy's new relative . . . *Oh, God, I've majored in messes!*

Kai knelt beside Gloria's chair. "It is nothing. Someone will tend to it later."

Tears blurred the chiseled features, the expressive eyes in this older version of Joy. Gloria nodded and tried to relax. Kai had taken control. It felt so good, so right, to place her trust in this woman.

Kai handed her another damp towel. "Here. This will feel good."

It did.

Again Kai checked Gloria's pulse. "Reverend, your wife needs to be seen. Please contact her physician. I suspect it's a virus, but let's be sure." Kai massaged Gloria's back with circular motions that strangely lessened the ache in her belly . . . and her heart. Each touch brought insight. Kai truly ministered through medicine . . . and compassion.

"But the police . . . Joy . . ." Andrew spoke in a pained, most un-Andrewlike voice.

"The officers haven't moved a muscle. See?" Pointing out the window, Kai reflected a calm that eluded the Powells. "You can apprise them of the situation. With this, on top of the earlier fainting spell, your wife must be seen."

"Mom? You fainted?"

Concern laced Joy's screech. *Thank goodness she doesn't totally hate me. In the midst of this mess, I've been gifted another blessing.*

"You can drive your wife to her doctor." Smooth-talking Kai addressed Andrew as if Joy hadn't interrupted. "There's no need for an ambulance."

Gloria jerked upright. "I can't leave Joy here! It's just an upset stomach!"

"I do not believe that is the case." Kai's comforting smile had set into stone. "I am concerned about you, Mrs. Powell. You need to see your physician." Her dark eyes narrowed. "If you are not . . . amenable. . . to my suggestion, I will ask the officers to call an ambulance. Liability concerns and health regulations will have them racing each other to the phone."

"Mom!" As Joy waved her arms, purple hair slapped her cheeks. "Just, like, go!"

"Joy's in good hands here." Andrew knelt on the other side of Gloria.

Gloria battled the urge to leap from the chair and slap them all silly for ignoring her right—her duty—as a mother to stay here. Whether Joy liked it or not.

"Trust me, Gloria. It is the right thing to do." Kai's lips had parted; the eyes were soft with compassion.

Gloria bowed her head, then lifted her chin and tried to mask her emotions. It seemed to work for Kai, who had nonchalantly pulled out a cell phone and offered it to Andrew. "Call her doctor. Now."

"Patrice Davies on West Berry," Gloria mumbled, just in case Andrew's brain had rusted, like his jaws. "I'd rather go to her than Carl." *Less embarrassing with a woman . . .*

Andrew returned the phone to Kai, who said, "I'll check in later. Dr. Davies may have questions."

"All right." Andrew moved to Joy, held out his arms, and then let them drop when she didn't budge. "I'll be back, sweetie, okay?"

Joy rolled her eyes and sighed, but the nervous jangling of a dozen bangle bracelets betrayed her nonchalant act.

"You'll be fine," assured Kai.

As Andrew left to update the officers, Gloria's stomach roiled again. *I won't be fine until Joy's fine.* "I love you," she whispered, though Joy had turned away, as if entranced by something across the room. Her newfound sister?

Kai stepped close. Gripped Gloria's arms. "I will take care of your daughter."

Gloria squeezed Kai's hand in appreciation, then got to her feet, hugged the teenaged statue, and stepped away. "I'll be back—we'll be back—as soon as we can." She managed to smile despite the space between her and Joy, which was three linear feet, though a million emotional miles. "You hear, Joy? Everything will be okay."

Joy's mouth fell open.

Is she that shocked that I'm hopeful? Gloria felt her lip quiver, but it wasn't because Joy was in jail or because her stomach was cramping. How long had it been since she'd presented Joy with anything but a smothering anxiety under the guise of concern? Gloria dug her nails into her palms. *Be still and wait,* she prayed, then spread her hands and stared at the indentations. She'd had this hand-digging habit all her life. The anxiety too. How many habits must she shed before the three of them again became a family?

Andrew returned to the room. "The cops freaked out when they heard about what happened. If we don't go now, they'll call the EMTs."

Again Gloria hugged her daughter. For the briefest moment, Joy pressed against her. A minor miracle. The first of many? As Andrew led her from the room, that was her prayer.

⌒⌒⌒

"Joy . . ." Kai inched closer, mustering techniques she'd honed to treat children petrified of doctors, their needles, and the pain they inflicted. She could not wound this child who possessed Father's brow, Mother's lips, First Daughter's lustrous hair . . .

Kai blinked. This child had knife-sharp eyes, a sneer the size of Beijing, and was shouldering Mount Tai–sized boulders on her petite frame. *Go slow. Lay a foundation.* Kai forced her eager feet to stop two meters from her youngest sister. "It is an honor to meet you." Kai extended her hand in the American way. "How I have longed for this moment."

Glistening pools of pain—of curiosity?—met her gaze and held it. "You longed for it?" Joy finally asked.

"With all my heart."

Joy crossed her arms and stood motionless. The door framed her as if she were a still life of a rebellious teenager, with her grungy jeans, goth haircut, heavily lined eyes, black blouse cut low enough to expose red bra straps, bra cups edged with lace. Joy desperately wanted to be noticed . . . or loved. Dared Kai hope it was the latter?

"Then why did it take you so long to get here?"

Kai recoiled as if the question had grown fangs and bitten her. Of course she had expected it, but that did not lessen the shock of being spewed with both spit and hate. Kai forced rhythmic breaths. Her muscles began to relax, her thought patterns to settle. Joy did not know the mountains she had climbed, the valleys she had traversed, to reach this point. *She surely suspects abandonment . . . or worse.* Kai resettled her gaze on the face of her sister.

"Why?" Joy swore. "Why won't you answer me? Can't you at least give me that much?"

Tell the truth.

Kai's scalp prickled as if a breeze swept the stuffy room. Was it the fates, speaking to her?

Tell the truth. It will set you free.

Was it Old Grandfather, delivering a message from the other world?

More curses. "Are you listening?" A wail whistled from those purplish-black lips. Joy crumbled to the floor, rested her elbows on her knees, and buried her head in her hands. "Why won't somebody tell me what is going on?"

Kai longed to wrap her arms around her sister and bathe her with all the tears that the Changs had shed for her. Instead, she rushed to the quivering pile of denim and lace, placed her hand on a thin, frail back, and stroked in sync with Joy's cries. *It worked with the mother. Perhaps it will work with her child.*

"I will tell you everything." Kai continued to massage her sister's back. "Everything you want to know."

Joy seemed to stop breathing. Then she lifted her head and fixed Kai with an all-too-familiar gaze.

Kai had seen sorrow engraved on the face of a Cultural Revolution denunciation victim, had heard sorrow in the screams of a Cambridge parent whose child lay dying in the aftermath of a drive-by shooting. Sorrow straddled racial divides and trespassed the houses of the rich, the poor, and everything in between. The capitalist, the Communist, and everything in between. Sorrow had taken residence in the life of her youngest sister. Tears filled Kai's eyes. Oh, that she could salve this pain!

"Is my mother alive?"

Kai shook her head.

Glossy lips quivered. "My father?"

Breath whooshed, so relieved was Kai to bring good news. "Yes! His name is Lao."

"Do I have sisters? Brothers?"

A gurgling brook rose. "Yes! Ling, aged thirty-nine, is the oldest. We call her First Daughter." Kai bubbled the joyous news. "Then me. I'm . . . thirty-five. Mei, Third Daughter, is thirty." She took a breath, longing to share her sisters' stellar qualities.

A tear blazed a path through Joy's makeup. Proof of her sister's pain threatened to burst the dam Kai had built to maintain control. Kai reached out. Her fingertip met petal-soft skin and absorbed the tear.

Joy raised her chin. "Why did y'all give me away?" was asked with such a strange mix of hush and intensity, Kai's control melted. She, too, became a heap on the floor. They half sat, half lay, shoulder to shoulder—for an eternity? For a minute? Then Kai found Joy's small, cold hand, cupped it between hers, and began to speak.

8

Something crashed into Kai's consciousness. Her eyes fluttered open. Had the Red Guards returned . . . again? She lay on the kang; fear prohibited even a nose twitch.

A rumble—thunder?—reverberated in her bones. It had been years since that awful day, when the insanity that had imprisoned Mother and Father came knocking—and reduced to shards the windows that Father had been so proud to install, the windows that labeled them as *bourgeois* pigs. Kai did not understand the insanity then and she did not understand it now, but it had taught her to sense the tremors preceding life's upheavals.

For five stomach-gnawing, back-breaking years, the sisters marshaled for battle, First Daughter the boss of Kai; Kai the boss of Third Daughter, Third Daughter the boss of the chickens and crows. Though Kai had argued a baby could not command, First Daughter insisted that Third Daughter actively engage. *"Everyone must feel important,"* she had whispered. First Daughter's words gave Kai the strength to rise each morning, the courage to trust in sleep each night. By the time her parents had hobbled home in 1973, Kai was sick to death of being important. But the time to be of real importance—massaging Father's emaciated limbs, rubbing lotus cream on Mother's scabs—had just begun.

Was this new insanity a dream? Kai stretched her legs across the kang's padded quilt until her toes touched First Daughter's safe, solid calf. She let out a sigh at the comfort of her sister's presence. A moon sliver cast shadows over First Daughter's lustrous skin. Perhaps calm would prevail.

Again thunder rumbled . . . or was it Father's voice?

A breeze whipped through the window and tangled First Daughter's hair. Kai sat up straight and pricked her ears like a nosy goat's.

Father was cursing Mother! Saying things that Kai had not heard since the day she had been forced to hurl stones and nasty words like *used shoes* at her parents. The very thing Father just yelled at dear Mother.

Last night's dumplings clumped in Kai's stomach. Had Father slipped back into the hateful spell that had imprisoned his mind for two years after his return? Kai pushed back her quilt and left its comfort. She must stop Father. After all, she had nursed him day and night until he became Father again . . . or a close relative of the man he had been before the Troubles.

Kai crept into the hall. Careful not to dishonor the calendars that bore portraits of Mao by touching them, she tiptoed past the kitchen to the door of her parents' room.

"How could you allow this to happen to us?"

"It is the fates." Kai strained to hear Mother's voice.

"The fates? It is your stupidity."

It took no effort for Kai to hear Father.

"I will not allow it."

"It is the fates," Mother repeated.

"Will it be the fates when they again beat you with chains and whips? Call your daughters cow-devil and snake-spirit counterrevolutionaries? Reeducate them in Tibet?"

Kai longed to skitter back to the kang, pull the quilt over her head, and pretend that the Troubles were not again stirring up dust that hid in crevices like evil spirits. But she must know what angered Father.

"That business has been discarded along with Mao pins and Madame Mao operas." Mother snorted, making Kai decide that a fever had affected Father's mind. "After what we suffered, they would not dare."

"They would not dare?" Father's mad demon laugh caused Kai to tremble. "Wild-greens dumplings and millet porridge have masked the memory of the rice husks and vermin's dung that we lapped from bowls. Do you not remember the beatings you endured because you miswrote one lousy character?"

Something creaked. Had Father risen? Kai skittered toward her room and then froze in the hall. Father would curse *her* if she were caught eavesdropping.

"Yes, you have forgotten all," Father continued, "now that Second Daughter monitors her class and spit no longer stains her face. You have forgotten, now that Third Daughter finds such joy in school and in the camaraderie of her classmates. If the village chief discovers the secret in your belly, your defiance of Family Planning pronouncements, he will fire-breathe his fury."

"I do not believe it!"

Father emitted a manic cackle. "You will. Fury lies

dormant, like a sleeping hateful dragon, ready to slay you with one noxious breath."

Kai's spirit slithered onto the floor though her bones kept her upright. Mother, pregnant? Oh, what would they do?

"You are wrong!" Mother hissed. "China has changed."

"China will never change. And I will never endure such suffering again. Not for a baby. There is no choice. You must abort this child to save our family."

Kai bit her lip, winced at the metallic taste, and fended off an image of a bloodied chicken. Its bloodied embryo. A bloodied . . . Mother. *A bloodied baby!*

"I will not murder a child."

A slap rang out.

Mother groaned.

Kai clapped her hands over her ears. It did not stop the sound of what she believed—what she *knew*—was her father striking her mother.

Numb, Kai worked her way back to her room. She moved as if she were dead, her feet not feeling the floor, her hands not feeling the wall. Was she floating, or had she died at the horror of hearing Father beg Mother to kill a child? Her future sibling?

"You can divorce me." Words careened off the walls and slammed into Kai.

"I will not divorce you."

"You must divorce me, for I will not kill a gift of the fates."

Something like a sob came from Father and froze Kai in place. So Father had not gone mad, at least not entirely.

"How can I divorce the one who picked lice from my hair as we lay, starving and shivering, in prison? How can I divorce the one who bore me such loyal children, even if they are daughters?"

"I will bear you another child. Perhaps this one will be a son."

A brother? Kai threw back her head. Banged it against the wall.

"Shh! What is it?"

Shivering, Kai again proceeded to tiptoe, ever so slowly, to safety . . .

"There are spies everywhere." Father's voice was a teapot hiss. "Our neighbor. A second cousin. We are treading water in a bitter sea of betrayal."

"China has changed."

As Kai crossed her bedroom threshold, her parents' voices thunder-rumbled. *Five steps, four steps, three steps,* she told herself, *and I am safe from what I have heard.* Kai climbed into the kang, but its quilted warmth no longer comforted. Until the rooster crowed, she tossed about, fomenting a plan to save all of them, especially a baby, full of innocence, of hope; things the Changs must preserve, or they, too, would die.

Kai leaned against the door of the juvenile director's office in Fort Worth, Texas. Though her head cleared, her heart ached from memories she had not wanted to remember, much less express in words. Yet teary-eyed Joy had hungered, had thirsted, to know . . .

"So I was the baby," Joy whispered.

Kai nodded. Should she reveal that only through her finaglings had Father relented? Could she chance staining Joy's first impression of a good man, a kind man—a man who only labored to protect his family in the hopeless situation that so often was China, so often was *life*?

113

"What made my father change his mind?"

A soft hand found hers with a surprising grip for someone so petite. Kai's skin tingled at the very touch. She smiled at Joy, who, despite grimy makeup, radiated an innocence that proclaimed survival of whatever China, whatever America, had done to taint it. *Joy deserves the truth, and I will supply it.*

"That night tears dampened my quilt. Yet my sisters—our sisters—slept as the innocent . . . and uninformed."

Joy leaned close. Cigarette smoke twitched Kai's nose. *Another problem to face, but not today.*

"At dawn, I peeked in on my parents, whom the fates had finally blessed with sleep." Kai stifled a cough. "I roused my sisters and dragged them staggering and sleepy-eyed to an old banyan tree." Memories birthed fresh tears; Kai swabbed them, hoping to rid herself of emotion. "I shared what I had overheard in the dead of night and begged my sisters to help me find a compromise that Father would accept."

Joy's eyes grew as wide, as rapt, as those of First Daughter and Third Daughter on that awful, wonderful dawn.

"As a red sun rose, we plotted our futures. The first step? We begged for the baby's life. We did it, Joy, for two reasons. The fates had given recompense for our suffering. We could not anger them by refusing their gift." Kai struggled to finish what she must say. "We also did it to save Mother, who could not bear another loss."

"But you didn't keep me. You sent me to . . . that place."

That place. Kai's shoulders sagged. So the neglect had imprinted Joy, despite how she and her sisters had tried to help by volunteering at the orphanage whenever possible. Her composure slipping, she called on a decade of memories to help her. The memories did not fail.

114

"We Chinese have a saying called yin yang. It does not translate well into English, but I will do my best. Yin yang is a quality that somehow incorporates opposite qualities into one being. Purity/filth. Good/evil."

Kai wiped sweat from her brow and searched Joy's face for a sign that recognition dawned. Joy barely breathed.

"Before, during, and after the Cultural Revolution," Kai continued, "China symbolized yin yang in a way I haven't seen before or since. I will never forget the day our mother limped home, half of her scalp shaved, the other half displaying a nest of hair so tangled, so filthy, it housed lice and dung beetles."

Joy shuddered; another good sign. She could still feel the pain of others. Their youngest sister did not hate them beyond repair.

"Even after news of Mao's death," Kai continued, fortified by the intensity in Joy's gaze, "the arrest of the Gang of Four, the reopening of schools, the return of sanity and a degree of peace to our home, yin yang struck again when Mother got pregnant. As I shared, the authorities would have forced Mother to abort you if they learned of her defiance. If a neighbor harboring grudges against our parents whispered to a Party member that a baby wail had penetrated a courtyard wall, that baby might have been seized and thrown into the river. But if—"

"Oh, how could they do it?" gushed from Lily.

As if innocents are not aborted every minute of every hour of every day in every country . . . Kai stifled the urge to defend her homeland, but for Joy's sake, she could not be sidetracked. "If," Kai continued, as if uninterrupted, "a healthy baby girl was left on the steps of an orphanage located in a nearby village, no harm would befall her." Kai waited for Joy to wipe her eyes and refocus. "That, my sister, was—is—the reality of yin yang."

Joy did not move. Did the child breathe?

Kai battled a sinking sensation. "We three sisters coaxed that compromise from Father and then swore on our ancestors' graves to penetrate those orphanage gates whenever possible."

Joy's hands, which she'd been digging into her wrists in the habit of her mother, plopped into her lap. "I remember one woman . . ."

Kai clutched her throat to suppress a cry. Did Joy remember how they had salved her chapped bottom? How they had slipped her caramels when an orphan's sickness—or death—distracted the staff? Dear fates, did Joy remember the Chang sisters?

". . . or maybe she was an older girl. Her hair shone like it was lacquered."

Nothing could stop Kai's lip from quivering. "First Daughter, your oldest sister."

"She always patted me on the back."

Akin to an American full-body hug.

"She brought me special treats."

"We all came, but First Daughter visited most." Kai again struggled for composure.

"So they let you in but wouldn't let me out?"

Kai nodded. "We planned to reclaim you when political winds changed. An old enemy of Father's destroyed our dream. Years earlier, father had complained about her poor work ethic. She had a cunning ability to pit friend against friend, inflamed by her love of snitching!"

Joy began tapping her foot, surely wondering what this had to do with her.

"Father's enemy wangled the plum job of orphanage director. Her insidious talent for sniffing out truth led her to suspect that we were your family. Oh, how that snake would fix her beady eyes on us when we came to volunteer!"

Joy froze. Did she remember that evil woman?

"Hints and innuendos slipped off the director's forked tongue! Despite our caution, she discovered—or intuited—that our family had left you on the orphanage steps. Before we could reclaim you, Lily . . ." Kai's cheeks flamed with embarrassment. She had done what she had intended not to do—call Joy by her real name.

Her sister paled. "My name was Lil-y?" She enunciated slowly, perhaps letting the two syllables roll about her mouth, her soul, to see how they felt. "I . . . I like that."

"*Bai he* in Chinese. It is a beautiful, and useful, flowering herb." Kai pressed on, afraid that she might break down if she paused. "Our plan—yes, we had a plan—was proceeding nicely. America opened its gates, as did Harvard, where I was studying medicine. Then a telegram arrived from China. *Mother ill. Return home.* With her dying breath, Mother begged me to go to you. Testify of our love." Kai did not mention Mother's necklace. A detention center was not the time or the place.

A tear escaped the corner of Joy's eye, yet her expression did not change. *Perhaps this story exhausts her as well as me.*

Kai breathed deep and exhaled. "The day after her funeral procession, I biked to the orphanage . . . in time to see you leaving with the Powells. The orphanage director—how I hate her to this day—smirked at me. She seized the chance to give you, our most prized possession, to Americans. I am sure it stuffed her pockets with *yuan*."

Tears cut deeper channels through Joy's makeup.

Kai hurried into the next part. *Oh, fates, please, help me!* "Do not blame your parents, Joy. They provided you with things we Changs did not have."

Joy tore at her hair. "But I didn't . . . I don't belong!" A wail escaped her throat. "Do you have any idea what it's like to have slanted eyes here in Cowtown? Do you have a clue?"

Kai's throat closed in frustration, from exhaustion. *Do I have a clue, my dear sister? I changed my name just to avoid having it butchered daily by those who would not bother to learn its pronunciation. I am a magnet for snide comments about Chink friends when I go out with Caucasians. I watched seriously ill patients stalk out of the ER rather than be treated by a "slant-eye."* She laid a hand on Joy's shoulder. "It will get better, I assure you." She did not lie. Truly, it had gotten better.

Joy buried her head in her hands. Kai longed to do the same but just sat there, spent, staring at her sister.

A horrible grinding sound split the uncomfortable silence. Hairs pricked on Kai's neck.

The door flew open. There stood Nicole, the juvenile director, pale as Joy, who'd leapt from the floor.

"Siren's sounding. Doppler's spotted a twister near here."

Twister? Texas slang for a tornado? Kai fought an instinct to grab Joy's hand and flee. Training triumphed. "Where do we go?"

"Uh, we just congregate in that main area. Where y'all came in."

Cubicle city? Kai swallowed hard. "Is there not a basement?"

"Welcome to Texas." Nicole gave her a weak smile and held open the door.

Kai grasped Joy's clammy hand and double-timed after

Nicole. They joined a cluster of employees who were either staring at the floor or exchanging high-pitched giggles. Scared . . . or happy to escape work. "It'll be all right," Kai whispered to her robotic sister . . . and then begged the fates that what she said would be true.

9

Record time for a doctor visit. In only ten minutes, Gloria had registered, peed in a cup, stepped on the scales, been cuffed and puffed. If this fainting spell were truly nerves, as she and Andrew had discussed on the way over, she'd be back with Joy, barring a traffic snarl, within an hour . . .

The examining room door opened.

"Hello." Smiling, Dr. Davies, the reed-thin female member of the practice, pulled Gloria's chart from a rack on the door.

Gloria returned the pleasantry, difficult with Joy in jail and her head pounding. She wiped soggy palms on her paper gown and tried to calm down. The sooner she got this over with, the sooner they could reunite with their daughter.

Dr. Davies adjusted her glasses and studied Gloria before opening the chart. "Your husband called at the behest of a Dr. . . ."

"Chang Kai."

Over wire-rims, the doctor's eyebrows arched. "Don't believe I've met him."

"Her. She practices in Boston."

"Hmm." Dr. Davies crossed her arms and cocked her head, as if curious about the circumstances that had led a Boston doctor to send Gloria for an exam. Who wouldn't be?

"According to your husband, you fainted and vomited." The doctor tapped her file. "I also got the lowdown on your daughter. I'm sorry."

Gloria blinked back tears.

"Your husband also believes your symptoms are stress-related." Dr. Davies sat on a metal stool, rolled it closer to the examining table, and pulled a pen from her lab coat. "Why don't you tell me what's been going on?"

Gloria clutched the paper gown. "I've made a mess of everything," she confessed. "Now I've caught a virus, though it's really a good thing, and—"

"Gloria." Dr. Davies smoothed her no-nonsense bob. "You're not making sense. It's good that you have a virus?"

"So we could leave Joy alone. With her sister and the police." Words mixed with sniffles. "I mean, her sister's a doctor, the one who had us call you . . ."

"I see," said Dr. Davies, though her blank look made it clear she didn't see at all. "Let's talk about that later. Now, lie back so I can examine you."

Gloria squeezed her eyes shut, but that brought images of Joy in the jail—*with Kai. Without me.* She stared at the ceiling until she heard the stool clank and Dr. Davies say, "You can sit up now, Gloria."

Someone knocked on the door, sending Gloria's heart off-kilter. She gripped the table. Her head spun, as did her stomach. Again.

A nurse handed a slip of paper to Dr. Davies and left.

Gloria rubbed her churning stomach and then smoothed her gown. What now?

"As the technician probably explained, I ordered blood and urine tests."

"Um-hum," Gloria mumbled, wondering if it would be rude to lie back down and curl into a ball while the doctor tried to talk to her.

"The electrolytes are okay. Your CBC shows that you are mildly anemic . . ."

"Um-hum."

"But, Gloria . . . Gloria?" Dr. Davies pulled off her glasses and set them on the counter. Her eyes gleamed strangely.

"Yes?" Gloria struggled to show interest in whatever excited her doctor.

"There is one interesting result."

"Um-hum?"

"That's the urine test."

"Um-hum."

"I'd like to do an ultrasound to confirm it—"

Gloria's skin tingled. Ultrasound meant a mass. A growth. Not stress-related.

"—but the urine pregnancy test was positive."

Gloria let go of the gown she'd been clutching. She kept hearing the word *positive*, but her mind wouldn't wrap around it and tie it in a bow. A pink bow. A blue bow . . .

"I'd hold off buying a crib, Gloria, but I won't hold off on congratulations. You're pregnant."

"But I can't get pregnant," finally emerged from a cotton-candy-sticky mouth.

"I hear that all the time."

Baby blue. Pretty pink. Colors swirled in Gloria's field of vision and obscured all of Dr. Davies but her toothy smile. Again she opened her mouth, tried to talk.

Something buzzed. A siren?

The doctor clasped the file to her chest, as if it were classified. Strange . . .

A nurse whirled into the room. "Tornado warning." She huddled with the doctor, as if to speak in confidence, but panic megaphoned her voice. "We've gotta get downstairs. Now."

Gloria's world tumbled, though she was still sitting up. She heard the doctor's terse whispers but couldn't get past the word *pregnant*. Had it been spoken a minute ago? An hour ago? Pregnant? She couldn't get pregnant!

"Get her husband in here," Dr. Davies ordered. "That stretcher in the storeroom. Bring it. Stat." Her voice crackled like a bad phone connection. Sinking fast, Gloria battled to hear every word. "Get her clothes on. That gown is a mess."

∽◦∼

"It's ridiculous to coop us up."

"Like a stairwell's safe."

"No kiddin'."

Gloria battled to open her eyelids, which felt as if they weighed ten tons.

"You know what it is? They're bored over at the National Weather Service."

"No kiddin'."

Something weighed down on her, warm and soft and soothing. A blanket . . . and a hand, grasping hers. Even with her eyes shut, she'd know that hand anywhere. Andrew. Dear Andrew. Her lungs settled into their familiar rhythm.

"What a crock!"

Gripping Andrew's hand, Gloria's eyes fluttered. They weren't alone!

People dressed in nurses' smocks and casual suits clustered

under a No Smoking sign, where two orderlies lit up nonchalantly. Gloria gripped the rails of . . . a stretcher? She was on it! Her lips tightened to combat a tremble that rattled metal rails. "Where are we?" She tried to sit up.

"You're okay." Andrew took hold of her shoulders and eased her back onto the stretcher. "But you fainted again. They wanted to take precautions."

She'd fainted when they'd told her—exhilaration fizzed every fiber. *Infertile, thirty-five-year-old me. Pregnant!*

"Andrew!" She tugged his sleeve. "Did the doctor tell you?"

His brow wrinkled. "The nurse just said you'd fainted."

She reached for his arm. Missed. "Andrew, I'm—"

"Just relax."

"I've relaxed for thirty-five years!" Words escaped in spurts. "We're pregnant!"

"What! The vomiting . . . you mean . . . but I thought we couldn't."

Vomiting, the jail, their daughter . . . Gloria sat up. "Andrew, I've got to tell Joy." She thrust her legs over the stretcher edge. "We've got to get her out of jail! Now!"

The smokers' cigarettes hovered midair. Folks coughed and spluttered, politely averting their eyes.

"Gloria, cool it!" While holding her down, Andrew raised his eyebrows, head nodded toward the crowd.

Gloria shoved away Andrew's hand and ignored a throbbing headache. *Who cares what these folks think? I've got to get to Joy, talk to her . . . tell her about . . .* Her mouth went dry. "How long have we been here, Andrew? What time is it?" All she could think about was Joy, who today had gained one sister . . . possibly another! How would Joy react to a change involving dirty diapers? Midnight wails?

"Around two thirty."

The splotched walls and clouds of cigarette smoke pushed in to create a pent-up feeling. "What are we doing in here, anyway?"

"There's a tornado warning." Andrew again checked his watch. "It's about to expire. Hopefully the doctor'll clear us. We'll head back to Joy."

Gloria sighed. How would Joy take the news? A big mess had just become a massive mess . . . or maybe not. Until Joy had dyed her hair and grunged her dress, church families called her to baby-sit, claiming the kids loved her enthusiasm. A baby sister or brother might smooth Joy's puffy-lipped resentment into a smile!

Gloria pictured Joy caressing a newborn's downy cheeks. Babies had revitalized stalled marriages, restored health to ailing grandparents. New life might resurrect in Joy a spirit of trust, of love. *A spirit I've smothered with my fear . . .*

Dr. Davies broke from the knot of mumbling employees. In her experienced way, the doctor pressed her fingers against Gloria's wrist. "You've been through a lot, Gloria. After they release us—"

"Release us?"

"Standard operating procedure for a tornado warning. We had two last week."

"Yeah," someone muttered. "What a waste of time."

"We'll do that sonogram when we're cleared to return, and a couple of other tests." The doctor nodded, as if convinced things were normal.

"But my daughter's waiting . . ."

Andrew massaged her shoulders. "She's in good hands, Gloria."

Good hands. Gloria remembered Kai's strong fingers, helping her up, Kai's soothing words, bolstering her resolve.

Kai, trained as a healer, would care for Joy. Gloria nodded agreement. Kai was the answer they had needed for a long, long time.

"You're in good hands too." Andrew draped his arm about her shoulder. "Let the doc take care of you . . . and our baby."

Andrew's tone soothed her nerves. *Thank you, Lord.*

"Amen!" someone hollered. Others clapped. Gloria leaned against Andrew and nodded thanks for the folks' congratulations. Yet she only had eyes for the upturned nose and tear-softened eyes of her man, who'd never asked anything of her except that she love him; who'd never done anything but trust God, before the gift of Joy, during the trials of Joy, and now. *Live for today. Live for this new life.*

Gloria bowed her head. *God, let me trust like him. Let me believe in your perfect plan. For Joy. Andrew. Our baby.* Again she massaged her stomach. The idea that life blossomed there cascaded warmth to every cell. God had provided. He would provide again and again . . .

A door scraped open. Before them stood a man dressed in a janitor's uniform. A walkie-talkie hung from a loop in his jeans.

"Storm's done passed over."

"Great."

"Headed east."

"I guess that means we gotta go back to work, huh?" The men standing under the No Smoking sign sucked a last nicotine hit. Someone mentioned a side trip to the restroom, but Gloria barely heard. The awful word *east* kept ringing in her ears.

East meant the juvenile center. East meant Joy. East meant Kai. There was not a blessed thing Gloria could do to stop another storm from threatening her daughter's life.

10

With Joy's help, Kai lugged a mattress issued by a detention center employee across cubicle city's floor. Though lumpy and smelling of sweat, the mattress could shield them from missiles of glass . . . steel . . . bone? Kai tried to ignore a twinge of fear. Surely the fates would not lead her to Joy only to fling both of them into a storm . . . or let the storm fling them.

As Kai and Joy sat cross-legged, their mattress a backrest, employees whispered fearfully into cell phones and cursed about the ruined day. One man cracked vulgar jokes. With desks moved against walls, the sterile space strangely burst with behavior that ran the gamut of human emotions. *Not a place to have a meaningful conversation with my sister.*

"Y'all need to settle." With a booming voice, Mr. Moore, the officer in charge of emergency preparations, ordered people about. A radio of gigantic proportions was set by the door. Sneezing, Kai leaned against the mattress. Could a thing reeking of cigarettes, sweat, and dust truly protect them from a tornado?

"This is so stupid! We're not in Kansas," mumbled a woman seated nearby.

"What's your beef?" countered another worker. "It's better than a staff meeting."

Mr. Moore knelt and fiddled with the radio, which crackled and moaned.

Kai monitored the histrionics of the grumbling south-wing employees. If tempers flared and a tornado blew in, this stuffy space would become unbearable . . . and potentially dangerous.

"How many times do we have to drag out these filthy things?"

"Every time, get it?" Mr. Moore fiddled with a walkie-talkie and burned the complainers with a stare. Kai didn't blame him. People's lives—including her Joy's—were at stake. Emergency protocol demanded disciplined responses. She kneaded her knuckles and sat up straight, trying to set an example for the others.

"Lockup's complete on the detainee floor." Mr. Moore drowned out radio squawks. "Take your positions."

Still sitting cross-legged, Kai tensed, ready to pull the mattress about her and her sister, as Mr. Moore had demonstrated. Joy huddled into Kai. Even mixed with cigarette smoke, the fruity smell of Joy's shampoo helped mask the mattress odors. "Like, are detainees prisoners?" Joy asked.

So you are beginning to see the ramifications of your actions, dear one. Perhaps this ordeal will be worth it. "We are fine." Despite a sinking feeling that the twister might be spinning their way, Kai managed a smile. "The detainees are just children." Kai lowered her head and fixed her gaze on Joy. "Like you. They are confused, hurt, and angry. But they are children."

Whimpers mixed with curses and laughter as folks disobeyed Mr. Moore and milled about. Kai crossed her arms and tapped her foot. *Typical Americans. Again, I am different. So is Joy. Perhaps that is a way to reach her: through our common differences.*

"Kai?" Joy's whimper joined others in the room.

The right hand pulsed. Oh, it was a blessing and a burden to so intensely feel another's pain. "What is it, Joy?" Kai asked in a soft voice.

"I'm . . . scared."

As Mr. Moore shooed the last rovers into their mattress strongholds, Joy's words soothed Kai's hand. *I am glad she is afraid, for it shows she has emotions . . . and that she will trust me with them.* Yet there was no need for fear, at least according to Mr. Moore, who kept assuring them that he'd never seen a "real tornado" in his life. Kai let out a sigh and tried to smile. She laid her hand on Joy's arm. "Listen to Mr. Moore. The man sounds like a tornado expert."

"Have you ever seen one?" Glare from the overhead light fixtures illuminated Joy's trembling nostrils. Fear: Kai had seen its many mutations . . . and had learned techniques to keep it from metastasizing to inhibit her work. She must busy this one—her dear, dear sister—with chitchat.

"No. My part—our part—of China has no such phenomena."

Joy clasped her hands and pursed her lips, as if desperate to still fears . . . and satisfy curiosity. "What . . . what is it like there?"

Kai struggled to rein in elation. How long had she waited for this moment?

Radio static buzzed, instructive words droned, but Kai willed away the intrusions. For Joy's sake, she must seize fate's timetable . . . and get it right.

Kai shifted on the cracked mattress edge. How could she

describe a country that had indiscriminately cut down trees, yet boasted the world's most fragrant flowers? How could she describe her childhood's blue velvet nights, when stars had winked at the Chang sisters and the moon man had slipped from his filmy-cloud home to say hello? How could she describe another night, innocence dying as she groveled at the gate of a neighbor, who tossed a flaccid turnip and two pencil-thin carrots into her face, then spit on her and slammed a heavy gate door?

Kai moistened her lips. She, fluent in Mandarin, Cantonese, and English, could not summon words to describe China. Yet this sister had waited seven years for an explanation. She must string together words to answer a logical question. Joy's well-being might depend on it.

As if to remove the neighbor's phlegm that had long ago stained her cheek, Kai wiped her face. "There is no way to explain China other than to say it is beautiful and ugly, generous and selfish, spacious and crowded. China possesses everything . . . and nothing. In my country, time has dragged for a century, has sped by in a day."

"Will . . . will you take me sometime?"

A thousand flowers blossomed in Kai's breast. Though she was leaning against a stinky mattress in a Texas jail, the spring Kai had so desperately awaited had come at last. Kai locked eyes with Joy. "Yes, Joy. Yes. If—"

An ear-splitting whistle froze Kai's words. A crackling sound and a *whoosh, rumble, whoosh, rumble* swelled and tumbled closer, closer . . .

Kai threw her arms about Joy and pulled her close. She zeroed in on the part line of Joy's hair, treasuring every silky strand, grinding her teeth in determination to protect this sister no matter what.

"At three fifteen Central Daylight Time, a tornado was spotted in the metropolitan Fort Worth area ten miles west of the intersection of I-35 West and 820." Crackles interrupted a robotic radio voice. "It's tracking east at thirty miles per hour."

A chorus of whimpers, Joy's among them, electrified the room. Someone screamed. Joy thrashed about, her elbow punching Kai in the ribs.

Though Kai winced in pain, though her teeth chattered and her brain raced, she begged calm to prevail and widened her eyes to battle a narrowing field of vision. To her best memory, they had not traveled on I-35. Perhaps there was no need to worry.

"On its present course, the tornado will impact the area east of Jacksboro Highway and 820—"

"Oh, Jesus!"

"That's us!"

The room erupted with cries and thuds and moans. Kai felt her lips tighten.

"This is a very destructive tornado," continued the mechanical radio voice. "Take necessary precautions immediately. Stay away from windows. Find the lowest part of—"

"God!" Joy shrieked.

Kai winced as pressure pummeled her eardrums. Oddly, sounds coming from outside the room had ceased. Nonetheless, Kai tightened her hold on Joy.

The mattress went sailing.

Kai scrambled, her fingers grazing their shield as it careened backward, flipped, hit the floor, bounced, and came to rest against a table leg. Desperate to reclaim it, Kai crawled forward.

"Take cover, I tell you!" Mr. Moore's voice mingled with that of Radio Robot and gasps and sobs and cries.

The room seemed to wobble. The air became soup. The hand Kai had extended to snag the mattress froze. As she struggled to breathe, the room went dark.

Collective gasps and screams coiled about Kai's throat. She forced herself to breathe slowly, basic protocol of emergency room triage.

Clarity returned as she realized that the tornado had claimed its first victim: the power supply. What would be next?

"Back up, you idiot!" Mr. Moore bellowed a command. "Get away from there!"

Kai swiveled her head.

A man skulked away from a plate-glass window. Kai succumbed to curiosity and let her gaze meander. What fascinated that man?

The sky was painted the color of wet green tea leaves. Telephone lines writhed, then popped, as if possessed by demons. Red-and-orange fireballs exploded into black ash. Insects swarmed in colossal dark clumps. Kai lunged forward and grabbed their mattress. Were these the end times that so fascinated her roommate Cheryl?

A rhythmic rumbling, like that of an approaching subway train, began to drown out the room's hysteria, the radio, and Mr. Moore's calls for calm.

Kai guided a trembling Joy into the head-to-chest position demonstrated earlier.

"Help me!" erupted from the mattress sandwich to their right.

"Stay calm!" yelled Mr. Moore, his voice anything but.

To shut out the cacophony of panic, Kai hummed into Joy's ear and manipulated Joy's frozen fingers so they interlaced about her head. As she burrowed with her sister under the mattress, she thumbed through memory files. Cheryl and her friends had linked the end times with wars and earthquakes. Not tornadoes.

"Oh, God! Oh . . . Kai!" Just enough light seeped around the mattress for Kai to see Joy's face. Tears had dissolved the crude black liner ringing Joy's eyes, had cleansed her cheeks of cheap blush. Remnants of purplish lipstick stained her chin and the corners of her mouth, giving her the look of a tragic young clown . . . or a child playing at dress-up. *Wherever she has been, whatever she has done, she is just a child.* Children must be comforted. Assured. Provided with better support than a nasty old mattress.

"I am here with you, Joy." Kai infused calm into her voice as she had done on countless clinical occasions. Again, protocol . . . yet those occasions had not involved the sister she had devoted her life to find. Every sinew in her body tightened. *If the fates inflict pain on this one, I cannot go on.*

Thrum-chug. Thrum-chug.

"My cell's dead!" someone shrieked.

"Avoid underpasses," came from the radio. "Repeat. A tornado . . ."

"Would . . . you . . . pray for us, Kai?" Joy had begun to pant. Sweat bathed a complexion that had taken on a bloodless pallor.

Kai startled as if she had been slapped. *To whom would you have me pray? The fates, which have proved so capricious that I am sickened to the point of nausea? Confucius? Buddha? Ones I have never accepted as gods?*

The heat, the mattress smells, swears and sighs and gasps and pleas, siren blares and ghastly splits and crunches, the glazed look in Joy's eyes, an eerie pressure that tugged at their mattress shield—it all funneled into a sucking fear that yanked at Kai's insides. The fates bore down with an otherworldly force!

"Please, Kai, please!"

Kai closed her eyes. Called on her experience, her training, her hopes, her dreams. Yet the vortex intensified and drained her of all she had ever known, thought, believed.

"Oh, where are my parents? I'm so sorry! Like, I'm . . . I'm . . ."

Kai covered Joy's trembling hands with her own and begged composure to return. Her training and determination were but useless puffs of wind. It was all puffs of wind compared to this indescribable force, whirling closer, closer . . . Kai's head dropped to her chest. *To think I tried to conquer fate and actually thought I could save this child. . . .*

Daughter! I am here for you.

Hairs prickled on Kai's arms. That voice. Again. Was it Old Grandfather?

I am Who I am. Do not fear.

"Wh-who?" Kai's composure slipped. "Who are you?"

Joy's hands flew to her face. She began to moan in a manner that Kai had heard behind curtains in emergency rooms.

Now her words had frightened her sister. Kai tightened both her grip on Joy and her resolve to never let that happen again. Yet the words of that unknown voice continued to fill her mind. Do not fear? In the eye of a storm?

Do not fear. I am with you always.

Though Joy continued to cry, though the thundering intensified, though the radio monotoned about taking cover, the strange words rallied courage and allowed Kai to focus on Joy. Careful to keep one hand on the mattress and the other on Joy, she whispered, "Do not fear," into Joy's ear. "I am with you always."

Joy's sobs ebbed. Convulsing shoulders stilled.

"Do not fear." Encouraged, Kai repeated the words gifted in an unknown way, by an unknown speaker.

Glass shattered. Sirens screamed. Screeches and grunts and moans of human fear tried to smother her voice. With Joy melded to her body, Kai hunkered into the floor, caring not who the speaker was. "I am with you always," she kept repeating.

A strange sucking sound filled the room, as did a cool breeze. *It is over!* The thought leapt from Kai's heart, yet she was taking no chances with the safety of Fourth Sister. "I am with you always," she whispered, and held tight to Joy.

$\backsim$

"Repeat. The tornado seems to have disintegrated near the intersection of . . ."

Kai let out a breath and loosed her hold on Joy. Had they escaped? Had the unknown speaker who whispered "fear not" been telling the truth? Shuffles—people walking?—and thuds from dropped mattresses mingled with the monotone of the emergency radio.

"Stay put!" yelled Mr. Moore. "That's an order!"

Kai massaged her taut neck muscles. If people were emerging from their mattress cocoons, surely the worst was over.

Someone whimpered.

Another.

Kai's heart leapt to her throat. People had been hurt, yet the one in charge asked that they stay put. She would effect a compromise. She edged from under the mattress to look about. If there was work to do, she could help.

Kai turned back to Joy. "Stay put, okay?" When Joy nodded from beneath the mattress still sheltering her, Kai said, "I will be back."

The storm's afterglow illumined glass shards that carpeted the floor. The room's occupants wore dazed expressions, as if they'd landed on another planet. Kai cupped her hands to her mouth. "I am a doctor," she called out, grateful that years of following emergency protocol amplified her voice. "Can I assist you? Does anyone need help?"

"I don't think so. At least not that I can tell." Mr. Moore ran his hand across his shiny bald scalp and slowly crunched in his rubber boots through water and broken glass until he reached the heap that was their mattress and Joy. "A man's bringing a mop."

A mop? Kai suppressed a laugh. *A mop to swab an ocean.*

"Just check for cuts, bruises, abrasions." His meaty jowls shook, as if Mr. Moore battled to suppress his emotions. Kai knew well the feeling. "Whew. It's nothing like what could've happened."

You have finally seen a tornado, Mr. Moore. Kai nodded away her thought, eager to begin work. "Do you have first-aid supplies? A kit?"

"Hey, Pete!" Mr. Moore yelled at the man standing nearby. "Get the kit." Pete began to dig through a bin, hopefully stuffed with supplies. Other workers, wearing jumpsuits, boots, and gloves, streamed into the room and gathered mattresses, a tree limb, two hubcaps, and mangled pieces of metal.

"We don't need NOAA anymore." A woman grabbed the squawking radio and turned it off. "Warning's expired."

Mr. Moore sighed, shook his head as if he couldn't believe their fortune, and then stuck out a reddened hand. "Where are my manners? I haven't even asked your name."

"Kai." She extended her hand. "Nice to meet you, Mr. Moore." This was no time for chitchat, even if it was Texas. "I would like to make sure everyone is okay. You have employees here, correct? Detainees on another floor?"

Officer Moore nodded. "We're basically a holding tank for juvies. Doris down in receivables is an RN, and she's checking things there. Near as she can tell, we don't need 9-1-1. They're swamped anyway." Mr. Moore scratched his neck. "So far I've just seen minor stuff. No signs of trauma."

Minor? Without attention, minor became major. Kai held out her hands, hoping that Pete would hand over the kit before she yanked it from him. "Despite no signs of trauma, we will need to assess everyone. If I can just have that kit . . ."

Pete straightened and shoved the kit at Kai. "You need a towel? Water? Soap?"

"Yes," Kai called over her shoulder as she walked to the center of the room, pausing to pull gloves from the kit and put them on. "My name is Kai," she announced, raising her voice in hopes that all could hear. "As I said earlier, I am a medical doctor and would like to help you." As she spoke, she pivoted, hoping her words would be heard by everyone in the room. "If you are experiencing dizziness or chest pain, please call out."

When no one responded, Kai stepped toward a woman who sat cross-legged, her head buried in her lap. "Are you okay?" she asked.

The woman raised her head, managed a bleary nod. Kai knelt beside her, checked her vitals. "It will be okay." She patted the woman's shoulder, then stood. "If you have cuts or abrasions, however superficial, please call out. If you are able, please check the status of those in close proximity. Other than that, please stay where you are."

"Ma'am?" someone called. A man's voice.

Kai whirled to her left.

"I think she's cut."

Kai's gaze riveted to a sweatshirt, pressed against a woman's arm. A blue sweatshirt, with no telltale red stain. Most likely a minor injury.

"Thank you, sir." She hurried to the woman and knelt by her. "What is your name?" she asked as she unwrapped the sweatshirt.

"Anna," the woman said through tears. Kai kept talking while examining the woman's arm. The tip of what looked to be a triangular glass shard protruded from the woman's wrist. Kai's heart pounded. *No wonder the poor thing is crying. Inches more, and there would be arterial compromise. A red river seeping across this floor.* Kai inhaled her little secret. "I know it is painful." She kept eye contact with the woman. "But please keep still."

"Can't—" The woman's teeth chattered. "Can't you get it out?"

Not for all the tea in China. Kai pursed her lips, as if it were a possibility, but recalled her ER training. *"Patients like to think their opinion deserves consideration. Do not send them into shock by reeling off dreadful 'what-ifs' or alienate them by spouting medical gobbledygook."* Kai smiled, both for Anna and the memory of old Dr. Ward. "It would be best done in a hospital. You have insurance, no?"

"Yes. Oh, yes." The woman's chest heaved with her eagerness to help.

Involve the patient. Another of Dr. Ward's techniques, to the rescue.

"So we'll just tape this up—"

The woman pointed at her foot. "I've got a place down there too."

Without letting go of the woman's hand, Kai leaned close enough to spot a laceration the size of a dime.

Kai furrowed her brow, as if she were in deep thought. "I am glad you showed that to me. However, I believe it will be fine. As soon as I get water and soap—"

"It's right here. Drinking water too."

Kai froze. That was Joy's voice. But it couldn't be . . .

Joy knelt beside her. A bucket and a soap dispenser thudded onto the floor. So did a crate of bottled water.

"J-Joy. Are you . . . okay?"

"I got up when you made the announcement." Something like a sparkle highlighted Fourth Daughter's eyes. "When I saw you working, I asked the man if I could help. He said for me to take these to my mother." She giggled, and it was a beautiful thing. "I didn't bother to explain."

As Joy handed Kai the soap dispenser, Kai noted a dramatic change. Gone were Joy's sullen eyes, pooched-out lip, imperious demeanor of— When was it? A lifetime ago? Kai checked her watch. It had been two hours since she'd first seen the sister whom she'd lost in order to save, the sister with an attitude the size of this state, the sister who just might be changed by a Texas twister.

As they finished up with Anna, another man called for help.

Kai turned to Joy. "Tell them I am on my way. Try to make them comfortable. Offer them a drink."

With a nod, Joy hurried across the room.

As workers continued to clean up the mess, Joy helped Kai bandage minor cuts and became a water girl. When they had seen the last clerk in the room, suffering only from a splinter in her finger, Kai began filling out the incident report given her by Mr. Moore. A spate of folks seemed to be on the phone, hanging up the phone, or getting out their phone.

The sight of people calling loved ones brought David to mind. Kai closed her eyes and imagined his strong jaw, his tapered, smooth hands. How she longed to spill out her heart to him, to let his gentle voice energize her, inspire her.

"Um, Dr. Kai?"

Mr. Moore clicked off his walkie-talkie and shifted his weight nervously.

Kai set the first-aid kit by Joy, who had collapsed into a chair near the door. "Yes, Mr. Moore." She mustered a smile. "What can I do for you now?"

"We have a problem. In the detention area."

Kai nodded. Joy's eyes got wide. *In other words, the jail.*

11

Another first in America . . . visiting a "holding tank" for youth. Noting Joy's wide eyes and sucked-in cheekbones, Kai took her sister's arm. They trailed Pete, who led them out of the elevator and onto the third floor.

Fluorescent lights cast a greenish tint on a room walled by cold cement blocks and a steel entry door with an eye-level window so thick, Kai suspected it was bulletproof. Pete pushed an intercom button and peered through the glass, drumming his fingers impatiently. While they waited by a drinking fountain, Kai shivered to think of Joy in such a place.

"Hey, open up, Hank." Pete's finger-drumming morphed to knocks and a wave at the window.

The door opened. Out stepped a guard, wearing the now-familiar jumpsuit, a holstered gun at his waist. Kai grimaced. Men with guns had whisked away Father and Mother and murdered Old Grandfather. Guns spoke a language of control, of power. Oh, that these officers would speak the language with the utmost of caution.

"Purpose for visit?" growled Holster Belt.

Pete threw up his hands and rolled his eyes. "It's Moore's doings."

"Well, I'll be—"

Holster Belt restrained his words but not his disdain. Kai felt her mouth go dry. Soon she and Joy would stand on Holster Belt's side of this enclosure. That thought trembled Kai more than the thought of prisoners.

Behind the Plexiglas wall, youths wearing blue shirts and trousers huddled in a corner of the room as if seeking warmth in a dank cave. Was that fear or despair in their eyes?

"Hey, tobacco breath." Pete tapped his boot against the floor. "She's a doctor."

"You're a doctor?" The man fiddled with his belt and squinted, whether out of disbelief or to mock her eye shape, Kai did not know. "That one a nurse?" His squint zeroed in on Joy as he slicked back his hair. "You two are gonna take care of this?"

"Never forget that you are a servant. That you must do whatever it takes to bring healing." Dr. Ward's words helped Kai mask her emotions. She must retain her dignity, honor her oath as a doctor, as a citizen. If it meant ignoring a rude guard, so be it.

"Only until the EMTs get through." Kai smiled grimly. "Mr. Moore says it won't be long." She cleared her throat, eager for the distraction of work. "In the meantime, Mr. Moore sent me here. Apparently someone needs attention."

"Waste of time, but go ahead." Holster Belt stepped aside.

"Hey, save your lip for someone who cares." Pete motioned for Kai and Joy to enter the restricted area. "After you, ladies."

Kai again pictured her sister inside this place. *Welcome, Joy, to the land of the not-so-free. Perhaps this assignment will prove enlightening to you . . . in more ways than one.*

Joy in tow, Kai stepped across the threshold. The door clanked shut.

One of the room's three barred windows had been smashed. By the storm? A man pushed a broom across the floor, collecting glass splinters. Bleach worked double-duty but failed to neutralize the smell of sweat, urine, and mold Kai knew so well from working at health care facilities. *Sickness, death, and misery cannot be easily scrubbed away.*

Breathing shallowly, Kai sneaked glances about the room.

Two additional guards stood, their legs spread out, their arms folded behind their backs, and gave curt nods from their position just inside the door.

Kai forced a smile. "Where is the patient?"

"Patient, my eye." Holster Belt nodded over his shoulder.

A lone plastic chair sat in the corner farthest from the windows. On the floor near the chair sprawled a young man with stringy dark hair. Like the other confined youth, he wore a baggy blue cotton shirt and pants. One pant leg had been pushed up. A cloth knotted his muscular calf. With his head cradled in his arms, Kai could not see his face. Perhaps he had something to hide . . . or was hiding from Holster Belt.

As Kai approached the detainee, Joy's shuffles . . . and snuffles . . . dogged her. To concentrate on the patient, she ticked off a checklist. Blood stained the makeshift tourniquet but did not pool above or below. Kai's heartbeat slowed. Signs pointed to nothing serious, at least with his body. Here was the serious question: *Why did guards not bandage this wound?*

Something slammed. A fist against the wall?

Kai cringed; the detainee jerked up his head to reveal a scarred face and dark goatee. His neck whipped to stare at her. "Told you, I don't want no . . ." Curses, and a reference to Kai's ethnicity, filled the air.

A movement niggled Kai's peripheral vision. Kai turned. Holster Belt's hand hovered near his gun.

So the detainee refused treatment. I am sure Holster Belt did not mind in the least. Keeping her eyes on the detainee, Kai backtracked and took the water bucket and first-aid kit from Joy. "Stay here," she whispered, though Joy's stiff limbs indicated little chance of her moving. Kai forced herself to breathe slowly, yet her heart galloped as she retraced her steps to the chair.

Kai stopped three feet from misery.

"Please." She crouched down. "I mean you no harm."

Hissing, her patient raised his head. With an arch of his neck, he flung hair out of hate-glazed eyes.

Kai shivered and then squared her shoulders. *Stop. Do not heap emotions on the situation. There is no reason for fear, not with guards and their guns steps away.* The right hand pulsated its yearning to help.

"Don't you touch me, you—"

Kai knelt by his side. "Fine." Her vantage point showed the words *Death Wish, Eduardo* and a skull and crossbones tattooed on her patient's leg. "You take it off." She pointed to the bloody strip. "We'll do this together."

An eternity passed as the boy—yes, he was a boy, now that she could see youth and hurt in his speckled eyes—scrutinized every inch of her. Then he slumped against the wall. The wrap slipped to the floor.

Kai motioned for Joy to pull rubber gloves from the kit. Kai stretched them over her hands, noted a deep laceration in the leg, and took a water bottle and towel from Joy, who shook visibly. *I know how you feel, dear sister.* After slipping the towel under the boy's leg, Kai gently poured water on the wound to wash away blood. She squinted. Blinked.

No debris. She bent close enough to see a tiny mole on the boy's calf. There would be debris. Never had she seen broken glass make such a precise, deep cut. Unless . . . *He is a cutter.*

Her windpipe constricted. She stretched as a ruse to look for clues. . . .

Two meters away, a bloody shard glinted red on the waxy linoleum floor.

Kai swallowed bile. Flying debris hadn't inflicted this wound. The boy had used a tornado's afterbirth to cut himself. Had he attempted suicide or tried to ease pain by a release of endorphins? Most likely the latter, as suicide victims generally preferred the more effective wrist-slitting. Kai shuddered. If it were suicide, what power had shouted, *Enough!* Could it be the storm whisperer who had earlier calmed her? Dared she believe in such a thing?

"You 'bout done?" snarled Holster Belt.

The boy wrapped his arms about his legs. His head dipped to meet his knees.

Order him to stop hurting himself.

A tic worked in Kai's jaw. Again she'd heard the voice. But to whom it belonged, she did not know. Kai extended her hands and covered the boy's fists with power infused by . . . that voice. "Do not do it again," she hissed, borrowing the boy's earlier tone. "It is a travesty to the body, soul, and mind." Her right hand trembled with a desire to smooth back the boy's most unmanageable strands of hair, which again veiled those eyes.

The boy snapped to attention. Stared at her.

A strange heat radiated from Kai and manifested itself like the beating of a thousand swallow wings. Something powerful. Inexplicable.

The boy was the first to look away. Power welled in Kai. The air seemed to whoosh with relief.

Eager to utilize the uncanny release of pressure, of strength, Kai treated and covered the wound, which would need sutures. As she worked, she murmured encouragement. When she was finished, she tweezed the glass from the floor, picked up the bloody wrap, stuffed it into a plastic bag, and stashed it in the kit. "Another will be in contact," she told the boy. "Someone who can help."

Kai motioned for Joy to follow her past the guards, through the door, and into the foyer. Back on the side of freedom, or the illusion of such. Back by the drinking fountain, where they waited for Pete, who apparently had returned downstairs.

"That was cool, what you did in there."

Though haunted by the boy's expression, Kai managed to shrug and smile at Joy. Drained, her back aching, Kai let the wall support her. Faces of patients flashed through her memory, patients she had treated with skills taught by Harvard's greats, perhaps her own bent for healing. Yet never had she experienced a presence like today, when a voice had instructed her in medicine. How could that be quantified or dissected? She was not sure if she would speak to David . . . *or anyone* . . . about this. Perhaps Dr. Duncan . . .

"Why didn't you tell the guard?" Joy asked in a husky whisper.

"Tell? Tell what?"

"That he cut himself."

Ice water raced through Kai's veins. How could a pastor's daughter detect a cutting episode that guards had not even seen? She struggled to recall what the policeman had said about Joy. Yes, this was her first arrest.

Joy leaned close. "They would've used it against him, you know. Badgered him into doing it again."

Kai's spine went rigid. Her fists tightened. First arrest or not, Joy knew things an innocent would not know.

"You don't look so hot." Joy offered her a water bottle, which Kai accepted with numb hands.

"I don't feel so hot." Kai swallowed, unaccustomed to bringing attention to herself in such a way. The emotions rushing through her were eroding her composure. It was an entirely foreign feeling.

"I tried it once, you know."

Joy's words swallowed the air in the foyer. The water bottle plunked against linoleum and poured out onto the floor. Kai opened her mouth. Closed it. Every cell in her body screamed, *Why? When?*

Fourth Daughter, whom they had saved from certain abortion; Fourth Daughter, whom they had nursed in the orphanage; Fourth Daughter, to whom she had come to test for PKD. There had been no more precious gift to the Chang family than Joy! To think she would end her life with a single slit! "How?" Kai hissed. "How did you do this thing?"

"With a razor." Eyes dulled—by remorse? Desperation?—met Kai's. Otherwise, Joy just stood there, as if she were dead. Her passiveness spurted adrenaline through Kai, who grabbed Joy's arm and shoved a mass of beads and metals off her wrist.

A plastic band snapped. Blue beads flew into the air and bounced off the tile floor, as if in rebellion to the insult. As well they should rebel! Life was sacred. How could a Chang do such a thing?

The pale scar, neat as an inseam in a garment, cut an acute angle into Joy's creamy skin. A scant two centimeters . . . yet enough to drain a body of its lifeblood.

Another miracle . . . or had Joy intentionally failed in her attempt?

Kai released her hold on Joy. One question answered, a million to go. How best to get answers? Her instincts screamed that the Powells must be present during such a discussion, yet Joy must know *this instant* what she thought. "We will address this, Joy. You must get counseling. This is not—"

As Kai stood, trembling and openmouthed, the elevator doors opened and spat out Pete and two men with a stretcher. Without comment, Pete picked up the water bottle and entered the holding tank, followed by the other two men.

Before Kai could broach the topic that had sucked the air from the hall, Pete returned, pulling a mop bucket. The other two men carried her patient on the stretcher, stopping near Joy. Kai stepped close enough to see her patient's speckled eyes, which seemed to beg her to do something.

The EMTs carried her patient into the elevator. Doors whined shut.

After Pete mopped up Kai's spilled water and returned the mop bucket to Holster Belt, he rejoined them in the hall. "We're done here." Pete wiped his hands on his trousers. "I'm taking y'all down."

"One moment." Kai strode to the holding tank and pushed the intercom button. Pete followed. Did he sense that Kai needed a monitor to deal with the guards?

Holster Belt swaggered to the glass. "Yeah?" Despite an air of indifference, curiosity gleamed in his eyes.

Kai cleared her throat. It was now or never. "As a physician, it is my opinion that the boy—my patient—needs counseling." She debated telling Holster Belt the truth and, heeding Joy's words, discarded the idea. "Please see that he gets it."

"Who do you think I am? God?"

Most definitely not.

Veins bulged in Holster Belt's throat. "They're all beyond help. Every stinkin' one of 'em. All the money *in Japan* ain't gonna fix 'em."

Heat rose to Kai's face. *Such ignorance, such indifference.* "If you are not . . . able to do so, I will report this myself." She made sure to shrug. "In detail, I might add."

Holster Belt's sneer showed stained teeth. "Are you threatening a guard?"

"Quite the contrary. You have a choice. I care not how we proceed."

"I'll see to it." Gumption swelled the voice of Pete, as if he was irritated by Holster Belt. Or was humane and kind.

Kai let out a breath. *Thank goodness.*

"It'll be on Moore's desk," continued Pete. "Yesterday."

Kai offered Pete a small smile. "Thank you, sir."

Together she and Pete moved away from Holster Belt . . . and the evil that seemed to seep from him. Kai took Joy's arm. The three of them stepped into the elevator.

His head shaking, Pete pushed a button. "Holy smokes, lady. I don't mind helpin' you out. But they're all crazy, you know?"

Kai battled a desire to scream. "So we stop trying?"

Pete shrugged. "Half of 'em try to kill themselves. Can you believe that?"

12

Pete mumbled good-bye and jetted from the elevator the instant the doors opened. Kai followed Joy into the foyer. She hoped Pete would honor his commitment to write that report—sooner rather than later. She'd follow up, just to make sure. But now she must speak to Joy.

Mr. Moore rounded the hall. Only his sweaty bald head and rumpled clothes hinted that a storm had ripped through. "That's the last ambulance run. They say there's nothing serious. Miraculously." He shook Kai's hand. "I can't thank you enough."

Kai smiled. "It is a privilege to be here." She cleared her throat. *So it will be sooner that I follow up . . . rather than later. Just as well.* "The injured detainee has psychological injuries." She furrowed her brow. "Pete, such a dedicated man, assured me he would file a report . . ."

"Glad to hear Pete's doin' his job." Mr. Moore whipped a pad and pen from his shirt pocket. A detail person. Kai's kind.

Mr. Moore scribbled, then stashed pad and pen. "Now about your daughter . . ."

Kai and Joy exchanged glances. "Actually, Joy is not my daughter."

An eyebrow peaked.

"She is my sister."

"Huh. Really?" Mr. Moore shifted about. "Do you have guardianship?" He fidgeted with his walkie-talkie, as if that would help him sort out things.

Kai shook her head.

"Hmm. She hasn't been booked?"

"No."

"Before she can leave, we gotta finalize the station adjustment. Her parents or legal guardians must be here for that." Mr. Moore swiveled, as if the Powells might materialize in the lobby.

"Kai?" Joy squeaked. "Have . . . have they called you?"

Kai smoothed her lapels in an effort to remain clam. What *had* delayed them? The tornado, or something they had learned at the doctor's? "I will check my cell."

"So . . . where did they go?" asked Mr. Moore, surely thinking *dysfunction.*

"Mrs. Powell fell ill," Kai answered. "Her husband took her to the doctor. We should hear from them at any time."

Joy's rasps signaled that any time needed to be now.

"If they have not called, I will call them." Kai slipped her hand in her pocket, where she had stowed her cell. Found *Call History.* Nothing. Pressed another button.

A fast-busy signal answered. She jabbed the thing again. Same annoying sound.

"Busy." She battled a frown. "The phone company's probably swamped." *Hopefully not with debris and water.*

"They'll get here when they get here. I'll tell Nicole what's going on." Mr. Moore fiddled with his walkie-talkie. "In the meantime, y'all stay put."

They were led into a lounge furnished with two sofas, a

folding table, and four chairs. Employees slumped in two of the chairs, their eyes glued to a television set. Exhaustion began to creep up Kai's spine, along with the knowledge of what she had to discuss with Joy and then the Powells.

As Mr. Moore left the room, she plunked down next to Joy, who'd sprawled on a sofa patched with duct tape and was biting her nails. With reluctance, Kai nudged her cell into the depths of her pocket. *To keep punching Redial and getting a busy will snap Joy's nerves . . . and mine. Besides, I must tackle this sticky-as-blood issue before Nicole arrives.*

Kai darted a look at the employees, who seemed hypnotized by the television. *Yet at the mention of self-mutilation, those ears will become elephant-sized.* Proceeding carefully, Kai smoothed her skirt. "We must address the . . . confidence you shared."

Joy would not meet Kai's gaze. "A confidence you won't keep, huh?" Though the words were biting, defeat hung on every word.

"You know the answer to that." The couch sagged as Kai twisted to better see her sister's face. "Your parents—"

Mr. Moore entered, holding cans of cola, glasses of ice. "I notified the front desk. They'll call Nicole when the Powells arrive. She'll bring them in here."

What had detained the Powells? Nothing short of an emergency would keep Gloria from this daughter she loved so fiercely . . . unless the tornado had whirled the Powells into its cyclone of death . . .

"Shop Rite-Way and start living today."

Joy lifted her head, as if wooed by the catchy television jingle . . . *Or else she's avoiding me.*

Perhaps the interruption is best, with this public setting.

Besides, my role is to keep an eye on her. What better way than to let the American squawk box hypnotize?

Joy joined the two workers to stare at the TV advertisement. Clerks dressed like candy stripers skipped down grocery store aisles to transform shopping into an amusement park experience. *If only my mood could be so transformed. . . .*

"We interrupt this program to bring you a special weather bulletin."

Kai's breath caught. If . . . the worst had happened, should Joy hear it via TV?

The screen flashed to a newsroom. An anchorwoman sat at a desk back-dropped by a Doppler radar map. "This is Andrea Phillips with a special report from KTVT, Channel 11, your station for the latest in weather." A grim smile hollowed the woman's cheeks. "When we establish contact, we'll go straight to Meteorologist Chris Turner, reporting live from the touchdown of what's being described by on-site weather spotters in southwest Tarrant County as an EF-5 tornado." The woman fumbled with her earpiece. "Chris, can you hear us? Chris?"

Fear gripped Kai. She cupped her hand over Joy's.

"Chris? There you are. It's Andrea." Relief plumped the newscaster's pinched cheeks and mouth. "What can you tell us?"

Joy sat up straight and cradled her stomach as if to steel against more pain . . . or had PKD begun its insidious creep? Kai edged closer to her sister until their shoulders touched. With effort, she shoved away thoughts of the illness that might be showing its nasty self to Joy. One step at a time, she would help Joy with whatever fate brought. Now it was the tornado. Whatever EF-5 meant, it didn't sound good.

Had Gloria and Andrew, on their way to the doctor, driven into a murderous twister?

The screen split to reflect two scenes: the anchor, still at her desk, and a curly-haired man who gripped a microphone. "This is Meteorologist Chris Turner, standing not twenty yards from where a suspected EF-5 tornado disintegrated a barn." The camera panned to an untouched telephone pole flanked by a swath of denuded field. "Though the twister blew a herd of goats and two dairy cows to smithereens, miraculously, not one single human life has been lost. At least that's what we've got for you at this point."

The man shook his head as if trying to convince himself that his report was true. "You have witnessed a modern-day miracle. The twister has whirled itself into oblivion." The reporter chuckled inanely. "I don't know what to say, other than the man upstairs took care of things. It's a miracle. There's no other way to say it. Though hundreds have suffered property loss, which is estimated . . ."

Kai tuned out the TV and studied Joy. If her parents had been spared, this tornado would prove to be a blessing. Joy had flung off the mask of defiance and exposed her deadly cutting secret. *Another area where she needs counseling. Attention. Help. Thankfully I have resources.* Thoughts pricked her. *A pastor has resources too, as Gloria so eagerly shared.* Had the Powells suspected Joy's self-mutilation? Why hadn't *they* seen the scar? Surely they hadn't ignored it?

Employees rose from their chairs, trading concerns, punching their cell phones, drifting out the door. *Finally we will be alone.*

Only when the door thudded shut did Joy turn to Kai.

"Do . . . do you really think my parents are okay?" Joy's thin shoulders shook.

Kai's stomach clenched at the thought of more pain inflicted upon this youngest daughter. *Joy needs hope. Something better than what fate offers. So do I.*

Forcing a smile, she gripped Joy's shoulders. "You heard the same thing I did. The man upstairs has taken care of things. No deaths have been reported."

"The man upstairs?" Joy's eyes glazed over. "Ha!" She tossed her head in disgust. Her mouth seemed torn between curving into a sneer, widening in surprise. "Tell me, do *you* believe in God?" Joy edged so close, Kai felt her ragged breath. "Does our family?"

Kai swallowed. Since Joy's parents were Christians, Kai must find a way to not insult them, yet be honest with Joy. Kai went through the motions of smoothing her hopelessly wrinkled skirt and begged the right words to come.

Answer a question with another question.

Kai raised her head on the strength of this voice. Whoever, whatever kept coming to her aid, she owed them a thank-you. How could you thank a spirit? A memory? Something a computer program, a lab experiment, could not explain?

"What I believe is of no importance." Kai's voice sounded flat. Void of the hope that faith would provide. Still, she pressed on. In this situation, there was nothing else to do. "What do you believe? That is the question."

∽

"What do I believe? You wanna know what *I* believe?"

Thankfully Kai had been trained to listen, for this sister of hers had much to say.

"That first Christmas in America, I stole Baby Jesus from the manger set up on our coffee table." Though employees slipped in and out of the break room, Joy ignored their comings and goings. "That little plastic baby got me past, like, the orphanage nightmares. Babies shrieking, like, 24/7. Babies with harelips and like, crooked backs." Joy sniffled. "They'd bundle 'em up and whisk 'em into this room down the hall." Joy waved her arms with abandon. "They never returned! Did you know that?"

Revulsion made a mess of Kai's stomach. Developing nations like China strained to care for healthy babies, much less those with special needs, but a dying room . . . Kai battled images of tiny emaciated limbs. Neither First nor Third Daughter had breathed a word of it. They could have done nothing anyway.

"I thought stained clothes, chapped bottoms, and canker sores were the norm. I went from wearing plaid tops, striped pants—whatever they gave me—to frilly pink outfits smelling like powder, not pee and vomit." Joy scrunched up her nose. "We'd go to church and read about Baby Jesus, talk about Baby Jesus, pray to Baby Jesus." Despite her pained expression, tears had dissolved the last trace of makeup, leaving a window into Joy's psyche.

"I was only ten, but I knew Baby Jesus got me outta there. That was all I cared about." Joy buried her face in her hands. "Oh, God," came out muffled. "Cookies and real milk. No screams at night, just prayers to Jesus. I even asked Him into my heart."

Kai murmured understandingly, though she was as perplexed by this statement as she had been the first time Cheryl used it.

"How could I not? He loved all the little children of the world." Joy raised her head. Strangely, her lip curled in sarcasm. "At first it was enough."

"So what happened?" Kai pressed on, seizing this chance

for a keyhole peek into Joy's soul. At any minute, it could close.

"Our church sponsored some Vietnamese. Our church—Christians, right?—puckered up at the boat people's soy and fish smells." Joy bounce-kicked the leg that rested on her thigh. "But they were clueless! Like kids, wanting to please the big white Americans and begin their American dream."

Boat people? Clueless? Kai's nausea swelled. Surely Joy hadn't lashed out against fellow Asians. Surely prejudice had not stained the heart of a Chang.

"The Vietnamese got baptized, giving these crazy grins, like those girls at school who get invited into these stupid clubs. They bought the whole fellowship-of-believers thing. Then they camped out on one side of the church with the whites across the aisle. Someone asked Mother why our family didn't sit with the other Chinese." Joy's chest heaved. "Can you believe that? They thought Hoc Nguyen and Bau Tran *were* Chinese!"

American carelessness, soothed with time. "Surely you understand their confusion."

"Confusion? No way. It was prejudice!"

"Prejudice?"

"There was a fire." Joy's face shone with an eerie light. "The sanctuary and back hall got roasted."

"Oh, how awful" was all Kai could think to say.

"The authorities said arson. By wax candles. Can you imagine that?" Joy screeched and bounced that leg. "But not just any wax candles."

Kai gripped the couch arm, unsure where this conversation would lead them.

"Candles made for one thing: to burn in Buddhist shrines."

"Surely an investigator could not determine the make of a wax candle."

"When they contain herbs found only in Saigon, they can. The candles had been jammed in a brass Buddha and arranged on the communion table."

"Someone placed an altar to Buddha in the sanctuary of a Christian church?"

Joy nodded. "The poor folks insisted they worshiped only Baby Jesus. You shoulda seen them, quaking in those black slipper thingies. They swore they didn't set up the altar. I believed them."

"So . . . what started as an act of worship ended in an accidental fire?"

"Investigators said the altar cloth and sanctuary carpet had been doused with diesel."

Kai felt her face pucker, as if she smelled gas fumes. Refugees had set fire to those who had provided them sanctuary? Never in her life had she heard such a tale, especially about the peace-loving Vietnamese. "Why?" she finally asked.

Joy began to drum a beat on the couch arm . . . and thudded pain into Kai's heart.

"Why would they try to destroy a church?" Kai repeated.

The irritating beat intensified. "They denied it, Kai. Like I said, they claimed to worship Jesus. They claimed to have left their incense and statues in Saigon."

"So they lied," Kai said dully.

"That's what everyone thought. Of course. Blame the gooks."

Kai winced. Why did Joy have to be so . . . in-your-face, as Americans would say?

"Daddy didn't believe it. He stood by the new members. A committee was formed. It sucked! Meetings, motions . . ."

Though she disdained Joy's language, Kai clucked sympathetically. This part she understood. To think pastors dealt with committees, just like doctors. *Poor Andrew . . .*

"I became guilty by associ-Asian. Churchies blackballed me from their stupid play groups. I got shuttled from one class to the next like a lumpy stuffed animal. Finally Mother kept me with her in the thirty-somethings group. You think I cared?"

Kai shrugged to hide what she longed to say: *Yes, dear one. I think you cared dreadfully. Otherwise your chest wouldn't be heaving, your arms waving.*

"Well, I *didn't* care. I didn't care at all. In fact, I was glad to see how phony the whole thing is. Like Santa Claus, American pie, the whole spiel they feed you. It's a crock, you know it? I'm not buying it." Joy swabbed at her spewing mouth. "Just like I don't buy the football games, the Friday-night dances. I'm not buying any of it!"

"You certainly aren't," Kai said, and then wished she had bitten her lip. Why fuel resentment? Hate? Hopelessness? Joy manufactured enough on her own . . . and might soon explode, right here. "So what happened, Joy? What did the committee decide?"

"Like I said, guilty by associ-Asian." Joy lifted her chin. Looked Kai full in the face. "They were wrong, you know." The eyes, so like First Daughter's, filled with tears.

Kai touched her sister's cheek, though what she longed to do was pull her close. Oh, to understand this child caught between two worlds! "Who was wrong, Joy? Why? Tell me!"

"Another church burned. Another. They had one thing in common: Asian refugees." A toneless quality had taken over Joy's voice. She looked past Kai, as if seeing her life, up in smoke. Kai shivered. Joy, too, was haunted by things from long ago . . .

"The police set a trap. Undercover cops posed as neighbor-hood drunks." Joy dabbed at her eyes. "Fourth time was the charm. They caught him. Guess what? No slanty-eyes! The

159

fire-lover was a vet, angry at gooks who'd killed his buddy. North Vietnamese, South Vietnamese, Chinese, anything-ese, they were all the same to him."

Kai settled trembling hands in her lap. No wonder Joy harbored deep-seated grudges. "That happens everywhere, Joy. People want an easy answer. A quick fix. Surely you understand . . ."

"Surely I understand that I've been fed a fairy tale since I was brought here. My parents can't handle that I won't sit in the pew and smile pretty for all the Bible-toters."

"Have you explained to them how you feel?"

"Have I explained to them?" Joy shouted. "Only a thousand times. They never listen. Why? Deep down, they're scared of me. Especially Mother. They cannot accept my eyes, my skin, and my accent—"

Something—somebody?—rustled near the door.

"Now my parents might be dead!" Joy wrapped her arms around her knees and wailed. "Maybe I killed them."

Another rustle. A click.

Kai raised her head. Locked eyes with Gloria, who, with Andrew, framed the doorway. Relief swathed Kai with shimmering warmth. They were safe! They could focus on Joy. Kai clasped her hands and rose. *Thank the fates* came to mind, but she discarded the thought. Whatever else she'd learned today, one thing was clear. The fates she'd hounded for years did not exist . . . or if they did, she no longer trusted them. They were as fickle, as capricious, as that tornado.

13

My baby. My Joy. Gloria trembled in relief. If Andrew weren't holding her up, if Nicole weren't here, surely she'd fall to her knees and thank the Lord.

Joy leapt to her feet, darted glances as if unsure of what to do, then threw out her arms and collapsed into their embrace.

Gloria buried her face in Joy's hair and inhaled Joy's sweet grass and tangy smell, the smell Gloria had learned—loved— on that first van ride. There was another odor—stale cigarettes. A problem . . . for later. Joy was alive . . . apparently uninjured!

A flurry of radio updates and Andrew's implacable calm had nearly convinced her of that, but words couldn't compare to holding Joy. The quaver in her lips, the tremble of her shoulders—proof that Joy cared—caused Gloria to swallow tears and fears. She flung her arms about Joy. Despite everything, Joy loved them. Again Gloria breathed deep and prayed, *Thank you, Lord.*

"We didn't know . . . we wondered if you had . . ." Sobs hatcheted Joy's words. Gone was Joy's earlier angst, her earlier anger. Or perhaps it had ducked into the dark alleys of her mind, to resurface on a stressful occasion, like hearing that she would have a sibling. Though Andrew had convinced her that Joy should be told—and now—indecision crept near. How could Andrew—and Dr. Davies—be sure? Gloria didn't know this new Joy. Lord, had she known the old Joy?

"I am thankful that you are safe." Kai's words rang true. "We heard everything was clear, but it is marvelous to see evidence."

Gloria nodded, and considered giving Kai a hug. *Not yet* . . .

"So you're . . . okay, Mommy?" Joy leveled a gaze her way. Her eyes, cleansed of sleazy makeup, sparkled. Her girl had a dynamite smile!

"I'm okay, sweetie," Gloria whispered. "How about you?"

"Good. Really. I helped Kai. Like a real nurse would. It was cool."

"Y'all woulda been proud of Joy." Nicole slapped her clipboard against her thigh. "They were *Chicago Hope*, right here in Texas!"

"No big deal." Joy pursed her lips, shrugged her shoulders . . . flashed another brilliant smile. It was a huge deal, apparently.

Andrew clapped Joy's shoulder. "I'm—we're proud of you."

"Me too." Nicole tapped on her clipboard. "Folks, that segues to the station adjustment." She stepped toward the door. "I know it's nearly five, but we don't do 'em on Fridays. We gotta nail this down . . . or hold Joy over the weekend. I don't want that, she doesn't want that—heck, no one wants that."

Amen! Gloria released Joy, though she yearned for more of Joy's touch, Joy's love. Oh, that things could be like they once were, when Joy listened to them and—

162

"*Y'all want me to listen to you, but y'all never listen to me.*"

Joy's theme song chose this moment to replay in her mind. Gloria's head drooped. She'd been delusional . . . for years. With a child on the way, a daughter facing a station adjustment, she'd better tune in to reality. She'd better *start* listening. Now.

⌒⌒

Kai followed the group to the same office where she'd first been reunited with her sister. *The greatest moment of my life . . .*

"It's a miracle no one was seriously hurt." Nicole continued the chitchat started on the trip down the hall.

Miracle. With the task I face, I could use a double portion.

They entered Nicole's office. With the sweep of her hand, Nicole ordered them to sit. Behaving like a true gentleman, Andrew pulled out their chairs. Kai pictured David, opening her car door, sending flowers. She missed him . . . and would call as soon as feasible.

Nicole pulled out a file and studied it. Gloria and Andrew sat, holding hands. Gloria had been transformed by a rosy glow, an easy smile. This mother, who surely died several deaths while waiting to see Joy, had been resurrected.

Eventually Nicole cleared her throat. "I appreciate what y'all have endured today. We battled Mother Nature. And won. Kinda."

They all chuckled.

"Joy, because of your record, or lack of it, I'm leaning toward a station adjustment. We're talking no sheet. A little service. Restitution." Nicole smiled. "Piece of cake."

Heat rose to Kai's face. Could Joy avoid serious repercussions? Another miracle.

"Normally Moore isn't too wild about 'em. And the paper trail stops with him." She tapped a pencil on the table. Her chair swiveled, and she swung her leg. "After today, he's singing your praises. I guess y'all soothed some freaked-out folks."

Joy slumped over but failed to hide blushing cheeks.

Kai studied her sister. *Deep down, this one longs to please. If only I can convince her, convince them all, of that. . . .*

"Anyway, thanks for helping. I got to see the real Joy. You confirmed what I'd thought all along. I had to twist Robbins' arm, but he's on board too, though he couldn't be here." Nicole waved her pencil. "As y'all can imagine, patrol's swamped with calls. Moore waived Robbins' scribble on the dotted line." With a triumphant smile Nicole passed copies to Gloria, Andrew, and Joy. "Sorry." Nicole shrugged at Kai. "That's all I've got."

Joy fanned herself with the paper. "I'll move over by Kai. We'll share."

Kai locked eyes with Gloria, who was clawing her hand. *She's uncertain about my role. I am uncertain as well . . . but I believe I can trust these parents of Joy.* Kai pushed away from the table and shook her head. "I would rather not be involved."

"Perhaps just Andrew and I should deal with this" was said with dignity, by a different Gloria.

Kai felt in her pocket for her phone and let the smooth plastic soothe her. She needed to hear David's voice, to tell him of the storms she had endured. He would murmur consolation. How she yearned for his affection, after staring death in the face . . . on that prisoner's leg, her sister's wrist. The images rocketed Kai from her chair. It was time to call Boston.

"Stop!" Joy flew to her feet and flung her paper to the floor. "Mommy, how dare you diss Kai?"

"Joy, I didn't mean it like that."

With sweaty fingers, Kai jammed her phone in her pocket. Joy majored in mood swings. Attitude. This time, manufactured from thin air. "You misunderstand."

"It's pretty—" Joy swore—"clear to me!"

"Joy, I promise, I didn't mean to hurt you or Kai. I'm sorry you misunderstood."

"I'm sorry too!" Joy stomped her foot and tossed her head. Purple-black hair swished. "Sorry you ever adopted me."

Anger paralyzed Kai. She could only stare at the ashen face of Gloria, so undeserving of this assault. Surely the latest of dozens.

Joy continued her tirade. Fueled by the hate in Joy's voice, fueled by knowledge of what Mother would have done to such an ill-behaved child, fueled by what Joy had been rescued from, Kai grabbed Joy's arm and squeezed. "Do not utter such unspeakable things." The words hissed like Kai's townhouse radiator. "In front of me. In front of your parents." Anger radiated to Kai's every cell. "Your parents sacrificed for you. In ways you will never understand. So did we, Joy." Kai paused when her lungs begged relief. "I have not traveled thousands of miles to hear a Chang talk like this."

Joy ducked her head and then lifted it. Red splotched her cheeks, her chin, even her nose. "Okay. Maybe I shouldn't have said that." Her tone had flattened. "But I will not sign any agreement unless Kai is involved. Do you hear me?"

"No." Kai shouldered her handbag. Stood. "You are not running the show, Joy." Anger smoldered. "I have calls to make. I will wait for you in the lobby." She strode to the door and turned to face Joy. "Sit down and do what they want."

The words hung heavy and seemed to pin Gloria and

Andrew to their seats. Only Nicole rustled about, her eyes riveted to her file as if its papers explained the meaning of life.

Surprisingly, Joy complied, and slumped against her chair arm. Perhaps the latest tirade exhausted her. *As well it should.*

After terse good-byes, Kai left the room. For now, those three could deal with Joy. Then she remembered the thing she must discuss with the Powells and darted a fearful glance backward. *It must be done later. But soon. Oh, what a mess!* Trying but failing to summon strength, Kai slogged down the hall.

The makeup's gone. Gloria darted looks at her daughter, who had slumped so dramatically, her rear end hung off the seat. *But the attitude's blown back in.*

Nicole plucked Joy's paper off the floor and plopped it into Joy's lap. "Well, all right, then." Gone was the breezy smile. Nicole sat down and turned to face Joy. Her wedge sandals clapped against the floor. "Here's the deal."

Joy picked her cuticles. If she heard, she gave no indication.

"You were accused of stealing a negligee and thong underwear from Sexy Lady at 11:00 on April 4." Nicole stared at her watch. "That's today."

"Sexy Lady?" Gloria's stomach knotted. Her baby had shoplifted sleazy clothes? "Why in heaven's name did you steal a negligee?" Her anger snapped Joy to attention.

Though Andrew clenched Gloria's knee, she wasn't stopping, no siree. "Are you sexually active, Joy? Answer me!"

Joy stiffened but otherwise didn't move.

"Gloria . . ." Andrew squeezed her hand.

"Don't 'Gloria' me! I need to know these things!" Gloria

166

slid off her chair and knelt by Joy, whose face had begun to crumple like a wadded tissue.

Gloria's anger splintered and showered onto everyone. Everything. How had Joy gotten so messed up? How had *they* gotten so messed up? "Well, are you? It's a simple question." She squeezed Joy's hand. Surprised at its fragility, its chill, she loosened her hold.

Joy shook her head but was losing composure.

"I need to hear the words!" Gloria's voice was escalating, but she didn't care. "Talk to me." If Joy'd had sex, she could be pregnant! The thought of her own pregnancy again washed over her. So new, so unbelievable; so polar opposite from this, though this was also new. Unbelievable.

"Mrs. Powell, I understand your concern." Nicole pulled out a pen. "I really do. But we have a different priority. We've gotta settle this station adjustment . . . or book her."

"What Nicole is saying, Joy—" Andrew pled in his altar-call voice.

Nicole tapped her pen on the table. "No offense, Mr. Powell, but it would be best if I handled this." A page rustled as Nicole fiddled with her clipboard. "If you don't cooperate, Joy, I have no choice but to let them book you. Understand?"

Gloria closed her eyes. *Father, let her see past her pain and accept this chance.* Joy needed help. It wouldn't come from her or Andrew. Not now. She wobbled to her seat.

An eternity passed . . . or was it a second? Joy nodded.

"Well, all right, then." Nicole leaned back in her chair. "What can you tell me about the allegation made against you by Detective Robbins?"

Silence reigned. Gloria wasn't sure what she hated most: that silence or the memory of her own nagging voice.

"We have surveillance tapes, Joy. Living color of your every move." Sarcasm now tinged Nicole's confident tone. Gone was the effusive praise and encouraging smile. "It's open and shut. There's two choices. We'll arrest you. Fingerprint you. Take a glamour photo."

"Can you explain 'station adjustment' again?" Joy asked dully.

"You confess. No muss, no fuss . . . no record. As long as you're compliant."

A phone rang.

Nicole made it to her desk in four strides. She picked up her phone. "Barton. Um-hum. Right." The phone rattled into its cradle. Nicole slid back into her chair. "Look. You've got two minutes to decide."

Joy raised her head. A hollow look had replaced her sullen stare.

Pain pricked Gloria. She could not bear this! She leaned across the table. "Joy, what can we do—"

Nicole slapped the desk with her file. "Please, Mrs. Powell. I know you're trying to help, but truth be told, you aren't."

You aren't. Gloria's cheeks burned from the slap of the words. From the truth.

"Joy's gotta accept blame for what she's done and move on. It's her choice."

Andrew rustled about. Gloria stared at the art on the wall, expecting it—and her nerves—to explode.

"I . . . I did it," came from behind a curtain of hair.

"Well, all right, then." Nicole's tone became giddy. "You have a real chance here. To turn things around."

Joy twisted to face Nicole. "What do I do next?"

Nicole pointed to the form. "It's all right here."

Joy pushed back her hair, ducked her head, and pulled the paper close.

For the first time, Gloria realized that Joy's glasses were gone. *Not sexy enough, I suppose.* She caught herself studying Joy's cute nose, exquisite eyes, smooth brow. When, oh, when had her girl needed makeup, dyed hair, and vulgar clothes to feel beautiful? Wanted? Had she ditched her glasses because she couldn't bear being called a dork? Why couldn't she see her smarts as an asset?

"Let's start at the top—FWPD Formal Station Adjustment."

Joy scooted her chair close to the table and set down the document.

Andrew picked up his copy and studied it. Gloria pretended to do the same but flitted looks between Joy and Nicole.

"You've already gotten off to a good start, here today, by helping with the cleanup. Confessing. Agreeing to the FSA."

Was that Joy, nodding? Gloria allowed herself to breathe. *Nicole knows her stuff. I should take lessons.*

"It's right there on the form, if y'all want to follow along." Nicole held up the paper, pointing to the first paragraph. "Obey all laws and local ordinances. Obey rules and directions of parents/guardians."

Gloria scanned the sheet. Boxes to check. Rules. *Joy won't even make her bed; she's suddenly going to comply with this?*

"Attend school and remain in good standing. No contact with—" Nicole penciled something on her form. "We'll talk about that later, Joy, in our one-on-one."

The creep for whom she's wearing the negligee? The one who talked her into scrawling graffiti on the school wall? Who taught her cuss words? *The one without a name, a face—at least for us?* Gloria held her breath so questions wouldn't spew all over the room. There'd be time for questions later. After she, Andrew—Kai? Yes. Kai.—talked.

Joy quirked an eyebrow. "One-on-one?"

"Every week. Right here. You and me." Nicole scribbled on her paper. "Or at— You go to Paschal, don't you?"

"We'll bring you over, Joy. It's no problem," shot out of Gloria.

Andrew squeezed her hand, a not-so-subtle warning.

Regret immediately pummeled Gloria. Too often she'd butted in when she shouldn't. *Perhaps Nicole can meet one-on-one with me.*

"Anyway, it's all there. Restitution. A letter of apology. Community service."

"Community service? Like . . . what?"

With her finger, Nicole traced the table edge. "Hmm. In your case, maybe the Harris welcome center."

Joy sat straight. "You mean the hospital?"

"Yeah. You'd probably start at the front desk. If things go well, you'll walk the wards. Deliver flowers."

"Hmm." Joy's leg swing belied the noncommittal utterance.

Gloria blinked. The medical thing. Again. *And you didn't have a clue.* After today, why should that surprise her?

Nicole unfastened her form from the clipboard, scribbled, and passed it to Andrew, who signed and handed it to Gloria.

Parent/Guardian_____

Date: _____

Parent. Not caretaker. Not prodder. Parent. Gloria grasped the pen as if it were a lifeline to Joy. *Can a FWPD form signal a new start? Not just for Joy, but for me?* Gloria signed the form, dated it, and prayed with all her might that it would be so.

Joy took the document. Scrutinized it. Gloria kneaded her knuckles. *She has no option; it's clear to us adults. But is it clear to Joy?*

Joy lifted her head. Set down the pen. "Is this what you want me to do?" Her voice had thinned, as if she were no longer sure of herself.

Andrew leaned forward. "Well, hon, sure. I mean, think what a record would do to your future."

"Joy, you have a future." Nicole's perkiness returned. "I talked to your advisor before mayhem descended. The only thing keeping you off the honor roll is your absences." A leg swing erupted. "Nip that in the bud, and there's no tellin' what you can do."

"Do you agree with that?" Joy's gaze penetrated Gloria, searching. . . .

For what? Understanding of me? From me? What I don't know about Joy would fill every file in this room.

"I . . ." Gloria pursed her lips, not sure what to say. But this wasn't a trick question. "Yes, Joy." She twisted her ring, oddly afraid to meet the gaze of her own daughter. "I think you should sign it," she told her lap.

"Then y'all will do your part?" Joy asked.

"Of course." Andrew smoothed into his preacher's groove. "We'll get you to counseling. Mom said—"

"No." Joy brushed her paper. "I know you'll do that. I'm talking about Kai. Treating her like my sister. Like she's part of our . . . family." Joy knotted her hands. "It's like when I saw her . . . everything changed. I . . . like, can't explain it, but I feel connected."

Nicole again checked her watch. "Well, yeah, sure. I mean,

I can understand that." She pocketed her pen and pushed back her chair. Her leg kicks became frenzied.

Andrew found Gloria's hand and squeezed it twice. Their code for *Let's do it.*

"Yes, Joy. We'll do our part. We'll make Kai feel welcome."

"You too, Mommy?" came out breathy. Desperate. "Do you promise?"

Gloria's head swam with contradictory images. Kai, helping Joy find herself. Joy finding Kai . . . and them losing her. She dug her nails into her palm. *God, is this of you or not? If it is, why am I vacillating like an idiot?*

Nicole kicked.

Andrew cleared his throat.

Joy began to mutter in her old rebellious way.

Gloria wiped sweaty palms on her skirt. *There's no choice. If I don't agree, I'll lose her.* "Yes, Joy." She stretched her lips into a smile. "You stick to your part of the bargain, I'll stick to mine."

"Do you really mean it?"

The pain in her daughter's voice stripped Gloria of doubts. Pretense. Her fingers writhed, so desperate was she to do this right. To tell the truth, yet help her daughter. "This is all new to me. I won't deny it's hard."

Joy's mouth gaped. Air whistled between her lips.

Is she that shocked to see me for who I am? Unsure. Imperfect. Real? Talk about time for a change. Gloria fisted her hands and took a breath. "I've loved you since the first time I set eyes on you, Joy. I will always love you. I want what's best for you, as does your daddy." Emboldened by the calm in her spirit, Gloria smiled at her daughter. "I . . . I think Kai can help us. I really do."

Joy's nostrils flared, her shoulders shook, in the way that always pulled at Gloria's heart.

"I was wrong to doubt Kai's motives," Gloria added. "Forgive me."

Joy's eyes filled with tears. Then she picked up the pen, scribbled with abandon, handed the paper to Nicole, and wiped her eyes.

"Well, all right." Nicole stuck the form into a file folder. Hand-shaking preceded their good-byes, as if a sacrificial pledge had been signed. And it had. The enormity of their commitment, of Joy's commitment, lodged in Gloria's chest. *We'll all be giving one hundred and ten percent. Without you, God, it won't happen.*

They left Nicole's office. When they neared the lobby door, Joy held back. "Mommy?" She used her little-girl voice. "Can I talk to you?"

As if afraid, Andrew scuttled away.

Her eyes downcast, Joy minced forward. "I . . . I haven't done anything."

Gloria's breath spurted. *Praise God.* She clapped her hand over her heart. *Then why did you steal come-on clothes? Who is the creep?* Questions tightened her chest.

"Like nada," Joy mumbled. "Zip."

The sight of Joy's bent head and contrite tone warded off questions. *Joy just gave up her independence to share what she hasn't given up.*

"Oh, Joy." Gloria cupped her daughter's face in her hands and looked into those lovely eyes. "Thanks for telling me." A smoky smell prompted a question, but she squashed it, then stomped her foot to celebrate her small victory. They'd discuss tobacco . . . later.

Though neither of them spoke, their shoulders grazed as they entered the lobby. Those million miles between them had just been reduced—dramatically.

Andrew rushed forward and draped an arm around Joy, the other around Gloria. "Everything okay?"

Gloria nodded and gave Andrew a tell-you-later hand squeeze.

"Yeah. Like, yeah!" As if freed from her burden, Joy broke from them and skipped toward Kai, who embraced her as if they were lifelong friends, not day-old sisters. Joy waved her hands, Kai nodded, easily interpreting, accepting each move.

Gloria's lips tightened. *They are naturals. Unlike Joy and me.*

"I've been thinking about how to do this." Andrew's breath tickled Gloria's ear and soothed her conflicted feelings. What would she do without Andrew to think like a Christian when she wasn't? Act like a Christian when she didn't?

"Kai needs to tell Joy about PKD."

Gloria battled prickles of fear. "Don't you think it'll overwhelm her if she hears about that and the new baby?"

"Joy needs the truth. Kai's obviously got her ear right now, so she's the one to tell her." Andrew scuffed the floor with his loafer. "If Joy has this PKD, a station adjustment's only the tip of the iceberg. She'll need a good doctor. A good sister. Plenty of support. Which God seems to have packaged in Kai."

Transplant. Dialysis. Snatches from that dreadful report Kai had shown them—was it only this morning?—ran through her mind. Gloria seized her husband's arm. "Andrew, I'm scared."

Andrew brushed hair wisps from her face. "We've got to give this to God."

How many times had she heard that? Ignored that? She nodded mutely. It was time to listen to her husband. Her preacher. Her lover. It was time to listen to her God.

As Gloria and Andrew made their way to the sisters, Joy threw back her head and erupted in laughter.

A thrill cascaded through Gloria. Twenty-four karat, every syllable of bubbling glee. *I haven't heard that laugh in . . . too long.*

A sunbeam poured in the lobby window and spotlighted the sisters. Gloria shut her eyes, begging holy warmth, holy peace, to melt her fear. She'd never believed in coincidences. Kai had been led here by God, who had perfect timing.

"Hey." Andrew lightly cuffed her shoulder. "Back to the plan, huh? Let's take Kai to her hotel. She probably wants to clean up." He glanced at the chattering sisters. "We'll go home, do the same, and then meet her downtown. Do steak. Mexican, if she wants it."

"Joy's stomach . . ."

Andrew's face fell. "Oh, yeah. Then steak it'll be. We'll celebrate, Texas-style!"

Gloria studied his face. "Are you sure we should tell . . . both of them?"

Andrew's eyes narrowed. "No, I'm not sure, but we just agreed—just promised—to include Kai." He let go of Gloria. "I'll see if that plan works for Kai."

Gloria felt the room whirl, as if the tornado had encored. How many years of her life had been spent in waiting? Worrying? For Daddy to come back home. For a godly man. For Joy. For Joy to fit in. She hadn't realized until now, but she'd never accepted the present time as a gift. She had never really lived.

As Andrew talked, Kai nodded. Joy nodded.

Gloria joined the nodding. With God's help, she'd fling off the smothering shroud of waiting, worrying, and live for today. Face the sorrows, the joys, the good, the bad—not only because it was right, but because she was sick to death of living the other way.

14

Four hours ago, a killer spun through here. Bone-tired, Kai leaned against the detention center's brick wall and watched cars zip down the freeway. *Now it's business as usual.* "Miracle." Kai savored the taste of the strange word. Gloria had allied with her, another miracle. Oh, that more miracles were in store for Joy.

Having declined a ride in the rolling trash bin, Kai waited for a taxi. She pulled out her cell phone to again try David. Strange, him not calling back on his day off. . . .

She started to push 2 on the Speed Dial that David had set up for her, wishing that his arm rested about her shoulder in his intimate yet proper way. As the sun beamed warmth on her face, Kai closed her eyes and let memories carry her to Boston. . . .

On a crisp autumn day, they'd strolled the Public Garden, a favorite—and rare—date stolen from impossible practice hours and nights on call. On a cobbled path, they'd met a little girl. Tears sparkled her wide brown eyes. A chubby fist clutched peanuts.

"What's the matter?" Kai asked.

"The ducks fly away when I try to feed dem." She stamped a sandaled foot. "Dey won't even talk to me!"

After a nod from a woman who stood protectively near, Kai knelt by the girl. "Perhaps they are busy. For that, they should be scolded. How could they not take time for a nice child like you?"

Earnest eyes gripped Kai. "Could I put them in time out?"

A giggle escaped. Oh, this one, full of spirit! So like Third Daughter. Kai clucked her tongue. "Well, now, that is an idea. But I have a better one."

The girl glanced at the woman, who nodded. A peanut fell to the ground. "Den what?"

"Give your time to ducks that won't leave." Kai's heart swelled to remember her first view of the waddling bronze ducks of Boston, so carefree, yet so sure, so safe. It was at that moment that she had fallen in love with America, where imagination so often chased, and caught up with, real life.

"Where are those ducks that won't leave?" the little girl demanded.

"I'll show you."

The woman shadowed the girl. Protecting? Waiting? Hoping? Kai did not know.

Time sighed sweetly, like the leaves that fell about them. Kai and David and the little girl fed peanuts to Mrs. Mallard and her eight ducklings. Content as house pets, the ducklings seemed to nose the girl's feet as she giggled with glee. The girl's mother stepped close. "I don't know your name, but thank you." She gathered a shawl about bony shoulders. "Her father just died. We've had a rough time getting her to sleep, getting her to do anything. She thinks everything will fly away and leave her." The woman shivered. "Just like those birds."

Kai wrote the name of a pediatric counselor on the back of her business card and reassured the woman that such behavior was normal.

When the two left, David pulled Kai near Mrs. Mallard. "Close your eyes."

Kai complied and tried to smile. *These Americans see unexpected surprises as good things. I will do my best to adjust to their way of thinking.*

"Hold out your hand."

Something smooth—plastic?—brushed against her palm. She opened her eyes. A cell phone lay in her hand. What Cheryl had insisted she get. What she had avoided. Was it not enough to have an answering service, a receptionist, a roommate efficient at message-taking? "It's . . ."

"I know, I know." David tweaked her cheeks. "You're trying to think of something nice to say." He grabbed the phone and punched 2 on her new gift.

Dreamy music—a nocturne?—muted the sound of their breathing. Kai's skin tingled. She touched David's arm. "What . . . where . . . ?"

Laughing, David pulled that music—and another cell phone—from his pocket. He held two phones. Hers. His. Kai's hands flew to her face. He had somehow programmed this thing, with the pressing of one button, to call her!

"Hello." He handed her one of the phones.

She tried to press a digital readout.

He laughed, then flipped open a cover. She held the phone to her ear, heard David's gentle breathing, and locked eyes with him.

"Hey, Kai. It's David."

She could not speak. Her voice . . . her heart . . . was held captive by every tender syllable that silly gadget projected.

Perhaps she did need a cell phone, after all. Just like she needed David. She glanced into eyes that echoed the love in his voice. Dared she hope that the doctor devoting his life to the care of cardiac patients would give his heart to her?

"I am just one ring away." David still had not blinked. Neither did Kai, so intent was she to preserve the moment. "If I am in surgery, on call, leave a message." His voice did not waver, nor did that gaze. "As soon as humanly possible, I will get back to you."

The air horn of an 18-wheeler on the Texas freeway obliterated her Boston memories. Blinking, Kai flagged down the cab pulling into the center's circular drive.

Dear David, you have kept the promise witnessed by Boston's elms and maples . . . until now. I have left you three messages over the span of three hours. Why, at a time when I crave the tone that lowers my blood pressure, when I need advice from one who has pulled lives from the other side, do you not answer?

After she hopped into the cab and gave the driver her address, she again jabbed 2 on the Speed Dial. "Please leave a message," informed a nasally voiced woman.

The phone snapped shut, as did her hopes for time with David.

Kai watched truckers streak by as the skyline of Fort Worth neared. She had left David not one but three messages. There was nothing more to say that could be communicated over phone lines.

⌒◯⌒

Another cabbie—this one wearing a cowboy hat.

"Could you take me to the Longhorn Palace?"

The man tipped his hat. His big-as-Texas smile showed

179

missing teeth. "Hang on, ma'am!" he bellowed. "I'll spur this baby on down the line. Getcha there in no time!"

While Kai gripped the armrest, the man regaled her with talk of looking for eight, apparently a score in the rodeo game, and "bucking Big Red." Kai comprehended enough to know that David would relish his stories. If only he were here. . . .

The cab pulled into a street crowded with what the cabbie called honky-tonks and slop-slingers. More Texas talk David would enjoy.

Glad to shut the door on unrequited hopes and crazy driving, Kai paid the cabbie and wobbled from the taxi. Christmas lights marked the perimeter of a building that resembled saloons on the sets of David's Westerns. A life-sized Plexiglas longhorn pawed and snorted from its corral by the entrance. Kai half-expected John Wayne himself, wearing a six-gun and cowboy hat, to shove through swinging doors. Kai smiled. Rodeo Cabbie, with his wild drive, had set the tone for dinner!

"Howdy, ma'am. Welcome to Cowtown and the Longhorn Palace."

Boots clomped across a planked floor as a greeter met Kai and led her inside. Laughter rose from a bar that spanned the long wall of the restaurant. A buffalo, antelope, and yet another longhorn gave her glassy-eyed stares. Kai's abdomen tightened. How much face would she lose with the Powells if she ordered vegetarian?

They wove through a maze of tables covered with checkered cloths and entered another room. Another. Remembering why she had come, Kai tightened her hold on her handbag. Was a room reverberating with *yippees* and *yee-haws* a place to discuss deadly disease?

"Kai! Over here!" Joy jumped up and then plopped back into her chair, as if she'd embarrassed herself with her enthusiasm. Still, a coquettish wave of her hand reflected the easy way they had talked at the jail, the way they had anticipated each other's gait, falling in step like . . . Kai's throat tightened. *The ways of First Daughter and me.* Seeing Joy made Kai hungry for the presence of Ling, Mei, and Father, who wrote seldom and called never, as they had no phone. *Oh, that we could reunite! Sooner and not later. . . .*

"Bye-bye! Enjoy y'all's steaks!" Curls cascaded when the hostess whirled and flounced out of sight.

Kai recalled the wall-mounted animals. *I will do my best. But do not count on it, Miss Texas.*

Joy waved Kai into the chair next to hers. Across from Kai sat Andrew; across from Joy, Gloria. A cowgirl in a miniskirt and pointed-toe boots sashayed to their table and distributed menus and Mason jars filled with water.

"We'll need a bit of time." Andrew, smooth as ever, chatted with the waitress. "How 'bout ah give you a holler when we're ready?"

"Yee-haw!" Andrew and the waitress high-fived. Joy rolled her eyes. Kai suppressed the same response and then decided to mimic Joy. America's let-it-all-hang-out philosophy just might foster community and humor. *Something this family needs.*

"Did you get a chance to kick back in your room?" Andrew stretched casually and sipped his water as if this were a social function rather than a discussion of Joy's future. *Not so different from the teahouse approach in China. A game I can play.*

"No. I called the office. They've survived just fine without me."

Andrew chuckled, then asked, "Is it a big practice?"

One of the biggest, the best, in the country, if not the

world. "Perhaps small by Texas standards." Kai also sipped water. "We are growing, slowly but surely."

"How cool is it to hold people's lives in your hands, like, every day?" Kai noticed that Joy had Nicole's habit of bouncing her leg.

Kai massaged fingers chilled by the frigid glass. "It is both a sorrow and a joy."

Gloria had begun to dig into her palms, surely fearing another sit-through of the Healing Right Hand's history. *Do not worry, mother of Joy. If—no, when—Joy hears about my gift, it will be in a more dignified place than the Longhorn Palace.*

Kai brushed at her sleeve. "That is a story for another time."

Andrew covered Gloria's hand with his. Kai could not help but notice how their fingers intertwined perfectly, how, with their freckles and pale skin, it was hard to distinguish between the two. So different in this way from her and David. As his parents loved to point out.

"A story you must hear, Joy," Andrew said.

"Yes." Gloria gave a polite smile. "Kai told us many, um, interesting things."

Joy's swinging foot clipped Kai in the calf. "Sorry. I'd love to hear them. Like, what's wrong with now?"

Andrew picked up his menu and ran his finger along its laminated edge. "There's another thing we want to talk about."

Joy crossed her arms, as if to set up a barricade. Teenaged attitude, striking again?

Andrew again took Gloria's hand. "When we got home, we told Joy about the doctor's visit."

Kai felt her face fall. They already contacted Joy's physician about PKD?

"Like, yeah, Kai, it's the best—" She clapped a hand over her mouth. "Oh, I'm sorry, Daddy."

Andrew swiped his forehead. "No, no, Joy. It's . . . Hey, you tell her."

Joy's face glowed. "Mom had a pregnancy test! She's gonna have a baby! I'm gonna have a brother or a sister!"

Kai's skin tingled. A new life. What glory—for Gloria! Then puzzle pieces—Gloria's paleness, haywire emotions, and nausea—interlocked. "How wonderful!" Kai thrust her arm across scattered menus for congratulatory handshakes. "When are you due?"

"November 20." Gloria had the glow of a new mother. "The sonogram helped pinpoint the date."

Andrew chuckled. "We survived a tornado and a sonogram in one day."

Kai murmured excitedly and put away questions of a medical nature. She would not play physician/patient with Gloria, who did not want it and did not need it.

Joy prompted Gloria to share a rambling stairwell story. Kai half listened, entranced by the color in Gloria's cheeks, the lovely tone of her voice. This new baby might revitalize Gloria and Joy—another miracle!

The waitress approached, order pad in hand. "I heard y'all hollering. Thought I'd better check in."

"We're havin' a baby!" Andrew's modulated voice had disappeared, as had his worry lines. This man loved his family. Loved Joy. Kai truly rejoiced for him.

"Hey, cool!" Light danced in the young woman's eyes as she pulled a pen from a shirt pocket. "This calls for a celebration. So what'll it be?"

Gloria shook her head. "We've been so busy gabbing, we haven't even looked."

"Should I come back?"

"Nope. We're shooting the moon on this one—or the cow, I should say."

Kai swallowed. *Despite your desire, forget vegetarian.*

"It's our treat, Kai."

"Oh, no." Though she demurred, Kai was secretly pleased at Andrew's gesture.

Andrew shook his head. "We insist, you hear?"

"Yeah, Kai," Joy chimed in.

After an appropriate time of protestation, Kai murmured, "Many thanks."

Andrew slapped shut his menu. "Whaddya say to T-bones? Man-size!"

Gloria groaned. Not Joy, who said, "Daddy! That's a great idea. Like the waitress said, let's celebrate. Have y'all discussed baby names?"

"Um, Joy, it's a little early for that."

Kai gave a smile of relief. *Gloria, you have nailed that one.*

Despite the chatter, a pit lodged in Kai's stomach at the thought of digesting a hunk of T-bone, whatever that was, but she'd rather swallow it whole than dim the gaiety. A gaiety that would be dimmed, soon enough, when she unfolded the papers in her bag and set them on this table.

***

Somehow she ate the whole thing. Well, not exactly. Unlike Andrew, she'd stopped short of gnawing the bone. Neither manners nor a finicky appetite stopped her. She, like every robust Chinese, sucked juice from rooster skulls, gobbled down chicken intestines, the reproductive organs of fish . . . especially at joyous feasts. But the Texas-sized portions, her anxiety, or thoughts of those mounted trophies kept her from savoring the food. Besides, there was something—someone—else to savor. Kai again framed Joy in her field of vision. This moment would be tucked away. Retrieved during hard times. *Which may start now, with PKD talk. . . .*

As if on cue, busboys removed half-eaten slabs of Texas toast, scraped-to-the-skin potatoes, and the funny T-shaped bones. Andrew swept crumbs into a napkin and folded it into a tight square. If only Joy's problems could be so easily removed.

"Joy, we have something else to discuss," he began.

Hair brushed Joy's shoulders as she bounced about. "Like . . . another surprise?"

Gloria fisted her jar and wiped off water beads with her thumb.

"Not . . . not exactly." Andrew didn't say more, only exchanged a wide-eyed expression with Gloria.

Kai pulled her folder from her bag. Someone must start this. Why not the doctor? She cleared her throat. "Joy, you asked earlier why it took so long for me to find you."

"Um-hum." A narrow-eyed wariness usurped Joy's gay mood, which Kai regretted. Still, this must be done.

"In fact, you asked twice. You also asked why we Changs left you at an orphanage."

A carefully guarded look entered Joy's eyes.

"I did my . . . best to answer the orphanage question."

No one moved. To keep from frightening Joy, Kai had infused her voice with calm. Still, this one must know the suffering of the Chang family. She extracted a paper from her file and laid it on the table.

"If you are willing, I would like to answer the question of timing now."

Gloria was absorbed with her hands. Andrew crumb-

gathered. Kai vowed to fix her attention on Joy. Ignore the rest of the world . . . including her phone, which was emitting the majestic ring tone that signaled a call from David. Kai closed her eyes and envisioned David's gentle voice. When her job here was done, she would relax in her spacious hotel room and pour out to the heart doctor all that had taken place this day.

The nocturne ended. So did the irritating beeps, which acted as an alarm clock for Kai. She straightened and fixed her gaze on Joy.

Joy scraped at a nail. "Yeah, um, sure" stuttered from her mouth.

Kai took a breath. "Our mother suffered great indignities during the Cultural Revolution. Father was not spared, either, but that is another story. Of all her ailments, the one afflicting Mother's kidneys caused her the most pain. After you were born, Joy, she took to her bed . . . and rarely left it."

Joy, her face crumpling, shook her head, as if she could not hear more. Who could blame her? "Did she . . . suffer?" she finally asked.

Kai moistened her lips. There would be no discussion of ankles swollen to the size of small trees, vomiting, lethargy, bloody urine, the sunken-eye, fixed expression, the itching, the twitching. If Kai had her way, she would never utter such things to this one. "I would like to tell you otherwise, but it would be a lie. Though I had been called to medicine at an early age, seeing Mother's suffering confirmed the vow I'd made at age eleven to be a doctor."

Joy knotted her hands. "Wow! Like, you were just a baby!"

Younger than you, but wiser in the ways of the world. Or so I thought.

"You will have to tell her about that too," interjected

Andrew with such enthusiasm that Kai turned to him and smiled. At least one Powell believed in her story.

To her surprise, Gloria nodded forcefully.

Make that two Powells.

"Ever since, I have stalked Mother's killer." Kai leaned across the table and handed Andrew and Gloria sheets identical to those she had given them earlier. She handed her last copy to Joy. "A year ago, I finally received Mother's file from Chinese authorities. A name was given to Mother's killer. PKD. Polycystic kidney disease."

Joy hunkered into her seat and seemed to study the medical-speak of the papers. Kai absorbed every lift of Joy's eyebrow, every turn of Joy's head. Could it be that medicine also called Fourth Sister? Despite the gravity of the situation, Kai allowed herself to dream of working with Joy, side by side, somehow, somewhere . . .

"This sounds awful."

I have only given a sanitized version, dear Joy. You should meet the patients hooked to the blessed, cursed dialysis lines. You should see the lists, pages of which could carpet hospital halls, of those begging for a kidney. You should have seen what was left after PKD ravaged Mother's body. Kai nodded yet pressed her lips together lest even one gory detail escape.

Joy set down the papers. Her lovely eyebrows displayed their full arch.

"I am sure you are thinking, What does this mean to me?"

Joy nodded. Gloria punished her fist. Andrew had removed every molecule of Texas toast from their tablecloth.

Here is the hardest part, dear sister. Oh, that I get it right. "I am sure you noted the third word on this document. Such medical terms often are unclear to laypersons."

Joy edged the word *hereditary* with a chipped nail. Her lovely forehead creased.

Angst assailed with such force, Kai leaned against the table. If only that wretched word could be scratched from the document and forever forgotten.

"Hereditary components play a significant role in PKD. So Mother's children are at higher risk of having polycystic kidney disease."

There. She had said it.

She knew by the creases in Joy's cheeks, her droopy eyes, that Joy understood.

"What are the symptoms?" Joy spat out.

Kai's heart swelled. *Oh, she is a smart one. An emotional one.*

"Well, now, Joy . . ." Gloria, who had been strangely silent, made her debut in the discussion. "We don't want to alarm you."

"*Moth*-er! If I have a disease, I want to know!" Joy crossed her arms, glared at Gloria. "How long have y'all known about *this*?"

"Now, Joy . . ."

Kai placed her hand on Joy's arm. It worked with Third Daughter, or at least it did years ago. Perhaps it would calm this one. "Your mother learned about PKD just before we met. Her health and . . . your predicament . . . did not allow her to share."

Gloria fixed her with that half-curious, half-grateful look. Surely she knew by now that they were allies in this battle.

Joy gave a sullen nod.

"We had begun to discuss testing when . . . we were interrupted by Officer Robbins. If your parents agree, I'd like to have you tested before we waste time on what might be."

Kai allowed herself a sigh. She had said enough. The Powells must make the next move.

Andrew laid his hand on Gloria's arm. Right below the elbow, as always. How comforting, to be able to predict your spouse's every move!

Kai imagined David, standing beside her, his breath warming her neck, his arms allaying the sights she daily viewed in the hospital. David and Kai. It sounded so right to her. How did it sound to David? To David's parents, who traced their ancestry to the Mayflower and snubbed all without red, white, and blue blood lines?

"I'm glad you brought up testing, Kai, 'cause Gloria and I discussed it." Andrew turned his head. "We'd like for Joy's Texas doctor to run prelims. Give Joy a physical. Right?"

Gloria nodded.

"The family medical history will be shared, of course. If there's any reason at all for concern, Carl will call. We'll keep you posted every step of the way. Right?"

Again Gloria nodded.

"First thing in the morning, we'll give Carl a ring."

"Hey, wait a minute. So . . . Kai?" Joy crinkled her eyes. "Like, this is your medical specialty, right?"

Smart *and* cagey, this one. "Renal medicine, yes."

"Is that a coincidence . . . or what?" Joy pushed back from the table. "Why don't we, like, just go to Boston?"

Gloria opened her mouth and then clamped it shut. Andrew and Kai exchanged glances. *Surely he will take the lead here. I am only her sister, not her legal guardian, as the police so aptly pointed out.*

"Joy, no use rushing things that can be avoided. I mean, Boston's a long way—"

"She's my sister. Don't y'all understand anything?"

More than you understand, dear one. Kai slipped on the hats worn by Joy's parents, something she'd done with dozens of patients. Another trick taught by old Dr. Ward.

"Your parents know best, Joy. It's time you accepted that as a fact."

"But—" Joy tossed her head and slung purple strands over violent eyes. A curse spewed into that stringy mop.

"Joy!" flew from Gloria.

Kai gripped her chair, gritted her teeth, and met the half-veiled gaze of Tornado Joy head on. "A Chang does not say such things." She swept her hand toward Joy's parents. "Neither, I am sure, does a Powell."

An eternity passed. Or was it ten seconds?

The teenager was the first to look away. And hang her head.

Kai released her achy fingers from weathered wood. "I concur with your parents' decision. There is also the matter of the police to consider. You are under a station adjustment, no? They may not allow you to come to Boston." *Though I ache for it*.

Andrew and Gloria again joined hands and exchanged glances before they smiled big. Their body language signaled another surprise.

"Gloria and I discussed something else. After the tornado."

Joy tensed, as if expecting yet another blow. Who could blame her?

"If you complete the requirements of the station adjustment and Nicole allows it, we will all visit Kai. In Boston."

Waves of elation swept through Kai. The Powells' trust had risen to the point that they would permit such a thing? Just hours ago, she never would have imagined a change of heart.

Joy bounced in her seat. Waved her hands. The spitting image of Third Daughter. Oh, it was a marvel!

"That is, if Kai can put up with us."

Kai bit back a desire to explode into a musical master-piece similar to the one recorded on her phone. "I would like nothing more."

"There is the police matter," intoned Gloria. "Your grades. Attendance."

"Yeah, yeah, I know. You'll see a change, really." Joy gripped Kai's hand as she had done during the storm. "Now that I . . ." She glanced toward her parents. "I mean, with two families behind me."

Andrew nodded. "I am glad you see it like that, Joy."

"Yes," Kai echoed.

"So . . . I'll be going to Boston?" Joy's eyes sparkled mis-chief and hope.

Dimming images of needles pricking Joy and CT scanners whirring over Joy's body, Kai managed a smile. "Massachu-setts, here you come."

"Can we go to the coast? Like, stick our toes in the Atlantic? And the Freedom Walk? Can we do that? We studied it in school."

Kai glanced sideways at Joy, suddenly so alive, so eager. Boston offered much for tourists. How she craved to shuttle them about the city that had embraced her! She stifled a sigh. How many patients bypassed sights because they must languish in a sterile dialysis cubicle?

"We'll just have to see, Joy," said Gloria.

I could not agree more. We will just have to see. Kai nod-ded. "Your mother is right, Joy. And your father—a thousand thanks for an . . . unforgettable meal."

Andrew puffed out his chest. "There's nothing like this in Boston, huh?"

I certainly hope not. "No doubt about it," Kai managed.

Andrew signed the bill with a flourish.

Kai adopted Andrew's habit of searching for minuscule crumbs. *The Longhorn Palace was not such a bad place for the PKD discussion. But I will not discuss the other thing here.* The waiter disappeared with the credit card. Table chatter waned.

"We must address one other matter." Kai fixed her gaze on a bucking bronco poster, avoiding Joy. "Would you mind if we went to my hotel?"

Question marks entered Powell eyes. "Sure," Andrew finally said. "Whatever you want, Kai."

15

She's with her sister . . . and on cloud nine. Gloria pretended to reapply lipstick but instead used the vanity mirror to study Joy and Kai, huddled together in the backseat studying the framed family pictures Kai had given Joy. The two looked like best friends. *Something I never had.* Or sisters. *Ditto.*

"That's Ling? She's beautiful!" Joy squealed.

"She has the round face of Southern Chinese. Much admired in our village."

Photos and family members crowded in with Kai and Joy, filling the car with old stories, laughter; filling Gloria with the sense of being an outsider in a reunion. *Joy has the family she's yearned for, at some level, all her life.*

Tears blurred Gloria's vision. *Joy's peace. I've been on my knees, begging for this.* Gloria hand-combed her hair. She was happy for Joy. So why did the sisters' laughs set off an internal barometer?

Because she's connecting with the sister she's known for one day better than she's connected with me for years.

A scene flashed in Joy's mind: Ten-year-old Joy, begging to dye blond the hair of the Asian doll she'd received as a birthday present. "So everyone will like her." Joy had stroked the doll's plump plastic cheek, such a yearning in her eyes that Gloria had turned her head. An hour later, pink balloons, tied to dining room chairs, nodded listlessly. Not Gloria, who fumed as she fussed and pretended to busy herself with Joy's hair ribbons. In homes where folks shelved Emily Post's *Etiquette* next to Junior League handbooks, not one of the mothers of the invited girls had bothered to RSVP.

Gloria, fearing something like this, had urged Joy to invite church friends. Even then—years before the fire—an inexplicable, indefinable divide existed between Joy and her church peers. Joy had refused to include several deacons' daughters who would've attended—if for no other reason than their parents told them it was the Christian thing to do. *I should've made Joy invite them.* Gloria berated herself for the thousandth time. *I should have told* Joy *that was the Christian thing to do. Back then, she'd have listened.*

Old Mrs. Browning, their next-door neighbor, and her pug, Charlie, had rushed over with a nosegay of roses. A frozen smile remained on Joy during the singing of "Happy Birthday" and the blowing out of candles.

Though they'd piped, "It doesn't matter," and "Surely a misunderstanding," though Gloria had pampered a stiff and sullen Joy, not a tear was shed.

Until the next day.

Gloria found the doll they'd scrimped and saved to buy stuffed under Joy's bed. Scissored hair exposed a pink scalp.

Sobbing, Gloria had lain on the floor, pounding Joy's braided rug, stroking that doll's bristly hair. Though her daughter had not cried, Gloria wailed for the shunning by Joy's peers, the loneliness that would lead Joy to destroy an innocent doll. She understood how her daughter felt. She'd experienced similar feelings when her daddy had walked out the door.

Joy never said a word about the incident. Neither did they. Andrew thought it might send Joy "over the edge." Gloria thought it strange advice from a counsel-happy pastor, but she had no rebuttal. She, too, neared the edge, though she hid it behind church functions, always smiling, smiling, *her* hair neatly combed and pulled into a barrette.

Unlike that doll's.

The church burned three years later, destroying Joy's last semblance of a sanctuary outside the four walls of their home. From that moment on, Joy had inched closer to a precipice. *And I'm just learning now how to lure her back to solid ground.*

A horn blared. Gloria startled. Andrew found her hand, squeezed it, and chatted about, of all things, the weather. All Gloria could think about was that doll and her Joy—suddenly chatty in the backseat—and the layers of dysfunction she needed to peel away to be a real mother. Most of all, she wondered why Kai, in her clipped manner, had requested one more meeting, this one at her hotel, before she returned to Boston.

Suede and leather chairs cozied up to a faux fireplace in the Wranglers Room. A cowboy painting, framed in weathered fence rails and barbed wire, hung above the mantel. Pocket doors had been slid shut. The staff had set a pitcher of ice water and glasses on a turquoise-inlaid table.

Kai balanced on her chair edge. With flawless skin and glossy hair, she presented the picture of a composed professional woman. *Everything I'm not.* Gloria tucked her hands under her legs to keep from gnawing her fingernails.

Kai bowed her head. "I want to thank you, Andrew and Gloria, for your kindnesses during a most tumultuous time."

Andrew leaned forward. "We owe you the thanks."

Joy nodded with vigor.

"There is one last thing I would like to discuss. Though it is not easy to say, I would be remiss in my duties as a physician, a sister, and I hope a friend . . ."

Gloria tried to swallow the anxiety lumping in her throat.

"During our time together, Joy mentioned a cutting episode."

The lump exploded and set Gloria afire. Flames leapt white-hot about the room. Gloria blinked. Saw that bald-headed doll with slashes on plastic wrists. She jumped from her seat, flew to Joy's side, and collapsed in a pile by Joy's chair. "Oh, Joy!" Tears rained. "You're so smart, so beautiful!" Flailing fingers found Joy's cold, stiff hands. "How could you do that to yourself?"

Bead and metal bracelets covered—what? Evidence, hidden under cheap baubles, that Joy had attempted to harm herself? *Once again you, her mother, don't know.*

She let go of Joy, gripped her throbbing head with both hands, and dug into her scalp instead of crying out. Bangles. Sweatbands. Gloria had thought her daughter was accessorizing. Stylizing.

Did she know *anything* about Joy?

A sob erupted from Joy. "I'm so, so sorry, Mommy. Daddy." Joy flung her arms about Gloria's neck. The smoke–bubble gum smell of her daughter cooled the fire. The room began to lose its white-hot glaze. "It was so wrong. So stupid!"

Thin arms tightened their hold . . . and smothered the last

flames. Gloria quivered at her daughter's touch. How long had it been since Joy hugged her with abandon? Years?

"Mommy," Joy kept saying as she stroked Gloria's hair. "I'm sorry."

Gloria could not talk, could not do anything but spill tears onto Joy's blouse and shake her head. She should be supporting Joy. Yet sprawling on the floor, having Joy hold *her* tight, filled a desperate ache.

Three years, she realized, answering her own question about Joy's hugs. When Joy started high school, she disdained even cheek pecks. "I've . . . I've missed you," Gloria managed. "I mean, it's me who's sorry." Gloria buried her head in Joy's breast. "I've done it all wrong."

Warm hands—Andrew's hands—massaged her neck.

Gloria closed her eyes, freeze-framing this moment, where Joy was safe . . .

"Um, Joy, Gloria."

Gloria squared her shoulders. *Not . . . not yet, Andrew. Just a little longer . . .*

Andrew gently pried Gloria from Joy, who wiped her face with her hands and glanced about awkwardly.

Kai rose from her chair. "Excuse me. This is no time for an outsider."

Andrew returned to his chair. "You are not an outsider. Please sit down."

"Yes. Please, Kai." Wiping her eyes, Gloria sat as well. No amount of thanks could repay the woman—the sister—who'd extracted Joy's darkest secrets . . . and shared them with a family that must seem problematic at best. This sister, who'd even brought presents—presents they hadn't bothered to open—had gotten only grief in return. Gloria rummaged for a tissue and blew her nose. That would change.

Andrew rested his hands on his knees. "I can't tell you what it means that you shared this with us." His voice was hoarse, his eyes bleary.

Kai lowered her gaze, as if she were embarrassed. Gloria knew the feeling well.

"Before dinner, as I told you, I checked in with my office . . . and got the name of a colleague, whom I called. I could not return to Boston without doing so." Kai spoke haltingly, as if in unfamiliar territory. "Adolescent behavior is not my field of expertise."

"You got ahold of someone this late?" Andrew asked.

"MRA has certain . . . connections in our city."

"What . . . what did they say?" Gloria blurted, darting looks at Joy's slender wrists.

Kai straightened. "Would you mind if I asked Joy a few questions?"

"Oh, please!" flew out of Gloria. "Ask her . . . anything."

"How many times have you cut yourself?" Kai asked in a clipped voice.

Joy rubbed her wrist—*that* wrist?—and clenched her fists. "Just . . . the once." Tears streamed down her face. "I . . . I didn't like it."

Kai nodded encouragingly. "That is a good thing."

"A very good thing," intoned Andrew.

Gloria rubbed her finger against her thumb. *Lord, how did we get to the place where it is a good thing our daughter only once slashed her wrist?*

"Did you use your razor?" continued Kai.

A nod.

"Did you pry out the blade or . . . ?"

Joy shook her head. "No! It wasn't like that!" She buried her face in her hands. "I . . . hated the sound! I hated the way blood snaked across my skin! Honest to God!" She clapped her hand over her mouth. "I'm sorry. I mean, like, it was gross!"

Gloria jumped from her chair and again knelt by Joy. She rubbed shuddering shoulders, cooed, as if she understood. She had to understand, or at least try. *Dear God . . .*

"It . . . was all wrong. I . . . I swore I'd never do it again."

"So you just used the razor," Kai monotoned. "Like shaving, only . . ."

"Uh-huh." Joy raised her head. Red-rimmed eyes sought out Gloria, then Andrew. "I swear, I'll never do it again. No matter what happens, I won't do that again!"

Gloria clasped her daughter's sweaty hands and smoothed hair from Joy's tear-ravaged face. "I believe you," she whispered. "And I believe *in* you, Joy."

"I appreciate your honesty," Kai finally said, when Joy had quit whimpering. Those calm eyes honed in on Gloria, then Andrew. "Though Joy needs to be seen by a psychiatrist—her doctor can refer you—it's my belief that she does not need emergency treatment."

"You mean, like, the ER?" burst from Joy.

"I mean a mental health ward." Kai's words slammed into Gloria. "It is one thing to want to die . . . I speak from experience."

Gloria spun about.

Kai had risen. Her handbag hung on her shoulder. Except for dark circles under her eyes, she could have been a graduate, fresh from college, ready for an interview. *Yet she's witnessed horrors I've only read about in history books.*

"It is quite another thing to attempt to take a life. Including your own." Kai stepped close to Gloria, who rose from the floor, and Joy, who rose from her chair. "Forgive me if

I upset you, Joy. I am saying these things as your sister, not as a physician. For that I might be criticized by some in my profession."

"I . . . I understand," Joy stammered. "Say what . . . you need to say."

Gloria opened her mouth to agree but could not find her voice.

"If you ever consider such . . . a thing again, think of those who would die for you." Kai pointed at Gloria. Andrew. Put a hand on her breast.

Joy's shoulders convulsed. Tears downpoured. She nodded in a frenetic way.

Gloria bowed her head, unable to keep looking at Kai's porcelain face, twisted by pain. In her soft-spoken way, Kai had opened her heart to them, dodging the medical protocol she'd prefer. *Kai would die for Joy.* A wave of guilt washed over her. *And I wouldn't even welcome Kai into our home.*

"Think of Mother," Kai continued, "who died, her last wish to reunite with you unfulfilled." In a way incongruous with her trembling lips, Kai dealt business cards.

"I . . . I will," Joy whispered.

Kai extended her hand to Joy. "I must leave now, dear sister." They embraced stiffly, as if both were unsure what would be appropriate after the bombshell Kai had detonated. "With your parents' permission, you may call me anytime, day or night, weekday or weekend."

Gloria nodded passionately. "Of . . . of course."

"I will give your names to my call service. They will be told to contact me, no questions asked."

Desperate to show how she felt, Gloria threw out her arms and then let them fall to her side. She gathered resolve and shook Kai's hand, praying her grip would convey what was in her heart. "We can never thank you for what you have done." This time, there was no need for Southern manners. Fervor emblazoned Gloria's every word.

⌒ 𝑜 ⌒

Ah, David. It seems like an eon since we've spoken. Cell phone in hand, Kai sat cross-legged on her king-sized bed. She rubbed a stomach aching from too much T-bone and vowed to fast tomorrow. It would not be as simple to purge the image of Joy's pale scar from her mind. Perhaps if she talked to David about it. . . .

Without bothering to listen to his message, she punched David's number. Oh, to hear his voice and then speak to him of Joy's potential, Joy's problems. David, a fifth-generation Christian, could help her relate to the Powells and their religion. Perhaps it was time to learn more about their God if He performed such miracles—

"Hello."

"David. It's you!" A breathy quality hoarsened Kai's voice. She barely recognized herself!

"Kai." Something—exhaustion?—had softened David's accent. Kai glanced at the digital readout on her phone. It was nine thirty—ten thirty Boston time. Early for David, who studied journal articles and played his classical music until well after midnight. She gripped the phone, as if the connection might be lost.

"I have so much to tell you!"

"So you met your sister."

Ground I covered in the earlier message, along with the near-disaster. Something sharp as that steak bone stabbed Kai. "Did you get my messages?" she asked softly.

"I did, Kai. Did you get mine?"

201

"No. I just . . . I just wanted to hear your voice. It seems like it has been forever."

"It has been a long day."

"Did they call you in? What happened?" Questions flowed, so eager was Kai to understand his day, have him understand hers . . .

"No, nothing like that, Kai. Just . . . things."

Kai's scalp pricked. "I see." Of course she did not see at all.

"Hey." A phony ring shrilled David's voice. "I double-checked your flight."

Thank you, Mr. Secretary.

"Three thirty tomorrow, right?"

"I have not had time to study my itinerary."

David cleared his throat. "Tell you what. If the ETA changes, I'll call. Okay?"

"That would be wonderful, David." Kai battled to keep bitterness from her voice. Perhaps a critical patient forestalled David gifting her with a nice long chat. *Just because this was your expectation does not mean it was his.* "If I cannot pick up, you can always leave a message." She winced at the irony of her comment.

David exhaled. "I'm sorry to sound abrupt, but I really can't talk right now."

Kai relaxed her death hold on the phone. *Even a perfect gentleman deserves a break. He does not know what I have endured. . . .*

They said good-bye. Kai pressed *Messages* and retrieved one from Cheryl, who was just "checking in." Curious about David's message, Kai again punched a button.

"Kai, glad you made it through okay. I'll pick you up, as we agreed, tomorrow at three thirty. Let me know if plans change."

Five times, Kai listened to three Yankee sentences. Was this caller the doctor with the heart, the man who usually hung on her every word? Had the heart doctor, in a matter of two days, had a change of heart?

The thought sent Kai reeling to the bathroom. Or was it the beef?

16

Can I drop by Tuesday? Another emotionless voice mail from David. As Kai bustled about her brownstone, straightening the glossy jackets of Cheryl's art books, she mentally replayed David's message, as if there were deep import in five clipped words. Was a terse message better than none—which is what she'd gotten Sunday and Monday ... *But who's counting?*

Kai clipped daisy stems at an angle and rearranged them after filling a vase with fresh water. She'd make the den warm, inviting ... everything that airport encounter lacked. *Encounter.* An unsuitable word for moments spent with one she ... loved.

David, a skilled conversationalist, had been a monosyllabic valet when he picked her up Friday at Logan, then begged out of a date Saturday, pleading emergencies. Suddenly David had many emergencies. Coincidence, or excuse? She would ask him that very question ... when he arrived for a chat. *The likelihood of having a cozy chat with David in his present state ranks up there with me finding a cure for PKD. A miracle.*

The teapot whistled. A siren joined the shrill and split the midmorning Tuesday calm that had settled over their Back Bay neighborhood. Loosing her tense fingers, Kai shook leaves into a French press and steeped the tea. Could an inviting room and fragrant aroma transform David into his old self? His *loving* self?

Someone knocked on the door with hollow booms. So unlike David's staccato raps, followed by, "Kai! I'm here!"

David might be standing on the other side of the door, but if Kai trusted her instincts, it wasn't the man who'd given her his phone number, his time, his heart.

She unbolted the door. Opened it.

There stood David, wearing the scrubs he usually stowed in his locker, the scrubs that he said reminded him of illness, of work. Where were his khakis, his loafers? With effort, Kai brushed away negativity. He was on call. Living a doctor's life. He'd traded shifts with a partner so they could have this chat. That showed concern.

Despite internal gongs that cautioned reserve, Kai rushed into David's fresh-scrubbed and lime scent and cradled her head just so . . .

As if he were a kind uncle, David patted her head.

Kai snapped to attention and tried to swallow a sickening feeling. She had diagnosed David, all right. *All wrong.* "Come in." She let him walk past her and enter the room, where he stood under the light fixture, his head swiveling, his shoulders hunched, instead of beelining to his usual spot: the glider rocker near the stereo.

Clamping down tears, Kai walked to the kitchen, pressed the leaves, and poured tea. "Make yourself at home," she managed, though every cell screamed that was impossible. As she carried the cups, tea sloshed onto her hand.

Heat scalded. Kai winced at the rush of fire. A bad omen, spilling *Zhu Ye Qing*, tea meant for special occasions. Something this would not be.

David sat on the edge of the loveseat and rested his elbows on his knees. His robust athlete's complexion had taken on a sallow cast.

Kai's right hand tingled. Had David taken ill? As Kai knew, physicians rarely took time to heal themselves. She handed David his cup and sat in the rocker that bore his aftershave scent. With effort, she cast off late-night memories of cuddling here, watching John Wayne save the West, and then strolling to the harbor to watch the moon surrender to silvery water.

She affected a casual pose, curling her legs beneath her. "What is it, David?" Pain radiated from her heart. "You don't seem like yourself." *I'm worried sick about you . . . about us.*

David set his cup on an end table and stared at steam curls as though they revealed the mysteries of the world.

All she wanted to understand were the mysteries of this man.

"That's the thing, Kai. I am myself. Therein lies the problem."

David, using rhetoric? *So unlike him.* She warmed her hands on her cup and vowed to mask emotions and words. David asked for this chat. He should do the talking.

David met her gaze. *Finally.* "Kai, I've never met anyone like you." His perfectly sculpted hands batted the air. "When we met, I thought God had answered my prayers."

Kai blinked away bitter tears. Religion erected this wall. She should have known.

"How could one person—a beautiful woman—share my love for music and medicine, movies and art . . . and respect my commitment to remain chaste until marriage?"

Even as he talked of purity, desire trembled Kai. When this man so much as pressed his lips to her temples, her whole body throbbed. Yet the weariness in his voice, the tension in his jaw, signaled she must quell her emotions or lose face. "We do share many common interests." The dry words and dousing of passion nearly choked her. She longed to add, *including sexual attraction*, but a Chang could not broach such a taboo subject.

David edged forward on his seat, leaning so close to his cup that tea steam added sheen to his face. "But not the main interest."

Kai nodded despite a wave of nausea. Intuiting this did not salve the pain. She sipped tea, her eyes on David. *Get a good look at your love. It may be the last.* She, a Chang sister, would suffer another blow. Would this one prove fatal to her soul?

"I can't see you anymore, Kai." The anguish on David's face wrenched Kai's heart. Oh, that he would suffer. She gripped her teacup and stared at the green-gold contents, unable to look at his quivering lip, the hollowness about his eyes. "It kills me to say that," she heard, "but God's made it clear what I need to do. My parents concurred."

Resentment tensed Kai's muscles as she thought of David's father, always pointing out flaws in the Chinese character, always lambasting "the heathens" that flocked through Boston Harbor. She bit back the comment sticking in her throat like a chicken bone: *Who swayed you most, David? The Christian God . . . or your family?*

"Please know that I care for you."

David's voice floated close. To keep calm, Kai focused on specks of tea leaves floating in her cup. *Things from China are beneath this heart doctor . . . and his family. Including me. But I will not play the victim.*

"Yes, David. I know that." Kai set down her cup and

struggled to her feet, though the pain in her abdomen, in her heart, made it a struggle. She stepped close enough to clasp David's hand, stayed far enough away to avoid his scent, the feel of his breath against her cheek . . . the essence of David that she loved. Others might ask him to expound on his reasoning, try to sway him, but she would not press the issue. It was not the Chinese way. It was not the Chang way. *It is not my way.*

"How . . . how was Joy?"

Kai bristled. *He did not bother to ask when I radiated "Joy" at the airport.* "She is fine." Kai rose to her feet, now unwilling to share life-changing confidences with this man who did not want to share his life. "Thank you for asking."

David's mouth went slack. With jerky movements, so uncharacteristic of the graceful man she'd known, she'd loved, he rose and jabbed his hands into his pockets. "Take . . . take care, Kai." Without another glance, he left 348 Beacon Street, which seemed to sag the minute the door quietly shut.

Questions about miracles, about that voice, penetrated Kai's stiff pose of resentment. Ironically, religious issues, the very subject that precipitated this event, remained unexplored. Untasted. Like David's full cup of tea.

Kai returned to her seat and sipped the soothing elixir that had provided antioxidants and sustenance and warmth to Chinese for generations. Yet the tea's lively bouquet failed to assuage her wounded soul.

How could a sizzling romance end faster than it took China's best tea to go stone cold?

⌒꤮⌒

Joy agreed to a date. Gloria peeked out the window by their booth in Jimmy's Café. *And the sun hasn't fallen from the sky!*

208

"Hey, Mom." Joy munched on thick-cut chips, gulped her Coke, set down her glass, and checked out pictures of local celebrities tacked on a water-stained wall. *A place to see and be seen . . . when I was Joy's age. An eon ago!*

"This was a good idea." Joy tucked a strand of hair into her French braid and dabbed her lips with a napkin.

Gloria's half of an egg salad sandwich hovered in the air, then plopped onto her plate. *I had a good idea? What a difference six days makes!* "I just thought, since you had to get out early anyway, it might be nice to celebrate." Gloria fanned herself with her hands. "I mean, not really celebrate. Like Nicole said in that e-mail—set little goals."

"Mom, you can just say thanks." Joy plunked her elbows on the plastic tablecloth and propped her chin on her hands. "You don't have to explain."

The smell of eggs assailed Gloria's nostrils and sent her senses reeling. She'd felt crampy and bloated all morning. Not PMS—thank goodness—but still . . . whatever had led her to order a mayonnaise-laden sandwich defied explanation—as did her inability to talk with her only child and make sense. Lord, may that change! "I'm sorry. It's just that . . ." Gloria dug into her palms. Dared she tell Joy how she really felt? It might set off bad thoughts, heighten Joy's insecurity.

"What, Mother?"

Gloria twisted her hands. Joy was . . . transparent now, from her well-scrubbed face to her pink Keds. That tornado had swept away the debris cluttering Joy's life and let her real self shine through.

"It's just that . . ." Words became hard as marbles and clunked in Gloria's mouth. What else should she expect? She hadn't talked to Joy like this in years.

Joy flipped her braid over her shoulder and settled back

in the booth like she had no qualms about today's appointments with Carl and Nicole. *My qualms make up for it! And I haven't even quizzed her about that shrink appointment yesterday.*

"C'mon, Mom. Just spit it out." Despite the brash words, Joy's tone, and yawn, showed a girl at ease with herself. *Trying to be at ease with me.*

Gloria licked her lips, as if testing the words, then took a breath. *Hey, if she can do this, so can I.* "I'm worried." She swallowed. She'd finish this. For Joy. *For me.* "But I'm proud at how you've responded."

The dark eyes gleamed despite a quirky frown. "It's only been, like, four days."

"Actually, six. But who's counting?"

Joy rolled her eyes, but her hand darted across the table and brushed Gloria's sleeve. "Oh, *Moth*-er." They smiled shyly, as if just meeting. *In a way, that's true.*

They settled into their booth . . . and into a good talk.

Finally Gloria checked her watch, surprised at how an hour had fluttered by. They'd done lunch, like real mothers and daughters. "Hey, we've gone an hour without a fight" came out before she realized what she'd said. But Joy just nodded, like it was okay. "Now we've got to scoot." Though the last thing Gloria wanted to do was move.

A frown creased Joy's forehead. "You haven't eaten, like, anything."

Queasiness struck at the mention of food. Why was she surprised? Since Sunday, even dry toast caused dry heaves. Strange how food issues had started only after her positive pregnancy test. Psychosomatic for sure. She rubbed her middle. Tenderness radiated to her breasts, but the empathy on Joy's face carried her past discomfort. "If you had morning, noon, and night sickness, you wouldn't eat, either."

Joy's smile lit up the photos in the dumpy old joint, which had never looked better. While having such a blast, Gloria could almost forget about the faint scar on her daughter's wrist. Almost.

17

Same table. Same Nicole. Same Warhol poster. Different Joy.

Nicole picked up a treat bowl, nabbed two Kisses, and passed it to Gloria.

Typically, Gloria would have been tempted by the dark, creamy goodness, but now she had to squelch the urge to retch. For heaven's sake! Even her love of chocolate had succumbed to this prenatal sickness?

"Your daughter came to session yesterday with a list of goals." Nicole munched on candy, tucked her hair behind her ears, flipped file pages, and grinned at Joy. "This is huge!"

A paper slid its way to Gloria and brought back memories of last week's meeting, in this very room. That had been huge too. A new start.

> Goals for the Week of 4/9 to 4/13
> Clean up room
> Write rough draft
> Meet with counselor about nursing program
> Research PKD

Call Harris H. about volunteering
Talk to Mother

Though the last item was written in the same concise print as Joy's other goals, the letters looped about Gloria's neck. Conversation with Joy had been reduced to an item on a to-do list? *I have no one to blame but myself.*

"Joy and I've been meeting during her free period. Her teachers sign off daily on a form. Part of the station adjustment." Nicole handed Gloria a paper. "Here's the ones from yesterday."

A different girl . . . revised her Thoreau paper . . . participated in class discussion . . . on time . . . work completed . . .

Gloria ran her finger along each teacher comment, letting the words infuse her with hope. "This is amazing."

"Cool, huh?" Nicole unwrapped another chocolate and popped it in her mouth.

"Flat-out amazing."

Joy ducked her head but couldn't hide a grin.

Gloria let out her breath. One response at a time, she'd learn Joy 101. Their family depended on it.

"So that's Joy's school progress." Nicole grabbed her clipboard and flipped back the page. "Yesterday, Dr. Peters and I spoke about Joy's emotional well-being."

Gloria tensed. Had Dr. Peters noted their failures as parents on a to-do list?

"Joy agreed to have her file released to me."

Heat crept from Gloria's neck to her face.

"It is Dr. Peters' opinion that Joy's cutting incident does not manifest ingrained self-hate or long-term self-destructive tendencies but rather evidences a one-time attempt to respond to disconnect at school. Unfortunate but sadly typical teen-aged teasing."

Gloria remembered the taunting voices of her own teen years. She, who knew how it felt to be ridiculed, could have helped . . . but hadn't known! "Oh, Joy!" She twisted to face her daughter. "Why didn't you tell us?"

Joy stared straight ahead. Did not blink. Did not seem to breathe. Yet her brow remained smooth, her gaze alert.

Her daughter had donned the mask of Kai. As a defense mechanism? To hide anger? Gloria battled a wooziness that seemed to be swallowing her. . . .

"Mrs. Powell, we are not here to discuss the past but to move forward."

"I understand" rushed out of Gloria's mouth. A lie, but something she had to say. She looked up, her senses whirling. The forest in the Colorado nature poster closed in. Warhol's poster seemed to be exploding, seemed to be splattering her with tomato soup. . . .

"What we want to discuss today involves Joy's education." Nicole crossed her arms and leaned back in her chair.

"Like, I wondered, Mom . . . Mom?"

Gloria raised her head and tried to focus on Joy's face.

"If I finish strong, like Dad says, would you maybe home-school me again? You know, like when I first came over from China?" The words ricocheted off the wall and pinged into Gloria. Suddenly her wooziness morphed into a painful pressure . . . in her groin.

"Like, the kids don't get me. They're either rah-rah about who's balling the jocks—sorry—or trying to smuggle weed into the bathroom." Frenzied hand waves—and more information than Gloria ever wanted to hear about Joy's school—stirred air molecules into a frenzy. Gloria gripped the table, wanting, needing the pain to stop.

"The Paschal environment really isn't Joy's thing." Nicole's voice became tinny. "We thought if Joy could homeschool . . ."

"Yeah, Mom! If I can do my own thing, maybe—"

A weight lodged on Gloria's bladder with such intensity, she crossed her legs. "I have to— Please excuse me." She wobbled to her feet. "I'll be right back."

"See?" Joy's words slammed into Gloria, but she couldn't stop. *Joy will die if I wet myself in public.* She'd expected bladder problems. Not this. Not at ten weeks.

"I told you and Kai there's no way she'd get it. She never gets—"

Get through the door. *It's hard to hold my bladder while striding out. How stupid I must look! But if I wet my pants . . . Yuck!*

Gloria passed the drinking fountain, grateful for signs that pointed the way. Never had the word *Restroom* looked so good.

Swish. Swish. Closer. She panted in sync with her steps. The bathroom door loomed like a mirage, something she neared but couldn't quite reach. *One more step. Yes, Lord, yes!* She lowered her shoulder, shoved against wood.

The door opened. Despite her squeezing, so did her bladder.

Liquid trickled into her panties. She struggled for control.

A weight plunged into her groin area, deeper, deeper, and scraped hard.

Gloria clutched her pants. *Lord, it's pulling my insides with it!* Still, she lumbered on. A silly tune swelled in her mind. Was she singing, or did lyrics pour from bathroom speakers? Not elevator, but bathroom music? Gloria slogged toward the first stall. *I've lost control of my mind . . . and bladder.*

Pee dribbled down her thighs. Desperate to make it, Gloria

stretched for the door. Yet the weight lit fire to her groin, her hips. She sank to the floor.

Pain belted her abdomen. Gloria gasped, laid her head against cool tile, and yielded to the pressure. Urine streamed, warm and sticky. Yet there was a strange relief . . .

The door banged open.

"Mommy! Mommy!"

Footsteps pattered.

Gloria shook her head and tried to cover herself with trembling hands. Joy could *not* see her like this.

Not one muscle roused to action.

"I'm sorry, Joy," she whimpered. "I'm so, so sorry." Her voice sounded as woozy as her mind, but try as she might, it wouldn't sharpen.

Joy knelt by her side, buried her face in her hands. "Mommy . . ."

The whispery softness of Joy's words wove a cottony blanket that spread over Gloria's pain. Though her eyes refused to focus, she smiled at the blur of flesh, black, white, and purple. Don't forget purple. Despite achiness that radiated from her core, she patted that funky, silky hair. She hadn't embarrassed Joy! Her Joy, here for her!

Joy raised her head. Her eyes were luminous moons, misted with tears. "Mommy! What happened?" Joy found her hand.

Her wet hand. Her red hand.

Gloria's breath caught in her throat, which had become a desert. "Joy? Joy!" She gripped Joy's wrist, then thought of that scar and let go.

Red stained Joy's creamy wrist. Gloria's mouth widened. Blood. She stared, uncomprehending, at her hand. Blood. Her eyes bulged . . . and riveted to the floor, where blood pooled. *My blood.*

Joy rustled closer. Took Gloria's hand. "Mommy, I'm . . . I'm so, so sorry."

Not just my blood . . .

A scream reverberated through Gloria, though clenched teeth trapped it inside. *It's my blood. Our baby's blood. God, no! It's our baby's blood and my blood!*

"Mom, you stay put." Joy steadied her with a bloody grip. "I'll get help. Then I'll be back, I promise." Joy's brow furrowed. "Do . . . not . . . move."

The door wheezed. Gloria freed the held-in scream. Rasped a cough. She clutched her throat, not caring that blood would stain her neck, face . . . whatever she touched.

She blinked. The bathroom walls had been painted red. Red dust motes floated in a random, erratic way. A hideous painter had broad-brushed her world. With death? "N-n-nooo!" Red motes spun, faster, faster—

"Mommy! I'm back!" Joy swooped to block out the hideous color, then clutched Gloria's shoulders and held her still.

Gloria sagged. Her baby had returned for her. Caring, not hating. Loving, not resentful. But that other baby . . . Great heaves shook her body. Tears poured from her eyes, her nose, her mouth, streaming, streaming, and washing away the hideous red.

"Mommy. Look at me."

Gloria smiled, cried, seeing nothing but that lovely purple hair.

"Mommy!" Urgency laced Joy's voice. Her grip tightened. "Listen to me. Now!"

Gloria swallowed. Joy sounded . . . like Kai had . . . when? Last week? Yesterday? Gloria cocked her head, as if she were looking at a stranger. "Joy?" She wanted, she needed this new Joy. She clenched her head, which was being sliced in two with pain.

"They asked me to check down . . . there." Joy gently laid Gloria back on the floor. "Be still. Breathe, Mommy. In, out, in, out."

"But—"

"No buts, Mommy. Just lay there. Help's on the way."

Help's on the way. Gloria breathed a sigh. *Joy, using one of my sayings. Sounding now like . . . me.*

Joy patted Gloria, as if anchoring her, then let go. As Gloria watched, Joy rustled to her feet, turned on the tap, and yanked towels from the dispenser. She laid them on the counter and began to wash her hands.

Gloria continued to watch as if she were seeing a film. Strange, the things that Joy was doing. But good. Definitely good. Even stranger, the cramping and achiness had eased. Also good. Good.

As she studied her daughter's every bend and stretch, Gloria's memory meandered. There was Joy, that first day in the van, trembling when their shoulders touched. Andrew, his smile big as Dallas when she announced they were having a baby. When was that? Heaves avalanched. Six days ago? For six days she had known the joy of being pregnant. Now . . . now it was over.

Sobs racked her body. She blinked, then studied Joy, there at the sink. "Joy? Joy!" She craved Joy's touch. Like before.

Joy whirled, the towels in her hand. "I'll love you forever," Joy sang. The words were whisper-soft. "I'll love you for always, as long as you're living, my Joy you'll be."

It was their old nighttime song, inspired by a Joy bedtime book, stowed by Joy into a memory box, pulled out just for today. "Joy. My Joy," Gloria cooed.

"Yes, Mommy. I'm your Joy."

My Joy.

She felt the downy softness of Joy's touch. Felt the rough, papery towel. Felt Joy's breath puff on her legs. Joy swabbed . . . and kept singing their song.

Gloria ran her tongue across parched lips, wanting a drink, wanting more this lovely, soothing music.

Rushing water joined the chorus, as did yanks at that dispenser, the sound blending with Joy's voice.

Time flitted about the room. Gloria did nothing to pin it down. *How can I, with these blood-stained hands?*

The door opened. Nicole entered, as did . . . paramedics?

Joy's singing continued. Men lifted her onto a stretcher. Joy walked alongside them, holding Gloria's hand.

It was blissful, having that warm, soft hand anchor her against the thud of the elevator, which muted Joy's song. Other thoughts seized control as they loaded her into an ambulance. Technicians argued with a livid Joy.

Why would anyone argue with a girl who had purple hair? Gloria again stared at her bloody hands and wondered about her silly thoughts. Had she lost her mind . . . along with her baby?

Ambulance doors shut. Her vitals were checked, but her silly thoughts would not stay at the jail.

She'd been there three times in the last week. Once she'd left in an ambulance.

That had to be a record, even in Texas. Didn't it?

 ⁓

Take it easy, the doctor said. See a counselor. Gloria again picked up *How to Survive a Miscarriage*, dropped off by a church friend, and flipped through its pages.

"At first you will be numb" caught her eye.

Gloria gave a silent nod.

"Then you will be angry."

Gloria stormed from bed. Stopped at the window.

Birds chirped hello to peeping babies. An occasional bee somersaulted midair, perhaps drunk on nectar. How dared they? Even the sunshine she craved like God's mercy mocked her. Their baby had died, yet nature celebrated! She rattled shut the louvered blinds, crawled back under her covers, found the book.

Let memories flow. Don't suppress them.

Gloria tossed down the book, both because it grated at her and because she heard Joy clopping down the hall, returning from school. She pasted on her best effort at a real smile. Joy didn't need phony or woe-is-me. Joy was improving. Her miscarriage could not stall Joy's progress.

"Mom." Joy slipped into her room, in the quiet way she'd adopted since the baby died. Yesterday.

Gloria's jaw ached from smile-stretching. "How was school?"

"Fine. Dad said to tell you he'd be home as soon as he could." Joy's hands were behind her back, as if she were about to curtsy.

Gloria shrugged, though the submissive posture of her daughter salved pain. "Really, I don't know why he's taking off early. I'm fine." She yawned, as if bored. "In fact, I was about to get up. Would you like a smoothie, dear?"

"Mom. You don't need to get anything for me." Joy thrust out her hands, which held a nosegay of pink and blue carnations.

Gloria's chin quivered. Baby pink. Baby blue. "Oh, Joy." Her insides shimmered, as they had that first time she had looked at Joy's perfect face. Her daughter understood what this stupid book had not. Her daughter understood that she was not mourning the loss of one she had known intimately. Her daughter understood that she was grieving for the one she had not been allowed to know. Her daughter, though she was only seventeen, understood the pain of not knowing whether she'd carried a girl or a boy.

"I thought . . . you might like them." Joy handed her the bouquet.

Gloria buried her nose and inhaled the heady, clove-like scent that she'd always preferred over pricey roses. She shoved away a bad Daddy memory, took another whiff . . . and remembered running along her grandmother's picket-fence line. Butterflies swooped down to inspect her pink dress before fluttering away. She saw her daddy, tossing her a ball, laughing when it bounced off her knee and dribbled onto the ground. A good Daddy memory.

A warm spring welled in an exquisite, painful way. "It's . . . perfect," was interspersed with a cleansing cry and streams of tears.

Joy sat on the edge of the bed and patted and cooed.

Gloria sank into the scrubbed-clean smell of her daughter, whose slender arms encircled Gloria and pulled her close.

Time was reduced to the inhales, exhales, of a daughter whose tears free-flowed onto her blouse, a daughter who soothed and hugged. She'd lost a child . . . to find a child. The thought birthed more tears. It was a painful truth, an inexplicable truth. Even as she questioned, Gloria knew it was of God.

Gloria gently pulled away. "How . . . how did you know what I felt when no one else has had a clue?"

Joy gripped the sheet and twisted it into a tourniquet. "Because . . ."

Through strands of hair, Gloria glimpsed lips bowed by

unspeakable loss, eyes heavy with grief. A jaw working to express the thing that no one had understood for six years. "Because, Mommy, I never got a chance to know my family either."

A moan tore from Gloria, who flung her arms about Joy and pulled her close. Joy trembled in sync with raspy breaths, matching the tremble in Gloria's soul.

"You must hate me for not understanding." Gloria battled an urge to tear her hair. "Why didn't I see it?" She paused . . . only to catch her breath. "To think I was jealous of Kai, who'll help you reclaim what you lost. Your sisters, your parents, your first home."

Joy wailed, as if in agreement.

"Oh, Joy, I'm sorry!" She again wound her arms about Joy and held on for dear life. Both hers and her daughter's.

The whimpering slowed. Joy dabbed at her eyes, then pulled her legs onto the bed and sat cross-legged. "Kai told me about my family."

My family. Gloria had feared those words for years. How she had squandered energy, emotion, opportunity. No more.

Gloria rose from her bed, padded to the bathroom, and returned with tissues. "I want to hear about them, Joy. But first I want to make tea. Fix you a snack."

"Are you sure, Mommy?"

Mommy. Another name used all too rarely . . . until this past week. How she loved the sound of it!

"I'm sure." Gloria tossed the tissue into a wastebasket and pecked her daughter's cheek. "About everything. I wish I would've been surer years ago. I might have saved us . . ." Gloria writhed her hands but could not find the words.

"If I forgive you, will you forgive me?" Joy uttered a perfect new saying . . . for both of them.

Nodding, Gloria hugged her daughter, who padded after

her to the kitchen. Suddenly starving for crisp spring air, Gloria raised blinds and opened a window, then set water to boil while Joy took charge of the snack, arranging cookies on a plate. It felt like a fresh start, a new season, a solace for the days of grief that would follow. *Right now, it is enough. Lord, yes, it is enough.*

18

"*Go in the front door, not the employee entrance. Cross the same threshold as your patients. Greet them kindly as they wait, scared, nervous, hating us for what we tell them, what we do to them.*" As Kai entered the lobby of Massachusetts Renal Associates, she adjusted the name pin on her lab-coat lapel and let words from Dr. Ward's last lecture inspire her. "*It will ground you when unintelligible insurance forms, dollar-sign-eyes drug reps, and computer glitches snarl your day. See those in waiting-room seats, just for a moment. Then rejoice that you have a chance to help them. That you are not ill.*"

Kai nodded at a slip of a girl, sitting in the chair under the Monet print—one of David's favorites—kneading her hands. Kai thought of Joy and tried to give a Texas smile, but she couldn't help but wonder, *Why is she alone?*

"Good morning, Doctor." Betsy, the receptionist, slid open the glass partition. "There's a call for you holding on line one."

Efficiency. Kindness. What Dr. Duncan demanded at MRA. Oh, how had one of the state's best doctors chosen her for his practice? "Thank you, Betsy."

"Oh, Doctor? Your nine thirty canceled."

Kai nodded, then turned and greeted poor Mr. Haynes, rifling through a *Field & Stream*, which she'd had Betsy order after he'd regaled her with fishing stories. Adventures he'd take only in his mind since dialysis chained him to machines three days a week.

An inner office door opened. Kai stepped aside for a patient exiting and entered the world of acidosis and kidney stones and Alport syndrome and PKD. Her world.

She strode the hall as if she were in the Forbidden City, every fiber twitching with the amazement that a mere village girl could work in such a place. The sight of her lit-up phone extension snapped her back to the present. She slid into her desk chair. It could be a hospitalist. The ER. A colleague.

Her eyes landed on the image of David, picture-framed and perched on her desk, his arm lounging carelessly about her shoulder. The two of them smiled for the jogger who'd broken stride long enough to grant their request to freeze-frame their love. Kai opened her file drawer and stashed the photo under her sweater. If only memories of David could be so easily hidden . . .

She jabbed at the phone button, then stared at her office wall. Though her heart begged otherwise, intuition drowned out its plea. *It will not be David.*

"Kai speaking."

"It's . . . it's Joy." Joy's voice scratched like leaves against concrete.

"Joy? How . . . how are you?"

"I . . . Oh, Kai." Joy began to weep. "Sorry, but I haven't had time to call!"

A black veil shadowed Kai's wall of accolades. "Joy? What is it?" She pressed the phone so tightly against her ear, she heard a low buzz. *Joy met with the doctor. He tested her. She has PKD.* Her composure threatened to splinter as her imagination careened out of control.

"You won't believe what happened."

"Yes, dear one." Kai heard her voice, though it seemed to have separated from the rest of her. Another glance at her diplomas confirmed what she must do. Joy did not need just a sister, but a sister and a doctor. One acquainted with PKD, which Joy was about to know in a horrid and intimate new way. "Tell me, Joy, what did they find?"

"What did they find?" shrilled back at her.

"What did the doctor find?" Kai evened out her voice.

"The doctor? He released her. Tuesday night. I guess they called you earlier."

Kai felt her eyes widen. Someone was released Tuesday? From jail? The Powells had called? It was so unlike Betsy to lose a message. Or had that answering service—

"Like, she's gonna be fine. But Kai," Joy wailed, "it was so awful."

Kai cleared her throat. "Joy, I do not understand. Tell me what happened."

"So they didn't talk to you."

"I just arrived at the office."

"Mother miscarried, right in the jail! During one of my sessions!"

Kai's mouth went dry, yet she loosened her hold on the phone. Gloria, not Joy, had suffered. "Joy. That is awful."

"I . . . I found her in the bathroom. Found the baby too." Joy's voice stretched into a screech. "Kai, it was . . . so tiny! So . . . helpless!"

Kai's stomach spasmed. "Oh, dear, dear," she kept repeating. "You found the baby." Her mind swelled with unwanted images.

A practicum session first introduced Kai to a fetus. Ten weeks old. Again she saw transparent fairylike arms, crossed in deep thought . . . or angry. Spindly legs were also crossed, though at the ankles, and drawn up to touch those arms. A thumb was forever frozen at a hint of a mouth; the skull, broad and disproportionately large, was filled with ideas and dreams no one would ever know. What power decided that life would end? Kai cleared her throat. This was no time to wax theological. "Oh, Joy. When did you say it happened?"

"We had a meeting with Nicole on Tuesday. Mother excused herself and was gone, like, forever. Nicole thought I should check on her. I found her on the floor . . . with the blood . . . the baby."

Memory of Kai's first ER call flashed in living color and throbbed blood to her pulses. "You found her first?"

"Uh-huh."

"I'm sorry you—and she—went through that. Thank the heavens you were there for her."

"I even cleaned her up. Paramedics couldn't believe I'd saved it."

Kai flattened her spine against her chair back. "You . . . you saved the . . ."

"The placenta was still attached." Joy began to cry.

Kai's arms prickled with such a strange mix of joy and pain, she battled the urge to cry herself. *Joy is a healer. I thought so at the jail. Now I know.* "Joy," she whispered, cradling the phone lovingly, as if she were holding precious Fourth Daughter instead of a communication device, "you have shown great bravery. You have done things grown women could not do."

"I had to. Because . . ."

"Because . . . Why, Joy? Tell me."

"The EMTs said to leave it intact. And . . ."

"And what?"

"It . . . it could've been me."

Kai's jaw went slack. "What do you mean?"

"I thought about what Father told Mother to do with me—what Father said she had to do. Like, I needed to help. Somehow. Oh, God!" Joy screeched. "I can't explain it."

Kai swallowed. "Some things cannot be explained. Still, the heart feels them."

"If . . . if you say so." Joy spoke in a muted tone. Begging encouragement. Hope.

"Your mother needs you now." Kai injected iron into her voice. She must finish this. For Joy's sake. And her own. "Even more than she needed that baby."

"You . . . really . . . think so?" Sniffles and words alternated.

As if Joy were in the room, Kai nodded. "Yes." She picked up her pen and began to doodle. "And you need her. She is a good woman, Joy. She cares for you."

"It's . . . like . . . it's strange."

Kai cocked her head. "Strange that you connect with her in a new way? That you . . . find you love her?"

"Like . . . whatever."

Kai winced. Did Chinese teenagers speak so flippantly about elders? From what she had heard, change was brewing in China. Old mores, discarded like used tea leaves. "No, it is not 'like, whatever.' Do not discount your role in Gloria's healing."

"My role?" Enthusiasm swelled Joy's voice. "You're not surprised about me helping Mom. It's like you knew I could."

The pen in her grip became a victim of Kai's tension. She sketched a kite, looped it in a careening path, and let out a sigh. Her mind raced from Boston to China. She had regretted not telling Joy this part of her story earlier. Should she do it now?

Her gaze returned to her certificates and diplomas, which expanded until they blotted out every inch of taupe on the wall. *Yes! Yes!* black calligraphy insisted. *Yes! Yes! Yes!* gold seals proclaimed. *It is time. She must know. Perhaps it is her destiny as well. A destiny to be protected. A destiny that must not end with a slit wrist and lifeblood streaming down a drain.*

As Kai scribbled on a notepad, the story of the healing hand raced across phone lines.

Joy listened wordlessly, breath-puffs the only evidence of her on-line presence. Kai finished. Joy said, "So, like, I was meant to do this. I know it . . . deep inside."

Sun rays dazzled the gold leaf paint Kai and Cheryl had rubbed onto Kai's certificate frames. Though Kai then closed her eyes, savoring the moment, glorious light seeped past her eyelids and into her very soul. "Yes," she whispered. "Yes."

"Doctor?"

Kai opened her eyes. There stood Deborah, an MRA nurse.

Kai startled, then nodded. Was it ten? Noon? Telling the story of her calling and answering Joy's questions had skewed her concept of time.

"Dr. Harrell's on line three." Deborah laid a file on her desk. "Should he call back?"

Kai shook her head. She had said what she needed to say. "Joy, something's come up at work that I need to address."

"Like, is it an emergency?"

This girl is what they call "something else." As though she were talking to a colleague rather than her sister, Kai skimmed a note clipped to the file. "I believe it is."

"Like, cool! I mean, not that someone's sick or anything. I mean . . ."

"I understand." *It is an inexplicable thing, Joy.* "Could we talk tonight?"

"Like, sure! I'll call you later, okay? Dad wants to talk to you anyway, about scheduling my appointment."

"Have you seen your local doctor?"

"He's been out of town."

Kai's stomach tightened. So PKD still hovers in the realm of the unknown. Kai pushed away black thoughts. "What time will you be calling?"

"Nicole couldn't meet till after dinner. Is nine too late? Or will you be in? I mean, like, it's Friday and all—"

No worry, Joy. Suddenly my weekends are wide open. "Nine is fine, Joy."

The two said good-bye. A bittersweet mood lingered. The tragedy of death. Poor Gloria. Yet hope, blossoming in her beloved Joy. Kai sunk back into her chair, exhausted, though her workday had just begun. She found the file, opened it, and took her call.

"So, like, I was meant to do this. I know it . . . deep inside."

Joy's words got her through her first Friday without a call from David, helped her slog through paper work, a conference call, a consult with a rather obnoxious colleague.

"So, like, I was meant to do this." She'd memorized Joy's words by noon as she munched an apple at her desk. *"I know it . . . deep inside."*

Certainly not the way Kai would state it. But it resonated deep in Kai's soul. *Dr. Ward would like it—no, he would love it. So do I.*

～

New findings. Clinical trials. Enough stats to birth a migraine. Kai set aside her work and caressed the smooth wood arm of the rocker where David loved to sit. *Never have I been so full of the latest data in my field, so empty in my heart.*

She hurried to the kitchen and set water to boil, intent on flushing self-pity from her system with a cup of tea. Cheryl's silly cat wall clock told her she had two hours, considering the time difference, before she again heard Joy's voice. Two hours to stop acting like a lovesick girl over her first weekend without David.

Her chin set with determination, she returned to the love seat, pulled a copy of a patient's chart from her briefcase, and found his latest lab stats. Stats that failed to show Mr. Rollings' twinkling eyes, a WWII shrapnel scar, the drive that led a great-grandfather, grandfather, and widower in agonizing pain to shuttle children to church.

The world of medicine—that means you, Kai—has done nothing to help him. Yet.

She flipped the page. Ran her finger across glucose, BUN, creatinine, GFR, CO_2, potassium, sodium, magnesium, albumin, and calcium readings. Neat, columned figures.

Nonsensical.

Just as the teakettle shrilled, Cheryl rushed through the door, her short auburn bob catching the light in the room. "Kai!" She tossed down her handbag and enveloped Kai. "Are you ever a sight for sore eyes!"

Kai's resolve to act the stoic crumpled with the touch of her first American friend. Cheryl had gone from a self-centered, fast-track Harvard journalism student to a caring, sensitive director of an international nonprofit organization after "being saved." Cheryl had played matchmaker for Kai and David, Cheryl's childhood friend. Though Kai rested her head on Cheryl's shoulder, it didn't alleviate the clamor rattling Kai's soul. Cheryl claimed God opened one to the needs of others;

David insisted God had closed the door to their relationship. Kai swallowed a gritty taste. This supernatural being was as unintelligible as Mr. Rollings' chart.

Cheryl eased away but kept her hands on Kai's shoulders. "I'm so sorry." Tears glistened in Cheryl's eyes. Beneath a smattering of freckles, her translucent skin glowed. Her heritage of tough coastal fishermen who carved a life along the rugged Maine shores had imbued Cheryl with peace . . . or perhaps it *was* her God.

Kai sniffed back tears. "He told you."

The teapot screeched at ear-splitting levels. *Yet I will not budge, for it would mean breaking the connection with one who loves me.*

"You sit down." Cheryl guided her to the love seat. Mr. Rollins' files were set on the floor. "I'll get the tea . . . on one condition."

Kai felt her heart leap. Surely Cheryl wouldn't avoid talk of David. It could be awkward, as Cheryl had known David since primary school. It might put distance between her and her roommate. *Can I withstand any more separation?*

"Of course," Kai managed wearily.

"That you don't grouse about how weak the tea is."

Sorrow lost its hold, and a giggle rose from Kai. *Laughter is a tonic, Dr. Ward, as you taught us. I should laugh more often.*

Cheryl joined her on the love seat and gifted Kai with a cup of steaming tea. "I talked to him after Bible study." In her New England way, Cheryl cornered the tiger lurking in the forest. *Such directness is foreign to me, yet perfect for my state of mind.* "He claimed he did what he had to do," Cheryl continued.

Kai set her cup on the coffee table. "What did you say?"

Porcelain thunked against porcelain. Two cups, side by side. Letting off steam. *Much like what I am doing.*

"Kai, this may be hard for you to get. It's hard for me to get." Cheryl leaned back, crossed her legs in the American way. "David felt your relationship was pulling him from God, his first love."

Kai felt her jaw tighten. God as a "sweetheart." A term of endearment David had used for *her*. Again the word *nonsensical* flashed in her mind, yet Kai would not question this dear friend.

Cheryl grabbed Kai's hands to form a knot of flesh. "God asks us to give Him our heart, our mind, our soul. To die to ourselves."

Kai's insides wrenched. She had heard political propaganda like this all her life. To think two of America's brightest deviated from logic in matters of religion!

"Then He can live in us . . . and offer a glorious new life."

A strange wind cooled the fire that was her gut. Kai fought a desire to shake her head. One minute, Cheryl's Christian language sickened her; the next, it revitalized her every fiber. "So the breakup had nothing to do with me."

Cheryl released Kai. "David cherishes you. But God comes first." Cheryl put her hand on her breast, as if pledging allegiance to this God. "In my heart, I know David's right."

Heart? Do not speak to me of the heart. You, David, and this God of yours are squeezing mine to death. Soon it will burst. Despite her irritation, Kai summoned the fortitude to nod.

"Can I pray for you, Kai?"

These Christians, always praying. To a God who says they must die to themselves. Kai turned from Cheryl, picked up her cup, and took a deliberate sip.

The phone rang. Once. Twice. Three times.

Kai stiffened, as if frozen by their talk. Having an unlisted number had freed them from cold calls. Perhaps David had changed his mind. . . .

"You have reached 946-9401. I'm sorry we can't take your call. Please leave a message." The recorder again beeped. Clicked. A buzzing sound scratched Kai's nerves.

"Hey, Kai. It's Andrew. Um, I tried your cell, but—"

The Texas drawl propelled Kai off the seat. She rushed to the kitchen. "Andrew." She exhaled, hoping to rid her voice of anxiety. She'd forgotten that Joy was to call. But this was Andrew . . .

"Sounds like I caught you off guard."

Kai eased onto a bar stool. "Of course not, Andrew. I was just—" *on the verge of exploding at your God*—"having a cup of tea with my roommate."

"That's nice." So congenial, so sincere, Joy's father. Also a pastor of this God. Kai sipped her tea. "I'm glad you called, Andrew. How can I help you?"

"Joy told me y'all talked."

Kai's grip tightened on the phone. Why had Joy not called herself?

"Thank you for being there for her, Kai. It means a lot to Gloria and me."

An image of the delicate blond woman flashed. "How is Gloria?"

"Better than I expected. She's . . . holding up. But . . . I think you know what this baby meant to her."

I know. Joy explained it in living color.

"Dr. Davies says she should be fine. I mean . . ."

"It is good there are no complications." Kai softened her tone in deference to the poor man, the kind man, and then felt her mouth tighten. *A man who also has died for the Christian God.* She forced a smile. "No infection. That is good."

"A miracle! Believe me, we've been on our knees."

Kai felt her eyebrows arch. Would she ever understand these Christians?

"That's why I'm calling."

Because you are on your knees?

"We finally got ahold of Joy's doctor while he was at his out-of-state conference. He just flew back today."

Kai held her breath. Joy's lab results were in. *That is why Joy did not call.*

"Dr. Carlson had the lab take her blood pressure. Other things."

What things? Kai pressed her palm against the counter and stared at the teapot, so silent on a trivet. No longer letting off steam, like she itched to do. "Have you gotten the results?" Kai closed her eyes, concentrating to pull every inflection from Andrew. Waiting. Waiting. She had spent her whole life waiting, but never had it gripped her like this.

"Yes. Some." Was it her imagination, or did a false joviality swell Andrew's voice? "Dr. Carlson isn't alarmed and doesn't want us to be." He cleared his throat. "But some of the numbers didn't add up."

Kai pressed her lips together. *The yin, the yang. A language I know well. So tell me, Reverend Powell, before I scream.* "Which ones?"

"Um, he didn't say."

So we know nothing. Absolutely nothing. And I cannot rest until we do.

"He did say we should bring her to Boston. Let you folks check her out." Andrew spoke with an ingratiating tone.

"Guess he checked around before he called. He said y'all are the best."

Kai rubbed her hand along the nubby kitchen wall. Her mouth had gone numb, as had her brain. She stared at that silly cat clock with the sweeping pendulum tail. *Swish, swish,* PKD. *Swish, swish,* PKD.

Kai pulled her gaze from the clock. So much had happened in such a short time, it was difficult to process. But she must. She tried to think. The Powells needed her to think.

"Will that be a problem, Kai? Kai?"

Thoughts dizzied her mind. She cleared them by picturing Joy, strolling in the Common. "Of course not, Andrew. I am at your service." She would grab Dr. Duncan early Monday, certainly before the staff meeting. Mr. PKD, she'd nicknamed him. No expense would be spared, no test would be overlooked. This was her Lily—her Joy.

"Carl wanted her tested, er, yesterday. Just to get ahead of the game."

"Of course."

"When can y'all see her?"

Kai smiled, remembering Dr. Ward's love of humor. "Yesterday."

Andrew's chuckle traveled all the way from Cowtown to douse the last of her tension. "We Texans don't time travel, but I'll get on the stick. How about we shoot for next Wednesday? I'll let you know ASAP. If you're not busy, I've got someone here about to have a conniption."

Kai pictured waving arms and purple hair. With a smile, she lifted her cup and finished her tea. This phone call gave her an escape from talk about David and the Christian God, which only muddled her emotions. Something she didn't need if she was to focus on Joy.

"Kai?" It was that lovely high-pitched voice. Joy! "Did you hear? Like, I'm coming to Boston! Could I take rounds with you? Oh, and I forgot to tell you this morning. I quit smoking!"

Kai smiled. Strangely, a conniption with Joy was exactly what she needed.

19

Cold coffee's the pits. And the pit is where I'm dwelling.
Gloria searched for nourishment in her daily devotion book,
her inky coffee, their cozy breakfast nook. Her appetite for
spiritual food—along with the church family's casseroles, her
thoughtful neighbor's cinnamon rolls—had died.

Just like . . . her baby.

She dragged along, wearing her robe and house shoes, then
clicked a smile in place when Joy and Andrew returned . . .
from work, school, the counselor's. They didn't need tears
and a mopey face.

Every phony comment and lying smile sucked out more
of her insides. If she didn't do something soon, she'd melt
into a puddle on this grimy kitchen floor.

She cringed. Would she ever see a puddle as anything but red?

With a push off the table, she rose to her feet and stepped
to the window.

Outside, birds sang and crickets chirped, surreal against the
sorrow in her soul. She gripped her middle, massaged with
deeper and firmer strokes. Not even a twinge. How could
that be? A baby had lived . . . and died in there.

Andrew and their old hand-me-down bed bore her grief. Never had he cuddled with her so gently, prayed for her so long, shed so many tears to match her own.

Tuesday, Wednesday, Thursday, Friday, Saturday. Sunday.

She turned from the window and smoothed her dress, the only thing, besides pj's and her robe, she'd worn since the miscarriage. This was the Sabbath, God's day, Andrew's day. It had always been so. It had to be so. At this moment, God and Andrew were holed up in the study, nailing down their sermon bullet points.

Would she be able to sit through it without falling apart?

She rested her elbows on Formica, let the weathered wood cabinet support her shaky frame. "God, get me through this. May I be Andrew's helpmate. He's sure been here for me. Get me over—" She bit her lip against the venom that roiled up, just thinking about that baby and why He would gift such a miracle, then snatch it away.

"Mom?" Joy stood before her, eyes wide, hands clasped.

Gloria winced when her hip banged the counter edge. Joy could read her with a glance. How could she allow such thoughts with Joy in the house? "Can I get you breakfast?" She sweetened her voice, just as she'd sweetened that cold coffee with spoonfuls of sugar. "How about oatmeal? There's a cinnamon roll—"

"Mom, I'll grab something." Joy pulled Gloria into a hug and the smell of bubble gum.

Gloria gazed at Joy, who wore a simple cotton blouse and a skirt patterned with zebras. Her hair had been pulled to the side and pinned with an ivory clip.

Gloria smiled. Joy, her Joy, looked like a million dollars.

Money. Shoplifting. A tremble began, deep in Gloria. "You look wonderful, Joy. Um, I've not seen that outfit before, have I?"

Joy's eyes narrowed, but there was no malice in them. Talk about a change.

"No worries, Mom. Dad dropped me at the thrift store after school. He gave me an advance against my job."

Relieved, Gloria leaned back. While she'd recuperated in a Harris hospital room, Joy had visited the gift shop . . . and the business office. "They already called you?"

"Uh-huh. I start right away. Only fifteen hours a week. But it's a start."

"That's why you're all dressed up. At least you don't have to wear scrubs."

"Actually, I do. I got those too." Joy wrinkled her nose. "It's kinda gross, wearing used work clothes. But it's all I can afford, at least for now."

"We could help you out. . . ."

"No, Mom." Joy's hands performed their dance. "It's something I have to do on my own. Like go to church with you today."

Tears sprung into Gloria's eyes. Joy hadn't set foot in church since . . . had it been two years? She tried to remember what had incited Joy's last exodus, but it jumbled into incidents of snubbing and sanctimony and legalism. "Joy," she finally managed to say past the expansion of her heart into her throat, "you don't know what this means to me."

"I think I do." Suddenly Gloria was staring into a gaze like Kai's. Level. Steady. Compassionate. *Just what I need.*

"So get your Bible, Mom. I'll tell Dad we'll meet him there."

⌒◌⌒

By the light of a red Boston sunrise, Kai sat at her desk and pored over preliminary findings of a daring clinical trial. Which MRA patients might benefit? She thumbed back a

240

page, searched for the inclusion criteria. Mrs. Connally. Mr. Devries. Near the end, barring a miracle. Words blurred as she searched for contact information and scribbled it on a pad.

Kai continued to read. Sunbeams blazed swaths across her gray carpet. The faint notes of birdsong penetrated closed windows. Hope despite so much despair. Kai rubbed her eyes. It was barely six a.m., and she'd zipped through files, plotted out her Monday. Amazing how a desk could be cleared when there was no David to occupy her time.

She shoved away a pang of sorrow and scribbled a plan of attack for Joy. By Wednesday, precious Fourth Daughter would be ushered into MRA with the fanfare they'd accorded that civil rights leader/patient . . . who had passed away last fall.

PKD.

Again.

Kai clenched the pen and stared at dust motes floating, helpless against the whims of physics. Here one minute, gone the next.

What every human faced, sooner or later.

"Kai?" Dr. Duncan, the forty-five-year-old founder of MRA, stuck his head into her office. "You're here bright and early."

Wearily, Kai rose. "Yes, with the birds." She affected cheeriness for her boss. "Good morning, Doctor."

Gaunt even in scrubs, with the hollowed-cheek look of a long-distance runner, Dr. Duncan waved her back into her seat. "What's it gonna take for you to call me Paul?"

Kai ducked her head to hide what surely were blazing cheeks. This man had hired her over a rumored pool of five hundred applicants. Imagine, such a legend, choosing a nearly penniless Chinese woman over the world's best young

241

doctors . . . then asking her to call him Paul! "I do not think it will happen, Doctor."

Dr. Duncan slapped a file folder against his leg. "One a' these days, we'll loosen you up, Kai. Hope I'm around to see it."

She smiled. "I hope you are around too."

Another guffaw informed her that she had said something funny. It happened constantly with her American friends. Though Kai was puzzled, she delighted in lightening their hearts, especially healers like this man, burdened with issues of life and death.

Dr. Duncan handed her a folder. "Here's the agenda. Sorry I didn't get it to you Friday. I had a 'take a look-see' that took . . . till midnight." A grin showed he didn't mind. Imagine, MRA's senior partner, still on weekend rotation, helping colleagues. An idea pricked. She tried to set it aside, but it wouldn't be dismissed. "Our meeting is at eight, correct?" This must be done carefully. One step at a time, as David always said.

"No, Kai. 8:05. If you don't behave, I'll tell Janine." They chuckled at the office manager's techniques to keep them punctual by scheduling meetings at odd times . . . like 8:05. MRA's efficiency soothed Kai's frazzled edges. She, Chang Kai, belonged to a practice where every hire oozed passion . . . or was told to clean out his desk.

"I am not keeping you from work?"

Dr. Duncan put his hands on his hips. "Whaddya want, Kai? Spit it out!"

Kai was tempted to dig at her hands, as Gloria did when "put on the spot"—another American phrase she'd conquered. "There is a personal matter I wish to discuss."

Did his dark eyes widen? Surely he wished at this moment

to flee what could be news of a tawdry affair, plagiarism, scandal. Something she would never inflict on this hallowed institution. She could not blame Dr. Duncan. He did not know her heart. "Yes, Kai. Of course." He pulled close the chair where her patients normally sat. Now her desk—and ethnicity, culture, experience, gender—separated them. Kai again fought Gloria's strange habit of punishing her hands. *Am I making a mistake by confiding in him?*

Dr. Duncan leaned back. "What is it, Kai?" Deep-set eyes crinkled, as if preparing to hear the worst. Not surprising, in their profession. She hoped to pleasantly surprise him.

"It is my sister."

"Your sister? I thought she was in China."

Kai looked out the window. The sky had been painted blue and spoke of hope. The blossoms of magnolia trees, planted in neat rows, braved the brisk spring breeze. She could trust this man with Joy. She must.

"I have three sisters. Two live in China. Years ago, our youngest sister was placed in an orphanage. She was adopted by Americans. Just two weeks ago we were reunited down in Texas."

"Congratulations" came out in a guarded way. Of course Dr. Duncan would dissect each word, for he did not yet know what she would ask of him.

"Yes, it was a Joy." She smiled at what David called a play on words, then cleared her throat when Dr. Duncan did not so much as blink. "But there are complications."

Skin stretched across that grizzled face, again preparing for the worst. She would not let him worry an instant longer.

"PKD runs in our family. She has displayed symptoms."

Dr. Duncan groaned. It was surely a groan for the millions afflicted—dear Mrs. Rodriguez, who could no longer leave her bed; precious little Sarah, whose body had rejected her donor kidney. It was condolence for the patients whose files bulged their cabinets. It was the doctor's response to a killer until a weapon was found to obliterate PKD from every people group, from every country. Until then, they would fight. Yes, they would fight. Though the numbers, perhaps the early hour, was numbing her brain, she straightened to refocus on Joy. "I will meet my sister and her parents Wednesday at Logan."

"What time?"

"Midafternoon."

With his jaw tightened, his nose sharp and beaklike, his eyes unblinking and bright, Dr. Duncan resembled a bird of prey. *A formidable ally . . . if he is on my side.*

"I'll clear my schedule, Kai. Three o'clock will be fine."

"You mean you would consider . . ." Of course she heard his answer; exactly what she had wanted. Still, his acceding to her wishes so quickly sucked the air from her lungs.

"I would like to see her." He rose. Jabbed hands into his lab coat pockets. "Have the Texas folks fax her records. Everything from vitals to when she said her first word."

Kai grinned. "Aye-aye."

"In the meantime, call Ruth at the transplant unit. Tell her your sister . . . What's her name?"

"Joy. Joy Powell."

"Hmmm. Joy. I like that." Dr. Duncan moved toward the door. "Ask Ruth for an appointment. She's gonna balk since we don't have her work-up, but get Joy on the list. In the system." The threshold frame was gripped with Dr. Duncan's powerful hand. "When I call in, they'll have a name." His eyes narrowed. "Make it for Friday. That's pushing it, but who knows? Maybe we'll get a miracle."

Kai grabbed the word from the air, glad to make re-acquaintance, then bowed low. "It is a miracle. I am privileged to have you do my sister's work-up."

Their senior partner chuckled. "Cut it out, Kai. That isn't the miracle. The miracle is we had a conversation about something besides work." He grimaced. "Kinda."

Wide-mouthed and clueless, Kai stared at her boss as he ambled down the hall. So he wished to speak to her about something besides work? Whatever could that mean? Shaking her head, she returned to her desk.

<hr />

"An apple a day keeps the doctor away," laughed Deanne, a single mother who'd waitressed through nursing school and brought humor and efficiency to MRA. Of a stellar nursing staff, Deanne, who now stood by Kai's desk, was Kai's favorite.

Kai set down her Red Delicious.

"Sure you don't want to join us?" Deanne handed Kai the requested file. "Monday's half-price pizza, not that you rich doctors care. We're talking Little Italy . . ."

Unlike her colleagues, Kai had resisted a love affair with cheese and doughy crust and in the past saved time for David by skipping lunch. That might change, but not today. "Ah, pizza." She encouraged Deanne with a smile. "Eat a slice for me."

"No problem there." With her robust figure, Deanne likely ate many extra slices. "Ya need anything else?"

"No, but thank you." Kai waved Deanne out the door and waited until all but a skeleton staff jabbered their way to lunch before she grabbed the file and opened it.

Transplant Donor Procedures.

Kai had no need to study the thick document, having updated it for her practice six months ago. She punched in the phone number at the top of the page.

"Transplant Unit. Ten South."

"This is Kai from MRA. May I speak to Jeanette, please?"

"Just one moment."

Kai was put on hold, with jazz music to settle her nerves. They needed settling.

"Jeanette speaking."

"Hello, Jeanette. This is Kai, Dr. Duncan's associate at MRA."

"Yes." The rushed Boston dialect braked. A pleasant tone took hold. "He left a message. Said to expect your call."

Kai opened and closed her mouth. So many times since she had stepped off that United Airlines jet, America had rolled out a red carpet. Unexpected kindness still took away her breath. To think that a man of Dr. Duncan's repute would make a call for her!

"How can I help you, Doctor?" An edge whittled away congeniality. After all, this was Boston. Monday. A busy hospital.

Kai picked up her pen . . . and vowed to adopt the Boston style. "Did Dr. Duncan explain our predicament?"

"Huh-uh. He just told me to help you out."

"I would like you to schedule an appointment for a patient."

"Have you got the preliminaries?"

"The patient arrives in forty-eight hours." Kai flipped open her Day-Timer.

"Normally we wait until prelims are in."

"We do as well." Kai smoothed into the next part. "This time we would like to make an exception."

The sound of a bell dinging crept into the silence. Mass

General's Transplant Unit surely pulsated with dramas that beat with the lifeblood of this great city. If all went according to plan, Kai's movements would integrate with the work, the sacrifice of others . . . and help her sister.

"What's the patient's name?" huffed Jeanette, suddenly blowing full-fledged attitude over the phone.

"Joy Powell." Kai pressed her lips together. *This one makes it clear she is doing a favor. The first of many I will need.* "I would like to request one more appointment." She kept her tone businesslike.

"Say what?" shrieked Jeanette.

"One more appointment. This one for donor consideration."

"A donor appointment? Without an official patient?" Suspicion crept into Jeanette's voice. "Dr. Duncan knows about this?"

Kai loudly riffled the pages of the handbook for Jeanette's benefit. "I have the TU procedures manual here. There is no limitation on an unsolicited donor—"

"Provided he or she completes the extensive psychological and physical screening and genetic marking work-up," Jeanette finished for her. *An efficient one. Not necessarily compassionate. Often a bad combination.*

"Which we will have the donor do. To save precious time, we would like to schedule an appointment. In the event a . . . donor is needed—"

"And all the prerequisites are completed . . ."

"Exactly." Kai battled irritation. She disdained the American habit of chasing another's words and brushing past them. Still, she was the one who needed a favor.

"So you want an appointment," snapped Jeanette. "Actually, two of them."

"Also for Friday. Or earlier."

"Well, I can tell ya, earlier ain't gonna happen."

"Fine. We will settle for Friday."

"Let me get this straight." Attitude blew out what little reserve Jeanette had retained. "You want something put on hold, like at Kmart. Blue-light special, maybe?"

Kai pressed her lips together. Another dislike: American fondness for sarcasm. In the Chinese way, she waited. Jeanette had a choice: irritate an MRA associate or cut a corner. Nothing unethical or immoral. Just a favor. For someone special. Like Joy.

"I suppose it's all right," the woman finally snarled.

An abrupt click returned jazz to Kai's ear. She sketched their banyan tree, the hill near her village—and stared at the paper. She had not drawn the banyan in years.

"Friday. At eight o'clock sharp. Take it or leave it." It was Jeanette, brasher than ever. *Ready to be done with me. I am ready to be done with her as well.*

Kai carefully copied the information onto her calendar, repeated it, and thanked Jeanette.

"The donor's name?" Jeanette spoke as if Kai were inefficient, stupid, or both.

"Chang Kaiping."

"*Chang . . . Kai . . . ping?*"

"Would you like for me to spell it?" Kai could not help but smile at Jeanette's spluttering. One day they would meet, and she would win this woman over. It would prove difficult, but she had forged other initially reluctant alliances.

"Yes . . ."

Kai complied. "Again, thank you, Jeanette."

"Wait a minute. You said Kai. Aren't you Kai? Are you Chang as well?"

"Yes."

"Is that one of those things, like, you know, Debbie Smith?"

"With over one billion people in China, there are many common names. In this case, Dr. Chang Kai of MRA and Dr. Chang Kai the potential donor are one and the same." With a third thank-you and a last smile, Kai hung up the phone.

20

Magnolia trees ringed a sleek glass-and-steel building that reflected orange blurs of cabs, the greens of those trees, and most of all, the glorious sun. *If only it would warm my ice-cold hands!*

Glass doors to Kai's medical building slid open noise-lessly. Gloria, walking ahead of Andrew and Joy, craned her neck, felt her eyes widen with wonder. The sky-lit ceiling of a two-story atrium anchored huge hanging baskets of massive spider plants and Swedish ivy. Tendrils tumbled and swayed in a soothing rhythm that slowed her breathing, her racing mind. This was a doctors' office? In Texas, they'd add shops and call it a mall.

A familiar dark-haired woman wearing scrubs rose from a stone bench centering the atrium. *It's her!* As the three of them hightailed it to Kai, Gloria heaved a grateful breath. To have jealousy and fear purged was as miraculous as finding magnolias up north.

Joy bear-hugged Kai. Another man, dressed in the same blue scrubs as Kai, stepped toward her and Andrew. "Reverend and Mrs. Powell?" The man had an athletic build and a deep tan. "I'm Paul Duncan, Kai's associate. Glad you're seeing Boston in the springtime." She and Andrew shook Paul's hand. "Our team here at MRA will provide Joy with whatever she needs." As Gloria savored the gravelly, guttural dialect first heard in Boston cabs and their hotel, surprise welled up. She'd expected courtesy from Kai, certainly warmth toward Joy, but never celebrity treatment for Texas hicks.

Joy's enthusiasm—and a tight grip—dragged Kai close to Gloria and Andrew. "It's just, like, wow! They've got Freedom Trail footsteps painted right on the street!"

Gloria beamed with pride at the day's new mercies, like Joy growing up. Then she remembered why they were here. *God, surely you won't take her . . . as you took . . . our baby.*

A fresh wave of grief hit, but Gloria drank in Joy's laughter as a tonic essential for her health and clung to Andrew. She'd get by. New mercies every day.

Kai and Dr. Duncan led them into a spacious lounge where they were greeted by half a dozen folks, wearing the same blue scrubs with the MRA emblem. Gloria took in walls softened by watercolor paintings of lilies and trees bursting with hot pink blooms before they were led by a smiling nurse into Kai's private office. Chairs and a small table offered a window view. Under the watchful gaze of those magnolias she'd marveled over earlier, Gloria and Andrew filled out enough forms—insurance information, background questions, release statements—to bulge a new file. Tiny print faded in and out, reminding her of other forms connected with her baby . . . and Dr. Davies' words at her checkup post-miscarriage.

"I know how badly you wanted this, Gloria. I'm sorry." Dr. Davies had drummed her fingers against the folder, which held clinical details of her little one's life and death, then

251

fixed Gloria with a compassionate gaze. *"There's a good chance it'll happen again."* Dr. Davies shut the folder. *"A guy in Houston is doing wonders with high-risk pregnancies. Problem is, insurance doesn't often cover it—"*

"Mom!" Right as tears threatened, Joy burst into the room, Kai trailing. Joy beamed as if she were strolling on the Freedom Trail instead of being tested for a disease. "I'm going back now."

Joy's and Kai's resemblance tugged at Gloria . . . and reminded her that she had no siblings, no one who shared her DNA, except her parents. She shoved up her sleeves, begging the thoughts to leave. "You'll do great, dear," she managed.

Kai smiled brightly. "The CT scans, the blood work, the complete physical will take most of the afternoon. Dr. Duncan estimates we'll be done by five. Four thirty, if this one cooperates." She playfully boxed Joy's arm. "In the meantime, you are welcome to stay in here. You did say you had eaten lunch, correct?"

Gloria nodded.

"Please." Kai swept her hand as if showing off her slice of the kidney kingdom. Her hospitality dimmed Gloria's memories. "Make yourself at home. Use the computer. The phone. The receptionist—Betsy—can help with anything you might need."

Andrew shook his head, surely in disbelief at the warm reception . . . or remembering the cold shoulder Gloria had offered Kai in Fort Worth. Oh, that she could rewind and replay those scenes!

"We can't thank you enough."

"It is no problem, Reverend Powell. I am honored to be of service."

"Um, Mom? Dad?"

Joy wants something. She'll more likely get it, with this smile and twinkly eyes instead of that old huff and frown.

"Can I . . . stay with Kai? Just tonight? She lives on the Back Bay, not far from here at all. She said tomorrow we could do that Freedom Trail. Then lunch." The gleam of sisterhood dazzled those gorgeous almond eyes.

Andrew caught Gloria's gaze, then studied his hands, clearly giving her the veto power. Affection, respect . . . her husband nailed his role in every way. Gloria shivered with desire. It had been too long since she'd showed him what he meant to her.

"Your parents have just gotten settled." Kai placed a restraining hand on Joy's shoulder, displaying the woman's admirable ability to mask emotions. *Surely she craves time with her long-lost sister, but she's putting me first. Or so she thinks!* "Perhaps another day, Joy," Kai continued.

"Why not now?" Gloria blurted, thinking of the sisters, thinking of her Andrew, *thinking of me.* "That . . . that is, if you don't mind, Kai."

The mask finally disappeared. Kai beamed. "It would be a . . . great joy."

They all laughed. Then she and Andrew huddled with Joy for a three-way hug, suddenly in vogue. *Lord, may it never go out of style!*

Dr. Duncan entered the office and touched Kai's shoulder. "Hey! Do I need to call a posse?" His eyes radiated compassion . . . for Kai, Joy, or both? Gloria studied the man's craggy handsomeness. Did Kai have a love interest, or was this part of MRA's VIP care?

After the sisters left, Andrew pulled Gloria into an embrace. "That was nice."

She studied his face. "What do you mean?"

"Giving them time together." Andrew began to nuzzle her neck.

Speaking of time.

Gloria gave Andrew a lingering kiss. "I didn't do it for them. I did it for us."

Andrew's breath quickened. "Does that mean what I think it means?"

"I don't know what you're thinking, but I'm thinking that king-sized hotel bed." She grabbed hold of Andrew's belt loops and pulled him form-fittingly close. "And much, much more."

⌒◯⌒

Kai tilted her face as sunbeams eased the early-morning chill. PKD would not ruin this time gifted by the Powells and the associate who had seen to her patients. A tremor shook Kai's hand. Time gifted by the Christian God? As Cheryl had prayed last night, had such a being truly brought Joy to their brownstone? To Boston? *To me?*

Joy ripped off a hunk of "the works" bagel, freckled with sesame and pepper and garlic, and slathered it with thick cream cheese. "This is amazing!"

Kai sipped what Bostonians called tea and grimaced. A café near the site of the famous Tea Party should do better. She pulled out their walking guide and tried to forget that David had introduced her to the Independence Trail . . . and to romance.

"There's our first stop!" Her words garbled by a mouthful of bagel, Joy scooted her chair close to see the map. "We'll start at the beginning and see where that line takes us." The very thing David had said. When would he stop barging into her life?

"Ooh!" Joy wiped her mouth and swallowed the last of her juice. "Like, let's go!"

It was First Daughter's spirit that enabled Kai to leave David in the marketplace of Faneuil Hall. *If only he'll stay here.*

~

"It's so cool!" Her hands extended like a tightrope artist, Joy minced along the two-brick-wide line to the Granary Burial Ground. Joy looked every bit the all-American girl, wearing faded blue jeans and a USA T-shirt . . . *if I ignore the purple hair.* Huffing to keep up, Kai followed Joy and camera-toting tourists into the fenced-off grassy cemetery.

Kai squinted to read *1652–1730* on a grave marker. She peeked over Joy's shoulder, curious about this Sewall, an unfamiliar name; one overshadowed by Franklin, Revere, and Hancock.

"'Sewall gained notoriety presiding over the Salem Witch Trials.'" They stood under a stand of trees, Joy reading as Kai tried to follow along. "'Few know he later apologized.'" Joy slapped the guide against faded denim. "That's what bugs me about religion. It's all about rules and values that in ten years are, like, obsolete."

Anxiety crept in. As she'd carefully stepped on this hallowed ground, Kai vowed to tread lightly on this volatile subject. She did not want religion to erect a barrier between them now that walls were crumbling like centuries-old grave markers.

"It is a difficult situation." Kai nodded slightly, a motion contradicting the waves that rocked her stomach. She must digress. "We all face difficult situations."

Joy puffed out her lips. Her hands flew to her hips. The

guide fluttered in the midmorning breeze. "What do you mean?"

"We stand on sacred ground." Kai panned the now-crowded cemetery. "Patriots choosing freedom." Determined to change the subject, she avoided Joy's eyes. "I cannot help but think of our ancestors, buried in such a different place."

As she had hoped, Joy's eyebrows met that purple clomp of bangs. "You mean, like, not a cemetery?"

Kai shook her head. "On a hill overlooking our village. Hallowed ground, just the same." Kai pictured lush green rises, the view of seven distinct villages, Father and the three daughters, carrying money and incense to be burned.

"Do . . . did you visit them?"

"Days are set aside to do so. A failure to honor ancestors brings the wrath of—"

Joy's countenance darkened. "More rules, huh. Figures."

Kai battled an urge to shake this impudent being. "It is an honor," she managed. "Something done out of respect, out of love."

As if in agreement, or because Kai had let indignity swell her tone, a flock of sparrows whooshed from the trees. Birdsong drowned out the tourist chatter and the rush of traffic on nearby Tremont. Kai had put Joy "on the spot," as David said. It was right where Joy needed to be.

Joy scuffed her tennis shoes against spring-green grass tufts. Was that remorse heightening the lovely blush of her cheeks?

"It is the Chinese heritage." Kai lowered her voice. She did not want to spoil this special time with lectures. "Your heritage. My heritage. Perhaps one day we will walk that ground together. Then you will understand."

Joy nodded, as if her heart were too full to utter a word.

Kai smiled and pulled the guide from Joy's clenched fist. "Speaking of walking, there is much ahead if we are to conquer the Freedom Road by lunchtime." With Kai leading the way, they continued north—Bunker Hill their eventual destination.

∽

One if by land, two if by sea. Old North Church, with its historic bell chamber, captivated Joy, who responded with wide eyes and oohs and aahs. Thankfully the flickering candles, sacred garden, and arched windows had not spawned more religion talk. Fatigue took hold of Kai as they soldiered on, Bunker Hill now in sight. Yet Joy's exuberant arm-waving acted as a tonic. Never had the word *cool* sounded so good. They crossed a busy Charlestown street and entered the park.

Joy, her hand a visor, faced the famous monument. "Like, that's amazing."

Amazing. Like. If Kai got a dollar for every time she'd heard those words, she could buy an airline ticket to China. She glanced at Joy. Make that two.

Joy's chatter and the lure of the granite obelisk coaxed Kai to soldier on. They browsed at a gift shop filled with flags, decals, and shirts, all in red, white, and blue. Liberty bells of a dozen sizes and prices festooned a table. One youngster clanged away, to the irritation of a harried clerk. Kai feasted on the boy's dimpled chin and impish smile. David's hints—which seemed to have occurred in another century—had led her to dream of marriage . . . perhaps even children. Another horizon, dimmed.

"Look, Kai!" Joy's squeal returned Kai to reality but did not ease the strange heaviness in her chest. "We can go to the top!"

Kai suppressed a groan. Cheryl's nagging about an exercise regimen just paid off. *A thirty-five-year-old should not be this out of shape.*

"Two hundred ninety-four steps! Are you up to it?" Joy grinned, showing well-formed teeth—a blessing to one born where dentistry was an unheard-of luxury.

Kai glanced at her watch. They had time before meeting the Powells for lunch. She squared sagging shoulders and mustered false bravado. "I am if you are."

Joy heaved open a heavy door. "One, two, three . . ." Her pattering echoed in the tight-spiral staircase. "See you at the top!" rang in Kai's ears.

Kai took a deep breath and gripped the handrail. *Maybe next year,* she bit back.

"A hundred ten, a hundred eleven . . ."

Kai's chest hammered, echoing in her ears along with Joy's counting. She stopped twice to wipe sweat from her face, to ease the burn in her lungs. The stairs wound so tightly, she could only see one staircase segment at a time. *Perhaps that is a good thing . . .*

No longer could she hear Joy calling out the step number for the buzzing in her ears. Surely Joy neared the top. *Will I make it?*

Her legs screamed, as did her lungs. She changed tactics and approached each step as an old friend, caressing it with the sole of her shoe, lingering as if it had something to teach her.

"Kai! I made it! Are you down there?"

Joy seemed to be calling from China.

Kai leaned against musty stone and summoned the strength to utter, "Um-hum."

"C'mon! It's so cool!"

258

Then I must hurry. Fortified by Joy's wondrous tone, Kai clambered on, her gaze nailing each weathered step. She began to mentally count the steps, for the breath to utter numbers had evaporated.

Around ninety-nine, an image of Father flicked in Kai's mind . . . along with a horrid thought. Perhaps Cultural Revolution indignities had not caused Father's stroke. Perhaps the Chang line had been cursed with heart disease as well as PKD.

Kai's chest heaved, both to fuel her movements and to expel the horrid thought. Mental counting—mental anything— stopped. Finally a rectangle of light carpeted the step above her foot. Though her lungs burned protest, her spirits rose. Joy. A view. The top.

Huffing, sweating, she stumbled onto the final step.

Joy whirled about. "Look! There's four of these!" Sun rays beamed through an oblong window and tinted Joy's hair brown-pink. "You can see north, south, east—" Her eyebrows crunched. "Hey, you don't look so hot. Are you okay?"

Kai nodded, not able to speak. To divert attention from her poor conditioning, she slogged to the south window.

The harbor unfolded. Squinting, she spotted the masts of Old Ironsides, which were solid, sure, still standing even after a war. Sunlight glittered the water. Kai's breath slowed. She rested her palms on the Plexiglas, drawn to this city—this country—that had opened its harbor to her and unlocked the treasure chests of education and career.

"When I look out there"—Joy's voice echoed across the space they were fortunate enough to see by private viewing— "I can almost believe there is a God."

Kai leaned forward, bent her knees, and arched her back until the window supported her. Religion had dogged them the distance of the Freedom Trail. Could she not escape it?

"You never said what you think about religion." Joy's words smacked Kai's back.

So we will discuss it, whether I wish to or not. Her face pressed against the cool window, Kai closed her eyes and envisioned Old Grandfather. Though it felt awkward, she begged him to help. Slowly she turned, shifting the support of her body to her arms, which were propped against cold stone. With all the honesty she could muster, she met Joy's gaze. "Like you, when I look out there"—she nodded toward the window—"I want to believe there is a God." Emotion swelled her achy chest. "When I make the rounds at the dialysis unit, I want to believe there is a God."

Joy stepped closer. Neither of them blinked.

"When I look at your face and see both the hope of tomorrow and what was good about our past, I want to believe there is a God. When—" Her throat closed. There was nothing left that language could express.

A breathy lunge brought Joy into her arms. With abandon, Kai drew her close, felt sobs against her breast, felt tears trickle down her face.

"Thank . . . thank you."

Kai drank in the priceless elixir of Joy's words. She had erected no new wall with religion talk. Perhaps she had further cleared the path to intimacy with this sister. Another miracle.

For the first time since discovering that word *miracle*, Kai did not question its reality. As she reveled in Fourth Daughter's embrace, two questions tugged at her consciousness: Was the Christian God the author of such miracles? If so, how could she thank Him?

21

They'd reunited with a rosy Gloria, a jovial Andrew, and ate what Joy called a "yummy lunch" at a Bunker Hill bistro. The cabbie had pulled by the Stanford to drop off the Powells and then weaved and honked his way past mounted police, a funeral procession, and harried motorists.

Kai checked her watch. Two hours until the consult with the Powells and Dr. Duncan. With Joy waving her arms and laughing, with the delightful spring breeze, Kai had convinced herself the seizing of her breath on Bunker Hill was stress-related. She had always enjoyed excellent health. If heart disease ran in her family, likely it would take years to develop. She walked more often than she rode, favored a vegetarian diet—

The cabbie screeched to a halt at a light, avoiding a collision with careless pedestrians.

Kai sat up straight. No. She would not take a chance. Father had had a stroke at age forty. Perhaps a genetic predisposition was a nasty accomplice to sadistic prison guards to foil Father's health. *Those genes might doom my plan of action for Joy. I must know. Now.*

The atrium's beauty failed to soothe her as usual. Kai

hurried in the back way, a rare avoidance of the waiting room. She stowed her handbag under her desk and checked her messages. Nothing pressing. Good.

Not bothering to change into scrubs, she pattered to the nurses' station. By the counter stood Deanne. Another miracle, though minor compared to the others she had experienced. Kai shoved down the anxiety that tickled her throat. "Good afternoon."

"Back at ya, Doc." Deanne jotted on a chart and stuffed it into an examining room rack. "I wondered if you'd ever come in. You're gettin' wild and crazy in your old age."

Kai grinned. This month, she had taken more vacation than in two previous years.

"Guess that happens when you meet a long-lost sister," Deanne continued.

Not wanting to talk about Joy, especially not now, Kai continued a silent smile.

"She's a doll," added Deanne, with a cheerful yet perceptive glance, then returned to her work. *Your sixth sense, Deanne. Another reason you are my favorite.*

"Thank you." Kai stepped to the counter and waited. It would not do to interrupt a nurse, especially with a personal request.

Deanne slung files into the out-box, called a pharmacist, then took a message for Dr. Salvadore. Again Kai yearned to claw her hands.

"Doc, can I help you, or are you looking over my shoulder, waiting for me to mess up?" Deanne's curls proved as lively as her wit. Kai chuckled to keep up a gaiety charade.

"You should be looking over my shoulder."

"Aw, c'mon," gushed her favorite nurse. "Spit it out. Whaddya want?"

"When time permits, could you check my blood pressure?"

"Time permits." Deanne cocked her head and gave Kai the once-over. "Now."

That's what I hoped you would say. Kai followed Deanne into check-in, partitioned from the nurses' area by a glass-block wall topped with pots of ivy. Kai sat at one of three vitals stations. Vines curled toward skylights and added texture and color to soothing gray walls. A prestigious architecture firm had designed their offices to nurture and heal via this organic, fluid design.

The design did nothing to calm the stiffening of Kai's muscles. *Please, Mr. Christian God, help me,* ran through her mind.

Deanne moved a monitor stand close to Kai. "So what's this about?" Big brown eyes probed and poked. *Better than needles.*

Kai crossed her leg. "You nurses know us best." She adopted a jaunty tone. "Physicians do not heal themselves."

Deanne craned her neck, as if checking the hall for big ears. "C'mon." She wore the expression of an irritated professor. "You gotta tell me more than that."

"I am sure it is nothing."

Deanne snorted, as if irritated to be excluded from a secret.

"How is Daniel?" To soothe the nurse's ruffled feelings, Kai asked about Deanne's son, diagnosed with Asperger's. "Still building model airplanes?"

"Seventy-six and counting."

A little boy, shut off from so many, yet desperate to fly. Kai managed a melancholy smile. "That takes perseverance. Intelligence. You should be proud of him."

Blinking, Deanne nodded as she adjusted the pressure cuff, took a reading, snorted, readjusted the cuff, and took another reading.

"Have you decided about his schooling?" The pressure-building silence caused Kai to talk, just to talk. *Day by day I become more American.*

For an answer, Deanne ripped the Velcro cuff from Kai's arm and tossed it on a counter. "What's normal for you?"

Kai gripped her knees. "I haven't checked in years."

"Physician, heal thyself." Absent was Deanne's usual humorous tone.

"110 over 78." Kai donned the mask of flippancy. "Something like that."

"Something like that, huh?" Deanne clucked her tongue. "I just took it twice. Both times it was 140 over 110."

Kai's arm ached, as if she still wore the cuff. Her pressure could be indicative of a problem. Essential hypertension, renal artery stenosis . . .

Deanne ran her hand through her curls. "You'd better see that heart doctor."

Kai winced as if she had been slapped. Of course they knew about David. Some had joked. Fished for nibbles. She had never bitten, had just given what David called her Cheshire cat smile. If any queried her now, she would continue to evade the question, unwilling to discuss the truth: There was no heart doctor now.

"Let's check that pulse." Deanne rested one hand on the back of Kai's chair, the other on Kai's wrist. She cast her eyes on a wall clock. "Hmm," she finally said. "Low, but I guess that's good." Deanne looked her in the eye. "I don't need to tell you . . . or maybe I do. Get this checked out."

"I am fine," Kai lied. "It is just the stress from traveling, of making arrangements for my sister. I have never done well with travel," she again lied. David hated her save-face lies. But David wasn't here. . . .

Deanne brushed her hands together, as if ridding herself of this matter. For now. "Fine or not, check this out. Hear me?"

Kai forced a smile so this competent nurse would leave her with her sorrow. "I hear you loud and clear."

Deanne left the room. Kai remained sitting in the cold, hard chair, her third lie cozied up next to her.

She had not heard Deanne loud and clear, for those numbers had nearly drowned out the nurse's voice. 140 over 110.

High blood pressure. Father's genetics. Kai rubbed the arm that had been cuffed. It made sense that she might inherit such a problem, but that did not assuage the blow.

She buried her face in her hands. High blood pressure blacklisted her as a donor. She knew the words, had *written* the words, had chosen the neat, scientific font for the transplant procedures manual. Unless Deanne, one of their practice's most competent nurses, had botched her job, she would never qualify as a donor for Lily. Never.

As she rose, a wildfire swept through her and crackled rage. She had so carefully planned for every contingency, so sure that she, with the resources of MRA, could transcend obstacles erected by—whom? If not fate, whom could she blame? Her foot flexed with an urge to vent her fury on the indifferent blood pressure stand.

"Dr. Kai, you have a call on line two," intoned Betsy over the intercom in an irritatingly efficient manner.

You are a doctor, she told herself as she returned to her office and sat at her desk. *Perhaps you will learn today that Joy will not need your help.*

She stared past the blinking phone button to her wall of certificates and diplomas, whose golden seals and loopy calligraphy now mocked her. They were all meaningless. For the first time since she had discovered the Healing Right Hand,

Kai doubted she could heal anyone. Not the five patients scheduled to see her today. Not her sister Joy, who would come in for her consult and test results. Not herself. Especially not herself.

❧

She's clinging to her daddy in her old happy-go-lucky way. Gloria trotted to catch up with Andrew and Joy, who were following Kai down a hall lined with examining rooms. *And I'm about to bite off my nails.*

A sharp right took them into a conference area dominated by a gleaming oval table. A serene seascape hung next to botanical prints. Tasteful. Soothing. Moneyed. Except for the presence of two doctors, it could've been a boardroom in any successful corporation—not the MRA office where they would learn if their Joy had PKD.

Kai rose, her mouth tight. Dark strands escaped her bun, usually so sleek and styled. Tension increased. Had Joy's diagnosis swept Kai into a tempest?

"Sit down, please. Make yourself comfortable."

Joy hurried to the chair by Kai. They exchanged secret smiles. Sister smiles. A perfect antidote for worry. Gloria sat next to Andrew, leaned close, and inhaled his comforting fresh scent. *Oh, God, get us through this. Whichever way it goes.*

Dr. Duncan nodded at Kai, who rose, closed the door, and returned to her seat. Though an Oriental rug muted the sound, every footfall thudded worry. At times like this, God seemed capricious, as if He relished holding lives by a thread. Death. Life. Sickness. Health. Gloria bit her lip. She sounded like a heathen.

"Here you go." Dr. Duncan passed out stapled copies of a report. *The* report.

Gloria recalled the station adjustment. Joy's life, again reduced to papers.

"Thank you for the privilege of examining Joy," said Dr. Duncan.

"Oh, we thank you."

Chattering teeth kept Gloria from voicing thanks, as Andrew had. She appreciated the VIP treatment, but enough was enough. PKD or not? She picked up the paper, studied rows of numbers, and set down the medical mumbo jumbo. *Tell me, before I scream!*

In her uncanny way of sensing emotions, Kai darted an encouraging smile. "We have good news, though there is one more avenue to be explored."

"But it's good news." Dr. Duncan rubbed his palms together. "Good news."

Recessed lighting seemed to brighten and halo the paintings. A soothing breeze swept through Gloria. For the first time in weeks, she breathed, really breathed. *No PKD? Say it, then! Scream it!* The retorts sizzled on the tip of her tongue.

Joy leaned against Kai, a childlike smile on her face. Tears misted Kai's eyes and made her look fragile, older, despite her classic Asian beauty. *Though she does it silently, she has been worried sick about Joy . . . just like me.*

"Well, that's . . . great!" Andrew's voice swelled. The papers in his hand rattled. "But . . . what exactly does it mean?"

Gloria longed to high-five him. *Exactly!*

"We did an exhaustive battery of tests." Dr. Duncan pulled glasses from his scrubs pocket and put them on. "First the basics. WBC, CBC. BP, 110 over 85."

Gloria ran her finger along the columns of data.

"BP—toward the middle of the first page—sends up a flare." Deep-set eyes peered over half-rims.

A flare. Gloria poked the nasty number with her fingernail. *Doesn't sound like good news to me.*

"Something we'll check out." With a wave from Dr. Duncan, the flare was extinguished. Air whooshed from Gloria.

"What's encouraging is the RFP."

Kai leaned past Andrew to nab Gloria's attention. "Kidney function."

Dr. Duncan nodded. "Glucose, BUN, creatinine . . ."

Gloria found the numbers on her page, followed along.

". . . GFR, potassium, at excellent levels."

Tears blurred. An internal hallelujah drowned out doc-speak. Gloria wiped her eyes, took in the list of elements and substances that God had used to form her Joy. *Before you were in your mother's womb, I knew you,* her soul sang.

"Normal, all of it," continued Dr. Duncan. "Absolutely normal. As to Joy's occasional upset and digestive disturbances, I would suggest that they are tied to stress. We'll order a colonoscopy if symptoms persist. Other tests."

A colonoscopy? At Joy's age? Gloria gripped the table edge. Surely they wouldn't be stalked by another disease. "Like . . . what? What would we be looking for?"

Joy tapped the table. Shorthand for "*Moth*-er!"

In her intuitive way, Kai again caught Gloria's eye. "Let us not put the truck before the pony."

A grin creased Dr. Duncan's tanned face. Joy's hand flew to her mouth, as if to squelch a giggle. Gloria let out a sigh and smiled. Kai and her colloquialisms! She wouldn't joke if the tests showed problems. Her Joy was going to be okay.

"To finish our pony ride—" Dr. Duncan chuckled, as did Andrew and Joy—"the ultrasound nailed it. On page three. . ."

Gloria obediently turned the page, though she longed to shred the report into confetti and toss it into the air. Nailed it: definitely good news! Nailed it! Then she remembered *her* ultrasound. Again the figures blurred. Indignant swipes got rid of tears. She was the epitome of selfishness, thinking about her loss when Joy—*the child that's alive*—had been freed from a pernicious disease. *Focus, you ninny. Focus!*

". . . no evidence of cysts. Normal-sized kidney for a young woman of Joy's age. No evidence of compressed or distorted nephrons. No sign of build-up or edema." Dr. Duncan took off his glasses and laid them on the table, next to the file. "Nothing thrills me more—" he glanced sideways at Kai— "than to issue Joy a clean bill of health." Dr. Duncan shifted in the chair. "I would suggest a work-up on that blood pressure. It warrants a look-see."

"Definitely," murmured Andrew. Gloria nodded.

"We've told you the good news." Dr. Duncan leaned back in his chair. "I'm sure Kai's shared the nature of PKD. It can pop up out of nowhere." Blond eyebrows pressed together. "On the flip side, we're not a hundred percent sure that Kai's mother presented with PKD, though from Kai's research, I'd say we're at 99.9."

Andrew grabbed Gloria's hand. Sweat squared. "What can we do to prevent Joy from having to deal with this later?"

Andrew, again taking the words from my mouth.

Dr. Duncan rubbed his chin. "At present, treatment for PKD in advanced stages is dialysis and transplant. A low-protein diet may slow progression. We'll recheck that pressure, follow up with a specialist, get it under control. Other than that, bolster Joy's immune system with a good multivitamin, fruits and vegetables. Common-sense stuff."

They all nodded, except Joy, who had harrumphed after the mention of fruits and vegetables. Besides that, Joy, the one most affected by PKD seemed . . . the least affected.

"Do you guys have any questions?"

Andrew shook his head. "Dr. Duncan, we can't thank you enough."

The doctor rose, patted Kai on the back. "Though I probably shouldn't swell her head by saying this, I'd do anything for Kai. She's a healer."

A healer. Gloria glanced at Kai, whose drawn face seemed incongruous with her relieved smile. If only Kai knew the Healer, who eased life's pains. If only Kai could meet the Love who righted all wrongs, even those like Kai's family had suffered. Gloria must tell her. Even as Gloria stood and thanked the doctor, along with Andrew, a plan percolated. If God allowed, she would witness to Kai . . . before they left Boston.

22

No-Name Restaurant. Kai bowed her head, following the lead of the Powells, but peeked at faded life preservers and splintered oars. Seafarer décor, a bay view, and Boston's freshest lobster highlighted the impromptu celebration dinner Deanne had helped her arrange. *A joint crowded with my sister, her family, scores of raucous locals and tourists. The perfect place to hide my floundering mind.*

"Dear Lord, we praise you for your mercy, your goodness, your glorious presence, in sickness and in health. Thank you for Kai's hand in all this. Bless her career here in Boston. We thank you . . ."

Kai kept fluttering her eyes. Once she spied Joy, peeking at her, as if wondering what she thought of the prayer. Despite her elation over Joy's escape from PKD, a troubled spirit dimmed Kai's joy. Since the first healing hand incident, she had never doubted that her hand was gifted by the fates as a weapon against suffering.

I no longer believe in the fates. Do I now believe my yearning to heal comes from the Christian God? If that is true, He lords over cancer, PKD—the hateful things I battle each and every day! Despite His power, the Christian God allowed such horrors; Andrew acknowledged it in the "sickness and health" prayer. Kai battled an urge to shake her head—and she might have, if Joy weren't watching. She who loved order, statistics, and logic saw no logic to the "sickness and health" philosophy. No logic at all.

"Amen."

I can breathe again. Kai smoothed her napkin into her lap. *Amen means the end. Not a moment too soon.* She spooned into Boston's best chowder, savored tender chunks of lobster, inhaled the grassy aroma of fresh chives, and pushed away thoughts of God. Dear Fourth Sister had bested PKD. Worry about cardio issues . . . and God . . . would be stowed away.

Andrew dipped a meaty nugget of lobster into melted butter. "We can't thank you enough, Kai."

Andrew's and Gloria's contented groans over the feast and Joy's chatter comforted Kai, like long-ago times in her childhood home. Her heart swelled to see Chang features personified by her lovely sister, whose skin had cleared, whose eyes shone. It was Joy, a descendant of her people, to whom she owed this gift. She scraped the last chowder bite from her bowl, slathered a second piece of sourdough bread with butter. She would forget low protein and low fat . . . for one night.

Joy inhaled her last shrimp and forked into a stuffed crab. Kai smiled. *She's tossed caution to the seas as well!* Kai bit into her bread.

140 over 110 flashed unwanted in her brain. Her feet ached, a second reminder.

Kai struggled to swallow.

Andrew set down his fork and sipped on the sweet tea that when ordered had rankled the brassy waitress. "You've done so much, Kai. Without your help, this would've been . . ."

"An absolute mess."

Kai's chin lifted.

Gloria's eyes had softened to the color of robin's eggs. An angelic smile rounded the angles of her face. With her hair caught in a clasp at her neck, she looked younger, more beautiful . . . gracious. *Gloria wears something new as well.*

Kai returned the smile. *So this is the face of Gloria, behind her mask of insecurity and fear. A lovely face.*

"It has been the greatest privilege to be with Joy." As she spoke, Kai felt her heart swell. "To get to know her family."

"Your family, Kai" came from Gloria, of all persons.

Kai's hands tingled. Did these followers of the Christian God mean what they were saying, or was this one of the American come-ons she so disdained, throwing out "I'll call you" and "Let's get together" as casually as the trash?

Joy, perhaps sensing her unbalance, gripped Kai's arm. "Sisters," she whispered.

Joy's words washed over Kai. "It is an honor to be included in your family." The words weighed heavy in her mouth, but Kai was glad she had said them.

Noise from surrounding diners filled a contented silence at their table for four . . . until Gloria began stabbing at her palms and Andrew scraped at his empty plate. Kai waited, sure an agenda was about to unfold from the Powell adults.

"Um, Kai . . ."

Kai nodded at Andrew. *Spit it out, newfound family member.*

"We were wondering—since you've got connections here— if there's someone up here that could check out Joy's heart. Get it behind us, once and for all."

Rich chowder pooled in Kai's stomach. Andrew's request made perfect sense. She'd had a heart connection . . . still did, on a professional level. David's group, like hers, was the best in Boston. It made perfect sense to have Joy seen by Lockhart & Associates. A nurse could schedule it. With reciprocity between the practices, L&A might work in Joy as early as tomorrow. David would not have to be contacted.

"My associate pastor's covering things at the church. If we need to stay over an extra day or two, we could change our flight. Maybe a nurse could call Joy's school, the juvenile director, and explain so they wouldn't think . . ." Andrew popped his knuckles. "You know—to make it official."

Gloria smoothed her hands as if rubbing in lotion. "We've asked you to do so much. Please, please, don't feel obligated to do this."

Joy tilted her head. Her eyebrows arched, her lips compressed, uncertainty tinctured with doubt. *Fourth Daughter does not yet know how and what I would do for her.* Kai rested her hand on Joy's shoulder. "It would be an honor to refer Joy to a colleague. Perhaps we can get her in tomorrow. Do not change that flight yet."

Gloria hand-ironed her napkin. "Oh, Kai. That would be wonderful."

"Andrew, should I call your cell when I have the information?"

"That'll be fine."

"Dad and I are doing one of those early-morning bay cruises." The sparkle had returned to Joy's eyes. "But we could cancel . . ."

Kai shook her head. "We will shoot for early afternoon, then."

"I know you must be swamped." Gloria writhed her hands. *Another request?* "But if you have time, could we meet for lunch?" The words rushed out. *Gloria's nervous. Like me.*

Kai felt her jaw work. Though they had been christened family, she and Gloria had spent little time together without the presence of Andrew or Joy. It might be awkward, even dangerous, depending on Gloria's agenda. She studied Gloria as she formulated her answer. *Am I being too skeptical? Perhaps there is no agenda.*

"I have morning hospital rounds. Appointments. Perhaps around one?" Kai scraped sourdough crumbs into a pile. "I'll give you Joy's file then. Assuming our plan works, you can take it to the cardiologist."

"Perfect!" Gloria pushed strands of hair behind her ears. "Since you're crunched for time, I could bring sandwiches. We could eat in that atrium."

Joy had stopped chattering about the cruise and settled her eyes on her mother. *This one suspects something as well.*

"Tomorrow, then," Gloria continued.

Kai nodded. *Tomorrow I will see yet another face of Gloria's. May it be as attractive as the one I saw tonight.*

Poor her desk, Kai watched the morning sun streak the sky pink and gold. Last week, she had waited for an opportune moment with Dr. Duncan, who just yesterday had heralded the joyous news that Joy had defeated PKD . . . for now. Today Kai would lunch with Gloria, perhaps strengthen their relationship. Still her stomach churned, her head spun. Again she must seek Dr. Duncan's counsel. So many painful things, pressing in.

To refocus, she jotted notes to have Pamela call to cancel her TU appointment. Thank goodness Joy did not need one! She opened her file drawer, spied David's photo, peeking out from beneath her sweater. *David, dear David.* Just thinking that Joy would be at David's office birthed tears. They had shared so much. Should she request that David see Joy . . . or not? Heartache answered. No. L&A had many excellent doctors. It did not need to be David.

Kai heard the outside door bang open. Shut. Footsteps clattered. A light switch clicked on, as did the machine that ruled MRA—the hall coffeepot.

Thuds intensified until Dr. Duncan stood at her door. "Why didn't you start the coffee?" He wore scrubs and tennis shoes and carried a briefcase. Part businessman, part doctor-athlete. Running for fitness, a demanding schedule. Running, running.

While memories of a heart doctor are hounding me to death.

"Forgive me." Kai rose and bowed in a mock apology. "We Chinese only know how to make tea." In a short time, she had gone from considering Dr. Duncan her boss to considering him a colleague . . . perhaps a friend.

"If it's that mossy stuff I see—and smell—in the break room, forget it."

"I will not waste emperor's tea on one who does not understand."

"Emperor's tea, huh? Sounds special. Did you serve it to your sister?"

Kai shook her head. "She prefers fast-food colas. I hope to change that habit."

"I think she's gonna be okay, Kai." A smile dimpled tan cheeks. "There's no swelling, and her cholesterol's great."

"Still, for a teenager to have elevated blood pressure is unusual."

Dr. Duncan slapped his briefcase against his thigh. "Could be a fluke."

"Would you call 140 over 110 a fluke?"

"I'd call that a myocardial infarction waiting to happen." His shoulders hunched, Dr. Duncan strode to Kai's desk. "What gives? Did you recheck her and get a bad reading?"

Kai gritted her teeth. This was more difficult than she had expected. "Yesterday I was not feeling well. Deanne checked my vitals."

"Well, I'll be . . ." Dr. Duncan eased into the chair close to Kai's desk and laid his briefcase in his lap. "When did you last have it checked?"

"I have never had a pressure issue." Kai's lip quivered but she steeled herself to finish. "As I dressed for dinner last night, I noticed swelling in my ankles. My feet."

Dr. Duncan's facial muscles tightened.

"I do not want to be alarmist—"

"Nor do you want to be stupid." The doctor rose. His briefcase thudded to the floor.

Kai studied her hands. "I thought it best to wait, at least until my sister leaves."

"Are you asking for advice, or did you just raise *my* pressure for the fun of it?"

Kai hung her head. It was not like her to be wishy-washy. Why had she confided in her colleague if she was not going to heed his words?

"I'm phoning in an RFP." Dr. Duncan jutted his finger at her. "After all these years, we'll see if I remember how." He chuckled hollowly. "I'll bet the lab has a spot right now. This early, they're twiddling their thumbs or checking last night's Red Sox score."

"Americans and their sport." Kai tried to be flippant. Failed.

Doors banged. Footsteps and "Good morning" greetings cut through the uncomfortable silence. Kai checked her watch.

It was time to be a doctor, not a worrier. Not a patient. "I have rounds this morning."

"Perfect" came out in a hiss, not sounding perfect at all. "You'll already be at the hospital. The right place at the right time. Couldn't be more convenient."

"There may not be time," Kai protested.

"Make time." Dr. Duncan retrieved his briefcase. "I'll call in that order." Lips compressed into a thin line. "If the numbers are bad, I'm ordering an ultrasound. Also convenient. A one-stop, one-shop hospital trip. Like your sister's fast food."

Kai rose from her chair. "There is no need for that, Dr. Duncan."

"Paul." A hint of a smile softened the doctor's eyes, yet a frown remained. "You've passed me a hot potato. Isn't it time you called me by my first name?"

Silenced by an odd mix of gratitude and fear, Kai waved good-bye, grabbed her handbag and her reminder notes, and stopped at the receptionist desk, where Pamela interspersed sipping coffee with stapling printouts. Pamela gave Kai her usual warm smile.

Desperate to regain composure, Kai smoothed her lab coat and handed Pamela her notes. "Could you cancel these transplant unit appointments? Make one for Joy Powell at L&A?"

"Your sister, right? She's your spitting image."

"Oh no. She resembles my eldest sister" came out, surprising Kai. Like the old Joy, she now rode a roller coaster of emotions and behavior. More American than ever.

"Well, she's lovely." Pamela set down her cup and looked at Kai curiously. *Is dread and foreboding stamped on my face?* "You off to rounds?"

Kai nodded. *That is part of the truth, anyway.*

Pamela checked her watch. "A little early, isn't it?"

Maybe too late. Kai exaggerated a shrug. "A doctor can never be too early."

"Yeah, right." Pamela rolled her eyes. "Tell Johnny I said hi, okay?"

Kai's insides wrenched to envision her youngest patient. "Yes. He will like that."

Johnny, in Stage 4 PKD, was one year younger than Joy. One inflicted, one spared . . . for now. As she walked through the atrium, the questions that had kept her tossing and turning last night slithered into her mind. A God that capriciously healed one, then inflicted another, was no different than fate. That did not explain the adoration glowing on the faces of Cheryl, David, Andrew. Transforming Gloria's face as well.

A swirling wind accompanied Kai to the taxi stand, as did queasiness and disquiet. It was time she asked more questions about the Christian God and His miracles. If her intuition and her symptoms were confirmed, she would need those miracles. Sooner rather than later.

❦

Kai had smiled as they'd drawn her blood. Nodded when they'd asked her to return in an hour. She had sleep-walked to the nurses' station to learn that patients were being cleaned, turned, and fed. Not a time for her to barge in, poking and prodding. She killed time in the cafeteria, shelling a hard-boiled egg and stirring a cup of tea. She dumped both, untouched, into the trash and headed for the staff stairwell.

Her footfalls echoed through the dank space and matched the pounding in her heart, the tremor in her limbs. An image flashed of soldiers kicking Mother's cabinet, of a saber slashing Mother's fine cotton quilt. Not since the Revolution had fear terrorized her like this.

At the second-floor landing, she commanded her training to stem a rising tide of hysteria. She tried to recall an old Dr. Ward-ism. Instead she whispered, "Please. No." But whom did she address? It took every bit of strength to open the stairwell door.

Meal carts clattered across industrial tile. She pasted on a smile for familiar and unfamiliar faces alike. Lights brightened, dimmed; call bells buzzed, stopped. Kai drifted toward the glass-windowed lab and opened the door.

The technician who had performed her work-up stared past her. Not a good sign. The hand that held one sheet—her future—shook as if he had seen a spirit. Or a death sentence. The room whirled like the videotaped TV footage of that Texas twister. Though the poor man stood silently quaking, he spoke loud and clear: *You have PKD.*

Without seeing the figures, Kai knew. The disease that had granted Joy reprieve had invaded her system. Kai took the paper from the technician. A glance at the sheet confirmed everything. She whirled about, unable to breathe in a room where blood was collected, reports were written, where—

"Doctor—um, Doctor?"

"You are first a physician, then a human being." It was Dr. Ward, calling to her from that stuffy lecture hall. Just in time.

She straightened her arms, adjusted the mask on her face, raised her chin, turned slowly so as not to stagger—for the room still whirled, though more slowly. "Yes." Her voice sounded like a mere echo, as it had in that stairwell, where she had nearly melted.

"I . . . I called Dr. Duncan, as per instructions." The technician moistened his lips in a way that made Kai want to console him. How awkward to give one further up on the hospital hierarchy bad news.

"Yes," Kai intoned. "Thank you."

"They're waiting for you in radiology." Perhaps emboldened by her courtesy, the hesitant speech disappeared.

Radiology. Poking and prodding, as those soldiers had once done. Proof that insanity had engulfed their village. Kai blinked. Proof that disease ate her kidneys.

Tremors returned with a vengeance. Kai smoothed her lab coat, focused on the young man's name plate, and looked past his clean-shaven face for his eyes, which brimmed with pity and unease. "Luke, thank you for disrupting your routine."

The man shook his head. "Oh, ma'am—I mean Doctor—it wasn't anything."

"Could you do me one more favor?"

The man nodded with such vigor, Kai wanted to shake his hand and thank him for his compassion. A trait she had long admired.

"Let Radiology know that I will be delayed."

Eyebrows rose in alarm.

"Just momentarily, Luke. I must first complete my rounds."

The man exhaled. "You're talking, what? Thirty minutes? An hour?"

"No more than that." Kai wobbled to the door. "If there is a longer delay, I will have a nurse let them know."

"Since it's early, we're probably okay." Luke shuffled files on his desk, surely eager to resume work, more eager for her to leave. She couldn't blame him. With a good-bye, she and her ominous report left the room, hurried into the doctors' lounge, leaned against the wall, and heaved a sigh. She could study her fate in private.

She stared at the clock on the wall, stalling. Then she thought of her patients, her promise to the technician, and let her eyes fall on the sheet.

Creatinine? Off the chart, as were the others that mattered. PKD.

She crumpled the sheet into a ball, hurried into the restroom stall, knelt, and emptied the contents of her stomach. "Help me." Her voice thinned into nothingness as she cried to . . . the Christian God? She knew of no one else on whom to call.

She gripped the toilet with such fervor, her knuckles ached. There was no guarantee that PKD would spare dear Joy, First Daughter, and Third Daughter. If such a tragedy occurred— and she of all persons knew the odds were heightened now— she could never be their donor. Perhaps not their *doctor*. As she leaned against the bathroom stall, her right hand throbbed as never before. Kai raked it through her hair. A lifetime had been spent in relentless pursuit of disease. Nabbing enemies one by one.

First it had been poor Father. Though he still walked with a limp, his mind had been restored after his stroke. Kai's quest shifted to public schooling, Yantai University, the gates of Harvard Medical School. She had marveled when assigned her cadaver, though she had concealed such macabre thoughts from classmates, who groaned as if they did not see that a dead body could be explored with dignity and used as a weapon in the war.

Kai wiped her eyes with a tissue.

Her life had changed when she was handed her first chart. Dorothy Jo Spears. A real patient, to soothe, to diagnose, to heal.

She still had a letter that the dear woman had sent after her hospital release. Before Kai had spotted her obituary in the *Herald*.

Dozens of faces marched though her memory; yet always

at the forefront was the sister they had given away, the sister she had found, the sister who was safe. Kai doubled over from a spasm of grief. *If Joy is free from PKD, why am I behaving like this?* Had she all along pursued disease in an egoistic way, thinking she could change destiny she had once relegated to fate?

If fate did not control destiny, who did? That was the question. She must find an answer, even if it meant walking the path that led to the Christian God.

She staggered from the stall, washed her hands, and splashed water across her face, not caring that her eyes had sunk deep and were rimmed with red. As she dried her hands, she stared at each finger, especially those of the healing hand. Was it the Christian God who had spoken power into each sinew, each tendon? Did power miraculously—that word again—pipeline from the Christian God into the body of one born in a poor village?

The paper towel became a wad in her hand . . . *the* hand. She would ask Gloria about the Christian God. Until then, she would lavish her patients with the mercy bestowed by the Healing Right Hand, even—especially—if it were a gift of the Christian God. A new mercy washed her heart, her mind, her soul; something undefined other than the certainty that it somehow mixed sickness and health, miracle and mundane. She would use this new mercy. Somehow. Some way.

Johnny would be first.

Kai left the lounge. Walked up the hall. Found his chart at the nurses' station. Entered his room. "How is Mr. Johnny?" She filled her voice with the hope, the dreams that a normal teenaged boy might have, though the chart she had just studied testified otherwise.

"Not . . . so good, Dr. Kay." With a muffled voice, the boy

mispronounced her name. Of course Kai paid it no mind. Jaundice had soured his skin. His puffy face was mismatched with twiglike arms and a body swallowed by a hospital gown.

Sorrow welled. She shoved aside sheets, found the boy's hand, careful to avoid his IV line, and sat on the edge of his bed. As if she were cradling life itself, she cupped her hands about skin scarred by insult after insult.

"May you be healed" poured from her heart. She spoke with such clarity, with such a melodious, strange tone, her eyes widened.

Words streamed on, as if from a port inserted into her chest.

Kai bent her head, but not before her tears fell onto the boy's thin arm. "May a miracle occur, right in this hospital." Huskiness made the strange voice—her voice?—sound even more mysterious. Yet the words flowed. Faster. Faster.

The boy's eyes fluttered. His breathing slowed.

The strange voice took on a rhythmic quality, reminiscent of Mother's lullabies.

When Johnny's mouth went slack and he breathed in the way of a deep sleeper, Kai gently arranged his hands on his abdomen and rose from the bed.

"Dr. Kay?" The gentle-breeze whisper sent a chill down her back.

She whirled. "Yes, dear Johnny."

He fixed her with the dreamy gaze of the babies Kai thrilled over at the hospital nursery viewing window. Babies she would likely never call her own.

"I've never had a doctor pray for me." When he smiled, a gap showed between his front teeth. "I like that. Thank you." Heavy eyelids ceded to tiredness.

A strange yet wondrous peace swirled about the bed though

the face was still swollen, the skin was still jaundiced, the boy was still dying.

Kai carried the strange voice to the room of Mrs. Ortega, the room of Mr. Daniel, the room of a critical, just called in.

Every patient thanked her. Every patient settled in, as though the strange voice had soul-healed in a way she had never read about in journals.

With surer steps, Kai went to Radiology. As she changed into a dressing gown, one thought teased her mind: *Will the strange voice soothe me during my procedure?*

23

Lord, help me find the right words. If it's your will, open a door. For privacy's sake, Gloria claimed a tiled table away from noisy lunch-bunchers and sat there, fidgeting with the bag holding Kai's sub. "Veggie, cut the cheese, add tofu," Joy had insisted. "Vinegar and oil." Her Joy, suddenly attentive to others' needs. Gloria could only shake her head and thank God for Joy's transformation, which was surely tied to Kai's appearance. *Perhaps I can reciprocate by introducing Kai to the One whose love never fails.*

"Hello, Gloria." Kai had approached unobserved. She gave her usual bow, wore her usual scrubs. Yet her skin had lost its usual glow. Her shoulders drooped. Joy's sister looked exhausted.

"Kai! Good to see you!" Despite her smile, conviction niggled at Gloria. *Kai traveled to Texas, rescued Joy—and me. She's ushered us about MRA and Boston. We've worn her out.* Gloria gestured for Kai to sit down. *She does more in a week than I do in a month. Maybe more.* "How was your morning?"

The almond eyes closed. Was it truly exhaustion . . . or sorrow? Gloria quashed a desire to reach for Kai's hand. Surely it would be presumptuous.

Kai managed a tight smile. "Some days are easier than others."

Gloria shook her head. They had simply visited PKD's neighborhood . . . and then fled. Poor Kai lived in it, day after day. How awful it must be! Gloria ran her finger along the pebbly table surface. "I can't imagine what you deal with. Death. Sickness . . ."

Such pain contorted Kai's face that Gloria bit her lip. This was lunchtime, for heaven's sake! "I'm sorry. Here I am ruining your break by bringing up stuff you probably want to forget."

Kai rubbed her temples with slender fingers. "One cannot always forget."

"Joy picked your sub with soy . . . I mean tofu." Gloria babbled about the food, desperately wanting to cheer the one who'd so cheered them. *God, take over here. I've stalled.* She slid the paper bag with the sub, chips, and a carton of soy milk across the table.

Kai raised her head. There was such hollowness in her cheeks, such a heavy-lidded, tearful sorrow in her eyes, Gloria's appetite waned. Perhaps a favorite patient had . . . passed, or medical politics had worn her down.

"What happened, Kai?" Gloria sidestepped her usual reticence. Joy's sister needed support. Though she was an unlikely candidate, she was the only one here.

Kai pulled her sub, milk, and chips from the bag and set them on the table. "It is best—" foil crinkling muted her words—"that . . . I not discuss it."

Of course. Privacy laws. Gloria followed Kai's lead and unbagged her salami and provolone sub, cheese fries, and a can of Diet Coke. Fat, preservatives, chemicals—as different as East from West to Kai's meal. "Forgive me for asking." Gloria smoothed her napkin on her lap, determined to help Kai. "I'm sorry for your pain."

Kai seemed to focus on her sub. She clasped her hands and rested them on the table next to her milk carton.

The bent of Kai's head was so forlorn, Gloria flung off caution. "Would . . . would you mind if I prayed for you?"

Kai did not move. Was she even breathing?

Chatter drifted their way from the atrium's crowded area. Gloria gripped the table. Had the direct approach offended Joy's sister? Perhaps they should just eat their sandwiches, chat about weather, tofu, the plants hanging nearby.

The Spirit whispered, *Be still. Wait.* Easy to hear. Hard to do.

After what seemed an eternity, the dark eyes caught her own. "What is this thing called prayer? What are these things called miracles?" Kai's elbows thudded against the table as she leaned forward. Her nostrils flared to match raspy breathing, as if the questions had exerted pressure on her body and had to be expelled.

Gloria's heart fluttered. Then peace decreed absolute stillness in her soul. She tilted her head back as sunbeams pierced the atrium skylight and showered their table with white-hot splendor. It was so good, so *God*. And it soothed Gloria's fears. "Prayer is talking to the One who created heaven and earth. The One who, through mercy and grace, saves those who believe in Him."

"So when I pray, I am talking to the Christian God?"

"You are talking to the one true God. The only God."

Kai looked past her, as if seeing . . . China? A terminal patient? A desire seized Gloria to pour out her heart. "Dear

Lord, thank you for Kai's gift of healing. May we see you as Great Physician, Savior, and Prince of Peace." Her voice rang with a fervor she rarely allowed others to hear. "Thank you for joining us in a most amazing way."

A warm wind swept over her. "Oh, God." Gloria's voice swelled. "You are worthy. Holy." The Spirit hovered closer, affirming her decision to share with Kai, reaffirming forgiveness for the way she'd earlier snubbed her. The Light of the World filled her with a warm glow. She traveled back in her mind to that pew where she'd sat as a lonely child, invited to church by a schoolmate. God had draped loving arms about her and pulled her into fellowship. The warmth! The joy!

Laughter from a nearby table pierced her communion. She opened her eyes.

Kai was studying her. The lines on her face had relaxed, though she held her motionless posture. "That is prayer, is it not?"

What little doubt had tried to wedge into Gloria's spirit evaporated. "Yes," she whispered. "That is prayer. A true miracle."

"That leads to my other question." Kai lined up her sandwich, milk carton, and chips with the table edge as if organizing her thoughts. "What are the things called miracles?"

Lovely mind-treasures unfolded. The Smythe preemie, now eight. A hardened lifer, convicted and saved. Andrew's stories, church praise reports, and college huddle group announcements all streamed through her brain with such speed, Gloria struggled to keep up. Would a doctor trained in science grasp things that were folly to the world? Something only God totally understood? "It is hard to explain."

The beginning of a smirk twisted Kai's lips, or perhaps

frustration. Understandable. Gloria fidgeted in her chair. If only Andrew were here!

He isn't. But you are.

Gloria toyed with her sandwich wrapper. "The best way I can explain it is a supernatural intervention of God in our lives. Like a healing. Like salvation."

"Like the mastering of a tornado?"

"Yes!" The table wobbled with a kick of Gloria's foot. She tried to rein in excitement that spurted adrenaline into her limbs. "God controls the weather."

"Our destiny?"

"Truly all things."

Kai unwrapped a straw and stuck it in her milk. "Is there a rhyme or reason to these miracles?" Though she spoke softly, her voice trembled. Gloria didn't blame her. How could she explain miracles beyond "He acts in accordance with His perfect will"? Her heart hammered as she again prayed for guidance. "Because He is a good God, a just God, we trust Him to perform miracles and pray that His will be done."

Kai's countenance darkened. "Is it His will for one the age of Joy to waste away in a hospital bed?"

Gloria fisted her napkin into a wad, knowing she needed to let God speak to Kai about His will in His time, His way. "Is that happening to a patient of yours? I'm so, so sorry."

Kai finished unwrapping her sandwich, as if done with conversation, but the Spirit again filled Gloria with the confidence to speak out. "I know we already prayed, but would you mind if I prayed for . . . what is your patient's name?"

The almond eyes resumed their relentless scrutiny. Then Kai nodded. "Johnny. Johnny is his name," she repeated, with such force, Gloria had an inkling of Kai's passion for healing. *Lord, that you would call her! Use her!*

Gloria prayed. Then they ate—or, rather, Gloria ate and Kai picked at her sandwich. Conversation lagged, but not in an unnatural way. After rewrapping her sandwich and stashing it in her bag, Kai checked her watch. "Thank you for lunch. I enjoyed our time." She pulled a file from her bag. "Earlier I called Andrew and told him I'd give you this, as we mentioned last night." Kai shook her head, as if surprised. "I am not myself, to almost forget the papers they will need at L&A."

Gloria took the file from Kai, though she longed to jump up and bear-hug her. When had she last wanted to bear-hug anyone . . . except Andrew and Joy?

"The receptionist clipped Joy's referral on there." Kai shouldered her bag. "I don't have a name, because they're working her in, but I assure you, Lockhart & Associates hires only the best physicians."

"Oh, Kai." Gloria abandoned her reserve and gave Kai a hug. She was pulled into a delicate, flowery scent. Feeling Kai's collarbones through the lab coat, she thought of vulnerability, fragility. *Lord, she needs you. Please take her in your arms.*

<hr />

Dr. Duncan, standing in my office? Somehow Kai murmured, "Good afternoon," before veering around her boss and sitting in her chair. It might be better to put solid oak between them.

The senior partner at MRA was a study in lines, from the ridges across his forehead to the way his arms had flattened against his torso. Her first thought ran to work quality, an error in the incessant, infuriating paper trail. Then she spotted the name on the file slapping his thigh. Of course. This was about her . . . and what she had neglected to do.

"I had asked that you stop by after your rounds." Dr. Duncan's Adam's apple bobbed. Though he spoke with his usual calm, there was no trace of his customary self-deprecating humor. Kai swallowed. He meant business.

"Please." Kai hurried to the chair in front of her desk that she'd filled with file folders and moved the folders to a cabinet. "Won't you sit down?"

"They faxed your results." Ignoring her request, he continued to slap the file against his leg.

Kai pretended to ignore *him* by straightening things on her desk.

"Did you see them, Kai? I had Pamela run you a copy." He pointed to her desk. "It should be right there."

Kai dug through a stack of papers. Nothing with her name on it . . . as a patient. So where was her file? Pamela had last made a mistake . . . *before my tenure here.*

"Maybe she put them in your box." Dr. Duncan turned toward the door.

Her renal function panel made an encore appearance . . . in her mind. "Do not bother checking my box. I got a copy at the hospital." *Which I tossed in the trash.* She lifted her chin. Met his gaze. "Same story with the sonogram?"

Nodding, Dr. Duncan raked tapered fingers through wisps of blond hair. "It's clear, blast it. Crystal clear."

Numbly Kai nodded. She had pored through enough RFs to confirm the intuitive dread she'd felt when Deanne took her pressure, when she'd spotted the swelling in her ankles. The tests confirmed what her body had shown. Just as it had been for Mother . . .

There is something I must tell you, dear sister Kai.

To this day, Kai remembered the opening sentence of that tissue-thin stationery. Heaven and earth had moved, not only for Kai to receive correspondence from China, but for First Daughter to get Mother to a Beijing clinic, where a diagnosis of kidney disease was given. The letter told of Mother's swollen limbs, skyrocketing blood pressure. Dozens of times, patients had presented with those symptoms. *It is the same with me.*

"I've been thinking about your options."

"Is it not a bit early for all of this?"

"It's late. Best guess is you're at thirty, forty percent functionality."

"They won't start the transplant procedure till it's below twenty."

"As you well know, that can happen in a week, a year, a decade, though my best guess is, with this rapid onset and few symptoms . . ." He gave her an exasperated look. "You just noticed the swelling, correct?"

Her jaw tightened. She would not ignore such a thing. "Of course."

"I suspect you are on a fast track." As Dr. Duncan wore out her carpet, sweat beaded his forehead. He bore the pained expression of joggers who had shuffled by her in the Common. Kai battled an insane desire to smile. Her boss was the one who looked ill. Who could imagine that Dr. Kidney himself would care so much for her?

"Please, Dr. Duncan. Sit down. You are making me nervous."

He fixed her with a stare but complied. The file became a drum for his knuckles. "This is a disturbing turn of events, Kai."

"But not unexpected." *Though I for one never envisioned it. How silly of me.*

"Have you considered your options? There's SRN out of

Cleveland, RAD in St. Paul—my college buddy works there. Some swear by a clinic in Switzerland—"

Kai shook her head. "I do not plan to seek treatment elsewhere."

Though Dr. Duncan grunted, he slumped in the chair and crossed his legs as if he'd expected her decision. "It might be awkward to be treated in-house, here at MRA."

"Why?" Conviction straightened Kai's spine. This was her clinic. In health . . . and in sickness. "MRA has offered me, a simple Chinese woman, only kindness." She folded her hands in her lap. "I have trusted MRA with my career. Since you run the practice, Dr. Duncan, I trust it." Kai realized that her voice was shrill but she did not suppress it. "Why should I not trust both MRA—and you—with my illness?"

Dr. Duncan seemed to study her from head to toe. Was he looking past her disease? Seeing her in a new way? In any event, it made her nervous. "If you are absolutely sure," he finally said, "I would like to take your case."

"I cannot allow you to waste your valuable time on me." She said what her parents had taught her to say, but it was a lie. To have an internationally acclaimed doctor ally with her . . . Kai blinked back tears.

"Ridiculous." Dr. Duncan waved off her comment. "PKD can't take one of my best out of commission."

"Money from your pocket." She chuckled, wanting to keep it light, but the euphoria she felt knowing that he would be her doctor was evaporating, leaving a numbness that was giving way to a bone-chilling cold. The awful reality of PKD, day after day after day.

"You're set to be seen over at TU." Dr. Duncan's eyes gleamed, as if he were advancing on the enemy. Then his shoulders slumped. "But that was for today."

"Yes. It was canceled."

"Make another one."

Kai's mouth went slack. It was clear where Dr. Duncan was going with this. She began to shake her head, and opened her mouth to protest, just as she had when Gloria and Andrew had spirited Lily away in that dusty van. Again, words failed her.

"You have other sisters, but they are in China, right?"

Kai nodded, though her mind silently screamed, *No! Not Joy!*

"They have no travel papers. No access to testing, right?" Dr. Duncan leapt to his feet. "Joy's your best chance. You know that as well as I do."

"They . . . the Powells are leaving tomorrow," spluttered from her mouth.

"The Powells can come back."

Trembling, Kai shook her head. Joy would not be involved!

Dr. Duncan slammed his fist on her desk. "Why? Tell me that. Why would you miss the chance for a perfect match?"

Kai envisioned Joy's face. "I have spent much of my life trying to reclaim what was taken from the Changs, the most precious of which is my sister Joy."

"And?" It was the casual shrug of his shoulders that propelled Kai from her chair. She leaned across the desk, her face a mere foot from his.

"I would have donated both my kidneys if Joy needed them."

"But she doesn't."

"She is at risk. I cannot allow—"

"You cannot allow?" Dr. Duncan's screech matched hers. "When did you start playing God?"

"Are you not playing God by deciding that a young girl—"

"Young girl? She is nearly an adult."

"She is seventeen years old. It is not legal."

"Seventeen soon becomes eighteen. Legal."

"No. I cannot allow it."

"Don't you think Joy should make that decision, with her parents' help?"

"Two weeks ago she was arrested." Kai's words hissed like steam. "Do you think she has the mental or the emotional acuity to decide such a thing?"

Dr. Duncan yanked a tissue from the box on her desk and mopped a sweaty red face. He wadded up the tissue, tossed it into the trash. When he missed, two long strides carried him to the tissue, which he slammed home.

She had never seen him agitated, had never even heard him raise his voice. He was her boss, could technically ask that she leave the practice. She studied her hands instead of his face. What on earth had gotten into her? Into him?

"This isn't getting us anywhere." He picked up the file from her desk.

Kai sensed his gaze upon her, but she did not meet his eyes. "If 'anywhere' means changing my stance on Joy, you are correct."

Dr. Duncan gave an exasperated sigh. "Promise me you'll think about it. She's here. In Boston."

"She must return to Texas. She has schooling issues, police issues—"

"And you have life-and-death issues."

Kai's blood boiled. *Yes, my issues. Not yours, kidney doctor of Massachusetts.*

Dr. Duncan massaged his forehead, apparently as frustrated with her as she was with him. "It's only fair that you

296

give Joy a say. How would you feel if she played God, like you are?"

More talk of God. *Yet it is all a mystery.* "You have understanding of God?"

Another sigh came from Dr. Duncan, this one tinged with regret. "God and I are at a stalemate, but I've seen enough in the OR to have a healthy fear of Him."

Healthy fear. An interesting concept. Kai lifted her chin. "So you neither believe nor disbelieve."

"I would like to believe."

A cold chill ran along Kai's spine. Her colleague, now her doctor, had repeated the thing said by her and Joy . . . yesterday. *Perhaps Dr. Duncan knows of these miracles that Gloria discussed. That I, too, have experienced . . .*

"Promise me this." He rapped on her desk. "While we reschedule TU, keep your options open where Joy's concerned. How would *you* feel if the roles were reversed?"

Kai pursed her lips and pretended not to listen, yet Dr. Duncan's words rang true. To hide such an opportunity from Joy might crush her hope. Her . . . joy.

Dr. Duncan nodded curtly, picked up the file—her file—and left, closing the door behind him. It was only then that Kai laid down her head and began to cry. For the decision she must make, for the China Chang sisters, whose chances for developing PKD had risen; finally, for herself. Though she hated each selfish tear, a fear that she couldn't shake settled into her soul. She had no medical expertise, no experience, to eradicate it.

Sounds of MRA business-as-usual seeped under the door, yet Kai ignored them in her urge to talk to the God she did not understand. "I do not know how to communicate. I do know that I need help. Please continue to smile on the life of my dear Lily." Would the Christian God mind if she used Fourth Sister's given name when they talked? "Please be with Gloria. Andrew." Tears clogged Kai's mouth and nose, yet if this God was as compassionate as others said, surely He would not mind tears. "Please protect Ling and Mei from PKD."

As she wiped her eyes, she remembered the way Cheryl and Andrew and the Powells finished their prayers. "Amen."

24

It's so hard to hurry up and wait. Gloria, Andrew, and Joy sat in leather club chairs arranged before historical harbor prints hanging on a wall painted cool blue. A sailboat model rested on a massive oak desk. Built-in bookcases were filled with everything from classics to anatomy texts. Stirring music poured from hidden speakers. The usual diplomas, announcing Dr. David Cabot's qualifications, hung near the door.

Andrew settled into his chair and sighed contentedly. If he was worried about Joy's heart, he didn't show it.

"Wonder what the delay is."

Gloria squeezed Andrew's hand, glad he'd filled silence with small talk. As always, Andrew intuited her thoughts. "Even us VIPs have to wait."

Joy smacked grape gum. "That's not the point! They got us in for my tests on, like, a few hours' notice." A purple bubble burst. "Y'all wouldn't believe their schedule!" Joy sucked gum into her mouth. "Kai visits Mass Gen twice a day. Last night she even *prayed* with her patients."

Lightning bolts shot up Gloria's arms. She opened her

mouth to ask questions, but Joy had gone off on a tangent about a boy who'd handed her his Walkman. A boy . . .

"Was his name Johnny?" burst out of Gloria.

Another bubble popped. "How did you know?"

"I prayed for him yesterday at lunch."

"Hmm." It was classic Joy, scrutinizing her . . . and her motives. "That's cool."

Suddenly prayer's cool? Gloria couldn't help but remember pouty Joy, makeup coarsening her features, filthy words spewing from her mouth at the mention of church. *Though we're at the doctor's, waiting for more results, I'm glad we've gone through this.*

Gloria and Joy traded smiles. *God used Kai to change us. Perhaps God will use us to change Kai.*

A man with freckled skin and a reddish-brown mop of hair entered the room. He had a lanky build, like Dr. Duncan, Kai's associate. Handsome too.

"Good afternoon, Mr. and Mrs. Powell. I'm David Cabot." He shook hands with Andrew, nodded at Gloria. "Joy, nice to see you again. Sorry to keep you guys waiting."

"Are you kidding?" Andrew drawled in his easy way. "They even offered us tea."

"Glad to hear it." Dr. Cabot smoothed his East Coast accent with soft-toned gentility, then pulled a chair from near the window and moved it next to Andrew's seat. He handed a file to Gloria before he sat down. "Here's Joy's original file. MRA said it was yours." An easy smile lit up a chiseled face. "It sure helped me get an overview."

"Kai had me bring it. She's been amazing."

The fine cheekbones hollowed, as if her words had pained him. Was it her imagination, or did his mouth droop as well? Gloria studied him curiously as he sat down, paper in hand.

Perhaps Kai and this doctor had had a run-in. Gloria tapped her shoe. Waiting had revved her already hyperactive imagination.

Dr. Cabot yanked reading glasses from his coat pocket and jammed them haphazardly onto his nose, giving him a lopsided look. A smile replaced his dazed expression. "Well, young lady. Your blood work came back normal. Ditto the stress test and echocardiogram." He arched his shoulders and leaned close, like he was sharing a good secret. "I went through Dr. Carlson's file and noted a fluctuation in your pressures." The paper was thrust at Joy, who snatched it up as if it were a treasure map.

"As you guys know, this morning her BP was close to normal." Now Dr. Cabot addressed them all. "With no presenting symptoms, I'm not ready to do a heart cath." The file shut. "Let's monitor things. Wait it out. My guess? Joy has a healthy, normal heart."

Gloria felt her body sag in relief. "Oh, God," she whispered. "Thank you."

"Praise the Lord!" came from Andrew. "Isn't that wonderful?"

Dr. Cabot nodded. "All glory to Him."

Andrew's face glowed, as it always did when God connected him with Christian brothers in unexpected venues.

Gloria glanced at Joy, who was still poring over her test results, and decided to risk her daughter's usual reaction. "So you are a believer?"

"Yes." A pensive look captured gray-blue eyes. "I accepted Christ while at Harvard."

Joy's head jerked as if she had been slapped. Her eyes blazed with curiosity and narrowed, surely calibrating and filing this new data. "How do you explain contradictions between science and faith?" Her leg bounced wildly, though her usual eye rolls and snorts had been left at home.

Gloria gulped air. God was at work in Joy, just like Kai.

A gentle smile made Dr. Cabot killer handsome. "Before I believed, God spoke to me through the complexities of the creatures I dissected in biology labs." He chuckled in a self-deprecating way. "I know, I know. It sounds sick."

"No!" Joy cried, and then slumped in her chair. "I mean, I get it."

"So you're a science geek too!"

"Yeah . . . kinda." Joy shrugged, as if disinterested. The gleam in her eyes said otherwise.

"It's not just science where He speaks to me. I hear His rhythms in etudes, nocturnes . . . even jazz." Dr. Cabot drummed his knee. "As to reconciling science and faith, I leave that to Him. Who can fathom His complexities? Yet I trust Him with them . . . and with my life."

"How can a loving God allow suffering? Stuff y'all deal with every day?" Yearning to know arched Joy's back, tremored her mouth.

Gloria and Andrew exchanged glances. Joy had sat through at least a dozen sermons on this very topic.

Dr. Cabot laced his fingers and rested them on his knee. "In this world you will have trouble." The Yankee voice boomed strong. "It is the path man chose, the path God allowed. It is a mystery, Joy. I understand your questions. But don't let questions blind you to God's goodness and mercy. New with every patient who walks in here. New with every experimental drug. New with discoveries on horizons we never imagined."

Joy sat transfixed, as if she were hearing the words for the first time. Perhaps her heart had been opened to *hear* for the first time.

A pager attached to Dr. Cabot's belt beeped. After studying it, he got to his feet. "Thanks for the chance to see your daughter." He shook hands with Andrew and Gloria, stepped close to Joy, and shook her hand. "You're a carbon copy of Kai."

Joy beamed and then asked, "You know her?"

Did that jaw again tighten? "Yes" came out husky. "Tell her I said hello, okay?" A tic worked in his cheek.

He knows Kai. Gloria continued to study the doctor's face and reconsidered the motive behind their VIP treatment today. *Are they friends? More than friends?*

"Keep digging . . . into lab manuals and the Bible. God can use you, Joy."

Though Joy didn't nod, a smile crept to the corners of her mouth.

They left the L&A offices and sailed, carefree, into a lovely spring day. Andrew pulled her close, Joy moseyed ahead. As pedestrians veered about them on the busy Boston street, questions flitted though Gloria's mind. How had Dr. Cabot known that Kai and Joy were sisters? Maybe it was in the referral. Still, something told Gloria those two had more in common than medicine.

It has been a day to forever remember . . . and long to forget. As Kai prepared to leave the office, her cell phone rang. Sure that it was the Powells, confirming dinner plans, she dug in her handbag, shuffled files on her desk, and finally tracked the ring to her lab-coat pocket. Breathless, she grabbed it and flipped the cover. "Hello. Hello?"

"Kai." The voice of heart doctor David sent *her* heart into crazy rhythms. "Kai?"

It is about Joy. Breathing raggedly, Kai backtracked to her chair, all the while listening to the lovely voice saying her name. *If ever I needed a heart doctor, it is now.*

"Yes, David."

"Are you all right?"

No, I am not all right, David. In a hundred ways, I am not all right. "I could not find the phone, David. I apologize."

"No problem. No problem." Kai fought a desire to tell David everything that was happening, including encounters with PKD . . . and God.

"I . . . I just wanted to let you know. Your sister's gonna be fine."

Fine! Kai's face crumbled with relief. Of all the doctors in L&A, David had seen Joy. Miracle? She struggled to hold her composure . . . and the phone. *Joy is fine!* Her intuition had whispered such, but intuition didn't equal squiggly echocardiogram patterns and stress-test results. "Thank you for calling." Pressure in her chest had returned . . . and strangled more talk. Besides, what could she say? That she missed him? That she faced a devastating diagnosis and needed him more than ever?

"Well . . ." David cleared his throat as he did when he was uncomfortable. This was unfamiliar territory. Fresh tears gathered in her eyes. She hated making him feel like this! "I just wanted to let you know."

She begged her voice to function. "Thank you, David," she eked out, "for seeing her on such short notice."

"Kai?"

Kai tried to say *yes,* but the word garbled.

"She has your eyes. Your inquiring mind. She's something else. Like you."

Something else. But not enough for a heart doctor. Again

she thanked David, slammed shut that phone, his first gift, and let it *thunk* onto the floor. She laid her head on her desk and tried to pray to the Christian God.

Sadness and anger thwarted her efforts. Sighing, she rose from her chair, picked up her cell, found her bag, turned off the light, and left the office.

～∽～

Gentle sniffles. Jowl-rattling snores. The beautiful sleep music of her Joy and Andrew, though how they could manage such slumber on full stomachs was beyond Gloria, who pushed back her covers and tiptoed to the hotel love seat.

Plush fabric cushioned her. She basked in the memory of the four of them, having another celebration, Italian-style. They'd passed steaming platters of fettuccine Alfredo, spaghetti with clam sauce. Andrew had prayed, Joy had laughed, she had snapped pictures, Kai—

Gloria sat up straight. Kai had barely eaten, had managed wan smiles. Having been there, done that, Gloria recognized someone troubled in spirit. With resolve, Gloria found her Bible.

The heater whirred as her family snoozed. Finally her weathered volume closed. Gloria moved to the hotel window and parted thick drapes. Someone walked a dog. Revelers hollered. Taxis honked. *I'm not the only one sleepless in Boston.*

Though she'd read Scripture and prayed, worry about Kai persisted. Perhaps a spiritual battle? A relationship problem? Dr. Cabot? Gloria smothered a yawn. Andrew would say it was her imagination, working on Eastern Standard Time. Andrew was probably right.

Gloria picked up her things and moved them to the hotel desk.

There lay Joy's file, the report from Dr. Cabot on top. Gloria skimmed the numbers, which meant nothing to her except, "Quit worrying about your daughter's heart." She thumbed through Joy's chart to file Dr. Cabot's report chronologically.

Two papers stuck together. She pried them loose. Stared at a Radiology report. Kai's name jumped out . . . as a patient. Gloria blanched. Kept reading.

```
Radiology Report, 4/20/97
Dr. Paul Duncan, MRA
Patient: Chang Kaiping renal ultrasound exam
History: Family history, suspected PKD.
Edema. High blood pressure.
Multiple cysts, enlarged kidneys observed.
Possible polycystic kidney disease.
```

Gloria's head spun as she stepped back. The paper slipped to the floor. When her calves hit the love seat, she collapsed into its cushiony depths and whispered, "Dear God, not Kai." She kept glancing at Andrew and Joy with the irrational notion that they should not sleep in light of such news.

As Gloria prayed, she watched a highlight film of Kai's pale face, her lack of appetite, her subdued behavior. Kai wasn't tired. She was sick.

Sheets rustled. "Honey?" Andrew craned his neck, displaying tousled hair and sleepy eyes. "You okay?"

Gloria stared at her hands. She would talk to Andrew . . . in the morning. "I'm okay," she whispered. Andrew promptly rolled over and fell silent. "But Kai is not," she whispered to the dead-of-the-night sleepers. And to God, who, of course, already knew.

25

"Kai?" It was Gloria on the phone, out of breath. Worried? Kai gulped air. Perhaps David had been wrong about Joy's heart. Why else would Gloria call now when they were to meet later today?

"Hello, Gloria." Kai paced the courtyard near the hospital entrance. "Sorry I couldn't take your call earlier. I was on rounds."

"Could . . . I see you?" Gloria's speech skittered. "As soon as possible?"

Definitely a problem with Joy. Nothing else would shrill Gloria's voice. Running her hand through her hair, Kai checked her watch. Eight thirty on a Saturday morning? It seemed like noon. She'd skipped her usual tea and porridge and gone in early . . . again . . . to catch up. Still she lagged behind. In two weeks, her world had been tilted, first by one event and then another. Two weeks ago, she would have blamed the fates. Now she suspected the Christian God. "I'm at Mass General. If you would like to meet here . . ."

"Yes. Yes, I would."

Kai swallowed. "I . . . I have an hour or so, Gloria. Will that give us enough time?"

"It'll certainly be a start." Strangely, resolve had steeled Gloria's whispery voice. Kai again bit back an urge to ask Gloria what was going on. *I will find out soon enough.* They agreed to meet in the hospital lobby in twenty minutes. Kai hung up the phone. As she hurried upstairs to see her last patient, her heartbeat sped to match her careening thoughts. Though she had endured Cultural Revolution travesties, bested million-to-one odds to enter Harvard's ivy-covered inner sanctum, and subsisted on cat naps and ramen noodles to obtain a Harvard degree, she suddenly doubted her ability to survive life's upheavals. If the Christian God could— would—truly help her, she needed to hear from Him. Now.

Gloria paid the cafeteria cashier for a diet drink and made her way to the hospital lobby. A gray-headed woman sat at a table, stirred coffee, and stared out the window. A toddler bounced on a man's knee, his chubby fist clutching an *It's a Girl* balloon. Four orderlies crowded around a table and scarfed down too-yellow eggs and crumbly toast as they regaled each other with their latest patient escapades. *A dozen tragedies and celebrations. I'm involved in a drama myself.*

"Gloria." Kai's voice echoed across the lobby and threatened Gloria's composure. She'd prayed through the night. At sunrise, Andrew joined the vigil. Over a room service breakfast that remained largely untouched, Joy added her voice to their pleas. After the three of them decided Gloria should come here alone—to avoid any awkwardness over Joy's presence—Kai had been called. Gloria straightened. *I represent the family here. With God's help, I can do this.*

308

"Kai." The women hugged. Though inwardly Gloria shuddered at Kai's fragility, she pasted on a smile. "Thanks for agreeing to see me."

A questioning look arched Kai's lovely brow. Her bleary eyes testified that she, too, had missed sleep. *And I know why*.

With difficulty, Gloria pulled from the embrace. "I know you don't have long. Is there a place we could talk?"

Kai jammed her hands into her pockets, nodded, and stepped through the lobby's revolving doors. Gloria hurried after her. They circumvented an ER entrance crowded with ambulances and service vehicles and cut across a swath of lawn.

Kai slid onto a concrete bench. Gloria did likewise. Wordlessly, she pulled the report from her purse and handed it to Kai, who barely glanced at it before fixing Gloria with a torrid look.

"Who gave you this?" Kai demanded.

"No . . . no one," stammered Gloria. "It was in Joy's file."

"Joy's file?" Kai's hands shook, as did the report. Then her face fell. "Dr. Duncan said he had put it on my desk. I must have stuck it in Joy's file. No wonder I could not find it." Kai cupped her cheeks, as if she'd learned a shameful secret.

"Kai, I am devastated." Gloria flung her arm around Kai. To her surprise, Joy's sister sagged against her.

Sympathy such as Gloria had never experienced for anyone outside her family swelled her heart and cracked the armor she'd worn to protect herself from hurt. Why, she'd rather go through this PKD herself than have Kai suffer! She stroked Kai's silky hair, so much like Joy's. "Last night I . . . I couldn't sleep for thinking about you." Every misgiving she'd had about Kai bloomed into compassion. "After last night, when we ate together and shared stories, I knew

God was doing something special." Tears stung her eyes, but she didn't take time to wipe them. She needed these tears; perhaps Kai needed to see them. "God used you to heal us. We're connected. Supernaturally."

A breeze swirled Kai's lustrous black hair and shadowed her face. "I feel it too."

"Then I found your . . . report." Gloria's voice broke. "Oh, Kai! Don't you see? God meant for me to find this. You can't go through it alone."

Kai raised her head and scrutinized Gloria with such intensity, she seemed to peer into Gloria's soul. Though it went against Gloria's nature to meet such a gaze, she held firm, praying that Kai would see not her but God.

"I must do it alone. Don't you understand?" Kai writhed her fingers. "Joy cannot know."

"Joy does know."

Kai heaved about, her teeth bared. "How? Why?"

Gloria's pulse careened. Kai would do *anything* for Joy!

"Why did you tell Joy?" A hiss steamed Kai's words. "She cannot be involved."

Gloria raised her chin and met Kai's gaze. As she and Andrew had discussed, they were done shielding Joy in the name of protection, which had alienated Joy from so many people, so many things. Including God. "You taught us about family, Kai. That's what we are." She scooted across the bench until her shoulders touched Kai's. "We'll help you through this."

Kai shook her head. "You do not understand. You do not understand at all."

The concern that had energized Gloria began a crazy backward spin. She planted her feet into dense grass. PKD was stopped only by dialysis . . . and transplant. Matches would be most likely with relatives. With . . . Joy.

Gloria clapped her hand to her forehead. *I . . . I think I am beginning to see, dear Kai. And I do not like it. Not one bit.*

Kai swept a leaf off the bench. "If you think Joy will stop at sending me a get-well card and a dozen roses, you do not know that daughter of yours, that sister of mine."

"She will want to . . ." Gloria's jaw worked, but the words could not be formed.

"Have you discussed with Joy"—Kai's face twisted like she'd eaten sour grapes—"the possibility of being a donor?"

"No. I . . . I hadn't really thought of it." *How stupid of me. I'll bet Joy has.*

"Did Andrew mention it?"

"N-no. I . . . I don't think he's even considered it."

"Well, someone most certainly has. She is five foot two and has the world's most beautiful smile." Kai folded her arms, suddenly a stern, unyielding judge. "We cannot allow it. She is seventeen and has a chance to live the American Dream."

American Dream. Gloria's parents had bought into an American Dream fueled by oil money. Gloria had chosen a different dream-ride for Joy: a safe religious bubble. Her parents' dream had run out of gas, her religious bubble for Joy had burst. No one but God would choose a dream for Joy. Though the last thing she wanted was to subject Joy to surgery—surely risky—she could not prevent Joy from considering such a thing. Kai had to know why this was reality.

With a force that surprised her, Gloria grabbed Kai by the shoulders. "We can't dictate a dream for Joy. She must follow God's plan. Of course Andrew and I will have to talk about it, and talk to Joy—"

"She is seventeen." Kai pulled from Gloria and planted her hands on her hips. "A minor."

Gloria laid her hand back on Kai's arm. "Minors grow up."

"I will not allow a young girl to make this sacrifice." Never had Gloria heard Kai shout. Until now.

"She's not just a young girl." Why, Kai was as stubborn as Joy! "She's your sister."

"That has no relevance."

"It has every relevance." Gloria leveled her tone and laid her hands in her lap. "That is why you found her. You wanted to save Joy from PKD. Now she has a chance to save you. We've gotta consider it. Deal with it."

A muscle twitched on Kai's face. "It . . . it was not my plan that Joy do such a thing."

Gloria exhaled, as did Kai. A passerby gaped at them, then beelined toward the hospital. Surely they looked like women whittled to exhaustion from a tough shift. Or quarreling colleagues. "It wasn't my plan either," Gloria finally said.

Words hovered in the air, along with the sound of a siren, shrilling closer. An emergency. A tense situation. Like this.

"We must consider the possibility that God wants this for Joy. Andrew and I will pray and see what God says."

Kai threw up her hands in exasperation. "Are you saying that a God in the heavens will speak to one on earth?"

"I'm saying He can, He will, and He does."

"How?" Kai leaned forward, as if about to stand, and then slumped against the bench. "It is one thing to pray to God." She began to shake her head, very slowly. "It is quite another thing to hear voices. In medicine we call that psychosis."

"I didn't buy it either, Kai." Joy's voice, coming from behind them, muted the sound of a distant siren.

Heat rushed to Gloria's face. She leapt from the bench and whirled about.

There stood Andrew, his arm about Joy. Their radiant smiles melted tension. Even Kai, who'd been trembling with anger, had risen and was bowing in her usual manner, though her forehead was still furrowed.

Then Gloria stiffened. Andrew and Joy were supposed to wait at the hotel. Why had things changed?

"So you and your father join in this family reunion," Kai said, then sat stiffly.

"Mommy told me." Her head bent, Joy rushed forward and knelt by Kai, who clenched her knees. "I'm . . . I'm so sorry." Joy threw her arms around Kai. The two became a huddled, heaving mass.

Though Gloria ached to hold Joy, she rose from the bench and let Andrew support her. The sisters had each other. As it should be. She had her man. As it should be.

Finally Kai broke from Joy. Sitting up straight, she smoothed Joy's hair, saying, "It is nothing, Joy. There are not even manifestations."

Gloria stiffened. *Kai's adopted my old technique of lying to protect Joy. It doesn't work, dear. But I won't tell you so. At least not now.*

Joy lifted her head. "So . . . you're feeling okay? Like, no problems yet?"

Kai nodded silently. Overcome? Sorry about lying? Perhaps still lying . . .

A smile erased Joy's worry lines. "So we've got time! It'll all be good!"

Time? Good? Gloria's heart galloped. Time for what?

"I've done research on the whole shebang," Joy continued. "The most likely six-point donors are family. Like . . . me and you."

Gloria squeezed Andrew's arm until he winced. Yep, no get-well card from this one. Joy planned to sacrifice her kidney to help Kai reclaim her health.

What a difference a day makes.

⌒⌒

Kai could not keep from trembling. Her secret had slipped from that folder, sprouted wings, and fluttered about like spring fever. She inhaled Joy's bubble-gum scent, which blended with the smell of the fresh-cut grass and the heady perfume rising from a nearby bed of narcissus to create a sensory experience every bit as eclectic as Joy. Kai gripped her arms. How could she think rationally with Fourth Daughter so near?

"I must go." Needing the safe haven of her hospital, Kai rose from the bench.

"Kai, wait!" Joy grabbed her arm. "I need to say something."

"Should . . . should we leave?" Gloria asked.

"No!" Joy's yell drew the attention of others nearby. "This is for y'all too! We're family. Remember?"

I cannot argue with something I agreed to. Finally Kai nodded and sat back down.

With a twirl, Joy spun away from Kai and plopped onto the lawn. Andrew and Gloria moved to stand by Joy. They smiled with such unabashed pride, Kai relaxed. Waited.

"Mommy, after you left, Dad and I had, like, a really good talk." Joy plucked grass blades and tossed them in her lap. "When I was little, you know, it was easy for me to accept Jesus. I . . . I guess I never told y'all how He seemed like an action hero. After all . . . the orphanage stuff, I needed a hero. Then . . . the fire happened." Huskiness added vulnerability to Joy's voice. "I blamed y'all. I blamed God."

"We should have been there for you," Gloria whispered.

"You *were* there, Mother. Let me talk, okay?" Joy's hand

waving stopped. "Please, Mom," she managed. Rudeness evaporated.

Kai tried not to notice the stares of passersby, surely entranced with a new daytime hospital drama.

Gloria nodded.

"Everything, like, blew up at school. I couldn't handle people hating me just 'cause I was Asian or nerdy or freaky looking or, like, whatever." The grass-plucking became frenzied. "I started hanging with the dark people, going to dark places."

Though Kai's gaze never wavered, she saw Joy in new angles. New hues. None of them included being a kidney donor.

"Then I, you know, got busted. Kai showed up. That tornado defied, like, the laws of nature to miss the jail." Joy tilted back her head. The sun chose that moment to highlight that zany hair. Kai raised her chin. *If this one continues to mature, she will bring great honor to our family. She must mature.*

"Not even to mention the aide position." Joy continued her soliloquy. "This morning Mom and Dad told me the truth about your results instead of, like, trying to manipulate everything so *Joy* wouldn't be disturbed." Joy glanced at her parents, as if for confirmation, and took a deep breath. "That's when I made my decision."

Kai nodded halfheartedly, not liking this new direction.

"Like, last month, I might've called this fate. The stars. Karma."

Kai squirmed on the bench. *Now it sounds like my old story.*

"Not anymore. I always wanted to believe in God, even when I . . . thought I hated Him." Joy's palms flattened against the ground. She leaned back. "Now I do believe. It's

315

like my heart opened to the possibility that He would work through things . . . if I'll get out of the way. That's why I have to know your plan to fight PKD—our plan." Joy zeroed in on Kai with an intensity that shuddered Kai's soul. *This is not an easy one to dissuade once her mind is set. So I will leave while I am vulnerable to this idea of hers.*

Kai made a show of checking her watch. "I must return to my patients." She darted her eyes about, as if concerned that nearby workers might overhear. "Now is not the time or the place for such a discussion."

"We've got to do it, Kai. Before we leave Boston." Joy crossed her arms. "That's tomorrow."

Despite being in the open air, Kai found it difficult to breathe. *Joy must not partner in this thing. Not now. Perhaps not ever. She, who had planned to sacrifice for Joy, was burdensome as a lame ox. The less Joy saw of her, the better.*

"I have missed a great deal of work lately." Kai stood and brushed off her lab coat. "This weekend, it would be best—"

Joy jumped to her feet. Blades of grass fluttered. "Best for whom?" With a *whoosh*, Joy crashed into Kai. Laid her head on Kai's shoulder. "Please, Kai," she sobbed. "Don't shut me out."

To now have Joy so near changed everything. She could no more ignore her flesh and blood than she could abandon a patient with a death rattle. She kissed Joy's part line. "If it is permissible with your parents, I will meet you at the Common entrance at five thirty today. Remember where we started our Freedom Walk? You will have your say."

They parted. After completing her rounds, Kai hailed a taxi and tried to pull her emotions together. The bay glittered with hope, but Kai could not shake the feeling that she had lost control—of her present and her future. She who had made a life of attaining goal after goal felt as powerless as the sailboats in the harbor, curving and fluttering at the whim of the wind.

The driver sped faster, faster, surely intent on dispensing with her and picking up a more profitable fare. Boats became white streaks, the water a blur of blue. Kai clung to the door handle, wishing *she* could dispense with this lose-lose dilemma. As a renal specialist, she had thrilled to uncover the mysteries of those amazing bean-shaped organs. She knew the ins and outs of their function. She knew the risk of infection, the odds of survival, in every documented kidney disease.

Her mind, her training, could not allow precious Fourth Daughter to undergo a transplant. Yet in her heart, her soul, she knew she couldn't stop her sister from pursuing her passion.

Kai leaned back and let her thoughts wander. She was under the shade of a banyan, where she as a young girl had vowed to be a healer. As her memory unfolded, no one stepped forward to say "I forbid it."

The cab screeched. Kai was jerked forward. She rubbed her eyes, as if she'd just awoken from a deep sleep.

"Can't you hear me, ma'am? I ain't got all day."

Neither do I, sir. Neither do I. With a tight smile, Kai topped off the fare with a generous tip and jumped out of the cab. Kai understood what to do to best handle her patients' needs. But what about Joy's needs? How should they be handled? At this moment, the answer eluded her. "God," she prayed as she strolled past the rustling magnolias, "they say you perform miracles. I believe I have seen them." She inhaled and begged the sweet magnolia scent to cleanse her troubled spirit. "Change Joy's mind." Heavy steps got her inside the atrium. "Or . . . change mine."

26

A cab's not the place for a meltdown, Gloria told herself. The driver swerved around tour buses and screeched to a halt in front of their hotel. Andrew paid him. Gloria and Joy headed to the elevator bank. Gloria jabbed the button. *Neither is a hotel lobby. So cool it.*

"Are you gonna hold up for Dad?" It was classic Joy, an eyebrow peaked, her mouth quirked. *She gets it.*

Let him climb the stairs! Gloria wanted to hiss . . . but didn't. She smiled sweetly, said, "Certainly," and prayed for guidance. This was fight number one in Parenting of Joy 102. She had to get it right.

Andrew joined them. They rode in silence to their floor. Entered their room. Gloria sat in the love seat, near her Bible and journal. A good place. Andrew fiddled with his cell and plopped into the chair by the table. Joy flopped on her bed and tossed a pillow. "Spit it out, Mom. Something's wrong."

She gets things Andrew's clueless about. Gloria glanced at her Bible. *God, help him "get it" without me "losing it."*

"I barely slept last night for worrying about Kai." *Good. Go slow, girl.* "I so appreciate all she's done for us . . . and for you, Joy. When you shared how God's changing your life . . ." Unable to explain further, Gloria grabbed her journal and riffled through the pages. "This is full of prayers for you, Joy."

Andrew had moved to sit by their daughter. Good. She'd sock it to both of them.

Joy darted glances between her parents. "So . . . it's all good?"

The journal slapped shut. "There is one little thing."

Andrew rubbed his chin in his philosophical pose. "What, dear?"

Gloria swallowed down her instinct to whine and imagined Kai dealing with this. "It hurt that y'all left me out of the chat about Joy's future. Y'all had said you'd wait here for me and we'd all three talk to Kai. Later."

Father and daughter exchanged "Who, us?" looks. In the past, Gloria would've burst into tears or backtracked. Not today. She dug her nails into her palms and waited.

"Like, it just came out so naturally . . ."

"Yeah, babe." Andrew avoided her eyes. "Kinda an impulse." Was he really getting it . . . or was he just afraid she'd erupt?

Gloria pushed aside her odd-mother-out feelings. This wasn't about her. It was about communication, which they'd need in megadoses if Joy took the kidney donation path. "If we're committing to this, we've gotta be on the same page. Like, communicate."

Joy played catch with her pillow. *She's nervous. Like I am.* "I'm . . . I'm sorry."

"Me too." Andrew put his arm around Joy. "We weren't thinking."

"Hey, no problem." Gloria felt her eyes widen. She sounded like Joy!

"So you're okay with it?"

Empowered by the lovely mix of respect and love on her daughter's face, Gloria shrugged. "Hey, like, it's cool. We'll see where God takes us."

Joy scrunched her nose. "*Moth*-er! You're talking, like, so weird!"

~~~

It's safe. Secure. Kai felt in her pocket for the box she'd stowed in her locker during rounds. *A symbol of all I hope for Joy, who's . . . right across the street!*

Would she ever feel humdrum about Joy? She thrilled at the sight of her sister's railroad cap, jeans jacket, pink shirt and tennis shoes. It was the same rush she used to feel when David entered the room. With effort, Kai pushed away thoughts of the heart doctor.

Andrew, Gloria, and Joy stood waiting by the Common's wrought iron gates. Kai tripped across the street, and Joy rushed forward to give her a hug. "Thanks for coming!"

Kai willed away the urge to bury her face in Joy's hair and cry in despair. Instead, she lifted her chin. "Are you ready to leave Boston?" she asked Joy's parents.

Gloria rested her head on Andrew's shoulder. "We love it here!"

Andrew nodded. "But it's time to get home." With arms draped about one another, the Powells resembled young marrieds on a weekend getaway. A pang of jealousy struck at their obvious contentment; Kai shoved it away.

"We've got one more thing to do." Gloria laced her fingers with Andrew's. "We hear you can't come to Boston without seeing the bronze ducks. Taking your photo with them."

"It's a must!" *That's what David once said, anyway.* David.

Her cell phone. Kai swallowed hard. Oh, the memories. "They're—they're in the Public Garden, not here. Just cross St. Charles. The swan boats are there as well."

Andrew pointed to the Common sign, several feet behind him. "How about we meet y'all back here in, say, an hour? I need photo proof of this trip for my deacons."

They all chuckled, like family, though Kai did not understand the joke.

"If you want flowers," Kai blurted, desperate to continue the community feeling, "there are tulips and redbuds." A perfect backdrop for the all-American couple.

"See y'all later." With silly waves, the Powells tripped toward St. Charles. Kai felt her tension release as she smiled at Joy's eye rolls.

"They're acting like teenagers," Joy complained.

"You are fortunate that they love one another."

Joy ducked her head. "I see that now. I see a lot of things." On the strength of that admission, the sisters strolled into the Common. Beech and elms and maples trembled with new growth. Kai's heart swelled to be showing off this city, her city, to Joy. Her sister. If only she could freeze this moment and suspend talk forever of the other thing. . . .

In a spontaneous way, Joy linked her arm with Kai's and lengthened her stride until the two matched each other's gaits. Kai closed her eyes and thought of the God whom she had heard so much about lately. *Thank you for this time with Joy. Somehow, some way, you are responsible. Thank you.*

Joy broke from Kai, headed toward a bench shaded by a majestic maple tree, and sat down. Sorry that their easy, natural rhythms had been broken, Kai did the same.

Silence—and the looming presence of PKD—began to

swallow nature's beat. Kai's chest tightened. Her hands fell into her lap. "You wanted to discuss something."

"Uh, yeah." *She, too, longs to reclaim our rhythm.* "I've read up on PKD. That file you gave my parents, stuff at the hospital."

Kai couldn't help but smile at the fire in Joy's eyes. *If this one's drive and energy is harnessed for healing, the enemy diseases will tremble with fear.*

"It's awful!" Joy shook her fists, as if PKD were walking by instead of a young mother strolling with her child. "When all they can do is dialysis or transplant . . ."

Kai nodded. "That is what we are reduced to at present. Things will change. They must."

Joy pursed her lips in her stubborn pose. "Until that change, I'm doing the genetic matching. They have a transplant unit in Dallas."

Kai shook her head. "You have been—what do they say?—a busy mosquito."

A lovely tinkling sound came from Joy, so incongruous with her brash manner. "Busy bee, Kai. Slang was hard for me too."

Again their arms linked. They inhaled, exhaled, in unison. Rhythms gifted through genes? Kai believed it so. "We have much in common." Kai kept her eyes on Joy. Kept her mind on their rhythms. "Much to share."

Joy popped upright. "Don't you see? That's why we're in this PKD thing together. If I'm a match, it's a no-brainer." Her eyes were filled with such longing, Kai turned her gaze to the Common expanse, alive after its brush with winter. Alive . . . like young Joy.

Kai felt her lips tighten. *That is the way out.* TU administrators balked at twenty-something donors, much less eighteen-year-olds. A memo from her as a renal specialist decrying Joy's involvement would end this fiasco. Joy would never know. "You are much too young to even be considered."

"One year and I won't be."

Kai stared at Fourth Sister. *She comprehends all.* Desperate to add levity, she quipped, "I was right the first time. You are a busy mosquito."

Joy rustled about. "The way I figure it, we've got time. That report puts you at thirty, forty percent function. God willing, we've got time."

Kai studied her hands. It was not right to lie to her sister.

"You're not going to support me in this, are you?" Joy, a pink-and-denim blur, jumped to her feet. "Are you?"

Kai looked at Joy but no longer saw beloved Chang features. Instead, she saw the village chief who tried, because of an age-old family feud, to bar her from the university, the officials who rejected her visa application—all those who had said, "You can't."

There had been an equal number who had said, "You can." It pained her to be seen as a negative person . . . by the one she loved most in the world.

"You can't play God, you know." Joy's voice became brittle. She scuffed her toe against dirt.

Twinges worked through Kai. *If Joy resorts to her rebellious ways, I will be to blame.* This situation called for careful reasoning. "How would I be playing God, to do what is prudent? To do what is best for you?"

Joy took Kai's hand and warmed it between her palms. "God's behind this, don't you see? Like, what are the odds you'd find me? That we'd survive a tornado without, like, even a broken fingernail? Can you just try, Kai? Try to trust Him on this?" Her desperation rent Kai's heart. "I mean, how many times does He have to tell you?" Joy's grip tightened and surged a tidal wave of emotion . . . and a question.

"When did this revelation come to you?" Kai kept her tone light. "On Beacon Hill, did you not question God?"

Joy's eyes blazed with a strange light. "Yeah. Things have changed. When Mom left this morning, Dad and I talked." Sweat slicked their hands, yet Joy held tight. "I recommitted my life to God, who never gave up on me, even when I was in that . . . dark place. It just, like . . . all clicked."

Joy released her hold on Kai. Snapped her fingers. "As I've learned about myself, I've kinda learned who He is. Though there's a bunch more to figure out." Joy possessed the rosy cheeks and electric energy of the children racing by, surely bound for the frog pond. "He's a God of miracles. Of love. A God who has conquered death."

"Conquered death." Kai battled a negative tone. "That is a God I want to meet."

"Then I'll introduce you."

The wind rustled through the leaves as Joy began to talk. Words about God coming to earth as a peasant's son shuddered Kai's soul. Her skin prickled, as though another presence, greater than nature, greater than humanity, had joined them. Though she could not see it, could not touch it, the presence was there . . .

"You can know Him, too, if you admit that He came for you. Died for you."

"This morning, did you admit such a thing?"

Tears filled Joy's eyes, which had lost their savvy look and bore the wide-eyed hope of young patients, trusting that the shot's sting would soon be gone. "Yes. I always believed it, like, at some level. Now I'm gonna live it."

They sat on the bench, full of the moment of being sisters

enraptured with one another . . . and something, someone else. God?

Birds chirped. Lovers strolled. The strange sensation of another presence faded.

Kai checked her watch, felt her eyes bulge to see that it was already six o'clock. Time itself had bowed to the strange words, the strange presence. "It is time to meet your parents, Joy. You have given me much to think about."

"Kai." Again Joy gripped her hand. "Open your heart to God and His ways. Open your heart to me. Please, Kai, please!"

"You are asking me to open my heart to things I do not understand." Kai again let her gaze fall on the Common as she thought of David, Cheryl, the Powells. An odd image— Chinese Evangelical Church flyers she'd seen tacked on utility poles—fluttered into her mind.

Kai faced Joy, who continued to grip her as if she were a lifeline. How strange that the sister for whom she had spanned seas and secrets had become *her* lifeline! *That is the problem: I cannot get past the fact that only by endangering Joy can I allow Joy to do would she feels called to do!*

Joy gave her a quizzical, penetrating look. "I know what you're going through, Kai. No matter what my parents said, I would not listen. This morning, it was, like, wow! God brought you to help me. Now it may be the other way around: Maybe I can help you. It blows my mind." Joy brushed off her jeans and anchored her cap on her head. "Please. At least think about it."

"It is time for us to go," Kai said, but she did not move a muscle. An unseen force had cemented her to the bench.

"Please, Kai." A single tear slipped down Joy's cheek.

Something broke in Kai, as it had when she had wiped away

Joy's first tear at the jail. She would think about it. She owed Joy that much. After she wiped away Joy's tear, she said, "I will ponder the things you have said. For you, Joy. After all, you are a Chang. The Chang I sought. The Chang I have found."

"Oh, Kai." Joy fell into Kai's embrace. "I wish . . . it had been me instead of you." Though Kai's jacket muffled the words, their import squeezed her heart. *Joy means it. Joy truly has a gift, a gift that has stolen my words. A gift I will treasure until . . .* She shoved away images of disease, of death, and instead basked in the sunlight, in Fourth Daughter's presence. *No matter what awaits me, it is enough. If you are here, thank you, God.*

Finally Joy lifted her tear-stained face and murmured, "I can't imagine what you're feeling, being a doctor and all."

Kai nodded. "It is strange, sitting on the examining table."

"Could I, like, be more than your sister on this?"

"What do you mean?"

"Like maybe a medical assistant?"

"You have the gift," Kai whispered. "You have a healing hand. Perhaps two." To add levity, she tried to laugh. Failed.

Joy bowed her head. "Yeah, I know. God told me that too."

Kai felt in her pocket. It was now . . . or next time. *With PKD looming, now is best.* "Speaking of gifts." Kai pulled out the blue velvet box that a Boston jeweler thought perfect when he'd appraised and cleaned Mother's priceless possession.

"What . . . what's that?" asked Joy.

"Mother's pearls. One treasure not destroyed by the soldiers. When Mother was on her deathbed, I promised her to one day fasten them about your neck." Kai's fingers trembled over the clasp. "That day has arrived."

"But—" Joy's face wrinkled like a dried walnut. She clapped her hands over her face. "I . . . I can't take them."

326

Kai ignored her tearful protestations and flung purple-black hair out of the way. "They are yours, Joy. We have always called you our jewel."

Joy's shoulders shook with such intensity, Kai could not fasten the pearls. "Shh, little one." She hummed Mother's favorite folk song until Joy settled. "It would be disgraceful to ignore our mother's last wish." Finally completing her task, she sat back and admired two Chang treasures.

"Don't you see?" Joy raised a tear-stained face. "You cannot deny me a chance to help." Again Joy grabbed her hands. "After what you've done for me, it's insane for you to shut me out!"

The creamy pearls, the chirping birds, Joy's bubble-gum smell—they all overwhelmed Kai's senses, as did an ephemeral hovering presence. God? Kai again linked arms with Joy. Perhaps it was He and not just Joy she had spanned seas and secrets to find.

"You've got to see the ducks!" After they walked Kai to her cab, Andrew grabbed hold of Joy and Gloria and pulled them to the corner. Twilight sun dappled his face with gold, gifting Gloria with another twenty-four-karat moment. How often had she prayed for times like this? Never had she imagined she'd find them in Boston.

"Why ducks?" Joy's bangs scattered, then settled. "We've got 'em at home."

"Not like these." Gloria handed Joy a book they'd just bought at a shop down the street. A silly little present, but a symbol of Boston. Kai. Their new start.

"*Make Way for Ducklings?*" Joy's snort became a giggle.

She's too cool for this book and those ducks . . . or so she thinks.

"Fine. Just laugh." Andrew herded Gloria and Joy across the street. "You'll see."

With Joy holding the book, years rolled away, as if the time in Boston, the time with Kai, had rubbed from Joy's face not only that sleazy makeup, but the last smears of rebellious attitude. Gloria skipped to match Andrew's enthusiasm. With Joy open to God and their family reading a chapter called trust, years tumbled off Gloria as well.

The first chick seemed to waddle close. Andrew broke into a jog.

"Dad! What are you doing?" Joy thrust her book at Gloria. Father and daughter dashed about, quacking. Gloria's happiness skyrocketed. Father, daughter, ducks . . . family again.

Because of Kai.

Gloria hugged the book. If Joy proved to be a genetic match for Kai, she would not stop her donor attempt. Both Kai's and Joy's lives were at stake. Though she and Andrew needed to discuss it, she knew what he would say . . . what they both would say. If God allowed it, they would obey. There was no choice.

Inhaling the fresh, crisp air, she hurried forward.

"This is amazing!" Joy screeched.

"I told you so!" Andrew playfully punched Joy in the ribs. "Say you're sorry."

Joy threw back her hand and laughed. Then her mouth twisted, and she hung her head. "I *am* sorry. For all I put y'all through."

"Oh, Joy." Gloria stepped forward, as did Andrew. They draped their arms about Joy, pulling her close. "It goes both ways, you know."

Joy found Gloria's hand and squeezed hard. "I know" came out in her new manner of speaking. Half sarcastic, half humorous, all truth. Perfect.

"This trip's given us a fresh start." Andrew reverted to his preacher voice to wrap everything up. Gloria didn't mind a bit.

"When we get home, Dad, will you baptize me?"

Gloria's jaw slackened. Another thing she'd prayed for since they'd left Customs with ten-year-old Joy. "Oh, Joy . . ." was all she could say. Again, it was just right.

"And, Dad, could we do it at a lake or something?"

Joy and Andrew kept talking, but Gloria quit listening. Tears pummeled her cheeks. She heard clicks, saw flashes, knew that tourists were photographing a woman having a breakdown by the famous bronze ducks, but she did not care. Shy Gloria was blubbering for all in the Boston Public Garden to see. Her Joy was in God's family. They'd spend eternity together. If that wasn't something to lose control over, what was?

"Mom!" Joy shoved her hair behind her ears and unbuttoned her jacket. "I've gotta show you something." Encircling Joy's neck was a luminous strand of pearls.

Exactly like the ones Daddy had given to . . . that woman. *His trophy wife.*

"They're . . ." Gloria's mouth felt as if it had been deadened for cavity-filling.

"It's my . . . our . . ." Joy ducked her head. Embarrassed. Insecure. Things that made Gloria find her voice.

"What, Joy?" Gloria gripped Joy's shoulders. "Tell me. Now." She added punch to her request. "No secrets. Remember?"

"They're . . . my mother's. Like . . . not my real . . . I mean . . ." A gargling sound came from Joy's throat.

Poor baby. Worried about me. As Andrew stood mutely, Gloria tightened her grip on Joy's shoulders. *God, help me here. Get me over Daddy and his new wife. For once and for all!*

Gloria focused on each pearl, a perfect symbol of irritation handled with grace. She rubbed her finger over surfaces smooth as . . . Joy's skin. "They're lovely, Joy." She kissed her daughter's brow, her cheek. "But not as lovely as you." Her hand still on the pearls, she said, "Every time you doubt that you are loved, remember this necklace. Wear it with pride. Never, ever worry about my feelings." When Joy's head jerked up, Gloria nodded so hard, her earrings grazed her cheeks. "Real family, birth family—call it whatever. Like, I'm your mom. Like, nothing's gonna change that."

"Oh, *Moth*-er!" Joy cried, and burst into tears.

27

"Lord I lift your name on high." *Could you lift me as well?*
Kai's feet swelled within her old shoes. Her hands were red,
lumpy messes. Yet she sang with the praise band as she sat on
the pew between Cheryl and David. Friends, both of them . . .
until Kai recalled how it had once been with David.

Since the diagnosis, Cheryl had expanded her roommate
role into chauffeur, errand girl, and spiritual mentor. She
had excelled in all roles . . . except that last one. It was not
Cheryl's fault. Kai ached to be at peace with God. Yet the
peace radiating from Cheryl, David, and the hundreds packed
in this elementary school gymnasium where their church was
meeting proved as elusive as Kai's attempts to battle PKD.

"You don't have to stand." Cheryl's words feathered Kai's
hair, which was dull, listless, and brittle. *Like me.*

Kai bit back an impulse to snap a retort. No, she would
stand, sing, attend Bible study, and slip her tithe into the
plate. God could not deny that she had done her best to woo

Him as she had once tried to woo fate. Though she longed to slump into her seat, she gripped the chair in front of her and redoubled her efforts at praise.

Somehow she stood through three songs, each with a more repetitive, more arduous chorus. Voices swelled, hands waved, the unmitigated joy creating such a yearning, Kai longed to clap her hands over her ears. She survived by studying the young woman slapping the tambourine against her hip, the man beating the drums with abandon, by following the words on the giant screen set up behind the platform.

Pastor Ed, distinctive with his salt-and-pepper beard and short Afro, activated the mike on his belt and stepped to the podium. "Let's pray."

Kai exhaled. His prayer finished, now she could sit, listen, and beg that the pastor would speak words to tame her restless soul. Or would the one-way courtship of God continue?

"Planes rumble into the air, our freeways pulse with traffic, even the harbor echoes the sounds of the great vessels that churn its waters." Pastor's Virginia drawl labeled him an outsider, but these Bostonians embraced him as if he were a Mayflower descendant. "It's static, all of it. How many hours a day do television, radios, and stereos blare noise into your home?"

"Can we count our kids?" someone called out.

"That's another sermon," chuckled Pastor, who went on to speak of Psalms 37:7 and 46:10. Kai thumbed through the pages of the Bible Cheryl had given her, knowing full well both verses were underlined. She had been still before the Lord. Yet God gave her no indication that He heard her. She gritted her teeth. She would keep waiting.

As always, Pastor preached beyond the noon hour. As always, Pastor apologized, blaming the Spirit for his delay.

Though David and Cheryl—indeed, everyone, it seemed—shrugged their shoulders and smiled as if they were coddling a cute but misbehaving kid instead of their shepherd, Kai felt her hackles rise at the mention of the Spirit, that hovering presence, yet another thing she did not understand. How could educated people truly believe a specter-like spirit could inhabit a human body?

"Let us pray."

Kai gripped her temples and bowed her head. *God, I want to know you. I want to talk to you.* She lost track of her thoughts, distracted by the pastor's impassioned plea for stillness, by the shriek of an infant, the creak of the gymnasium doors, and finally gave up pretense of a heavenly communication.

A tear slipped onto her cheek. She thumbed it away. Another Sabbath, and nothing new had happened. Could she be still and wait another week? Another day?

The pastor's amen stirred hundreds from the chairs. Conversation buzzed from row to row, attendees apparently rejuvenated. Church members shook hands, patted backs, spread good will and affection. "Bye," "Call me," "Don't forget" rose from the aisles.

"Meet you at Reuben's?" Cheryl asked a plump and smiling woman.

Kai stifled a groan. Reuben's was their normal, and usually enjoyable, Sunday tradition, except today Kai just wanted to get home and crawl under her quilt. But she would not be alone. PKD would snuggle up next to her.

Reuben's suddenly sounded "yummy," as Cheryl would say.

David and Cheryl continued canvassing stragglers who might need fellowship and a mealtime recounting of the sermon. Every week, it had gotten harder to fake smiles, pretend to eat Chinese or pizza or subs, all loaded with salt, all straining her overloaded kidneys. Perhaps she could claim a need to work. Head to the office, where it was quiet.

Except there she couldn't avoid patients' files, holding evidence of PKD, shouting, "You cannot fight us!" Including her own file.

Kai smiled and waved at a woman in their Bible study, then averted her head to avoid conversation. Since Dr. Duncan had reduced her patient load, Kai struggled to keep busy during working hours, much less weekend office trips. Though difficult, she would join the restaurant crowd. Play the game.

Kai bookmarked both the Psalms verses with bulletin inserts and made her way to the nearest aisle. Though she'd lost fifteen pounds since January, with every step, she felt as if she carried a backpack filled with rocks. *A burden called PKD.*

"You ready to eat?" Cheryl bounded up, followed by David, whose eyes captured hers in the way that made him not only a beloved physician, but an on-fire witness. Yet gone was the spark that caused those eyes to linger on her face.

David stepped close. His sleeve grazed her arm.

Sparks ignited as his scrubbed cotton shirt brushed her linen jacket. Most days, logic reigned and allowed her to see David as merely a friend. A colleague. Today was not one of those days.

Because of David's and Cheryl's long-time friendship, Kai guarded what she told Cheryl about David. Yet one as intuitive as her roommate surely understood how difficult it was to forget her first love. Perhaps her last love . . .

"Come on!" Cheryl grabbed her arm. "Mustard's on my mind! Pastrami!"

Does Reuben's have an entrée that will tell me how to be still and wait? As Kai linked arms with Cheryl and followed

David to his car, she nodded in sync with Cheryl's animated chat, but it was all an act. In fact, she starred in a macabre play, dragging from scene to scene, dreading the climax. Was PKD draining her of passion, or was it her failure to find God's peace? Despite relentless digging in the Bible, questioning of her more-than-willing mentor, Kai simply did not know.

FALL 1999
FORT WORTH

"You wouldn't believe my lab!"

Twisting the phone cord, Gloria leaned back in the kitchen chair and stretched her toes until they touched the sliding glass door. "Oh, yeah?" She pictured Joy, arms waving, mouth a perfect circle, now embracing college just like she'd embraced youth group and biology club her senior year. "Try me." Gloria rubbed her toes against glass warmed by September sun and sipped her Diet Coke . . . but drank in her baby's voice.

"We've already dissected a rat. Next week it's a cat."

Gloria made a face at the phone. "Like someone's pet?"

"*Moth-er!* It's anatomy class. If I go to med school, I'll have my own cadaver."

Gloria sat up straight and pushed away the plate that held her half-eaten sandwich. "Tell me about it, then." Med school. Nursing school. Lab technician. Thanks to Kai's input, Joy could choose from a smorgasbord of options. Gloria spied the framed picture on their baker's rack that captured a Boston spring day two whirlwind years ago. Before Kai lost weight. When purple still streaked Joy's hair.

Gloria let Joy regale her with the latest Collins Hall dorm tricks. Another miracle, one that she had prayed for: Joy attending Baylor University, where she and Andrew had met and fallen in love.

"It won't be that long, you know. I'll be taking the MCAT and—"

"Just savor each moment, okay?" Memories of giggly dorm girls gifted Gloria with another smile. "Make sure to get some sleep."

Joy's sigh made it from Waco to Fort Worth. "Kai's already reminded me."

Kai. Again Gloria glanced at the photo. "I haven't talked to her lately."

"I have! She e-mails nearly every day. It's so cool—if I've got a medical question, there's an expert in the family. Isn't that the coolest?"

"What's cooler is at the rate you're going, we'll have two medical experts in the family."

"*Moth*-er!" Joy shrieked, in her good way. Her very good way.

"Joy, thanks for calling. I love you."

"Me too, Mom. Bye." From Joy, "me too" was a mountaintop proclamation.

Gloria hung up, set aside the letter she'd just received, and dialed Kai's cell, private work number, home number. Like yesterday, she got only voice messages. She soothed the prickles running up her spine by studying that letter with all the exotic stamps and dreaming . . . all over again.

~

It was Tuesday. Kai pushed open the door at Boston's best bakery and set off the usual jingling bells.

"Hey, Doc!" Frank pulled on a server mitt. "The usual?"

Kai watched a little girl press her face against the glass

display. "No. I want whatever's caught her eye." Bending over, Kai studied maple-leaf cutout cookies, frosted in oranges, reds, and browns. *If those can't lift my spirits, nothing can.* "Low-cal, low-sugar, right?"

"Yeah, right. Cream cheese icing's slathered on, baby! Tell those nurses it's protein, okay?" With his bulky mitt, Frank grabbed a cookie and waved it like it were a blue-ribbon county-fair entry. As far as Bostonians—and Kai—were concerned, it was! "Two dozen?" he growled, apparently noticing the line snaking to the door.

"Better make it three dozen." Kai dug in her pocket for money. "Those nurses take bribes. And some of us get hungry." *Unfortunately, not me.*

"Know jes' what you mean." Frank rang up the sale, tied twine around the box, and handed it to Kai.

"Frank, you're always hungry." Kai grinned big for her baker, patient, and fellow PKD sufferer. Too bad his schedule didn't align with hers. He livened up the center.

Smiling, Frank patted his heart. "You hang in there, Doc."

"Right, Frank. You just don't wanna lose your best customer."

"Nor my doctor." Frank waved her out the door and into a brisk fall wind. Kai's jovial voice and smile disappeared, leaving her alone with a box of festive cookies, her cab driver, and the awful truth that PKD had gotten into the cab with her.

⁓

"Good morning, Doctor." Erica, the manager of the renal care facility, bustled to the front desk after Kai rang the bell. "Glad you showed. It's kinda dead today."

Kai rolled her eyes in mock anger. "Get it straight." The bakery box plopped onto the counter, her briefcase on the floor. "It's Kai, not 'Doctor.'" Kai faked tug-of-war with the treats, as if threatening to reclaim them. "Or I'll keep Frank's treats to myself."

"In that case, I'll call you whatever you want."

"That's better." Still chatting, Erica buzzed open the door to the treatment floor. Though Kai's thrice-weekly dread descended at the sight of twenty recliners, twenty stands, twenty dialyzers, one of which would suck fluid—and energy—from her, Erica's joviality helped. Subjection to dialysis had sharpened Kai's humor, dulled impatience; things that would make her a better doctor, a better human being. If God let her survive . . .

"Hello, Kai!" Shereen, a petite woman with big brown eyes, was swallowed by the lounge chair, a comforter, tubes, and the massive cleaning machine. With a tiny hand, Shereen waved in her shy yet warm way.

"Hey! Wanna cookie? It's Frank's butter recipe, slathered with icing!"

Shereen shook her head. "Maybe later."

Or not. Like Kai, PKD robbed Shereen of her appetite. Unlike Kai, who still worked part time, Shereen could no longer hold her executive position at an insurance company. Shereen's name—and her life—had been posted on the transplant waiting list. Shereen played the waiting game. *To a lesser extent, so do I.*

"You'll be on five." Erica hustled to the station nearest the window with a view of a small garden. Pots of butterscotch-colored mums stair-stepped a ladder. Whimsical statuary, oblivious to Boston's winds, rose from a foundation of grass and rotting leaves. Kai's favorite was a chubby baby, forever tossing flower petals to heaven. Surely God would respond to such joyous wooing!

"You ready? Kai? Kai!" Erica touched Kai's shoulder.

Nodding, Kai focused on Erica's tender smile so she wouldn't feel the two needle stings. Of course she wasn't ready. This was her fourth treatment since they'd implanted her fistula. Not one four-hour session had gone "according to plan." Twice her blood pressure had plummeted, she'd fainted, and they'd had to pump blood back into her body, causing unexpected swelling. Twice her blood pressure had skyrocketed and stretched four interminable hours into five.

Unlike Mr. O'Malley, who had for thirty-five years juggled dialysis with a clerk job, or Mrs. Bastrop, who had driven herself to treatment for two decades and went to the beauty shop after her Friday dialysis, Kai experienced nausea, chills, and a tiredness that creaked her bones. She inhaled, exhaled, and whispered a prayer for help. If God answered, she did not hear. Perhaps she was not flinging her petals high enough.

As Erica finished hooking Kai to the dialyzer, David rushed into the restricted area, bypassing an aide talking on the phone. Gone was his congenial air. His complexion was flushed, his lab coat rumpled. "Kai!" His hands on his hips, he rushed to Kai's lounger, then stepped back when Erica lasered him with a glare. "What are you doing here?"

"Plans changed." Kai tried to infuse her voice with gaiety.

David glanced toward Shereen, who had buried her head in a fashion magazine, pretending, at least, not to listen. *Right.*

"What happened to the carpool plan? Me or Cheryl?"

"Something came up." Kai exaggerated a shrug. It hurt to see webbed lines about David's eyes and know she caused him pain. He caused her pain as well, though he could not help it. "Erica worked me in." She widened her eyes and sent an SOS to Erica.

"As you see," Erica said crisply, "we're not exactly

swamped." She winked and smiled. "Would you like a cookie, Dr. Cabot? Looks like you need sweetening."

David ignored Erica and tapped his shoe. "Hmm. Any objection to me staying till you're done and taking you home?" *Is he staring at me . . . or ignoring Erica?*

Kai felt her insides quiver, and it wasn't because the arterial line was draining her blood. Nor was it because of the slight hum of the pump, doing its work. Kai struggled with David in his friend role as she struggled with dialysis. Having him sit here, out of pity or a need to be a Christian brother, wreaked havoc on her emotions. What could she say, with Erica holding her breath to hear the dialysis drama, with Shereen's big eyes peeking over that cover girl swathed in furs?

"You can stay, David—" Kai grabbed her briefcase, which Erica had set on an end table by her lounger—"and watch me study patient charts. I will take a cab home."

"We'll see about that," growled David.

"Good morning, Doctor." Erica's voice shrilled.

Startled, Kai looked up.

Dr. Duncan, holding a bouquet of violets, strode onto the treatment floor.

Heat rose to Kai's face. The poor man had spent enough hours covering her calls, covering her *case*, having Janine juggle the schedule to accommodate her treatments. To come here on his day off was beyond the call of duty . . . and downright embarrassing.

"What is this, an American Medical Association meeting?" Erica threw up her hands in mock disgust. Or maybe she *was* ticked. This was no place for a lounge-type chat.

"How's my favorite manager?" asked Dr. Duncan.

Erica reached for the flowers. "Tell me if those are for me, and I'll let you know."

Dr. Duncan reddened. "Actually they're for Kai. But there's always a next time."

"For me?" The burn spread to Kai's neck. Surely Paul didn't remember her fondness for Joy's former hair color? She had heard, through office scuttlebutt, that Paul had been a devoted husband who'd thrown his passion into the practice after his wife's death. Now Kai believed every snippet. Here he was, pampering a lower-level colleague. Wasting his valuable time. Still, he'd brought . . . her favorite flowers. "They're . . . beautiful," she stammered.

Erica raised a can of Pepsi in a mock toast. "Here's to next time," she growled, yet her coy smile revealed affection for Dr. Duncan.

Though Kai also longed to toast, she could only manage a weak wave, already feeling the cramps and chills that were constant companions here. She tried to smile, for Paul's sake. The man needed a break from the bean-shaped organs that consumed his life. "How are you, Dr. Duncan?" Kai managed.

He held out the flowers and half-set, half-dropped them in her lap. For a moment he wore the expression of a lost child. Strange, here in his element. "Do you know David? Dr. Cabot?" Kai rushed her words, eager to soothe whatever worried her boss.

Paul gave David a curt nod, which was returned. Kai swiveled her gaze between the two men, whom she had assumed got along. Obviously she had been mistaken.

Shivering, Kai opened her mouth, wanting to say something witty to smooth the suddenly chilly room. Or was her body temperature plunging in response to medicine's best attempts at purifying her ailing renal system?

"Kai?" Dr. Duncan knelt, one knee on the floor, and pressed

his hand against her pulse. She closed her eyes, unable to continue the charade that all was okay.

"One-thirty and climbing." Dr. Duncan turned to Erica. "Bring her chart, please."

Kai swallowed hard. She could not cry in front of David, in front of Paul, in front of Erica, who labored to please at this thankless job. Rebellious tears trickled down her face. It was maddening to have her weaknesses exposed for the world to see.

Paul approached David. "Would you mind if I spoke to Kai in private?"

David's mouth twisted. Nonetheless, he wheeled, strode to the door, and planted himself at the monitor station. Erica joined him, got Kai's chart, and then admitted a new arrival. Only Shereen seemed to track every movement of Paul, who sat next to Kai.

Kai worked up a smile. *At least I am distracting Shereen from dialysis.*

"We've put you through four of these." Concern stretched tan lines on Paul's angular face, making him look every bit of his forty-seven years. Still, he had a craggy handsomeness she seemed to be noticing more often. Perhaps he had begun a new exercise regimen. "The fistula's not doing any better than that catheter."

Painful surgery and weeks of healing, down the drain. Nauseous, she glared at the machine. *Like my blood.* More tears pooled. It was torture to worry the man she admired more than anyone . . . except old Dr. Ward, who was in the grave . . . or perhaps in heaven.

"You know what we need to do."

Kai shook her head. Felt her lips tighten. *Not that. No.*

"Why do you resist?"

Paul's question gobbled up Erica's banter, the new patient's chatter. David and the aide zeroed gazes at her. Shereen's magazine plopped into her lap.

Heat again rose, though Kai shivered as if packed in ice. How strange it was to be assailed by temperature extremes. And mood swings.

Paul's chair creaked as he leaned close enough for Kai to see silver hairs woven in dark eyebrows. He cupped her hand in his warm palms. "This isn't working, Kai." His thick accent deepened. "Unlike others, you have an option. A slam dunk."

"I cannot do that to a young girl."

"She is of age; ready, willing, and able."

Kai jerked out of his grasp. "You talked to her?"

Paul sighed. "No. I just guessed. Looks like I hit the bull's-eye."

"You're certainly a sports fan today," Kai snapped, all pretense of keeping her health issues private melting away. Like her control . . .

"Should I contact her, or should you?"

Kai gathered her blood lines and moved gingerly to avoid painful tugs. "You cannot do so." A triumphant smile fell flat. "You would breach privacy agreements, state law. Not to mention receive the censure of the hospital ethics committee . . . of which you are a member."

A sneer flirted with his mouth. "So you will sue me? File a complaint?"

Kai struggled to keep her composure. How dare he meddle in her affairs? To rip Joy from her idyllic campus, where she was acing tests, joining clubs, making friends—Kai eased her arm onto the recliner armrest. No. She would not allow it. "Look for another donor," she finally managed.

He clenched his fists. "That makes no sense when we have a hole in one."

"Now you have taken up golf."

"This is no joke." He leaned close enough for her to study the color of his eyes. Gray-blue. Or were they blue-gray? "It's your life." He rested his hands on her shoulders and looked at her as if they were the only two people in the room.

Her breath caught, seeing his tight jaw, the muscles cording his neck. No wonder patients, colleagues, staff—she was three for three—idolized this man.

"With Joy, you're six for six. It can't get any better." A tic started in that jaw. "It's a travesty to our profession for you to disregard a perfect match."

His hands tightened on her shoulders, causing discomfort, as did the truth. If she sought an alternate donor, she would rob a kidney from another desperate soul. She battled an urge to pull at her hair, but that would rip both lines from her arm.

"Promise me you'll think about it, okay?" The tan lines softened, the tic disappeared, as if he knew her very thoughts. He would. He had hired her, had supervised her, and now was doctoring her.

He sounds like Joy. I'll tell him what I told her. "I will think about it."

"Let me amend that. Like Nike says, just do it."

"So you can just up and change things?" She would have sat up straight . . . but her body would not let her.

"You've been thinking about it." Strangely, his voice was tender. "For two long years. It's time to act."

"Okay . . . Paul." She spoke his name, wanting him to know what a . . . friend he had been to her. Not just her boss, her doctor, but . . . her friend.

He again took her hand. "Will you think about one more thing?"

At his touch, she tensed from head to toe, not easy when

hooked to a machine. Had he blinked during this entire conversation? She had not. "Maybe," she managed.

"Call me Paul more often."

After he left, Kai ran her fingertips along the soft petals of Paul's violets and stared out the window at her statue baby. Oh that the God of heaven would reach down, pull her close, and tell her what to do! About Joy as a donor. *About this other thing as well.*

David broke her reverie and sat in the seat Dr. Duncan had vacated.

Kai's chest tightened. *Here sits that other thing I must deal with. Apparently sooner rather than later.*

"I couldn't help but overhear what you two were discussing." Now David, with his slender tapered fingers, cupped her hand.

Kai risked a glance at Shereen, who was videotaping the dialysis drama with those wide eyes. *Great.*

"You should listen to your doctor," continued David.

Which one? Her jaw tight, Kai studied the heart doctor who dared act as if he had a say in the matter. "Both of them?" she spat out.

David's eyes narrowed. "All of them. Not counting yourself. I understand where you're coming from, but it's no good. For your sister. For you."

Resentment melted. *He does care. They all do. That does not help.*

"But what does God want?" Kai spewed, then clapped her hand over her mouth, surprised at the intensity that welled. "Isn't that what matters?"

Confusion made a rare visit on David's pleasant face. As did speechlessness.

Kai settled back in her lounger. *So Christians do not have all the answers about their God. Yet somehow that does not provide the comfort that I hoped it would. I must navigate my own way in matters of the heart. At least for now.* "Thank you for coming, David." The decision clicked in place and brought a strange settled feeling. "I appreciate it. As I said earlier, however, a cab will take me home."

Shereen gasped.

David tottered, as if unsure whether to sit, to stand, or to leave.

He took the third option.

Kai sat alone, except for that strange feeling of closure. She curled into her recliner, stared at her flower-petal baby, and drifted to sleep.

28

Gloria sipped the last of her coffee. Caffeine and the lingering warmth of Andrew's good-bye hug staved off a November chill and a touch of empty-nest blues. Last week, they'd driven to Waco for homecoming and experienced all that parents of a freshman could want: Joy, in her lab rat costume, throwing candy from her "cage" on the Biology Club float, a chatty lunch with Joy's roommate Caroline and her parents, the Bears, pulling off a win for Andrew and a stadium full of frenzied fans wearing the green and gold. Memories of Joy, wearing a silly "frosh" beanie, made Gloria grin.

The phone rang and cut through the bubbling of the stew she'd fixed for dinner. She'd best get organized if the position they'd prayed about, she'd dreamed about, came through. She picked up the phone. It could be the director. "Hello."

"Have you heard from Kai, Mom?"

Gloria fell into the kitchen chair. Kai seemed to return her calls during Wednesday night service or her lunch volunteer shift. Gloria suspected Kai's phone tag wasn't coincidence. "Actually, I haven't. Have you?"

"Huh-uh. Just e-mail. She hasn't been calling me back."

"I'll try to get through to her." *Or Cheryl.*

"Something just doesn't seem right."

Gloria rubbed the shiny surface of their new portable phone. Like Kai, Joy majored in analytical thinking. "What doesn't seem right?"

"I ask her about her symptoms, and she just tells me about her patients. Not lying, but not telling the truth."

How well I know that act.

"I've been reading up on PKD. It can get bad fast. Maybe it's bad."

Joy at her best. Blunt . . . but good. "I'll call right now." Gloria jumped to her feet, flew to the sink, grabbed a rag, and scrubbed the counter with a vengeance. Her motherly side had prayed this day would never come, but she had known, deep inside, that it would. They would help Kai, no matter what it cost.

"Thanks, Mom. Call me back. Promise?"

"Of course, Joy. Bye." Gloria hung up and punished the counter, as if it were the horrid PKD, which, like germs, could not be eradicated. At least not yet.

~~

Kai balanced a sack full of takeout food on her knee while she unlocked the apartment door and hurried inside. There stood Cheryl, hands on hips. Staring. With a slam, Kai shut out a biting wind that had ended a week of Indian summer weather. *Looks like I've run into another storm front. This one named Cheryl.*

"I've got Chinese." Kai unloaded containers of ginger chicken, peppercorn shrimp, and steamed dumplings and pulled plates out of the cabinet. She glanced at the phone, which blinked news of four messages. *Will Cheryl notice if I tiptoe over and delete them?*

348

"You're not supposed to be eating that."

"I had them hold the MSG and salt."

Cheryl shook her head, as if to say she didn't believe a word of it. "Speaking of holding things, you've got a few calls." Cheryl pulled chopsticks and napkins from a drawer and slid onto a barstool. "And I am *not* covering for you."

Kai studied her roommate, her mentor . . . her best friend. "It's just so hard."

"To do the right thing?" spurted from Cheryl.

"I asked David if it was the right thing."

"When?"

Kai made a show of studying her watch. "About five hours ago. When he stopped by the dialysis center."

Cheryl arched her eyebrows. "I thought you'd changed days."

"An opening came up. I just called a cab."

"Why do you refuse our help? Why are you shutting out the Powells?" Cheryl pointed a chopstick at Kai. "Don't tell me they aren't family or I'll stab you with this."

"It's not that easy." Kai's voice broke as she mounded steaming food onto two plates. "I've got Joy to think about."

"Yeah, that's right." Cheryl jumped from her barstool, pulled glasses from the rack, filled them with water, and slammed them down. Water sloshed onto tile and drew a sigh. "I'm sorry. Let's pray. We should've done that to start with."

Kai hung her head, sorry that she'd involved her best friend in this mess.

Cheryl took her hand. "God, I thank you for my friend Kai and all she's meant to me over the years. Make clear the paths for us to walk. Grant us wisdom, courage, and the peace that passes all understanding." Cheryl squeezed tight. "Lord, I pray in the name of Jesus that you heal Kai, by whatever route you choose. May the food nourish our bodies. May our conversation honor you in every way. In Jesus' name, amen."

They shoveled food onto their plates. Though Cheryl ate with her usual gusto, Kai poked at a shrimp and made designs with rice kernels. The phone call she needed to make obliterated hope for a festive dinner and the return of her appetite.

Kai stared at the blinking light on the answering machine. Finally Cheryl set her napkin beside her plate. "I've thought a lot about how to say this, Kai. You know I want only what's best for you."

"I do know that," whispered Kai.

"It is wrong for you to lie to Joy."

Kai gripped the bar's tile edge. "I am not lying."

"Don't! I can't abide it. Lies by omission are still lies." Cheryl's tapping against the counter clawed at Kai's nerves, as did her words. "God is a lover of truth. I truly think what you're doing is a sin, not to mention a poor example for a sister who idolizes you." Cheryl curled her toes around her stool rungs. "Put yourself in Joy's shoes."

"How can I pretend to be nineteen?" Exasperation spewed out, as did resentment. Though Kai had struggled to deny it, she knew that Cheryl spoke truth. Something she was not doing . . . and must find a way to do.

"Joy is an adult. When we're talking life or death—and that is what we're talking here, Kai—Joy's age isn't the key."

Kai groaned off her stool and paced their tiny den. "What is the key?"

Cheryl swung about and leveled Kai with stony eyes. "How many times do I have to say it? Joy is family. Family deserves involvement. Family deserves the truth."

Kai stared at knotholes in their wood floor. She'd evaded, hedged . . . lied. If Joy had done that to her, she would take the first flight to Texas and ream her out in person. "You're right."

"Never thought I'd hear you say those words."

"I may not say them, but I have thought them many times." Affection for Cheryl welled up in Kai. She hurried to the bar and gave her roommate an uncharacteristic hug.

When the two separated, Kai was surprised to see tears in the eyes of the usually unflappable Cheryl. "You're so thin."

Kai nodded. She now weighed ninety pounds, counting a sweater and clunky boots. PKD had stripped her of more than weight. Day by day, hour by hour, PKD stripped her of dignity, pride, and pretense. "I'll be in my room," she said over her shoulder.

"Going to Texas in your mind?"

"Cowtown. When this is all over, we'll have to visit."

"You can count on it. And me." Cheryl's voice steeled her for what she was about to do. Kai whispered another prayer, shut the door, and dialed the Powells' home phone.

It has to be done. Now. Gloria sat on her bed, the phone in her hand, a prayer on her lips. Andrew pretended to sort the bills and business cards in his wallet. *Funny that while I'm dealing with stress by prayer, the preacher is playing with money.*

Gloria dialed the number she'd memorized the day Joy got her dorm assignment.

"Hello?"

"Joy. How are you?" She added a lilt to her voice, as if this were a mom check.

"I know, Mom."

Oh, God. Gloria's fingers clawed the air instead of her fists.

She had to somehow release tension. *Help me get through this. It's starting . . . now.*

"It's okay," continued Joy. *My daughter, soothing me.*

"Tell her." Andrew hissed and paced, in a most impatient, un-Andrew way.

Gloria inhaled. "We'd like to drive to Waco tomorrow. Discuss things."

It sounded as if half the dorm occupants were in Joy's room, giggling, conversing—things college girls should be doing rather than contemplating surgery with lifelong implications. Pressure built in Gloria. What was Joy *thinking*? Why didn't she *answer*?

"Yeah. Yeah." Gloria could barely hear Joy for background noise.

"Did I interrupt something?"

"What?"

"Sounds like quite a party, Joy."

"It's just a floor meeting. Hey, y'all!"

Gloria held the phone away from her ears and shrugged at Andrew, whose face had contorted into a frown. They were paying tuition for *this*?

"Hush!" Joy screamed.

Shushes and rustles and moans whooshed through the receiver. Gloria again cradled the phone against her shoulder, then held it to her ear when things settled. At least in Joy's dorm room.

"Sorry. I've got a break between noon and two. Meet for lunch?"

Tension loosed its hold. "Great! Should I bring stuff for a picnic?"

"Sure. That'd be nice. And your cookies, okay? Caroline loves 'em."

They said good-bye. Gloria hurried to the kitchen and set out butter to soften, found the jumbo-sized package of chocolate chips. She'd make all of Joy's favorites, though what they had to talk about was certainly not picnic fodder. "Lord, give us wisdom to say the right words." She sifted dry ingredients, set them aside, and beat the eggs. "Not my will here, Lord, but yours. Guard my daughter's heart . . . and her body, Lord. May we be an instrument to reach Kai."

Gloria made the chocolate chip cookies Neiman Marcus had made famous. For the first time ever, she didn't nibble on the dough.

It looked for all the world like a festive occasion. Gloria had packed a checkered tablecloth, sandwiches, chips, and drinks into their warped old basket. Tins held six dozen of Joy's, Caroline's—and apparently half the dorm floor's—favorite cookies. Joy chattered and Andrew nodded as they spread the cloth on Burleson Quad's lawn. Pansies winked, just for them. Live oak leaves whispered pretty nothings. Gloria acted carefree and smiled pretty, but nothing was pretty about PKD and their reason for coming. Despite her misgivings about how it might affect Joy, it was time to quit playacting and make plans.

One look transmitted her message to Andrew. They'd prayed as they drove this morning on I-20: for God's will, for peace, for the right words. Gloria distributed sandwiches, making sure Joy got the one with double cheese, pickles, and no mayo. Andrew tore his sandwich into bites and sipped Coke. Coeds strolled by wearing everything from green and gold fleece, Greek and Baylor T-shirts, to heels and designer dresses. Lovely tower bells pealed over laughter and chatter, the whole quadrangle oblivious to the Powell drama.

Andrew cleared his throat. "Mom said you talked to Kai."

Joy nodded, her mouth full of chips.

"She told you she's at end stage?"

Another nod. Except for a rogue gust blowing about Joy's hair and that munching jaw, their girl didn't move.

"We've been praying about this, Joy."

Joy swallowed, slugged her drink, and wiped her hands on a napkin. "Yeah, me too. Like, our whole floor's really into it."

"I don't think we have any option but to take the next step."

Joy shook her head wildly. Hair slapped her cheeks. "There's no need for that."

Gloria studied her hands. Who could blame a young girl, who might carry the deadly genetic marker herself, for having doubts? Joy, so desperate for friends just two years ago, now had the world—or at least this campus—eating out of her palm.

"I know we haven't talked about this for a while, but after Boston and our Christmas get-together, I thought we agreed—"

Joy bit off more sandwich. A pickle slice plopped onto the cloth as Joy waved her hands . . . and her food. "You . . . don't . . . understand." Words mixed with chomps.

Gloria's heart sank yet pressure eased from her chest and let her breathe. It was awful to want Joy safe in the Baylor bubble yet to know in the depth of her soul that Joy should help Kai. She gripped her Coke can, as if its chill could cool questions setting her afire. Had Joy's faith cooled so quickly by the collegial atmosphere?

"Joy." Andrew laid a hand on her knee. "Chew that and then talk to us."

The perfect eyes narrowed. Then Joy nodded, bowed her head, and cleared her throat. "Sorry," she managed as she wiped her mouth.

Gloria's heart swelled. At times, Joy looked just like Andrew.

"It's all settled." Joy shrugged, as if they should know what she was talking about. Gloria pulled her knees to her chest and gripped her legs with all her might. Would she ever understand this child?

"What . . . what do mean?" Andrew also played clueless. *Looked* clueless.

"I'm a perfect match—y'all already know that." Joy tossed crumbs to a bold blue jay. "Caroline—she's from Dallas, you know."

Gloria felt her head begin to shake, as if it were not connected to her body. What did Joy's roommate have to do with any of this?

"When I went home with her last month . . . um, like, we skipped class on Monday."

"Okay . . ." Andrew's voice was calm despite a tightening of the lines about his mouth. Gloria sat as still as the statue of Pat Neff to keep from crawling across the lawn and shaking Joy. They were paying all that money for her to skip class?

"Like, I'd called the week before. Made an appointment at the medical center TU. Transplant Unit." Her words mixed with bird tweets and laughter. "The people in Boston hook up with the people in Dallas, just like they did with the genetic matching."

"Okay" seemed to be the only thing Andrew could say.

"You wouldn't believe what they put me through. Enough questions to drive me crazy. They have to do it. I mean, it's a national standard."

"What are you talking about, Joy?" Andrew screeched.

"The prelims for donors. To make sure I know what I'm doing."

"They didn't call us?" flew out of Gloria, whose palms ached from her digging.

"I'm of age. One of the committee members had doubts 'cause I'm so young and all. But I explained how Kai sacrificed to find me, how she's my only link—right now, at least—to China. They're big on reclaiming heritage, you know?"

No, I don't know. But apparently you do.

Joy picked chips out of her bag and stuffed them in her mouth. "There's a few more hurdles—all in Boston. A CT scan, a meeting with the medical director and a social worker—you know, to make sure I'm of sound mind."

Gloria felt her eyes widen. Listening to her, who could doubt Joy was not only of sound mind, but ready to run a major corporation? Or plan for med school . . .

"After the final cross-match, we're good to go."

"What . . . how . . . What's the time frame?" Andrew's words garbled. *Like my mind.*

"A minimum of two weeks. I've got our flight booked already—used that emergency charge card y'all gave me. We've got twenty-four hours to cancel, like, but we can't. You know." Joy slapped her hands together, as if that settled it.

Andrew and Gloria stared openmouthed at each other. No, they really didn't know, at least not yet. Joy seemed to know enough for all . . . four of them.

As Gloria unraveled the hem on their tablecloth, they discussed a thousand loose ends. Paper work, deadlines, tests, phone calls. Joy had made the decision about her kidney. Worked out details. *And we support her.* Despite anxiety that robbed cravings for even one Neiman Marcus cookie, Gloria's peace matched the idyllic Baylor setting. In the strangest way, Gloria saw the past, present, and future here under a canopy of live oaks. With Joy's decision, Kai had a chance for a future. It was right. So right.

29

It was just a hospital room. Abstract prints. A television mounted on a beige wall. The window view showed spindly branches and rooftops spattered with snow. Kai lay under a thin blanket in the same standard-isue bed where dozens of her patients had waited. With Joy holding her hand, the scent of violets masking Mr. Clean's ammonia smell, a mountain of cards, drop-in visits by Paul, David, nurses, and aides, Kai might have been ensconced in a luxury hotel. The love of friends and the Powell family cushioned her from what lay ahead . . . mere hours from now.

"I've gotta go." Joy kissed Kai's forehead.

Kai nodded. Joy's coaxing of a Chang story had drained Kai's last energy reserves. Oh, that all the Changs could be here, for Joy's sake! She shoved away such sentiment. First and Third Daughters and poor Father had seen enough, had smelled enough, of death. If . . . *when* she and Joy returned to China, death would have been bested.

At least temporarily. Kai shuddered. Death could not be defeated . . . except by God.

"We'll be real close soon." Joy blew a kiss as she headed for the door. "Literally! Like, up close and personal!"

Kidney to kidney. Kai smiled. It was impossible to stay mopey with Joy around.

Those precious bow lips puckered into Joy's serious look. "I'll be praying."

You and David and the Powells and Roberta at the nurses' station and Cheryl . . .

Christian co-workers and church members who prayed had not surprised her. The one who had surprised her was Paul. *"I've done all I can do,"* he'd whispered as he'd brought her another bouquet of violets. *"Even graced the church doors."* Kai had experienced a strange tightening of her throat to hear of Paul turning to God, just for her.

After Joy left, Kai tiptoed around sleep, flirted with time, passed seamlessly from America to China. Nurses bustled in to check her vitals. Peasants nodded as they shouldered their sickles. The face of old Dr. Ward appeared in her dream-wake state, as did Father's face. One moment, she stared at a blank TV screen in her hospital room; the next, her toe tested the swift-flowing waters of the river near her childhood village. . . .

With her sisters, Kai skipped through rice paddies. Each footstep splashed liquid diamonds onto First and Third Daughters, who giggled and showed perfect dimples. Father waved from an adjacent field. He had the unlined but tanned skin of a young laborer. As he worked, he sang, "Little swallow, little swallow, comes here every spring."

Kai waved to him as she ran faster, faster, away from their village, away from First and Third Daughters. Determined to find the sun, she climbed grassy slopes. The shop owner's wife called, "Stop! Stop!" but Kai paid her no mind.

Her lungs burned as she climbed higher. Occasionally she stumbled, but she struggled her way to a plateau. "Where are you?" she cried to the sun, which hid behind a cloud. Tears mingled with sweat. "I have fought for you. I have labored for you. Why will you not shine your light on me?"

A white-hot ray beamed onto Kai's outstretched hand with such intensity, her skin became translucent. She saw white-gray bones, pink-red muscles. Fear triggered a desire to run, yet the flash of heat and light rendered her incapable of moving.

Second Daughter.

Kai leg's turned rubbery, though she neither fell to the ground nor sagged. It was Old Grandfather's voice, or what she had always assumed was Old Grandfather's voice.

I am not Old Grandfather, though he is here with me.

Kai inwardly trembled; oddly, not a muscle moved. Was God speaking to her now? Had He often spoken to her, though she had not known it was Him?

I created your inmost being. I knit you together in your mother's womb. I crafted that Healing Right Hand! I am that I am!

It is the Lord! Truth assaulted Kai, along with a splendid booming sound, pure and holy like the white-hot light. Still she could not move.

You ask why I have not shone my light on you.

Kai dared not speak, now that truth had been revealed. She dared not even nod.

You have not asked me, Little Kai. How I have longed to shine my light, not only on you, but in you. But you have not asked. You have not believed in the Spirit. Most important, you have not died to yourself so I can live in you.

360

As Kai stood motionless on the plateau, a terrible force pressed against her. It was akin to a giant hammer, attempting to pound her into the ground. The force pummeled her head and shoulders.

Yes! I need your light! I want your light! Tears streamed. *I believe!* Kai labored to speak the words screamed by her heart. She could not make a sound.

The heavens parted. A ball of light exploded and filled the sky with white-hot light. Kai's heart expanded with joy, then shrank with fear.

I am Jesus, Son of the Living God. The voice pierced Kai to the core. Images from the past throbbed into her field of vision. Little Kai, stealing candy from her sisters, Little Kai, lying to Mother. Kai, peeking at a classmate's exam answers. Kai, too stubborn and proud to seek help. Though Kai still could not move, the sky, the air, even the plateau whirled. Time flitted away, as did Kai's very sense of being. *It is as if I am dead...*

If you believe in me, you will not perish, but will have everlasting life.

But I am not worthy! Kai screamed, still unable to move.

A howling wind whirled Kai into a black funnel. Debris blinded her, choked her, scratched her skin. Still she could not move.

The tornado made a sucking sound. With a thud, Kai was thrown to the ground. Trembling, her breathing raspy and excruciatingly painful, Kai wobbled to her feet.

Through the blood of the Lamb, you are a new creation.

A humming such as Kai had never imagined energized the air. Bees buzzed. Birds chirped. A warm glow filled Kai, who extended a tentative finger.

The sound swelled, as did a wonderful power within. Kai

stretched toward the white-hot light. "I am free!" At first her voice was tight and hoarse, but it loosed to shout, "I am free!" Kai spread her arms and leapt, as she had on that long-ago day, when she stood on the roof. . . .

As she sailed through the air this time, powerful hands cupped to catch her. The wind whistled, the clouds whirled, but Kai was safe. Oh, safe! In His hands . . .

Someone shook Kai's shoulder. She startled awake.

Gone was the bright light. Gone were the hills of her village. She stared at the wall-mounted television. Yet so vivid was her dream memory, she extended her arm, looking, feeling . . .

There was no translucency. No radiating light. Yet Kai knew her soul was now white-hot clean.

"Oh, Jesus," she whispered as nurses explained what came next. Strong hands slid under Kai and scooted her onto a rolling stretcher. "Praise Him." Her eyes fluttered. She was in this world but not of this world. She had died but was alive. What a glorious feeling!

Doors whooshed open. The stretcher clanked. Bells rang. Orderlies told her they were taking her to surgery. Perhaps Joy was already there. . . .

Strangely, or perhaps it wasn't strange at all since she was a new creation, she smiled at the ceiling tiles of the hospital wing hall. No one knew it, but God was going with her into surgery. Whatever happened, they would be together. Forever and a day.

$\sim$

Gloria set down the book she was pretending to read on the waiting room table and studied her watch. Three hours and five minutes. A sigh loosed hair she'd pulled into a messy wad and clipped. Wow. Two minutes had crept by since she'd last checked.

Andrew yawned and stretched his legs. "You want coffee?"

"I'd say yes, but my bladder would shoot me."

"Want a mint?"

Gloria fisted her hands. "What I want is for them to be done."

"Wanna neck?"

Despite the time bomb ticking in her chest, Gloria nuzzled Andrew and kissed the man who constantly detonated her nerves. Until she saw her girl, touched her girl, nothing would help, but she could fake it for Andrew.

The surgeon stepped through the double doors that had swallowed up Joy. Kai. He no longer wore a mask, cap, or the blue scrubs of . . . three hours and ten minutes ago.

Gloria leapt to her feet. His having changed into his lab coat was a good thing. Wasn't it? Wasn't it?

She clattered across the waiting room to meet him in the hall. Her ears pricked to hear every sound. Her eyes zeroed in on wire-rimmed glasses, a square jaw . . . a smile.

"Both surgeries were successful." Behind the glasses, eyes twinkled. "Both patients are in recovery."

"They're . . . okay?" Gloria could tell that she was shouting, but she could not stop.

The doctor nodded. "Kai's already produced urine." He shook his head, surely in awe of the body's amazing properties. "As far as Joy, she's a trooper. Given the resilience of youth, I expect she'll be on her feet tomorrow, though as I told you earlier, her operation was actually the more complicated of the two."

Gloria did not remember but nodded. Who cared, anyway? They were okay!

Andrew shook the doctor's hand. "You don't know what this means. Thanks."

"I should thank you. It would be a different unit without

Kai. And your daughter . . . she's done a brave thing. Impossible without your support."

Gloria's knees began to wobble, as they had so long ago, when she'd first met Kai. Unlike that first time, when she'd flat-out fainted, she straightened, whispered a prayer to God, and let Andrew and the exhilarating news sweep her away.

⌒⌒

"Kai?"

She groaned. Pain stabbed her body.

"Kai!"

Try as she might, she could not open her eyes.

"I can only stay a sec. Technically, I'm not even supposed to be here."

A warm hand touched her cheek and caressed skin aching for his touch. She smiled . . . then winced at the pain. She was so thirsty. So tired.

"All morning, I've been with the chaplain. The strangest light came through those stained-glass windows. It was almost like . . . God was in there with me."

"Doctor, what on earth are you doing in here?"

"Uh-oh." His chuckle rippled pleasure through Kai. It felt so good to be free. She had told no one about her freedom . . . except God. Right now, that was enough.

"Do you want me to write you up?" Mock anger swelled the nurse's voice.

The doctor stood to leave. "You'll have to catch me first."

Will you catch me? Kai smiled and drifted to sleep.

30

China, five years later

Hurry up and wait. My life story.

For five years, China had wooed Gloria with new policies, new procedures to ensure adoption was legitimate, well-documented; the antithesis of that first trip. Despite all of its shortcomings, how could she criticize that first trip? It had given them the Joy of their lives . . . given Gloria the career of her dreams . . . as a liaison with an adoption agency.

"God's in control, Mom." Joy, intuitive as ever, drummed an offbeat cadence on Gloria's back as they were led into a room on the second floor of the Civil Affairs Bureau. "Stop it!" Gloria hissed, but she wasn't really angry. Just annoyed that Joy had more patience than she did.

The seven of them, five adoptive family members and two social workers, had been shoe-horned around a table designed for four. Dust-clouded windows framed an open-door suite. Chipped plaster, file cabinets, and a teacher's desk pulled Gloria back to memories of school rooms. Yet a waist-high wall of cardboard files—adoption folders?—outlined the room's perimeter. The smell of sweat and garlic, dust motes the size of mosquitoes, nervous titters, and Chinese rat-a-tat between social workers Apple and Fanny, reminded Gloria she was a long way from Fort Worth. Again.

Humidity partnered with a 100-plus-degree temperature to bathe Gloria in her own sweat. *Forget first appearances. There's nothing dry to wipe off with.* While Gloria dug her fingernails into her palm, she cast a look at Joy, in another world with her iPod. *Wish I could orbit . . . until they give me our baby.*

The other adoptive couple held hands and sweet-talked. Gloria patted the file folder that contained copies of a sheriff's report, FBI fingerprints, DCFS license, family pictures, birth and marriage certificates, medical physicals, I-171H, passports, their invitation to travel, letter seeking confirmation; copies of every scrap of paper certified by both the state and the Chinese consulate that comprised their dossier.

Good thing she dealt with mountains of paper work in her new job.

Andrew held a diaper bag filled with the wrapped trinkets they'd been "requested" to bring the officials. The stuffed bag also held baby clothes, diapers, a Tupperware container of Cheerios, a water bottle. These items insured against last-minute problems. Didn't they?

She tugged on Andrew's shirt, unable to stuff her anxious thoughts in that bag. "It's been over an hour. What's going on?"

Andrew shrugged. "Paper work's snarled. The babies blew out their diapers." He leaned close to her ear. "They're delaying things just to irritate you."

"It's not funny, Andrew!"

The social workers darted glances at Gloria. Consternation widened their eyes. "Is everything okay?" Gloria finally asked Apple.

Apple jumped to her feet. "I will check, Glor-i-a, though I assure you, everything is a-okay."

Up to this point, Apple . . . and the adoption process . . . had been efficient, organized, reliable . . . a polar opposite of their experience adopting Joy. Yet an hour's wait in a stuffy room made her hands ache to hold Jing-Wui, their fourteen-month-old daughter. Jing-Wui purportedly loved fish and meat puree, steamed eggs, and rib soup. Jing-Wui purportedly was active, lively, and smart, loved smiling, could at six months rock "forth and back," and at age twelve months clapped her hands excitedly when experiencing new things. It was all in the document entitled *The Growth and Development of Jing-Wui*.

That document told her everything . . . and nothing.

Gloria dug into her hands, her bad habit encoring during this trip. Had her daughter randomly been assigned the name meaning "Little Bird," or was that truly the name chosen by her birth mother before she set Jing-Wui in a cardboard box near the entrance to a crowded train station, as the written history had explained? Gloria longed to know.

The sound of footsteps seeped around the sturdy wooden door frame.

Gloria's hands trembled. Surely they would have news. *God, let it be soon!* She wrapped her arms about her dossier as if it were a shield.

Apple entered the room. "The bus was delayed leaving the orphanage, that is all. They will be here any minute."

Gloria bit back a harrumph. *And I'm the Queen of Sheba.*

"I will prepare for their arrival." With a slight bow, Apple left.

Andrew leaned close. "How do you want to handle things?"

They'd gone over this ad nauseum. But chatter might keep her sane.

"You shake the officials' hands. Mine are too sweaty."

Andrew treated her with a slippery grip. "And mine aren't?"

Gloria cast her eyes about the room, and images invaded her mind of the orphanage that once held Joy, over a decade ago. "It's so different."

"Yet the same old waiting."

They shared nervous laughs.

Something thudded. Gloria gripped her file. Was that a cry?

Fanny straightened. The other couple gasped. Joy horse-shoed her neck with her earphones, dug in her backpack, and found her camera. Calm and collected as a medical school student should be.

Their room door opened. Apple stood at the threshold. "The babies have arrived." Her smile and a beam of light mesmerized the dust motes. "They will be here any minute." Apple moved toward the opening into the suite, as did Fanny.

Sounds swelled into baby screams and warbles and set off a clattering in Gloria's heart. Andrew collared her with his arm, and it was a good thing, for Gloria debated leaping from her seat and sprinting down the hall to find the baby with the pixie ears, the bowl-cut hair, the curious eyes, the wispy brows . . . or should she, like at least one of the babies, just scream at the top of her lungs?

Andrew tapped her shoulder. "So I'll do the greetings? The gifts?"

"I'll get the baby." Gloria's words hissed like steam. She was on fire to touch their new daughter!

Two officials wearing blue suits stepped into their room from the adjoining suite. One—Gloria assumed the notary public—made his way to the teacher's desk, pen and files in hand. Apple and Fanny pattered forward and shook hands with the men. The four bowed, spoke Chinese, every word stretching Gloria's nerves to the breaking point.

Two women, dressed in clean but faded dresses, entered the suite.

Gloria's hands writhed. Two nannies. Two babies. She locked eyes with the smaller one, with wispy brows, pixie ears.

"That's our Gracie." Andrew had repeated the words pounding in Gloria's skull, brimming her eyes with tears. *Our Gracie.*

Grace twisted her perfect body, clothed in a pink jumper, to bury her face in her nanny's chest. Gloria hugged herself. *Oh, God,* she whispered, *Gracie's world has been shattered. Please open her heart to our love. Let her sense that she is safe.*

"This is Grace Ann." Apple, speaking nearly flawless English, moved to that perfect pink bundle. "Will the Powells please pick her up?"

The room tilted, brightened. Everything took on a pink cast. With Andrew guiding her forward, Gloria took Grace from the nanny.

Little Gracie screamed as if she'd been dropped.

"Jing-Wui," Gloria whispered. "Jing-Wui. Mommy."

As Gloria gently bounced her baby, snippets and sounds streamed. Lights flashed.

It was Joy, taking pictures. Their older daughter, preserving their first moments with . . . their younger daughter. Gloria's lip quivered. Again she was the happiest mother in the world!

The other couple's baby trumped introductions and pleasantries with hollers that surely would deafen them all.

Andrew took her arm. Guided her and Grace to the notary's table.

Fanny joined them. The official stood and spoke foreign words.

"Mr. and Mrs. Powell?" Fanny translated.

Gloria nodded till her head ached. She'd been well schooled on Gotcha Day's last step.

"Here is your baby," Fanny intoned, after the official's words. "Take her back to your hotel and see if you like her."

Gloria wanted to scream, "Are you crazy? I love her!" She bit her lip. *Don't ask questions. Don't say more than necessary. Everything you need to know has been given to you.* Thank God for Apple's and Fanny's careful instruction.

"Give her something to eat, to drink. Spend time with her," Fanny continued. "Come back tomorrow and tell us if you want to keep her."

As if Andrew understood her feelings, he tightened his grip. Gloria combated a desire to sing to the heavens by kissing Grace's spiky black hair, by comparing Grace's appearance with Joy's. Rounder eyes, more pointed ears. The same gorgeous skin . . .

Gloria breathed in the smell of soy sauce and fresh-scrubbed baby. "You are my Grace," she whispered into that perfect pixie ear.

"Are you sure about that name?" Andrew teased. Gifts from the orphanage director filled his hands.

"I've never been this sure of anything since I married you."

Joy, who'd heard it a zillion times, rolled her eyes . . . which were filled with tears.

Gloria fought a sniffle. Joy hadn't cried during Kai's surgery. Kai's baptism. Kai's wedding. *Oh well. A med student has to lose it sometime.*

They were both doctors, used to tragedy. Exhilaration. It did not help. As wails throttled her ears, Kai longed to hide in his arms, but her upbringing would not allow it.

He patted her. Shivers raced through her veins. Four years of marriage, and he anticipated her every need. Another miracle. How many miracles could a village woman with a transplanted kidney expect?

At least one more, this miracle held in the arms of a smiling nanny. Though she exercised her lungs with vigor, the girl dressed in a yellow sun suit, hat, and dainty white shoes was their Faith. Kai marched forward to present the gifts, as they had decided, since she spoke Chinese. A cement tongue made it doubtful Kai could say a word.

He took hold of her arm. "Kai, I'll do the paper work. You get our baby."

Words were spoken by the notary and the social worker, but Kai let her husband deal with them. She held out her arms and received . . . the most beautiful baby in the world. She had dimples in her chin, on her cheeks, on her arms. Why, the way she was screaming, she had dimples—and wrinkles—everywhere!

"She has your chin." Delight shrilled his voice. "Praise God! Just look at her!"

He is *absolutely, unequivocally serious.* Kai giggled but did not look at him. That would mean tearing her gaze from Faith. *Faith.* Something she and this man had learned, hand in hand. Were learning . . .

He bowed to the officials. Pulled her forward. She nodded and even managed to sign papers without releasing her hold on Faith. Just let anyone try to take her now!

When they were done, the three of them embraced. Faith

shivered but did not pull away . . . and quit screaming to fix them with curious eyes as they prayed for her.

After collecting Faith's things, they boarded the bus and posed for pictures with the Powell family. Their family . . . and Faith's godparents. They would eat, then rest before the next leg of their journey. It was a long trip to the village. What would the Changs think of Faith? Her husband? Would they see her changed heart?

Be still and wait, whispered the Spirit.

Kai leaned against the bus seat, woozy from the miracles that had unfolded. A woman with a disastrous medical history approved for adoption. Arrangements allowing them to travel to the Chang village before that final stop at Shamian Island in Guangzhou. It was enough that all four sisters would breathe the same air. Dear Father would meet his first granddaughter and reunite with two daughters. *Be still. Wait.*

Feeling like packhorses, they exited the bus and entered the hotel. They said good-bye to the Powells and found a table in the dining room. Suddenly the high chairs lining the dining room wall, ready steeds for young charges, made perfect sense. Like the tourists and love-crazed parents they were, they took turns snapping photographs. When Faith began to fuss, Kai took her from the high chair and held her close.

"It's okay, Faith Lily." While rubbing their baby's sweet little back, her husband hummed a lullaby, off-key and with a Boston accent.

She had learned to love his voice.

"You okay?"

She nodded, unable to speak.

He outlined her lips with his finger and then kissed her

long and hard, right in front of their waiter. So un-Chinese. But she did not care.

"Welcome to China, dear Paul." They both kissed Faith as the obliging waiter snapped a photo. "I cannot wait till you meet the rest of our family."

Author's Note

At age eleven, a brave young girl promised her two sisters that she would become a doctor and restore health to their parents, whose imprisonment during China's Cultural Revolution led to horrific mental and physical abuse. Eventually Harvard Medical School allowed that promise-maker to pass through their ivy-covered gates and obtain several degrees, including her M.D.

Over forty years later, the story of the woman I will call Dr. Chang trickled down to me after my mother, Ann Qualls, was treated by Dr. Chang. The story took a poignant turn when Dr. Chang learned that my mother, along with my father, had served as missionaries in the late 1980s in part of China; an even more poignant turn when Dr. Chang diagnosed my mother with cancer.

Story pieces for *Reclaiming Lily* continued to interlock when friends Shereen and Hossein Rastigar shared their personal battle with polycystic kidney disease (PKD). Friends Tom and Amy Koranek opened their homes, hearts, and file folders bulging with information about their China adoption experience to finish the puzzle.

Though these three sources and more than twenty-five research books comprise the inspiration for *Reclaiming Lily*, this book is fiction. I pray *Reclaiming Lily* honors those struggling with PKD, those with a passion for the magnificent land of China and its people, where millions are on fire for the Lord, and most of all, those who long to experience, and ultimately celebrate, the quintessential sacrifice: that of Christ on the cross in His unimaginable and most perfect gift of salvation through grace by faith.

Discussion Questions

1. According to Rita Soronen, executive director of the Dave Thomas Foundation for Adoption, "nearly 50 percent of Americans either have adopted or have family or close friends who have." How has adoption touched your family?

2. In the prologue, God transports a naïve Gloria Powell from her native state of Texas to the exotic countryside of China. Have you experienced international travel? If so, compare and contrast your "adventure" with that of Gloria.

3. Has your community been blessed with the arrival of immigrants from other cultures? Discuss the impact and changes that have resulted from such inflow.

4. This novel immediately throws two women with vastly different personalities and passions into the "fighting ring" over which one has the right to decide what's best

for a seventeen-year-old teenager. Did you find yourself rooting for Kai or Gloria? Why?

5. How does a Texas tornado provide the catalyst for emotional cleansing and a fresh start for Lily, Gloria, and Kai?

6. Trace the development of a heartfelt and genuine relationship between Gloria and her daughter. What do you think had created the disconnect that existed in the Powell household before Kai's arrival?

7. Does this novel change your perception of the Chinese Cultural Revolution?

8. Though *Reclaiming Lily* centers on the actions of Gloria, Joy, and Kai, there are also three male characters: Andrew, David, and Paul. Discuss how the men promote or delay the women reaching their goals.

9. When to sacrifice for others and when to allow others to sacrifice for you recurs as a consistent theme. Discuss any application to your own life.

10. Do the novel's settings—China, Fort Worth, and Boston—heighten your sensory experience in reading the novel? Give examples.

11. Compare and contrast the faith journeys of Kai, Gloria, and Joy.

Acknowledgments

Again, a village—Boston horticulturists and park rangers, prison officials, medical aides, Chinese nationalists, and interested readers—teamed to help this novelist. However, I couldn't have written *Reclaiming Lily* without Trina Scott and Barry Slotky, medical doctors who went "on call" for a writer. Amy Koranek opened her heart and her files to demonstrate the roller-coaster ride called international adoption. Hossein and Shereen Rastigar fielded questions to help me understand PKD. Bless y'all!

Thanks to Dana of Barnes Jewish Hospital's Transplant Unit (where Shereen received her brother's kidney) for outlining donor-recipient procedures; J.R., a health-care professional, who outlined signs, causes, and pathophysiology of self-mutilation. Meteorologist Jeff Desnoyers, you weathered a storm of writer's questions. Thank you.

Dave Warner, lieutenant at Normal Police Department and honorary novelist, you've cowritten three books! Nicole

McCall, also of the NPD, you unraveled the complexities of station adjustments with passion and patience. Thank you!

Special thanks to soulmates Cammie Quinn and Sara Richardson, who pored over rough drafts and labored to help me find the voices of Kai, Gloria, and Joy.

Sue Wang, how can I thank someone who for seventeen days was tour guide, translator, banker, and fellow adventurer as China unfolded? Thank you, Mama and Papa Wang, for five blessed days in your courtyard, reading and sipping green tea; for five splendid nights, letting China breezes and the kang's comfort soothe my weary bones.

Natasha Kern and David Long, thanks for believing in this story.

A thousand hugs to my family, who with the birth of dear Lily, put up with even more writer histrionics than usual. Love y'all—Alan, Thomas, Sarah, Josh, and Laura!

Thank you, Mom and Dad, for sharing your stories, especially those about China, your life, your love.

Thank you, Spirit, for whispering this story.

If you enjoyed *Reclaiming Lily*, you may also like…

When dark memories surface of their ill mother—and their father's desperate choice—is the silence these sisters keep hurting them more than the truth?

House of Secrets by Tracie Peterson

traciepeterson.com

When Samantha finds herself face-to-face with the man who broke her heart, will she continue to play it safe or decide to take another chance on love?

A Wedding Invitation by Alice J. Wisler

alicewisler.com